SASSAYWOO

SASSAYWOO

TRIAL BY ORDEAL

JOSEPH AKOI ZEZE

Printed in the United States of America
ISBN 978-1-958434-85-7 (sc)
ISBN 978-1-64133-711-3 (hc)
ISBN 978-1-64133-712-0 (e)

Library of Congress Control Number: 2022904436

Horror | Thriller
2023.01.25

MainSpring Books
5901 W. Century Blvd
Suite 750
Los Angeles, CA, US, 90045

www.mainspringbooks.com

PROLOGUE

IN THE MIDDLE OF the dark night under the branches of the trees that enveloped the forest, he suddenly emerged out of the mist of the fog, like a creepy shadow partially illuminated by a thin reflection of the moonlight filtering through the little spaces through the branches. He stood 6 feet tall, with a muscular frame, imposing fear and conveying havoc. Like an executional, he held a long cutlass in his right hand. Caught up in a grisly scene, was a woman, in her mid-thirties, snatched at midnight from a farm somewhere around the western Weala belt, between Margibi and Bong Counties. As her life hung in the balance, she was terrified for every second she breathed, as it brought her closer to a gruesome murder that the ghostly figure was about to commit.

He ripped off her blouse, made of an expensive African fabric, shredding both blouse and wrapper, exposing a pair of red bra and red panties on her curvaceous body. Then he slid the cutlass underneath her bra, tearing it off and exposing the woman's large round breasts with such protruding nipples as the tip of a snail shell. She fought back and cried out for mercy, as her voice echoed through the forest, but help seemed very far away. She now reverted to sobbing for the terrible predicament she was in. Naked and strapped to a tree with hands and legs tied around the trunk, she reflected on her mistakes and felt sorry for herself.

She should have remained in her hometown, where kidnapping her was going to be impossible, but it was out of fear that she unexpectedly made herself vulnerable and this is now happening to her. At the thought of this, she cried out loud, but she could no longer hear her own voice; too much screaming had made her hoarse.

With his large red eyes behind the dancers' mask that hid his face, he stared at her enticing breasts, dangling teasingly whenever she quivered with the agony he had inflicted on her. Her perfect body, that always aroused an irresistible desire that brought men to their knees, now trembled to the nasty stare of a pair of cold and terrifying eyes through which she saw the sting of death.

She was a good woman and a pride to her parents and her town. But she had brought disgrace to her ancestral land, by spreading her legs before a stranger which result produced a son, whose birth, in the eyes of this behemoth, was a woe for breaking a century-old tradition that he has vowed to uphold from the day he was born.

"Gbeh vay?" she asked, sobbing, her voice increasingly becoming hoarse, in her native Kpelle language, meaning: "Who are you?" which she assumed he understood, as she desperately sought to set the basis to reason with him.

But she was shocked, when she finally recognized him at first glance, when he came closer to her and removed the dancers' mask from his face. He was someone from her hometown and she had known him her entire life but did not know that he was this evil. She was now aware that she was going to pay the price for the decision her father, the town chief and the elders of town made to allow strangers to explore their sacred land, which the man standing before her was against. And one of the strangers for whom this decision was taken, was her son's father who was the key architect.

She was now faced with the hard truth that her personal affairs and that of her hometown were inseparable. She had thought that her personal affairs for having a son for the man who was seeking to venture into their secret habitat should not have been the basis for his influence on the town people. And for that reason, she left her hometown and was always reluctant to return. Confronting her now, was the part that made her frightened; the man before her was what people said he was. An evil being, a phantom who would ravage her entire hometown as the punishment it took against his interest.

She watched as he took a couple of steps backward and disappeared into the fog. And within a few seconds, he re-appeared with the necessary materials to build a furnace made of earth mound, a special kind of wood that emits extreme heat and a brand-new cutlass. These were the accessories he was going to use to condemn his unfortunate victim. It's the Sassaywoo, his trademark ordeal of trial and Judgment that the poor woman will have to face for the abomination she brought upon herself. This will begin the initial step for the long-awaited atonement to cleanse the woe that betide their land by destroying the ovary and then the seed, including all the other accomplices.

"Your innocence is betrayed by your woe and your woe is the source of your fear: for the radiance of the steel to consume your flesh for the abomination you have brought upon yourself."

He chanted the ordeal's verdict code in an enigmatically loud and melodious tone. Then he robbed a certain white clay all over her body when he again stood before her with the brand-new cutlass now very hot, which radiance turned the blade orange and green, because she was a woman. He first tested it on himself by pressing the hot metal on his forehead, his jaw and his left arm. But it did not burn his skin, which signified his innocence, and the only one ordained to perform the ordeal to those responsible for desecrating his sacred ancestral land, and this technique of justice was not a lie. It was the way of the ancestors.

She suddenly screamed with all her might to the extent that the veins on her neck became so visible as if they were about to force themselves out of her skin, when he pressed the cutlass into her breast. The steaming blade instantly separated one of her breasts from her chest. Then she screamed for mercy as the hot metal penetrated the flesh around her hips and thighs, exposing the pelvic and thigh bones now partially covered with churned flesh.

In the midst of her agony, a couple of hard truths filtered into her mind in obedience to the swift reflection of a person's life that occurs when they are at the point of a sudden death. She will never see her son again, neither her father nor her brother, and they may never know what happened to her.

As a young mother, she always told friends that she'd prefer a quick and peaceful death, rather than dying from the miserable conditions that often come with terminal illness. She wouldn't want her family members to endure the pain of watching her die in a slow and painful way. But she had never thought of departing this world in such misery, nor had she even imagined that death would throw itself upon her in such a vicious and tragic manner.

CHAPTER 1

MAILA IS A SMALL town located about 25km northwest of the former Mining Town of Bong Mines, Lower Bong County. Unlike Haindii and other surrounding towns in the region, most of the people in Lower Bong County do not even know about the existence of such a town as magical as Maila. The town is ideally situated along the St. Paul River, with a magnificent scenery of unique arrangements of waterways, dotted islands and beautiful crystal lakes, adorned with lush vegetation on the banks. The view is picturesque and dreamlike as a scene in a western fairy tale movie. The townspeople considered it a sacred place. They have preserved and worshiped the land for many generations.

According to legend, Maila was discovered by Chief Kerkulah Maila, a roaming Jorquelleh Kpelle warrior, hunter, and farmer. The story goes that Kerkulah Malia was seeking an alternative settlement far away from a Jorquelleh Chiefdom, because of overpopulation and the scarcity of arable land to farm.

He also discovered that the surrounding areas were inhabited by some Gola people who were spread along small fishing villages on either side of the St. Paul River. Apart from fishing, which was the principal way of life of the Gola, they grew small gardens next to their little villages. And the stranger was amazed that the crops produced more than expected.

"What a fertile land!" marveled Kerkulah Maila, convinced that he would make this place his new home.

But first he must find a way to lure the current inhabitants for permission to settle. Fortunately, the Gola Chief, Gbokai Lamine, was his *'stranger-father'*. Chief Gbokai Lamine was impressed by kerkulah's mastery of clearing and crop cultivation, so both men bonded instantly.

"There is a risk of living only by fishing and not by engaging in large farming activities. One day, you may never know that a severe drought might come and remain for a long period of time. The waters will dry up and there will be no more fish to catch and eat. You and your people will starve," he warned the Gola chief. "Allow me to settle here and teach your people how to farm, and to store enough food in case we experience such drought."

Having consulted his elders, the Gola Chief gave Kerkulah permission to settle, in return to teach them his special farming techniques. To further ensure his commitment to such agreement, Kerkulah Maila proposed to his hosts that in order to effectively deliver on his part of the agreement, he'd have to invite at least a few of his kinsmen with similar farming skills to come over and support him.

The Gola granted Kerkulah Maila his wish. But instead of a few men, hundreds of people from his former town started moving into the new land. Among them was Sengbeh Gbelema, a blacksmith and trusted friend, who specialized in fashioning durable farming tools. Kerkulah Maila soon became overwhelmed by the influx of the mostly unwelcomed settlers. Now he was going to be blamed for all of this, as his hosts were already feeling insecure by the continuous arrival of more people.

While this was happening, resentment was building between the two tribes. And adding to that, were a number of factors, such as, the Gola felt overlooked by the Kpelle because they were not skillful farmers. In fact, the Kpelle viewed the lack of knowledge and inability to farm as a grievous depravity, which would eventually lead to extinction. And so, everyone endowed with the dexterity to secure a sustainable livelihood through farming will look down on others who don't.

Also, the Kpelle were always reluctant to allow their disciplined and hardworking daughters to marry Gola men because they were not members of their poro society. In the beginning, the Kpelle people were submissive to the Gola as their hosts, but, and as soon as their numbers began to swell, they no longer had any regard for the people they once regarded as their stranger fathers, which the Gola saw as being ungrateful.

The Gola Chief Gbokai Lamine, complained to Chief Kerkulah Maila on several occasions of Kpelle encroachments on their land. What was more troubling was that the Kpelle had instituted their Poro society customs, a sacred bush school system, which prohibited the Gola tribe from participating in it.

"Your people are becoming too many and they are quickly taking over our land. Our people are now restricted from accessing certain parts of their own land on grounds that they are only meant for members of your *Poro Society*. Why must we always run indoors when your *country devils* are coming out?"

"I think you are mistaken, my noble stranger-father," said Chief Maila. "There are some of my people who do run indoors when the devils are out, so it is not only your people."

"Yes but, as soon as those of you who run indoors become members, they no longer do, and my people are not allowed to become members, which means we will always run indoors. This is humiliating to us. And it was not part of our agreement."

One day, Kerkulah Maila gathered his people to discuss the issue of a new influx of their kinsmen when the Gola chief, Gbokai Lamine complained again and demanded that the new group must be sent back to where they came from, and to abolish the Poro society from their land.

"Oh, my dear friend and brother. We have labored on this land for many years, and we're enjoying the fruits of our labor," Sengbeh Gbelema stood up and spoke. "Seeing that we have enough here, it will be cruel to turn our backs on our kinsmen who have come from afar in search of a better life. This land is big enough to host our two tribes. Maybe the Gola are not aware of the vastness and abundance of their own land."

"And we will never abolish our bush schools," added an old man. "How do we educate our young men and women to take after us?"

Alarmed that the Kpelle have surveyed their entire land and claimed to have vast knowledge of it, repeated warnings fell to no avail, and so this animosity grew beyond proportion as the Gola realized in horror, that they were slowly losing all their land as more land hungry Jorquelleh men and their families crept into their territory. War eventually ensued between both tribes.

The conflict lasted for several years. And in a great battle, led by Sengbeh Gbelema, the blacksmith, Gbokai Lamine and his people were eventually overwhelmed. They were driven away from their land and pushed all the way beyond the south of Haindii.

The entire territory now belonged to Kerlulah Maila and his Kpelle tribe. They made him chief and the settlement was named, Maila, in his honor. Years following the battle, Gbokai Lamine, with his people severely reduced, lived a quiet life. But some of his men, bitter for the loss of their land, organized raiding parties and harassed the Kpelle by laying siege on remote villages since they were not strong enough to confront their enemies directly.

"The only way this will stop, O chief, is if we capture and kill Gbokai Lamine, himself!" Sengbeh Gbelema once suggested to Chief Maila when he had captured and beheaded a group of Gola raiders.

"Gbokai Lamine was my stranger father. He allowed me to settle here and we have driven him out. So, I will not kill him. But the more we capture and behead these raiders, the more they are robbed of their strongest men to give us further trouble. And they will eventually accept their defeat," replied the chief.

But since its establishment, the town has remained a secret for fear of overpopulation from their kinsmen from the jokoleh and other Kpelle chiefdoms.

The town has since survived, even with an attempt to recapture it by a grandson of Gbokai Lamine several years later. But the beauty of this town remained a secret up to the founding of the Republic of Liberia and the establishment of many other municipalities around the area. The first foreigner to discover the beautiful scenery of Maila was a German Geologist and explorer named Alan Zeptter. Hired by Bong Mining Company (BMC), a German steel giant, to explore the area several kilometers west of the Bong Range to connect to the St. Paul River to build a power plant, he stumbled upon this magnificent paradise.

Impressed by the ideal location of the area, Alan Zeptter informed James Boima Barclay, a young and brilliant Liberian student, studying Geology at the University of Gutenberg in the then West Germany where Zeptter worked as an associate professor.

After Barclay graduated from the university, he was recommended by Zeppter to work as a senior mine geologist for BMC in Liberia.

"You will marvel at the uniqueness of this land. The day I will take you there, you would have never thought that your country is blessed with such a beautiful place," the German Geologist told his friend, one day while they both sat at the BMC Mess Hall having lunch.

"But I observe that the people are over protective of their land and are sensitive to foreigners," said Barclay.

"That is why I believe that there is more to what I saw when I stumbled on it. We can conduct a secret exploration and take an inventory of the magnificent scenery. Then we can devise a way to convince the people of how valuable their land is and how it can bring immense wealth to them."

The men conducted the exploration secretly but very carefully and soon discovered that Maila was more than just a town situated along the St, Paul with natural waterways, crystal lakes and dotted island. Certain parts of the lakes included natural hot springs, some filled with the abundance of fish that occasionally jumped out of the water. Some parts of the vegetation were natural flower orchards of many varieties that exude sweet fragrances, making the atmosphere conducive for leisure and relaxation. They also discovered species of water birds in certain parts mixed with water lilies and trees of different kinds of naturally decorated foliage with a pleasant aroma. Some of these places looked like a natural park covered with acres of lawns that reflected the color of leaves and wildflowers making it perfect for a golf course. Alan Zeptter and James Boima Barclay had discovered another wonder of the world and were prepared to transform this place into one of the best resorts on planet earth. This would certainly be one of the keys to Liberia's development.

Both men planned what they needed to do. The first step was finding a way to convince the people of Maila that the place was worth a lifetime fortune for their entire generation, if the town's people allowed them to seek the necessary investment to transform the land into a world class resort.

After the 1980 coup, J. Boima Barclay was appointed as General Administrative Manager by the military government. Key to his new portfolio was to represent the Government of Liberia interest at the Company.

In this position, J. Boima Barclay worked very hard to gain the trust of the people of Fuamah District. Through his influence many of his people were employed, some with BMC, others, especially the people of Maila worked on his rubber farms while he empowered some to acquire their own rubber farms and helped them sell their produce to Firestone or the Salala Rubber Corporation. He was also instrumental in encouraging Bong Mines Company to construct the road bypassing the mountain to connect to Weala and then the Kakata-Gbarnga Highway so that the people in the surrounding towns of Haindii, or Popota would not have to travel to Gbarnga by way of Kakata-Bong Mines Road.

The town chief, Johnny Colomea Lomeh was a descendant of Kerkulah Maila. Despite all the things Barclay was doing for them, he initially rejected the General Administrative Manager's request when he once expressed his interest to explore their land, and to transform it into a tourism paradise.

"We are bound by a strict traditional prohibition to protect Maila and its environs from strangers," replied the chief, suddenly becoming suspicious of the most senior ranking officer of the company who one day confronted him on the issue. "These are the exact words of my people. And they have warned that they should not be the ones to remind me of this."

Sensing that the time was not yet ripe to consistently engage the town's people, Barclay did not pursue his request further. He quickly informed Zeptter about the latest setback. Both men were again drawn to employing another strategy to convince chief Lomeh and his council of elders to change their minds.

"The people of Maila hold dearly to a deep-rooted traditional prohibition regarding opening up their sacred land for investment opportunities," said Zeptter. "We got to think of another proposal that may interest them, and gain more of their trust."

"I will offer to build them a school," Barclay suddenly snapped his fingers and suggested, after a long thought. "Let's educate their children so that as their minds are developed, they will be the ones to convince their parents. I know this may take years, but education is a powerful tool for transforming minds and shifting opinions."

Chief Lomeh and his people agreed when Barclay presented to them the idea of building a school.

"The world is changing and your children need to be educated to face the many challenges that are bound to come. Building a school in your town is a way to start. This will in no way disrupt the bush school system," Barclay told the people in a town meeting.

But out of suspicion, the chief and the elders agreed that it'd be best to begin with an elementary school. In the early eighties, the Maila Elementary School was built. It started with 25 students including the chief two children, Peter and his sister, Esther Gorpue Lomeh. Some of the elders held back their children for fear that they may abandon their tradition. But they later noticed that they were wrong when they saw that the other children who attended the school were learning how to read and write with great excitement.

Late in 1984, something happened that allowed the strategy to somehow work, but in an unexpected way. Esther Gorpue Lomeh, the town chief's daughter, upon completing the six grade, had left Maila to continue her Junior High School Education at J.D.K Baker Episcopal Mission School, in Nyenen, a small commercial town South of Bong Town, the main concession area of BMC. She was in the eighth grade when she was impregnated by Barclay. This happened at the time he had resigned and was running as representative for Fuamah Distinct.

Chief Johnny Colomea Lumeh was disappointed at first but when he saw that Barclay was popular and was definitely going to win, which will be good for the people of Maila, his anger subsided. Whatever the case, he was about to have his first grandchild whose father was going to be a powerful representative.

"I am so sorry that this has happened, my chief. But I will make sure your daughter continues her education. I will also make sure that your grandchild is fully educated as well. The child will have a foreign education and will come back to Maila as a true blood to foster its development," the formidable candidate told the chief in a meeting with Esther and her family.

A year later, on the day all of Fuamah District was celebrating the victory of J. Boima Barclay, Esther gave birth to a bouncing baby boy. He was named after his father, J. Boima Barclay Jr. to the delight of his maternal grandparents who nursed him to give Esther a chance to go back to school. Barclay Jr. later spent a portion of his primary education years at the Maila Elementary School.

As their representative, Barclay served the people well. More especially Maila. Through him, the number of citizens of Fuamah District employed with BMC quadrupled. More roads were built connecting all the rubber farms. And more people were owning rubber farms. Most of its children were graduating from Maila Elementary school and were attending any school of their choice in Bong Mines on the representative Scholarship where they continued until they graduated from high school. Through his instrumentality, a number of them were enrolled at the BMC vocational training institute where upon graduation they would be employed by BMC as staff members.

"O Chief son of our ancestor, Kerkula Maila," Gualee Tartee, one of the most respected elders, addressed the chief one day, when the council of elders gathered at the chief quarter. "We have decided to listen to Representative Barclay concerning the proposal he once told you about."

Surprised, the chief immediately convened a general meeting and invited the representative. Also in that meeting was his trusted friend and aid, Koikoi Pewee who was affectionately called 'Siegie'. Siegie was instrumental in helping Barclay to win the election. The elders in attendance were Kotee Sumonlor, Galakpa Jawoe, and Gbelemu Dormeyahn. These men were the descendants of the founding fathers of Maila.

Everyone was seated, except Sengbeh Gbelema, the town's blacksmith and a great-grandson of Sengbeh Gbelema, the blacksmith who was a close friend of Kerkula at the founding of Maila.

"Where is Sengbeh," asked the town chief, amid growing murmuring as everyone anxiously waited for the meeting to start, after waiting for an hour and a half. "Without him, we cannot proceed as the protocol demands."

"Here he comes," announced Gbelemu Dormeyahn just as a huge and muscular man, with bushy hair and beard, entered the palaver hut. He took his seat far from the rest of the elders.

There was silence as everyone's eyes were on the blacksmith who seldom spoke or mingled with the town people. Like his ancestors, people bought the tools he made because they were durable. They will visit his work kitchen, in the front of his hut to buy their farming tools. But he entertains conversations with no one.

The meeting finally began. The chief told the people about the purpose of the meeting, then the floor was given to Honorable Barclay.

"My intention is to bring life to this great town of yours. There are monies in this land that you all can benefit from. If you agree I can find the right investment to make this place look more than Bong Town. So, I need your permission for me and my friend Zeptter to explore your land to conduct a feasibility study. This will enable us to showcase the elaborate natural features, and estimate its total value. There are people around the world that are looking for a place like this to invest in. Together we can turn Maila into a tourism paradise, and the name of your town will be famous in Liberia and the outside world." Honorable Barclay explained to the people.

"I vow never to allow my ancestral land to be given to strangers," rejected the blacksmith, pointing his fore finger towards the concrete floor of the palaver hut. "Doing so, is spitting on the blood they spilled to acquire and protect this land."

"This is nonsense," stomping to his feet, the chief replied angrily. "The ancestors of every one under this palaver hut have also bled to protect this land. Not yours alone. And your altitude showed disregard for their efforts."

Everyone in the palaver hut stood still. There was total silence. The chief looked into the faces of the other council of elders, waiting for them to buttress him.

"I think it is time that we set aside some ancient traditional prohibition so that our town can realize its true potential for the betterment of all of us," interjected Gualee Tartee, thus breaking the silence.

"Maila doesn't need to look as beautiful as bong town is, to strangers. This town has a binding tradition that must be held. No matter what," insisted Sengbeh Gbelema.

"Count me in, O chief. Maila must be developed," added Kortee Sumonlor, a slim and tall man who stretches his eyes to show he means business whenever he speaks.

"Also am I," said Galakpa Jarwoe, a stocky man. "We cannot hold back the development of this town.

"With the chief's permission, I agree with the honorable man. It's time that we move past tradition," Gbelemou Dormeyahn stood up and spoke.

"Unless the chief has forgotten the vow Kerkulah Maila made to my ancestor, Sengbeh Gbelema, which the true sons of Maila had kept all these years, he will never understand because he's not a blood descendent of Kerkulah Maila," the town's blacksmith ranted.

Chief Lomeh froze upon hearing this. The black smith had struck a chord. The last son of Kerkulah Maila did not have children, neither to say, boys. He had no brother, but a sister who had a son. On his deathbed, he named his only nephew, this sister son as his successor, and that was how the chieftaincy of Maila shifted to the Lomeh, a great grandfather of chief Lomeh.

"You suppose to know, Colomea that only a Maila of paternal bloodlines may revert the vow made to my ancestor, but not a Lomeh whose intention is to seek personal interest when in fact he has given his daughter to the honorable man for the sake of money. The money you and the rest of the elders have received to sell Maila," growled the town's blacksmith.

"Leave my daughter out of this, Sengbeh," warned Chief Lomeh, raging with anger.

There was a sudden uproar when the black smith made this statement. The people immediately turned against him. The chief stood up and made an attempt to charge at the black smith, but he was held back by his elders.

They hurried with him into his house and had a closed-door meeting that lasted for about thirty minutes. They came back outside while everyone was still waiting under the palaver hut. Then they made the decision that the land must be explored, and that was it. After the verdict was announced by the chief, the black smith stormed out of the meeting. People tried to stop him, but he invaded them.

"Let him go," shouted Koikoi Pewee, the aid to the honorable man. "Gone are the days that tradition will hold back the development of the people. We will invite the magistrate on anybody who will hamper the development of this town or even Fuamah District as a whole."

The black smith upon hearing this, suddenly stopped and looked back. He studied the expression on the faces of the elders. This told him that they were all in agreement with Koikoi Pewee's statement. Then he looked at the chief, who also looked back at him, sternly. 'What a fool he has become,' he thought. 'From his great grandfather who first succeeded the Maila, up to his father, the vow had been kept'.

"All of you must pray to die before the waft that will come upon you," Sengbeh warned the people, in a sterned tone. "And you all will regret this woe."

"Sengbeh Gbelema," The chief called after him. "*E leh. Leh ka tee,*" he responded in his Kpelle dialect, meaning, 'it is a lie'.

Sengbeh Gbelema continued to live in the town doing his normal black smith work. Like everybody else, he would leave the town early in the morning for his farm, and return late at night. Just when the people thought that he had finally accepted the town's verdict, he suddenly ceased going to his farm, and also stopped making farming tools.

Then, one day he disappeared from the town without a trace. Thinking that he may have gotten lost in the bush, the chief organized search parties but he could not be found. After three months, people reported seeing him in the bushes of Bong Range.

"Sengbeh has chosen to banish himself from his own town," said the chief once in a meeting with his council of elders. "If he sees the reason to come back, even after this town has developed, we will welcome him."

In 1986, Representative Barclay informed Alan Zeptter, now retired and residing back home in Germany of this development. He responded that he was not too well, but will return to Liberia, when his health improves. In April 1989 Zeptter returned to Bong Mines and began surveying the town of Maila. Unfortunately, he did not accomplish much. The project was soon aborted when the civil war started and the fighting between the government forces and rebel fighters was nearing Bong Mines.

A rebel faction entered Bong Mines, and briefly occupied BMC concession areas, and the company was forced to immediately shut down. Zeptter and all German citizens and other foreign nationals working for the company were evacuated immediately. Hon. Barclay and his family fled to the United States as the war intensified.

CHAPTER 2

THE CIVIL WAR HAS ended. 4 years afterwards, Maila, like other towns, was still reeling from the carnage that took place during the conflict. Unlike other towns and villages along the main motor roads of the county, Maila did not experience any structural damage, even though some of its citizens who dare to venture to other parts of the country like Kakata, Gbarnga, or Monrovia, experienced first-hand some of the mayhem. But the town remained intact, hopeful that the transformation that was to have taken place will one day come. Hon. Barclay was still alive and throughout the war he had been in touch with the town's people, sending messages of courage and determination and always sending food supplies for their upkeep.

The town was saddened when they received news of Zeptter's death right after the war, but before that, the old German geologist and Hon. Barclay had completed a sketch of their land and the little details, including stunning ones the people of Maila did not even know about.

Tonolah Wuamah was born in Maila. He had survived the war, especially the hardship it brought. He was one of those who were optimistic that, now the war has ended, their town will finally be transformed to the resort that was promised by the investors. In fact, he has recently been in touch with Barclay's son who is currently residing in the United States with his aging father. He has sent word that he'd soon return to Maila to make his father's dream a reality.

Wuamah has known J. Boima Barclay Jr. as the toddler who briefly attended the Maila Elementary School. Before the war intensified, his father used to bring him to Maila whenever the representative was visiting. He also knew Easter Lumeh, the boy's mother who he practically grew up with. They all attended the Maila Elementary School together.

He and the current town chief, Peter Lomeh met young Barclay Jr. in Monrovia twice: the first time was in 1991, when the first interim government was established, but he could not go to Bong Mines because the country was still divided and that part was controlled by the larger rebel faction. The second time was after the 1997 elections. Again, he did not go to Bong Mines as the warring factions were not yet disarmed, and so he had to send for both men on those two occasions.

Since he learned of this latest development, a year and a half after the 2005 elections that brought a total end to the war, every morning he would saunter along the banks of the St. Paul and would suddenly fall into a reverie of how their town would look like.

He would see people, rich people of all nationalities riding in boats, skiing or swimming in the river and taking sun baths along the banks. He would imagine skyscraper hotels, bars and restaurants stretched along the banks and surrounding areas with its wonderful vegetation. He would see himself and other locals rushing to work early in the morning, and their kids going to nearby schools equipped with modern facilities even more sophisticated than the ones he used to marvel at back in the day at the Bong Mining Company Schools. As a young boy, Wuamah would often accompany his mother to sell roasted groundnuts and bananas at the school's gate.

He would see the town at night displaying magnificent lights illuminating the many hotels and resorts, and the bars and restaurants with the aroma of different kinds of dishes permeating their immediate surroundings. Wuamah remembered seeing these places only on television by peeping through the sliding glass window whenever he visited his maternal uncle employers' house in Bong Town. This uncle, John Dormeyahn, worked as a gardener for a German family. Wuamah also remembered the scent of delicious and exotic foods that oozed out of the Germans' kitchen.

He would daydream for hours and sometimes ignored greetings from fellow town dwellers as they passed by, while on their way to their farms or to fishing in the nearby tributaries. On many occasions, when he awoke from his fantasy either by himself or by some neighbor suddenly tapping his shoulder, Wuamah would revert to exploring the surroundings, venturing here and there to inspect and appreciate the scenery in anticipation of all the areas the development would be.

One sunny morning, he arose late from bed to the vigorous pounding on his door by Flomo, his 11 years old cousin, who by doing so had disrupted his sleep as he was deep into another fantasy.

"You made me jump from my sleep," he complained when he opened his door, stretching and yawning. "What's the matter? You want me to leave in my sleep?"

"You said to wake you up early to be ready in time for the meeting with Peter Lomeh, the Town Chief," replied the lad, rather startled. "And this was my third time knocking on your door. Look at the sun; it's already up."

"Ok but next time don't knock it too hard, people can die in their sleep for that."

"But you are the same person who told me to make sure you wake up," persisted the kid. "And look at how the sun is fully up and Chief Lomeh passed by and told me to inform you that he will be early on his way to Varney Town and . . ."

"I say don't knock on my door like that next time," he interrupted the kid, suspecting that the argument that was building up was not going to end, thus, increasing the likelihood of not meeting Chief Lomeh, his childhood friend, on time.

Wuamah watched as his cousin displayed his usual posture of still wanting to justify his action as he returned to the outside kitchen next to his aunt's mud house where he was helping her with the fire, while she prepared a breakfast of cooked cassava with fish and hot mashed paper, drenched in palm oil. He was reminded of the meticulousness of Flomo, as the kid would always go to lengths to justify his action on anything he thought was right.

"Since I told you, you will be a good lawyer in the future, you never cease from arguing with me. Thank God this is not during the civil war, where arguing with rebel fighters was going to be too bad for you."

"Why are you scolding your little cousin for doing exactly what you told him, Wuamah?" his mother inquired as soon as he entered the kitchen, made of sticks and palm thatches on the roofs.

"He did more than what he was told, Mamye," he answered, calling his mother by her name. "He made the whole of Maila know I woke up late this morning."

"Which is bad?" little Flomo interjected. "Maila hearing that you woke up late, or missing an important appointment with Chief Lomeh?"

"Or which is bad?" countered Wuamah, his attention now fixed on his cousin. "Still wanting to bring up a long argument that will make your aunty late for her garden and for me to miss Chief Lomeh?"

There was silence in the kitchen for some time. Little Flomo had searched all possible counter-arguments in his head to fire back at his older cousin, but there was none; his cousin has cleverly entrapped him to prevent another futile argument. Discerning Flomo' s thoughts, Wuamah started smiling again. His mother had finished cooking and had given each his portion of the cooked cassava breakfast and started eating hers. Wuamah took the small plastic bowl with his breakfast inside the house, wrapped it neatly with a sizable piece of country cloth, put it in his bag, and got up to leave.

He had left his single room mud house plastered with cement. As he walked through the town in rapid steps, he mused at the appearance of Maila; it has not changed much. There was still a mixture of huts with palm thatched roofs and mud houses plastered with cement, and zinc roofs just like his. There were few concrete houses, especially around the chief's quarter, built by Hon. Barclay. The avocado, pear, orange and paw-paw trees planted in the back yard of homes along with the cassava, sweet potatoes, pepper, and bitter balls backyard gardens still convey a sense of the identity of Maila.

He reached the ruins of Maila Elementary School and passed by it. To his right was the half broken down mud house with a dilapidated outside-kitchen in front of it. This was what was left of the old black smith house and the kitchen where he used to work. After school, he and his friends would be playing on the road and shouting while on their way home, but as soon as they reached the back smith work kitchen, they would suddenly be quiet until they walked past it, especially when he was there, working.

He suddenly felt uneasy, while passing by it. Sometimes Wuamah wondered what has become of him, since he left the town. And then he would conclude that maybe he died during the war.

"Why didn't Sengbeh just remain here or come back from wherever he went, doing the war?" he stood and asked himself, shook his head, and resumed walking.

At this time of the day when Maila is quiet; people are highly seen around the town center, except few older persons sitting by their houses and some lads in short pants and running about shirtless; everyone has either gone on his farm or has gone to tap latex on the surrounding rubber farms. After meeting with his friend Chief Lomeh, Wuamah will go tap some rubber on old man Kpaingba's farm. He will set off for his usual wandering along the banks of the St. Paul and into the surrounding vegetation.

Entering the chief quarters, he met Chief Lomeh at the front of his house, which was constructed of mud bricks and plastered with cement with beautifully designed paintings of artistic works depicting an ancient traditional Jorquelleh village. The town chief, a fair and average built man was attending to his motorbike, when Wuamah greeted him.

"I hope I did not keep you waiting, my young chief."

"No," replied Chief Lomeh, stopping what he was doing and watching his friend coming towards him. "Your cousin is effective in executing instructions."

Both men suddenly burst into laughter.

"Yeah, if I were going to allow any argument from him, your instructions could not have been carried out effectively," Wuamah said, offering a handshake as he neared the town chief while both were still laughing.

After the handshake and laughter between the two men, Chief Lomeh gestured to a bench on the side of his house for his friend to sit and resumed attending to his bike. He opened the top cover of the gas tank and shook it.

"This gas cannot take me from here to John Hill and back," he said. "Let me top it with the balance gas I have been keeping."

"From here to Varney Town is 3 hours. Can this gas you are adding take you there and back?" Wuamah asked as he helped his friend to steady the bike while he poured the gasoline from a white 5-gallon container, into the tank.

"Maybe, but I will get gas when I reached Varney Town," Lomeh answered. "The absence of network in this area is killing us. And I have to go, because Boima will be calling late this evening. He said he got a message for Siegie."

"From whom?" asked Wuamah, suddenly becoming concerned.

"From Hon. Barclay."

"A Message for Siegie?" Wuamah asked again.

"Yes, my friend. Koikoi Pewee. 'Siegie,' that pastor. Remember him, right?"

"Yes," Wuamah admitted with a deep sigh. "That pastor who won lots of Lorma votes for Hon. Barclay during the election. I wonder what that is about."

"Well," Chief Lomeh took a deep breath as he held Wuamah's left shoulder in a gesture to assure his friend. "That's why I am going for the call. And I will tell you. My nephew Barclay is serious, Wuamah," Chief Lomeh continued. "You and I have met him, right? Do not worry about Siegie. If I am reading your thoughts, we can rest assure that Boima is going to complete the survey his father and that German man started. He is bringing all the necessary equipment including boats. Remember what he said the last time we met him in Monrovia. He will start building the river docks where the boats will be stationed to explore the other parts of our waterways."

"I know," Wuamah said with a smile. "That boy is our own son from Maila here. We can trust him. But I fear that Siegie will start putting politics business in your nephew's head to start thinking about running as representative for Fuamah District in the next General and Presidential elections, and that will stall the development of our town."

"I don't think my nephew is interested in politics now, Wuamah," the chief told his friend.

The two friends beamed at this, and they suddenly turned to look at Maila and the landscape including the direction of the St. Paul and the nearby vegetation, beyond which, lies the impeccable wonders of their land.

"And there is something I must tell you before I forget," Chief Lomeh brought his friend to attention. "You have been hiding the issue of your Uncle Dormeyahn from me, knowing that I was not going to allow you to rescue him from the predicament he's in now. The fool knew very well that he was not able to mobilize the right men to tap Nathaniel Kpaingba's rubber, but he took the contract and time is now catching up with him. I learned that some of the tappers were inexperienced; they damaged almost a tile by slicing the trees, using the V Shape method. Kpankpa's latex leaked, until all dried out and killed the trees."

"Those guys damaged about 1,500 trees. If you divide that by 450 trees per tile, you are talking about 3 tiles. That alone is two pick-up loads of cup lumps every two weeks," Wuamah corrected the chief, rather appealingly. "You know it is because of my cousin, Flomo, I am doing this for him. Dormeyahn had that contract and he never told us, knowing that his son is living with us. I just didn't want Mamaye to feel bad when she asked me to help her only brother. That's why I agreed to recruit the right men for the job and those guys have been working for a week now and we will be concluding today. They have replaced all the damaged trees with new breeds of bud graphs from Firestone. And Nathaniel Kpaingba is happy about this."

"The same Nathaniel Kpaingba was happy when the trees were producing that whole week. But when he noticed that they could no longer produce and were dying, he started blaming Dormeyahn. So, he just used your uncle's stupidity to rejuvenate half of his farm with cheap "labor", interrupted the chief as lines of disappointment appeared across his forehead. "I have never seen a stingy Kpelle man like that."

"When he saw the work I did, he offered me the foreman position but I refused before he could say anything else."

"I know," laughed the town chief." "With the thing that's about to happen in Maila? Who wants to waste their time tapping rubber for Nathaniel Kpaingba."

"So Chief I am sorry for not bringing this to you before I accepted to help him."

"Okay my friend. Just that your uncle is very foolish. All that time he was working with the white people in Bong Mines, still no sense is in his head. He allows Nathaniel Kpaingba to convince him that nothing good will happen to Maila."

"Kpaingba will see for himself," added Wuamah. "There will be a time when Maila begin to boom, he will get no one to work on his farm."

"Time will tell, Wuamah," the chief said and gestured to his friend as he mounted his bike. "I will be passing by Cooper Dennis farm; I can drop you at Kpaingba's junction."

"Let me rush to speak to your old man. I will not be long."

Wuamah hurried into the old chief's house at the rear of the chief's quarter and greeted the now frail old man he was surprised to see sitting on his bed rather than always lying-in bed, and refusing to eat anything heavy and with palm oil in it. For some strange reasons, the old chief has started putting life in himself, after his son and Wuamah met the young Barclay for the second time.

He thought continual mourning for his wife, and the refusal of his daughter, Esther Gorpue Lomeh to return to Maila, years after the war, was having a toil on the old chief. Quite recently, as Wuamah observed, the old man had been caught kneeling before his bed and meditating.

While he and the chief rode on the bike on the rocky and rough laterite road heading towards Cooper Dennis farm, he wondered where Esther might be now. Throughout the war, there had been no bad news about her. Some people from Bong Mines saw her briefly at an internally displaced camp along the Kakata—Weala Highway just before the fall of Gbarnga. Since then, no one knew her whereabouts.

She refused to visit her parents in protest when they asked Representative Barclay to take his son to Monrovia when government forces lost Gbarnga in 1990. She blamed them, especially her father when the Law maker fled with her son to the United States, without consulting her. In 2003, when the war officially ended, puzzling to Wuamah, Esther did not return to Maila for the burial even when her mother died. This was a year after the general and presidential elections.

"Wuamah. This time you are not daydreaming. What's the worry I see on your face?" Chief Peter Lomeh asked, when they reached Kpaingba's Farm Junction, and noticed that his friend seemed to be lost in consternation.

"It's nothing," denied Wuamah.

"We have reached Kpaingba's Junction and your workers are on time."

They met a group of men who he suspected were the men who his friend had recruited from all the way to Mawah to complete the work on Kpanbgai's farm. Recognizing that it was the Town Chief of Maila who was riding the bike, the men greeted him.

Wuamah disembarked, and they all waved as Chief Lomeh continued his journey to Varney Town in Central Bong Mines. Then Wuamah gathered the men, briefed them on the work for the day, their payment plan and they all started on foot to the farm.

"Your men completed the work sooner than expected, today," mused Nathaniel Kpaingba, just after midday while he and Wuamah were standing near one of his rubber storage bungalows with a bag of money in his hand.

"Yes. It's time to get paid so I can be on my way."

"Oh yes, sure. But, what about the foreman position I offered you?"

"I am not interested."

"Yes. I almost forgot. You and the development of your town that has gotten over you lately," chuckled the average-built man. "Here. Take the money. Just so you know, I have hired most of the men."

"Just make sure you always pay them well."

The workers were paid and some of them had left. The ones who Nathaniel Kpaingba had talked to about hiring them, decided to wait around to finalize the agreement with him. Then came Lawuo, the Lorma lady who always sold fresh palm wine to them. She had brought some filled in a black five-gallon container.

They all gathered at the old rubber weighing station where she usually sat and sold it. Wuamah was about to leave when he saw his uncle, Dormeyahn amongst the men in a heated debate. Dormeyahn also saw him and waved, but Wuamah nodded slightly, a way to tell his uncle that he was not happy with him.

"Gentlemen, please let me ask Dormeyahn something I have been observing about him since we came to work on this farm," shouted Tokpa Moie, one of the tappers, thus bringing the rest of them to attention. "Why this John Dormeyahn man always talks about things only he can attest to?"

The men burst into loud laughter.

"You see now. Some of you were not around when Bong Mining Company was here operating. If some of you have seen Bong Town that people used to call 'Small Germany', you guys will not be sitting down here laughing. I say people used to come all the way from Germany and America to Bong Town for vacation. I used to live with the white people I was working with in Bong Town where there was 24 hours electricity and all the homes had Air Conditioners. I spoke German and I ate good food. Not like some of you who are still eating bamboo worms in this bush."

"With all of that, the German people you say you were living with did not take you with them when they were leaving, but they carried other people and here you are tapping and hauling rubber from village to village," another tapper, Harris Yasiah interrupted.

"And this same Dormeyahn man who's talking about us eating bamboo worms can himself eat rubber disease, the worse one," added Tarwo Cammue, another rubber tapper, and the rest of them exploded into another laughter as he meant that Dormeyahn eats the larvae of the ordinary weevils that are found in dead rubber trees, unlike the edible and nutritious larvae of the Red Palm Weevils found in dead palm trees.

Wuamah joined them, trying not to laugh. He ordered a cup of palm wine. After drinking it, he paid Lawuo and left.

"My nephew was just here. I expected you fools to ask him about me," he heard his uncle say, as he walked across the farm and took a path that led down to a tributary of the St. Paul.

"Dormeyah stop fooling yourself before thinking about fooling us. You think we are stupid to believe a liar who will say 'my witness was here, but no one asked him?'" replied one of the men, and another lighter erupted.

Wuamah chuckled.

He reached the waterside, a busy crossing point noted for its daily commercial activities. On a second Saturday like this, business often booms. People would come from Monrovia to buy a variety of food stuffs including palm oil and charcoal from farmers who brought their produce from across the river to trade. There's often busy traffic of motorbikes loaded with these goods which are transported to the parking station in Varney Town which is a transit point, and are loaded on transport vehicles and taken to Gorbar Chop Market in Red Light, Paynesville, outside of Monrovia to sell. Also, most of the nearby rubber farm owners pay their tappers. With cash on hand, the rubber tappers buy their goods and then they mery make with the consumption of the best palm wine.

This waterside comprises a waterway which headed north towards Maila which was the shortest way from Kpaingba's Farm. The southern part, which was the busiest one, joins the St. Paul and heads southwards, towards Dobli Island in Haindii. The few canoes ferrying to and from the direction of Maila were all out so Wuamah had to wait. He sat at a palm wine station, near a small rubber weighing, selling and buying station where people with small rubber farms from across the river ferried their latex to sell to the large plantation owners. To kill a little time, he ordered a cup of palm wine.

He took his first sip, and tried to compare the booze to Lawuo's, and would have loved to continue drinking more of hers because the taste was refreshing. But he was forced to hurry out of there, when the workers were making fun of his uncle. Unfortunately, he was distracted by a serious grumble that suddenly erupted at the rubber weighing station between a group of small rubber farmers who had transported their cup lumps and dried latex from across the river and the weigher.

"I will not accept that kind of rate you are calculating for the Dry Rubber Content. No way," vehemently protested one of the rubber farmers, pulling a 100 lb rice bag full of cup lumps from the scale. "Tarpeh. You will not cheat us today."

"My man, don't come cause problems here. That's the correct rate I am using to calculate your DRC," Tarpeh rebutted, using the abbreviation for Dry Rubber Content.

"You lie," rejected the farmer, and turned to the others. "He's taking a huge portion of the DRC as water so he can calculate a lower selling price. What will we carry home to our family? In fact, let the man get down from the scale, until Kaba-kollie can come to weigh our rubber, properly."

"I always told you people that this Jackson Tarpeh man knows nothing about the rubber weighing business. Now you have seen it," retorted another farmer.

"Even with Kaba-kollie, the rate will still be the same. I know what I am doing. I am not stupid. I went to school."

"That school business we're talking about here?" raged another farmer. "You think sawgrass will be gashing our skins, hauling our rubber from the bush for you to be cheating us like this? Let's get him down from the scale."

Immediately, they all rushed to pull Jackson Tarpeh, a bright and tall man, down from the weighing platform. This further aggravated the grumble and resulted into a fray when Tarpeh, clinging onto the scale, refused to get down. Later, Kaba-kollie, a fat man came rushing to the scene, breathing heavily, and put the situation under control.

Tarpeh watched as Kaba-kollie reweighed the disenchanted farmers' rubber much to their satisfaction.

"You, Tarpeh. That school business we are discussing here? Ever since the war ended, why can't you go back to your county to carry book business there?" a farmer, who has just gotten his rubber weighed, and was paid satisfactorily, addressed Tapheh, prompting the others to laugh at him.

"Tarpeh used to be behind those rebel boys in Varney Town harassing people to pay taxes to the rebel government, during the war," one of them said. "You think we are in those days where you did anything you like?"

Wuamah wanted to laugh as the farmers made fun of Jackson Tarpeh. This reminded him of his uncle.

Before the war he and Dormeyahn were close. Wuamah always visited his uncle when he was living with his German employers, and they did eat good food. Dormeyahn had not been the laughingstock people thought he was. He was a responsible and trusted boy to the extent that his employers took him as their son.

When he graduated from high school, his intention was to go to Monrovia to attend the University of Liberia, but because he failed one subject in the National Exam, he was going to wait for a whole year to take the re-sitter for that subject, pass it before entering the University. His employers advised that he should instead enroll at the Vocational Training Center and after graduation, he would be able to work for the company. So, he did, and was trained as a heavy-duty equipment mechanic.

He was in his senior year and was on his first Job training, assigned with the heavy-duty maintenance crew that operated the huge U-Clays and other heavy-duty equipment up the mountain, when the war came and entered Bong Mines. After the rebel faction that broke away from the main rebel group entered Bong Mines, the company shut down and its staff evacuated immediately after this rebel faction left and headed for Monrovia. Thinking that the war would not last, most of the staff left their tenants in their homes to secure them until their return. Dormeyahn employers asked whether he could do the same and he agreed.

Bong Mines was quiet for some time as most of the fighting was concentrated around Monrovia. Dormeyahn would pay occasional visits to Maila and sometimes he would bring things for his sister who he knew as his mother because she took care of him when their mother died. He would also take Wuamah with him to spend some time and would bring him back to Maila. One day Dormeyahn introduced Wuamah, who was 12 years old at the time, to a beautiful woman.

"She is Rebecca Habbah. From now on, you must see her as your aunty. She and I will get married after the war," he told his nephew.

Rebecca Habbah was dark in complexion with large breasts, small waist, wide hips and big legs. She preferred her hair cut low and always wore purple lipstick and large earrings. She was from Bong Mines, but had been living in Monrovia. For fear of the fighting there she had returned to Bong Mines. At first, she visited for almost a day and would return to Nyenen. It didn't take long before they started living together, especially when it was clear that the war would not end anytime soon and his employers would not be coming back to Liberia.

Whenever Wuamah was spending time, at night, he would hear strange noises coming from the room where his uncle and Rebecca Habah slept. These strange moans and screams, which were mostly his uncle's voice, sometimes echoing in rapid succession were often in high, medium and low pitches. And as a kid, he was afraid that his uncle was reeling with pain and wondered why it must always happen whenever everyone was asleep.

What startled Wuamah most was the noise would last for a few minutes and then it would subside. He would wait for a while, and thinking that something had happened to his uncle, he would creep into his room only to find Dormeyahn and the woman sound asleep. What was confusing to the kid was that the next morning his uncle would appear like nothing was wrong; he would appear exhausted, but somehow rejuvenated.

This night there were these strange grunts again. Instead of waiting for it to die down, he hurriedly tiptoed towards his uncle's door which was usually left ajar, and peeped inside. Fear suddenly gripped him. He saw Rebecca Habah on top of Dormeyahn, riding him like hell, her pumpkin- size breasts brushing his face.

He stood, spell bond, watching his uncle he thought was helplessly screaming in his sleep, as this woman performed this strange ritual on top of him, until she caught his eyes and ordered him back to his room with the direction of her index finger. In no time the kid was back in his bed with his heart pounding profusely as his body continued to shiver with fear.

Even now as an adult who has experienced and understood what was happening then, glimpses of that scene still flashed into his memory. Whenever he saw a woman with a low haircut, large breasts and wide hips, he would wonder whether she could do the same. The following week, with his urging, his uncle took him back to Maila. His mother, who became concerned, asked why out of a sudden he was eager to return to Maila, leaving the luxury of Bong Town where he had always wanted to visit. He told his mother that Rebecca Habah was a witch who always performs a strange ritual on top of his uncle that caused him to scream in his sleep in the middle of the night. His mother confronted her brother about this and after he told her it was simply nothing to worry about, she smiled and told him to always lock his room door whenever he and his girlfriend went to bed.

"Let that man just stay here now, Mamye," Wuamah heard his uncle saying. "My little nephew wants to be foolish now."

Dormeyahn and Rebeca Habah continued to live together at his employer's house in Bong Town. Things were going well for them. There was sufficient food and a steady income to satisfy their material needs. Dormeyahn was fortunate to be part of a skeleton team left to keep the Company's heavy-duty equipment intact to resume operation when the war ends. The Company power supply was still intact and everything appeared to be normal. But the fighting in Monrovia raged on even after the President was captured and assassinated. The Economic Community of West African States, (ECOWAS) and the rest of the international community started making efforts to broker peace between the warring factions but the main rebel group objected to these deals leading to numerous peace summits with still no agreement reached. More warring factions began to emerge especially, a new rebel group that was formed in Sierra Leone whose aim, according to them was to threaten the main rebel group on the west in a bid to force its leader to abide by the peace accords.

As the uncertainty of finding a peaceful solution to ending the war loomed, the main rebel group began to enter Bong Mines. Many of their fighters were occupying the concession areas now largely abandoned by the local staff as most of them had fled the country to neighboring Ivory Coast or the United States. Dormeyahn and few others were still living in Bong Town when one morning, a rebel group led by one Alfred Mantee, a rebel elite Special Forces sent to take control of Bong Mines, entered the Manager Quarters where he and Rebecca Habah were staying.

CO Alfred Mantee, a huge and extremely muscular man with an overgrown beard, ordered his bodyguards to take over the entire quarter. He also secured the house in which Dormeyahn was living and gave him three days to vacate. However, he later changed his mind when his senior intelligence officer informed him that Dormeyahn was a good heavy-duty mechanic, and they needed him to dismantle the heavy-duty equipment up the mountain as there were other plans in the pipeline for them. In the first few days, Dormeyahn watched with horror as the heavy-duty equipment he was dismantling were loaded on trailers and taken away.

He also observed that CO Alfred Mantee was making advances at Rebecca Habah. From being his special cook, the rebel commander had started inviting her in his bedroom, without first inquiring who she was to Dormeyahn. Many times, he would ask Dormeyahn to do the cooking when he took Rebeca Habah along with him to Gbarnga, whenever he was summoned by the head of the main rebel movement.

At night, Dormeyahn could not sleep, whenever he heard the same screams, this time more than the ones he used to make, coming from the same room he and Rebecca Habah used to sleep in. This had a psychological impact on him, especially when Rebecca Habah, who at first wept bitterly with him the first time it happened, now seemed to be comfortable with the situation.

This worried Dormeyahn. He began to lose weight due to the loss of appetite. As the thought of finally losing Rebecca Habah wore him down, he began to lose concentration. The tools he worked with started slipping from his hands, prompting his colleagues and even some of the fighters to ask what was wrong with him. Some asked him whether he was sick and if so, he needed to do something about his health.

One day, when he could no longer bear it, he gathered his personal belongings and took to leaving. CO Alfred Mantee learned of this that same day and feeling disrespected that Dormeyahn did not inform him before leaving, ordered his boys to find and bring him back. Dormeyahn was spotted around Botota, while crossing the train tracks to enter Varney Town and was detained.

"CO Mentee. If I will die today, so be it, but let me tell you the truth," Dormeyahn had lamented, tears flooding his eyes as he addressed the rebel commander. "I cannot be sleeping in the same house with and at the same time cooking for you when you are sleeping with my woman, Rebecca."

"So you are brave to tell me this?" CO Alfred Mentee suddenly rose to his feet, shouting. "That woman business we are talking about here? You sit and do nothing while we are risking our lives, fighting this war for you people? You see. You Kpelle people are very jealous and deep. Are you now against me for woman business?"

"I am told he's a Jorquelleh man, CO," interjected one of the rebel fighters who arrested him.

"I see. They say Jorquelleh men can chop people with their cutlasses for women's business. If I did not have a gun and was surrounded by bodyguards, this other one was going to butcher me. In fact, take him away and have him executed."

"CO we still need him. He's doing a good job for us up the mountain," pleaded another rebel fighter, who was the provost, spear-heading the work up the mountain. "And we still have more to do."

"Have you not been useful, I would have executed you," Co Mentee said, suddenly calming down. Dismantling the equipment was a strict mandate from Gbarnga. "Have him flocked and jailed. I will decide when to release him."

"Let's tie-bay him," ordered a fighter who was the ground commander.

"No, if we tie him like that, it will injure his arms, making it impossible for him to do our work," the provost refused.

Dormeyahn was flocked. And as he was led into this cell, he caught Rebecca's eyes and instantly felt betrayed; he saw no sense of remorse, but that he was an embarrassment to her. All she did was to frown and turn her face. CO Alfred Mentee also looked at her, scanning her beautiful and enticing body with extreme Jealousy. The rebel commander had never experienced the erotic pleasure he was having with her, and so he will not allow a "stupid Kpelle" civilian like Dormeyahn to enjoy it anymore.

Maymye and her late husband, Klemenni Wuamah, the father of Tonolah Wuamah, learned of this and paid a visit to the rebel commander to appeal on his behalf. Because CO Mentee knew his folks, and how they were very nice people who often brought him farm products whenever they came to visit Dormeyahn, agreed to free him on the condition that he must erase Rebecca Habah out of his mind and must never be seen near her. He is free to stay in one of the houses in the Managers Quarters.

Dormeyahn agreed and swore upon his traditional bush school fraternity that he will erase Rebeca Habbah out of his mind, and that he will continue to work on the heavy-duty equipment up the mountain, but begged not to stay at Managers Quarter. He'd rather stay at one of the cabins used by the mine securities who were referred to as Mind Guards. CO Alfred Mantee agreed, after more urging from the Wuamah and Dormeyahn's wish was granted.

He continued to live and work up the mountain, dismantling tons of heavy-duty equipment. Even though he did not want to see Rebecca Habah again, for fear of his life, Dormeyahn missed the good times they shared together during normal times. The rebel faction that was formed in Sierra Leone had attacked and overran the territories of the main rebel group from the west of Liberia, eventually capturing Cape Mount, Bomi and Gbarpolu Counties. Bong Mines was now a target when people in the vicinity of Haindii were giving accounts of spotting strange armed men parading the surrounding bushes along the banks of the St. Paul on Gbarpolu side.

Bong Mines became tense, when there was intelligence of an imminent attack by way of Haindii. CO Alfred Mentee was too busy up and down Bong Mines-Haindii Road, ensuring that security was beefed up and sometimes going to Gbarnga, whenever he was summoned by the leader of the main rebel group.

Dormeyahn became hopeful that the rebel commander would soon abandon Rebeca Habah in the midst of the increasing pressure on him to ensure that Bong Mines did not fall to the enemy rebel faction. He and Rebecca started seeing each other again, when it was apparent that the rebel commander was no longer residing at the Managers Quarter, and Dormeyahn soon forgot the pains he bore when he had lost her.

Haindii was eventually captured and the enemy rebel group was moving fast towards Bong Mines. One day, while up the mountain, there was news that Nyeanblia, some 3km from Varney Town was under attack and people were fleeing from nearby Benuma. Dormeyahn immediately left the mountain and hurried to Bong Town to get Rebecca Habbah so they could flee to Maila, but when he got there, she was gone. Again, he became a broken man, this time very disoriented and frustrated when he later learned from some retreating rebel friends that CO Alfred Mentee had sent some of his men for Rebecca and they had taken her to Kakata where he had now retreated. He was also advised to stay clear of the rebel commander who swore to order his execution whenever he sees him.

Dormeyahn's life had never been the same. Rebecca had again broken his heart. In the last few weeks, they were again together, he experienced far more pleasure than previous ones. She had told him that it was because of the pains and humiliation he bore for her sake, and that he was a nice man and could forgive her, after all what she had done to him. She swore that CO Alfred Mentee would have to drag her dead body if he ever tried to take her, again.

Now that she had gone back to him, and only left him with the memory of the pleasure that has since taunted him whenever he went to bed, he had known no other woman that could satisfy him. Back in Maila he had been from one relationship to another but none lasted as none gave him the pleasure he was used to from his beloved Rebecca.

Once, during the days of the occupying rebel group that captured Bong Mines, he met Gayduo, a Lorma girl who was displaced from Kakata. She had gone to Haindii to buy palm oil which she converted into torborgee oil and sold them at Katata Market, when the opposing rebel forces attacked. She remained hidden in surrounding villages and later moved to Bong Mines when there was some calm. Because the road from Bong Mines to Kakata was blocked, she remained in Varney Town, selling her torborgee oil in the market.

They met at a mechanic shop where Dormeyahn repaired vehicles used by the fighters to haul the spoils from the conflict. Gayduo was slim, and fair in complexion. She was quiet, submissive and looked nice to him, though she did not bear the enticing physique like Rebecca Habbah.

Dormeyahn took her to Maila and introduced her to his folks and they all liked her. She stayed with them while he was between Maila and Varney Town. Soon she got pregnant and gave birth to a boy who they named, Flomo. Initially, the thought of Rebeca Habah had diminished from his mind, but after some time, he started thinking about her again, and began to imagine the pleasure she gave him.

He and Gayduo started having problems when she could not agree to do the things Rebecca did to satisfy him on grounds that she was not a street girl and that it is the doing of street girls. This got to the point where Dormeyahn vowed to end the relationship, if she continued to give him problems and their relationship eventually ended. Gayduo later left for Kakata when the Economic Community of West African States Peace Monitoring Group (ECOMOG) assumed control after the Octopus invasion, and when she learned that her parents were still alive and were longing to see her.

Flomo was three years old, too young to travel all the way to kakata with her. At the urging of his aunt and uncle, she left without him and promised to return when things got better. Dormeyahn did not bother at first, until he visited Kakata when Flomo was now four years old. In kakata, he learned from her parents that Gayduo was now living in Monrovia with a Nigerian ECOMOG Soldier. When he also inquired of Rebecca Habbah, his main aim of visiting Kakata, some people he knew from Bong Mines told him that CO. Alfred Mentee had taken her along with their twins to Nimba where he was operating a Diamond Creek.

"Rebeca gave birth to twins?!" Dormeyahn wept. Since then, he returned to Maila a broken man and had never recovered.

A Canoe had arrived from upstream loaded with some farm produce from the direction of Maila. A group of marketers rushed a few yards into the water to help haul it ashore. When all the produce was offloaded, Wuamah and three other women along with their children mounted the canoe, negotiated with the young canoe man who agreed to ferry them upstream towards Maila. Wuamah watched as the canoe man steadily steered the canoe upstream, which was the most difficult part, once steering a course against the current. He himself was an experienced one. Satisfied that the young man who he barely knew, was doing a great job, he reverted his attention to viewing the natural scenery on both sides of the river.

Again, the thought of his uncle seized his attention, but he struggled to fight it off. He has done what he was supposed to do only for his mother's sake. He didn't need to worry about a fellow who has become more useless even in the midst of the little opportunities he always had to put himself back together.

Dormeyahn always sought contracts to operate vehicles on most of the surrounding rubber farms due to his background in mechanics. Sometimes he would win contracts to hire people to tap rubber and would never complete the job and would fall into trouble. When confronted, he would boast of his knowledge of the German language and his skills in heavy duty mechanics. He has always blamed his folks for letting Gayduo leave in the first place. They should have by all means settled the dispute and convinced her to stay, but they allowed her to leave. That was where he and Wuamah did not always agree.

The canoe landed at a small village, a few kilometers west of Cooper Dennis Farm and the three women and their children disembarked. It then continued until it reached the last turning point right before an elbow where the river turns left and enters the St. Paul. Wuamah disembarked. It was nearing the evening hours now. He watched as the young canoe man turned the canoe around and peddled back downstream to take the one-and-a-half-hour ride towards the crossing point at Kpaingbai's Farm. When it had gone far off and was almost out of sight, Wuamah started off on a path that would take him a 45 minutes' walk to Maila.

The Maila native continued along the path bordered by a stretch of young bush on both sides. The sun, which was at first overhead, was gradually setting towards the east. The birds were tweeting in the nearby trees, as crickets chirped from the undergrowth. He was occasionally alerted to rustlings in the grass, caused by small bush lizards, squirrels or snakes getting away to the sound of his approaching footsteps. As a kid who roamed the nearby bushes of Maila, he had learned to tell whether the rustling was caused by the bush lizards, rodents or snakes.

He had walked about 10 minutes when he reached an intersection where one path headed south while the other headed north. Continuing eastwards would lead him to Maila, but he did not wish to go home now. Chief Lomeh may still be in Varney Town and will be returning to Maila late. He wanted to hear from him as to the outcome of the call with J. Boima Barclay Junior. Both men enjoyed discussing Maila while eating and drinking. So, he took the path northwards to check on his palm wine tree.

He continued for some minutes, until he reached the mouth of another tributary of the St. Paul. For some time, he strolled along a trail littered with fine whitish clay soil close to the banks. He turned right, leaving the larger St. Paul at his rear, headed on for some time and reached a spot where he scooped under rows of layers of cascading branches of trees on both sides of a shadow brook as he turned southwards. He reached a clearing of whitish clay sand where stood a structure in the form of a small gazebo made of sticks, bamboo and palm thatches. He removed his bag from his back and hurried into a low bush and later came back hauling a beautifully decorated canoe.

Few minutes later, Tonolah Wuamah was paddling out of the shallow brook. He turned left, making his way into the tributary and kept on a steady course towards the direction of its mouth where it enters the

St. Paul. The sun had descended eastward, casting its bright orange rays on the far horizon of the river thus giving the waters a golden color, a pleasant scene that always captivated him. He paddled gently up north on the St. Paul for a couple of minutes until he reached the mouth of another tributary on his right. He entered it and steered downstream with less paddling as he relied on the current.

He reached a point where the river split and curved around a small and beautiful Island of palm grooves and ferns. Wuamah peddled on the left side where the current wasn't strong and navigated through the coordinated patterns of ripples. He entered the Island through a small creek bordered by algae covered rocks. He gently glided on, where the creek flowed a few meters into the Island and landed at a suitable spot. He anchored his canoe with a tiny rope tied unto the nose of a stick, got his backpack and disembarked. He walked a few meters along a path covered on both sides of its border with low growing field grass and whitish brown soil. He could hear from the distance ahead of him, the steady roar of the current where the two halves of the rivers from both sides of the Island rejoined, forming a much larger one that headed southwards downstream.

Wuamah entered a small swamp with some palm trees. After removing his Timberland booths from his feet, he waded through the ankle-high shallow waters covered with green algae, taking few careful steps until he reached his palm wine tree with a tree climber tied unto it. Wuamah used it to climb to the upper most top and first observed the base of the branches attached to the crown shaft to make sure no snake was lurking between them. Inexperienced palm wine tappers are sometimes bitten by poisonous black mambas. Then he inspected a small white three-gallon container attached to a chopped off stalk of a branch with a small 12-inch-long tube protruding from the top of the container into a portion of the trunk. He was satisfied it was full with fresh palm wine.

On the shores of the Island, he sat on a bamboo bench looking northwards at a distributary that connected to a network of shallow brooks and small rivers. He tasted the wine, and as usual, it was refreshing. The taste of the wine from this Island was appetizing and refreshing as compared to other wines in other parts of Lower Bong County. It was so alluring that if care isn't taken people became addicted to it.

Wuamah always hoped that this would be one of the trademarks of Maila when the town eventually opened up to Liberia and the tourism world for business. Only a few people in Maila knew of this palm wine with such a magnificent flavor. To him this was one of the hidden successes of Maila.

He later left the Island and was paddling on the distributary that led to the network of waterways leaving the St. Paul westwards at his left. The sun was still steadily setting and the orange red twilight had now fully descended on the water and the surroundings which told him that darkness will be less than three hours away. He mused at the fact that he still got little time to peddle around some of these networks of water channels enjoying the exquisite scenery.

Still feeling the refreshment of the wine as he rowed on, he began to feel drowsy due to the gentleness of the current, coupled with the mesmerizing sound of the ripples as they hit the sides of his canoe. Wuamah suddenly doused off as he lay, face up, into the canoe after uttering a loud yawn.

He was suddenly awakened when the front bow of the canoe hit against a huge rock which formed part of a cluster of rapids sparsely separated from each other. Wuamah realized that the course of the canoe had been interrupted by the rapids which extended a few feet to the shore of a cliff. This place looked strange as he looked around him with apprehension, and concluded that he may have been drifting for about two and a half hours. He looked up and saw that a cliff of about 1000 feet high covered with vegetation of layers of green moors and low trees stood before him.

This cannot be a part of Bong Range, he thought as he assumed that the mountain range was northeast of Maila, extending towards the western tip of Weala District with a distance of about 60 to 70 kilometers away from the town. He had been on a steady course northward and he believed it remained that way while the canoe was adrift. A streak of beam suddenly covered his face as it appeared to him that he had discovered another wonder of Maila.

Wuamah managed to carefully navigate his canoe between the rapids and landed on the rocky shore of the cliff. He made his way up the cliff with ease, but with little time. It won't take him long to scan this place. He reached an area where the trees were taller, with wide branches that provided a perfect shade. He continued walking towards the far edge and looked down. He could see a river that snaked through the foot of the cliff on the far left, but he wasn't sure it was the St. Paul or one of its tributaries.

The land below showed a plethora of beautiful scenery. Not quite satisfied as his curiosity grew, he continued walking but now turned his attention to the right where it looked darker, but he could see his way through as the trees on this side of the cliff were spread wide apart thus, allowing reflection from the sky.

He reached an area where the land descended down a steep and rocky slope. He could see running water flowing out of a crevice on his right. He took careful steps on the rocks as he descended along the edge of the running water. He suddenly marveled with disbelief when he reached a place where the running water cascaded mid-way of the slope and landed into an opening amongst the rocks thus forming a beautiful waterfall pool. He had seen another wonder of

Maila. Wuamah sat on one of the rocks and began to sob as the pride and joy of discovering this part of the bushes of Maila captivated him.

He wiped the tears from his eyes with the back of his hands and scanned the terrain ahead of him. It was increasingly getting dark but he could still manage to see. Then something suddenly caught his attention. There was an object lying against a tree a few meters from where he sat. He immediately sprang to his feet and started walking towards it when it appeared that it was an iron or an object made of steel he was looking at. And if he was correct, it would mean that someone else had been here.

As he moved closer to it, the glee he had just exhibited was increasingly turning to disappointment when it was actually an object he was looking at. It was an old and rusty AK-47 rifle. He also looked on the ground and was appalled to see bullets scattered all over. Someone was here and had been shooting.

He could hear his own heartbeat, as it pounded. His head also started swinging as sweat profusely ran down his body. It's like he was going to pass out. About two or three meters ahead, there were human remains tied to a tree. It appeared like it had been there for long as the clothes on the skeletons had all worn out. What was left of the trousers this person was wearing was military issued; the cargo pockets on both sides were still intact. There was a pair of military booths on its feet. What was more troubling and increasingly unbearable to see was another human remains tied to the tree in like manner. Lying on the feet of this one was another rusty AK-47 rifle. Wuamah noticed that some pieces of what remained of the clothes they were wearing appeared like they were burned together with human flesh. More frightening was that some parts of the skeleton, especially both sides of the skull and the rib cage were burned like someone used a hot object on them.

"What happened here, so?" muttered Wuamah, frozen with fear.

He was suddenly plunged into the fear and trepidation he once experienced as a kid, the night he saw Rebecca Habbah on top of his uncle when he stumbled over a mound of about 2 feet high made of clayish material with the ashes of a special kind of charcoal scattered at an opening at its mouth. Wuamah immediately recognized that it was a furnace used by black smiths. The thick charcoal was made out of a special kind of wood that produces immense heat used for smelting iron ore.

In traditional historic accounts, it was the Jorquelleh of Maila who experimented the use of such a furnace. It was used by a certain blacksmith to fashion iron spears and machetes to defeat the Gola once in a war. It was never meant to be used on human beings as the burned cloth with traces of burned human flesh suggested. Wuamah soon realized that he missed something. On what remained of the clothes on all the human remains were traces of a brown chalk which now looked dusty.

"It must have been a ritual," Wuamah thought. Someone was performing some kind of ordeal, and he tried to make sense of it.

"Gbeh Vey?" he suddenly shouted with a deep chilly voice in his native vernacular meaning, who is it? Upon seeing a very huge shadow that appeared to be emerging from the dark.

He immediately took off with a heavy speed stomping his feet against the roots at the same time falling down, hurting himself and quickly getting up, when the shadow appeared to be quickly advancing towards him. Wuamah reached the waterfall pool in no time, and started crawling up the rocky slope, surprised at the unhindered efforts he was applying, as his ten fingers clawed at the slippery rocks, helping to pull him up.

Unfortunately, when he had reached mid-way to the top, he slipped and started sliding down the slope. He tried to stick the nose of the timberland boots he was wearing into the small spaces between the rocks to stop him from sliding further down, but that could not stop him. The soil between the rocks was wet, due to the continual splashing from the running water that flowed down the slope and the slippery algae that covered the rocks.

He made frantic efforts to stop sliding and to find his way back up, but it was proving more difficult. In the frenzy of ensuring that he did not reach the bottom of the slope, he started rolling, this time hitting the rocks, bruising himself against the sharp edges.

He hit his head against a large one and sustained a concoction. This caused him to give up fighting and finally landed down the slope. He uttered a sharp cry and groaned as he struggled to roll on his back. He made an effort to open his eyes slightly as his body became weak. He could not even move his legs or his hands anymore.

Wuamah managed to see the shadow which now appeared to be standing over him, but he could not tell what or who it was, but was certain it was something dangerous. All he knew he was going to die. He was going to face the same ordeal as the unfortunate souls tied to the trees. Who were they? The question came to him. What were armed men doing in a place that had been kept a secret for decades, from the time the Gola were defeated? What or Who was about to seal his doom? Faint tears rolled down his cheeks.

CHAPTER 3

H AINDII MARKET DAY, APRIL 1993. Just before noon, the sun was up and the town on the edge of the St. Paul River was bustling with commercial activities. People were bringing their produce from the surrounding villages to the market to sell. Canoes were busy ferrying goods to and from the nearby Dobli Island. Plumes of dust filled the air as the road to Bong Mines was busy with traffic. Pickup trucks, loaded with goods and passengers on board, repeatedly blew their horns, as they sped past young men and women walking on both sides of the road, toting their goods on their heads, making their way to the market ground.

Battle worn trucks with arm men on board also sped to and from the town. Few motor bikes were plowing this route hauling gallons of containers, some empty, especially the ones entering the town while others, filled with palm oil heading towards Bong Mines.

The market ground was crowded and filled with the euphoria of bargaining and trading between the marketers and their customers who came from as far as Monrovia. Palm wine stations were full of young men and some fighters of the main rebel group, drinking, while others were seated around makeshift structures filled with the mixture of locally made and imported alcoholic beverages, also drinking amid heated arguments and laughter, and agitation. In other parts of the town, some rebel fighters, toting Ak-47 rifles, were roaming about, sometimes questioning and harassing people they suspected as enemies' collaborators.

Halfway across the river at the edge of the Dobli Island facing the distant bushes of Gbarpolu County, a brigade of rebel fighters of the main rebel group was positioned as they lie in ambush, with their AK-47s, RPGs, and BZTs locked and loaded as they monitored the quiet shorelines on the Gbarpolu side. They were responding to intelligence of an enemy rebel incursion in the bushes on that side of the river.

They had been dispatched to scout the terrain to ensure that their position was not infiltrated, arm bushed and attacked. That would lead to the subsequent attack and capture of Haindii as Cape Mount, Bomi and Gbarpoplu Countries were already overrun months ago.

Sergeant-Major Eric Gonpue, the youthful commander of the rebel brigade who appeared to be in his early twenties carefully crept out of his concealment and positioned himself behind a tree. He was of average height and light in complexion with a deep scar that ran from the left side of his forehead down his cheek. He peered through a pair of binoculars and scanned ahead of him to the west, north and south of the river. He sensed that at any moment, there were going to be movements along the shore lines in anticipation that the enemy forces may attack Haindii at any time. Sergeant-Major Gonpue and his men were in full readiness to defend Haindii, if it was attacked.

The enemy forces had a tendency of invading territories on market days, when people were busy doing business. It was hard times for the main rebel group who once controlled about 90% of Liberia, but had started losing territories after it launched an operation in 1992 to take Monrovia. Unfortunately, they were bombed and driven out by ECOMOG with the support of remnants of the Liberian armed forces, and a pro-caretaker government militia and also the opposing rebel group which was now believed to be right across the river. The main rebel group had been driven from the northwest to the southwest, comprising Lofa County from the north and all the way down to Cape Mount County, at the south.

Sergeant-Major Eric Gonpue joined the 1990 revolution when government forces, upon receiving intelligence that dissident forces had crossed the border from Ivory Coast and had infiltrated the eastern tip of Nimba County, raided his village. He had participated in many battles and had had many experiences.

He was one of few junior commandos conscripted when he was discovered roaming the thick jungles of eastern Nimba County, when he was separated from his family following the government forces attack. He and some young boys, had run into dissident forces ambush when they were attempting to cross a river bordering the Ivory coast. There, they were trained in guerilla warfare and had since been fighting. He participated in the attack that led to the capture of Buchanan City from government forces in mid 1990. He was also a part of the battle group that led a sustained assault on forces of the First Infantry Battalion at Camp Schieffelin along the Monrovia-Roberts Field Highway that forced the government troops to retreat to Monrovia.

The Schieffelin assault was a difficult experience for the child soldier whose initial role was providing ammunition to the older and experienced fighters, as the government troop they were fighting was one of the best trained. At one point in the battle, when they had sustained heavy casualties, they were forced to take part in active combat, and that was when young Sergeant-Major Gonpue experienced first-hand the retreating techniques of the government troops; retreating at the same time with their M-16s, LARs or M203s on their shoulders pointing towards the enemy who was chasing them and firing or launching with a great deal of accuracy.

This was where he saw most of his comrades die, some of whom were conscripted with him. He had also experienced the effectiveness of how an enemy sniper fire can pin down a whole battle group as with the encounter with 2nd Lieutenant Sumo P. Korvah, a veteran who was part of the Liberian contingent of the UN Peacekeeping Forces, during the Congolese War in the 1960s. This army Lieutenant, along with his men managed to hold back the advancing rebel forces for hours with the accurate use of sniper fire using M-1 single barrel guns until the entire First Infantry Battalion completely retreated. 2nd Lieutenant Korvah was mid-way into his retirement process when the war started.

Three years later, and now he was tasked with the responsibility to protect the strategic central western front of the main rebel faction, assigned to him by his Commanding Officer, CO Alfred Mentee. Watching how he fought in Buchanan and Schieffelin, the CO trusted his ability. Alfred Mentee was his training commandant when he was conscripted. The enemy forces he was about to confront consisted of former members of the government forces they fought at the onset of the civil war.

Not still satisfied when there seemed to be no activity across the river as Sergeant -Major Gonpue continued to spy into the binoculars, he suddenly signaled to his second in Command, Junior Commando Takpoh Duo, a muscular and huge fellow, who immediately crept out of his concealment and joined him behind the tree.

"Look to your right, and try to see what I am seeing," he said, handing the binoculars to Duo.

"I see one; two; three; four; five; ten canoes with men inside. I think they are heading this way."

"Good. Look to your left."

"Oh Chief!" exclaimed Duo, suddenly breathing heavily. "I see another 10 canoe with men inside. I think they have discovered our position and they are trying to encircle us."

Takpoh Duo immediately focused the binoculars on the western side of the river as Sergeant-Major Gonpue signaled to his radio man, a child soldier who immediately left his concealed position and ran towards him with a radio on his back. He was accompanied by two other fighters with one carrying an RPG and the other, an AK-47 built with a grenade launcher under the barrel.

"Bush dog. Come in for Dog Killer," he called, at the same time looking in both directions where the canoes appeared to be advancing towards them.

Takpoh Duo was still peering into the Binoculars with great deal of interest, as he repeatedly scanned the river from the north, the south and then the east.

"Dog Killer, Dog Killer," a voice sounded when the radio suddenly screeched as static feedback blurted through the speaker. "This is a Bush Dog."

"Advise on the situation at your end. I am seeing movements on the right and left of our position."

Sergeant Sackie Binda, the leader of the Bush Dog squad, who had emerged from an undergrowth from the surrounding jungles in the south of Haindii along with his radio man carefully scanned around him with suspicion. The rest of his Bush Dog Squad was still in their concealment as each was dressed in green country cloth with yellow and brown linings designed like dry leaves in the jungle. This provided them with perfect camouflage. They were all positioned with their weapons pointed as their squad leader took careful steps surveying the grounds beneath him.

He was widely known as "Sackie Dirty Water". And, had been scanning the bushes south of Handii to track enemy forces movements for weeks. It was obvious to him that the enemy forces would not have crossed the river on the Dobli Island side as they would have been easily spotted, and so upon his suggestion, the Bush Dog Squad was organized to comb the southern jungle along the St. Paul as far as the forest of Todee district.

His squad mostly consisted of Haindii lads who grew up within these brushes and their sole aim was to defend their historic town. It had been made known to them by the leader of the main rebel group who visited Haindii, following the fall of Gbarpolu County that the enemy rebel group comprised people from Guinea and Sierra Leone and it was incumbent upon all of them to defend their land.

He observed the looks and formations of leaves and pieces of dry sticks on the ground and then stopped when something caught his attention. The dry leaves and sticks were trampled on. This was not done by animals or local village hunters or farmers. It was a sign of massive troop movements, days ago. Alerted, he quickly hurried back to his concealment, a couple of yards from where he squatted for risk of being spotted by the enemy, he now suspected of using the route he was investigating.

"Dog Killer, Dog Killer," he whispered into the mic of the radio upon receiving it from his radio man. "The enemy has infiltrated. A bulk of them have crossed the river and are within the vicinity of Haindii."

"Roger that," responded Sergeant-Major Gonpue, suddenly becoming apprehensive and shaken with nervousness at the same time rubbing the scar on his face. His heart leapt when Takpoh Duo signaled to him that there were more canoes with men that appeared to be quickly advancing their way.

"All units open fire . . . All Units open fire," yelled the young commando with all his might.

The sounds of Ak-47s and light artillery immediately blasted the waters to the north, south, east and west of their position. Some of the fighters had even crept out of their covers running towards the river banks with suppressive fire as it seemed to them that they were not hitting the canoes which seemed to be advancing closer. Sergeant-Major Gompue was also firing his Ak-47 and when he realized that their bullets were not hitting the canoes, he began running towards the banks of the river too.

The entire battle group had rushed to the river banks, some of whom were a few feet into the shadow edge of the water firing and changing fresh cartridges with the ones they depleted. The young sergeant-major was suddenly overwhelmed with guilt and fear for the consequences when he realized that he had made a great error.

"Cease fire, cease fire, return to your positions. Return to your positions," he shouted at his men, almost weeping. His voice was barely heard as the thunderous sounds of guns and artillery from his men roared.

Across the river on the Gbarpolu side, an enemy rebel commander, wearing a camouflage and a green beret with the insignia of a Major, offered a broad smile as he peered into his binoculars. He was seeing clouds of smoke from the barrels of the guns of the enemy forces firing from the distant Dobli Island. Large droplets of water littered the banks of the St. Paul as bullets and shells landed into the river while some were skipping on the surface at rapid speed, like tiny flying objects. His smile became broader when he observed that his men in the canoes were not hit. They were way out of harm's way.

"They have taken the bait," he turned to a few of his fighters standing behind him and said with an ominous grin "Their positions have been exposed."

This commander, Major Jacob Saydee was a former member of the Liberian Coast Guard with years of experience patrolling the coastlines in search of illegal fishing vessels and other water crafts. He was also part of a group of Coast Guard personnel routed from the Coast Guard base in Monrovia by forces of the independent rebel group. With urging from his men, they surrendered to the Field Marshal, the head of this rebel group, but unlike most of them he refused to join any rebel group and fled to Sierra Leone.

There, he joined this opposing rebel group whose ideology was to force the leader of the main rebel group to abide by the peace accord to end the war. He was in charge of the operation to attack Haindii from the banks of Dobli Island.

He had used his experience in determining and distorting the positions of water crafts by taking advantage of refraction rays from the sun to lure Sergeant-Major Gonpue and his men out of their concealment. The refracted rays, with the right angle of incidence in which the canoes were positioned, made them appear closer than their actual positions. This was a simple stealth tactic Coast Guard patrol men used to sneak on illegal vessels and water-crafts operating the Liberian territorial waters.

His walkie talkie attached to his side suddenly blurted and he heard the voice of one of his men in the canoe reading the estimated coordinates of the shoreline of the Island. Major Jacob Saydee suddenly signaled to his artillery unit to position their big guns as he shouted the coordinates to them. The trees lines in front of them were immediately cleared, giving them a perfect view of the distant island, and soon a barrage of 106 artillery and mortar fire began smoking the edge of the island.

As he continued to peer into his spying glass, the body parts of enemy forces were seen in the air including their weapons as each drop of shell from his artillery hit their position. Some of the fighters who were in the water firing at the canoes had started retreating back into the bushes of the Island, but as they ran, they were being hit by landing shells launched by Major Saydee's men.

Sergeant-Major Gonpue who had not been hit was lying flat on his stomach, his Ak-47 lying across his arms with his feet partially in the water. Body parts were afloat and some were scattered along the banks. The shallow edge of the water was filled with blood and turned the dark green color of the water to red.

He raised his head a little to look ahead of him. Among the pieces of body parts of chop off limbs and heads were his radio man, the child soldier, chop off into half by the enemy's shell and the two fighters, the one with the RPG and the other with the AK-47 grenade launcher, both with their stomachs split criss-cross with their intestines pouring out. He tried to look further to recognize from the chop off heads, his second in command, but a shell landed close by, forcing him to dock his head as the dirt from the blast partially covered his body.

Drenched with the mixture of fear for defeat, pity for he and his men, and anger over the hard truth of the bravado of the enemy commander across the river, he remained where he was as he listened to the thunderous sound of artillery shells landing ahead of him and into the forest of the island. The shelling gradually subsided when there were no more movements from his men, except the cries and groaning of the injured and the dying.

Sergeant-Major Gonpue immediately began to crawl his way back to the bushes of the island, sometimes rolling over body parts and the steel of what were the barrels of AK-47 split in half by shrapnel. He knew that the men in the canoes would soon be landing on the Island to finish off the wounded or to capture fighters who may have managed to survive the shelling.

He managed to reach the tree where he stood to monitor the river, and squeezed himself behind it when it was safe to get up. He looked towards the river. The canoes were now too many on all sides and were advancing slowly as the shelling of artillery from across the river resumed. He sensed that the resumption of shelling was to provide cover for the approaching enemy forces, and his next move was to hurry back across to the Haindii side.

As he waddled through the bushes, he could see the bodies of some of his men lying about. He could also hear the cries and anguish of some of them lying under fallen trees hit by landing shells. He left the bushes and got on the trail that led to the crossing at the Haindii side. Along the way he caught up with some of his men, about ten of them who had sustained light injuries, suggesting that they were not part of the group that ran out of their concealments to the edge of the island to fire at the canoes.

"E-r-i-c," a familiar voice, with strenuous effort, called from behind.

He turned to look and saw that it was his second in command, Junior Commando Takpor Duo coming towards them with a wounded comrade in his arms.

"I thought you were dead," said Sergeant-Major Gonpue, with a glee on his face as he examined his friend, the only surviving member of the group that was conscripted with him who now stood before him covered in blood.

"I thought you were, too," he responded, after shaking his head no, and then his attention was suddenly fixed on the rest of the surviving men. "Why are you guys not taking the wounded?"

"No need for that now," lamented the young battle group commander, "They will slow us down and the enemy forces have by now landed on the Island. We got about 30 minutes to get to the waterside. We need to move now."

Out of a sudden, they all sprang to the ground and scrambled for cover, upon hearing the sound of an RPG. Each of the fighters remained motionless as their hearts violently leapt up and down their chests as they listened to the flight of the projectile overhead in a desperate hope that it landed way ahead of them.

Unfortunately, Lyee "Tekete" Kabbah, a fighter of the opposing rebel group fired the second one from the position half way between his right knee and ankle, and then docked back for cover. The projectile took a very low flight path as it tore through the undergrowth. Debris of leaves, sticks, wood shards, dirt and pebbles filled the air when it landed. Three of Sergeant-Major Gonpue's men were hit. Their body parts, chopped off from the blast, along with their weapons, spinning with the debris, as leaves and shards of three trunks were splattered with blood. Another two of Gonpue's men were rolling on the ground, crying in anguish.

After a few seconds of quietude, mainly, from the brief exchange of gunfire, except for the screaming of severely injured and dying men in the distance ahead of him, the young enemy rebel fighter who launched the second RPG crept out of cover and was slowly lifting his head to watch out for any enemy movement as he and his team of fighters anticipated that those who might not be hit would get up to run.

Lyee "Tekete" Kabbah, born and raised in the neighborhood of JJY Community in Gardnerville City, outside of Monrovia, earned the nickname "Tekete," due to his ruthlessness in soccer as a kid who played in the defensive position. Before the war, he participated in the Liberia Football Association league at the 3rd division level, playing most of his games under the Gardnerville Sub-Association. As the war neared Monrovia, he and his family fled to Guinea by way of Sierra Leone. The now dark skinned and medium height teenager, wearing dreadlock bedecked with beads, was recruited from Guinea and had spent a year fighting with the opposing rebel group.

He was suddenly alerted to a rustling in the bush ahead of him, indicating that the surviving enemy was getting away. He was fully out of cover with his Ak-47 rifle in his hand and was about to point it while his RPG now hung on his back, when a bullet fired from the rifle of Sergeant-Major Gonpue, pierced his forehead. It tore into his skull and fractured it instantly. His team scrambled back for cover as the lifeless body of "Tekete" riddled with bullets fired from Gonpue's remaining men, reeled backwards, the dreadlock on its head all covered with blood, bones and brain. Gonpue, Duo and five of their remaining men sprang to their feet and started retreating with high speed at the same time throwing a couple of hand grenades towards the direction of their enemy after ceasing the suppressive fire that was pinning them down. In about 15 minutes, they had increased the distance between them and the enemy as they sped towards the direction of the water crossing for Haindii.

It was mid-way into the afternoon, and Haindii was gripped with fear and confusion, following the sounds of heavy gun fire from Dobli Island. The market day was disrupted as all the sellers and buyers had fled. People who ventured to remain in the town were locked up indoors while most people had left for their villages. The town was quiet and tense. Rebel fighters were roaming about and taking defensive positions. Some people were arrested and line up for questioning for suspicion of helping the enemy to infiltrate. Old man, Rennie Kamara was one of those who was arrested and dragged to the G-2 headquarters on grounds that he was harboring a group of enemy fighters, on his farm, most of whom were his kinsmen on his father side.

Suddenly there was an uproar of confusion when Sergeant 'Sackie "Dirty Water" and his men entered the town from the Haindii-Bong Mines Road on the east. Upon hearing that some citizens of Haindii were rounded up for questioning and some of them were flogged, he and his men had rushed to the G2-headquarters and were demanding their immediate release. Commando Michael Saye, the G-2 commander was refusing on grounds that the people of Haindii had been deceitful, but after some heated arguments and verbal threats between his men and the squad leader of the Bush Dog, Commando Saye agreed to release all the men in his custody except old man Rannie Kamera. The Bush Dog squad insisted that all the townspeople must be released, and again the commotion resumed especially when one of Saye's men tore off the clothes of the old men and was about to flog him.

Just at that moment, one of Sackie Dirty Water's men, who was called Semou, opened fire on the rooftop of the G-2 headquarters with his General Machine Gun (GMG).

Sackie Dirty Water and the rest of his men joined Semou and started shooting above the heads of Saye's men at the same time yelling and cursing and threatening to shoot directly at them. Commando Saye and his men soon retaliated and were doing likewise. Semou, a huge and muscular fellow wearing a sleeveless country cloth designed like a vest and short khakis with one of those angle high pairs of black steel toe boots that were won by Bong Mines workers, reverted to shooting at the ground, closed to the feet of Saye's men as the dirt from the ground flew in their faces.

The bullets from his GMG ricocheted as they hit the stones. Sergeant Dirty Water and the rest of his men also joined him in shooting at the ground. Saye and his G-2 men also retaliated. At one-point Saye and his men became overwhelmed by their attackers and started moving backwards as the bullets from Sackie Dirty Water and his men were landing very close to their feet.

"If you don't free Mr. Kamara, we will dig your ter-toes," screamed Semou, meaning they will riddle the toes of the G-2 commander and his men with bullets.

"Order your men to cease fire," screamed Saye.

"You order your men to cease fire or we will all die here today," Sergeant Dirty Water refused.

In the midst of the commotion, Sergeant-Major Eric Gonpue who had managed to cross back into Haindii along with Tapkoh Duo who was forced to abandon his injured comrade, and some men rushed to the scene, firing warning shots in the air.

"Everyone cease fire!" he yelled.

Sergeant Sackie Dirty Water stopped shooting and signaled to his men to cease fire.

"What's the fuck going on here?" demanded Sergeant-Major Gonpue, with his attention fixed on his G-2 commander. "You guys don't know the enemy has taken the island and we are here trying to kill each other?"

"This stupid man accusing our people of conniving with the enemy and arresting them. I demanded that they be released but he refused," Sergeant Dirty Water explained.

"Saye. Let the people go now," Sergeant-Major Gonpue ordered, without entertaining any explanation from his G-2 commander "It was Bush Dog that informed us that the enemy had infiltrated, even on this side. At any moment they will attack from the Island with their artillery."

At that moment Semou, after re-belting his GMG with ammunition, rushed into a clay house where the suspects were kept, stepped the door open and ordered them out. Old man Rennie Kamara, along with the others who were detained were helped out of the detention room. He was clothed and together with the other detainees, asked to leave as fast as they could.

The elderly man did not know his father, who according to his mother, was one of the few men from Monrovia that entered Handii as administrators in the 1920s when the Liberian Government was extending its municipality in Lower Bong County. He stayed for a short time and was later transferred to Gbarnga. His mother, a local of Haindii, whose parents were lodging this man, known only as Kamara, was pregnant by the time he left and was never seen again. Rennie Kamara grew up in Haindii and even joined the Poro society. He attended the Booker Washington Institute. Upon graduation, he apprenticed at the 9th Judicial Court in Kakata as a clerk and now served on the town's council.

As it was approaching the evening hours, all the fighters of the main rebel group were taking up positions to make Haindii the last stand. As Sergeant-Major Gonpue instructed, they formed defensive lines along the banks of the St. Paul, facing the direction of Dobli Island in anticipation that the enemy forces were heavily reinforcing to lead the assault on Haindii.

The young commander had radioed the Bong Mines Command which also was sending reinforcements, military-technical, and artillery pieces that will be used to smite the island from the Haindii side in a bid to harass and frustrate the enemy. CO Alfred Mentee was on his way to Haindii with a large group of fighters to provide a protective corridor along the Bong Mines Haindii Road. Other rebel fighters, headed by a strong commando named Tongor, had also formed defensive lines a few meters into the bushes on the south of the town, predicated on information from Bush Dog that there may be an attack from that direction. The bushes at the north of the town were left open to provide an escape corridor in case their defensive parameters were breached.

It was approaching the late evening hours. The town was relatively quiet, and increasingly tense, except for the occasional firing of single shots by the fighters who were shooting the town's livestock for food. Sometimes a commotion would erupt between them and the Bush Dogs squad. At the waterfront, the few people who live in farming villages on the island were crossing the water in canoes with their belongings for fear of the enemy forces, but were being screened before they were allowed to enter the town. Sergeant-Major Gonpu, Takpor Duo, and Sackie Dirty Water were moving about inspecting the defensive lines to ensure that they were intact.

A commotion erupted at the waterfront, resulting into the exchange of gun fire in the air between some G-2 fighters and Semou, Gbato, and two other members of the Bush Dog Squad, prompting Sergeant-Major Gonpue, Takpor Duo and Sackie Dirty Water to rush to the scene. It started when Semou opened fire in the air with his GMG when some G-2 fighters were attempting to confiscate two bags of rice seeds from a farming couple, after it was searched and cleared.

"Nobody will take the rice seeds. The people need them for planting!" Semou cried out. "We will not sit here and allow you to starve our people after defending our town, no way!"

As the three fighters were making efforts to calm down the fray, two shots, in sequential order, were fired from a Light Automatic Rifle (LAR) from the direction of Bong Mines Haindii Road. Before the fighters could realize that it was a signal from the enemy rebel fighters, a barrage of artillery shells coming from the island and the southern side of the town started raining down on the town, hitting the waterfront and the defensive lines to the south. Rebel fighters defending the perimeter were hit as the cries and groans of the wounded and the dying filled the air, following the blast of each landing shell. Some of the fighters were returning fire with AK-47 and RPG.

Sergeant-Major Gonpue, who managed to escape the onslaught of rocket fire was at a safe spot behind an abandoned house at the edge of the north of the town along with a radio man. He had radioed the artillery group that was on its way several times but there was no response. The only thing he heard was the blustering of the static sound effect of the radio at the other end.

Becoming frustrated, and apprehensive, he looked towards the direction of the waterfront and saw some of his men retreating, many of whom were wounded. A shell landed in their midst, leaving scores of them dead or severely wounded. Few of them survived and kept running up the hill towards the direction of the Sergeant-Major.

He waited until they were safe from the enemy's artillery reach and left his cover and ran to them, with his radio man following. He caught up with Sackie Dirty Water, Takpoh Duo, Semou, Gbarto and some other fighters who survived the blast with a desperate and inquisitive expression on his face. Tarkpor Duo, covered with blood from dragging the wounded to safety and breathing heavily, informed him that the defensive lines at the waterfront had been beaten, and there's an urgent need for artillery support.

"They are not responding, either," informed Sergeant-Major Gonpue after tying it for another time and was still receiving the static feedback.

"They had been ambushed," Sackie Dirty Water said and suddenly becoming very shaken. "Haindii will fall!"

Just a few kilometers before reaching Haindii along the Bong Mines-Haindii Road at a particular curve near Sherman Farm, where the road is bordered on both sides by a hill of about 25 feet high, Caporal Charles Bryant, an AWOL soldier of the Liberian Armed Forces, fighting with the opposing rebel group, was lying flat on his stomach in ambush position. He was pointing his LAR rifle at a column of destroyed battle wagons and artillery pieces which belonged to the main rebel group, ambushed while on the way to Haindii on high speed.

The bodies of rebel fighters who were accompanying the heavy weapons were lying on the road and in the pickup trucks on which trunks mounted the big guns. The ones who survived managed to flee into the nearby bushes and back on the road to Bong Mines and were being pursued. The windshields, frames, and tires of most of the Technicals were riddled with bullets as blood smear, human organs, veins and arteries were scattered in and around the bullet riddled-vehicles.

Corporal Charles Bryant was focused on a particular pickup truck with a radio inside and an anti-aircraft weapon mounted at the back. The rebel driver inside was wounded and had apparently lost consciousness. He came to himself, but while still in a state of delirium due to the excruciating pains from his left shoulder wound, he remained head down, half way under the steering wheel, making frantic effort to ignite the engine.

Cpl. Bryant, known by his colleagues as the soldier with no warning shot, was well positioned at a spot where he was directly facing the passenger side of the front of the double cabin Pick-up truck. He shook his head in pity for the unfortunate enemy fighter who lifted his head slightly above the shattered window and then took the shot hitting the enemy driver from the left side of his head. Blood and brain splattered in the car. Three frightened fighters quickly jumped out of the back seat and started firing and yelling, but they were gunned down. Immediately, fighters of the opposing rebel group came running out of the bushes on both sides of the road, jubilating and at the same time firing into the air.

Cpl. Bryant came out of his concealment and found his way from the hill down the road. He was wearing an army issued fatigue uniform with a red beret. He was an extremely slim and tall man in his early 30s, and was part of a group of elite soldiers trained by the Israelis Special Forces. In 1990, he was assigned at the Alligator Base somewhere near the James Springs Payne Airfield, about a quarter of a mile from downtown Monrovia, where they constantly held back rebel forces from entering the Sinker belt. It was the shortest route to the Executive Mansion from the east.

He got in contact with the opposing rebel faction through his commanding officer, Capt. William Toe, a founding member of the group. Capt. Toe was wounded in one of those fierce battles to prevent rebels from crossing the air field. Corporal Bryant later accompanied Capt. Toe to Guinea to seek treatment, after the first interim government was formed.

As Cpl. Charles Bryant walked to the damaged war vehicles, slightly hopping on his right leg, an injury he sustained while on a mission to rescue the president in 1991 when he was captured by forces of the independent rebel faction, the fighters jubilated, as they shouted "No warning shot, no warning shot," at the same time firing in the air.

Then they inspected the vehicles that were still operational, including the big guns and started removing the dead fighters. The fighters among them who were mechanics were working on some of the Technicals. There was more jubilation when a large group of their men joined them from the nearby bushes.

When the vehicles and guns were ready, the group split into two as Cpl. Bryant and others headed towards Haindii while the rest, heading to Bong Mines, was led by a young, tall and well-dressed Lieutenant in his camouflage with all the necessary gear. This Lieutenant was also a former Arm Forces of Liberia personnel from the E-die 90 group, named Mamadee A. Donzo or otherwise known by his men as Mandingo Marine.

It was late in the evening. The battle had been fought for more than three hours. The defensive lines of the main rebel fighters at the waterfront had been breached and they were driven back along the road almost to the center of the town. They have tried several times to re-establish their defensive lines, but enemy rockets were landing on the perimeters of the water front and so they had to retreat to safe distances away from the landing shells thus, making the waterfront a no-go zone.

At the south of the town, fighters commanded by Tongor, and Cooper Twazamah, his assistant, whose war name was 'Disco Rebel' were holding the defensive lines. Leading the charge, Disco Rebel, who earned the name for the way he would come out of his concealment, only when they were under heavy fire, and danced to the sound of the enemy guns, at the same time firing back, initially expanded the perimeters further into some acres into the bushes.

Unfortunately, the opposing rebel group, positioned in the nearby hills had refrained from firing rockets when they realized that Tongor and his men were advancing towards them despite their heavy fire power. They were only able to hold them back with sniper fire.

Rockets launched from the Island across the river were not hitting the town itself, except for a few stray ones that landed on the houses, and setting them ablaze.

For some time, there was a loll in the fighting as the artillery fire from Dobli Island had subsided, except the sporadic exchanges of small arms fire by the enemy snipers positioned at nearby hills south of the town, and the return fire from Tongor and his men who were holding the defensive lines.

Some town people were taking advantage of this situation and were leaving their houses and sneaking their way to their farming villages on the north side of the town while some brave men were fighting to put off the fire on the rooftop. Women would occasionally sneak out of their houses, rushed into their outside kitchens to collect food and water. They would slip back inside to the sound of gun fire or retreating rebel fighters.

Sackie Dirty Water and some of his men were roaming the town advising their people to stay indoors as they were poised to defend their town. He had lost eight of his men who were among those holding the defensive lines at the waterfront to enemy rockets. Another two, the youngest on his Bush Dog Squad went AWOL at the urging of their parents who whisked them away to their farming village when the fighting subsided.

From a squad of 15 men, they were now down to five. The Bush Dog Squad leader watched as the last of his men was hurriedly buried behind a clearing a few yards into the bush behind a house and then hurried to join Sergeant-Major Gonpue with Semou, Gbato and the last three members of his squad following him.

The young commander and his second in command were sitting on the floor of the town's gazebo, a few meters from the defensive lines at the south of the town to avoid exposing their heads to enemy snipers, when Sackie Dirty Water and his men joined them. Sackie could tell from Sergeant-Major Gonpue's face that he was petrified. He had not yet received any radio contact from the artillery unit on its way and the re-enforcement they were expecting. Details provided by G-2 officer Michael Saye showed that they had sustained heavy casualties and they needed more men to hold the town. Moreover, CO. Alfred Mentee's radio was also tried but there was no response.

"Dragon fire. Dragon fire," he called, again, his voice sounding like he wanted to cry, and his expression showing a damping spirit as he did not anticipate any response at the other end. "Come in for Dog killer."

Sergeant Joseph Chabeor, a battle group commander, also an E-die 90 conscript, charged with the responsibility to flank his opponents from the east was riding along with Cpl. Charles Bryant in the captured pick-up truck whose driver's head was blown off by the AWOL soldier. They had stopped when they were in striking distance from Haindii and had positioned and calibrated all the captured artillery pieces, including theirs in striking range on a hill along the Bong Mines Road, overlooking the town when the radio blurted. He looked at Cpl. Bryant who nodded when the call came again. He then picked up the mic and said something in his Krahn dialect in an ominous tone and laughed in an eerie manner.

Sergeant-Major Gonpue at the other end, who also understood a little bit of Chabeor's dialect, interpreted it as 'Fire from hell'. Immediately the barrage of artillery fire from the eastern flank and the Island across the river resumed. The grounds of Haindii shook as shells from some of the big guns landed. Rockets fired from the captured anti-air craft guns tore through the branches of orange and mango trees in the town.

Some of Gonpue's men thought the reinforcements from Bong Mines had arrived, and they were the ones launching the artillery from their rear. So, they started running towards them, yelling that they must adjust their range to hit the Island because the enemy forces were concentrated there. But before they could realize that the men operating the big guns weren't the reinforcement they were expecting, Chabeour's men opened fire and killed all of them.

"We got to leave now!" cried Sergeant-Major Gonpue. "The enemy have captured our big weapons and are using them on us!"

Semou started weeping when it was obvious that his town was about to completely fall. He grieved at the idea that foreigners from Guinea and Sierra Leone have taken over their precious town and would destroy their heritage forever.

"No," this cannot happen!" he cried, and reloaded his GMG.

Semou left his cover and ran up the hill towards the enemy forces, at the same time firing and yelling in a manner strange to them. Gbarto, and the three remaining fighters of the Bush Dog squad, seeing that the enemy was not returning fire, became emboldened and joined him, also firing and shouting in like manner. The other fighters immediately regained courage and joined the Haindii fighters.

With Semou leading the charge, the group of fighters that joined him, about 20 in number, continued the suppressive fire of mostly Ak-47 and two RPGs. The enemy were somehow taken aback by the strange wailing and yelling of Semou, Gbarto, and the other three Bush Dog fighters by his side. Shells from the enemy artillery were flying over them and landing directly at the south of the town, where

Tongor and his men were causing some problems for their forces docking at the nearby hills.

Sergeant Chebeur ordered his men with the Ak-47 and other light automatic rifles to hold their fire, until Semou and the advancing group of fighters got closer. A LAR shot was fired, as Semou and the group closed in on the enemy. He suddenly stopped and staggered backwards when the bullet caught him in the center of his chest. Cpl. Charles Bryant, who was positioned on top of a termite hill overlooking the road, took another two shots with an interval of two seconds each.

The bullets pierced Semou's left ventricle further staggering him backwards, but this time convulsing as he fell to the ground with his finger still clinched to the trigger of his GMG. One of the fighters of the Bush Dog Squad was caught in the leg as the gun danced in the lifeless hands of Semou while still discharging the bullets. Then Sergent Chabeour gave the order to his men to open fire. The rest of the group started retreating, when they saw Semou falling.

Gbarto was hit in his left thigh. He dropped to the ground and crawled into the tall elephant grass along the side of the road. Cpl. Bryant watched the wounded Bush Dog fighter creeping into the grass and was heading for the bushes at the north of the town. He made a face with an unusual mixture of grin and pity. The shot he took was meant to pierce Gbarto's muscle, but not necessarily to fracture his thigh bone which might be too severe and could cause fatality. He needed him alive.

Sackie Dirty Water who could no longer hear the wailng and yelling of Semou, whose gun fired for some time and then stopped, began to cry as he sat where he was with his head buried in his hands. Semou and the others that died under his command were childhood friends.

Some of them were even his relatives who joined him to defend their town.

Though he was born in Nyenen, his parents were from Haindii and so Sackie always visited the town. He loved to tell stories of the beauty of Bong Town to Semou and the other kids who would gather around him to listen with amusement.

The part of Nyenen he was born in bordered Bong Town on the south by a little creek. The concession area including staff's residence was not fenced, enabling Sackie and peers to tour Bong Town every now and then.

He was a troublesome kid. His father, Moses Binda worked as a laborer at the pellet plant, shoveling spilled iron ore into the conveyor belt. Sometimes they would work along the rail ways providing support to the engineers that repaired and maintained the tracks. His mother, Nowei, was a market woman who at one time got into trouble with the youth of Nyenen for her advocacy and campaigning to turn the only soccer field located right after Bong Town main gate to a market ground.

Sackie earned the name dirty water when he almost drowned at a place called Dirty Water, a location in the concession area where when the iron ore were washed, the chocolate brown water passed through gigantic pipe systems and entered into a small river that snaked out of the Mountain. Tons of Iron ore debris filled the sides of the banks and sometimes piled up on the river bed, thus turning both into a dangerous muddy quicksand.

Other parts of this river were also the host of the company's septic lines where the waste was dumped and spilled over into nearby streams that resulted in the breeding of sizable varieties of succulent species of cold-water fish and frogs. Sackie and some of his friends often roamed this area to fish and to catch frogs and sold them in front of Bong Town supermarket.

One day, while he and some lads, with their fishing lines and their two-prong frog spears in their hands were walking over a dead tree trunk that laid across a narrow brook that connected to the river, he spotted a large spring frog about the size of a soursop resting on top of a dead stick that protruded out of the water. He suddenly balanced himself and threw the spear at the frog in an attempt to pierce its back. But he slipped and fell into the running water.

It swept him some meters downstream where the brook became wider and the current was less. He however managed to swim towards the banks. But out of a sudden, he began to sink into the muddy ore debris, just before wobbling out of the water. Sackie cried for help; he was sinking very fast into the mud. He had gone under, but fortunately he was rescued by some of the Mine Guards stationed nearby who came rushing when they heard his friends running and calling to them for help.

He was pulled out and was made to lie on his protruded stomach. He could not breathe easily. He had taken in a large quantity of dirty water mixed with mud. He vomited some of the mud and dirty water out when the Mind Guards applied some emergency first aid technique, and was later taken to Bong Mines hospital where he spent nearly two months taking antibiotics and other treatments. It was then that he became known as Sackie Dirty Water by his friends who joked of his vomiting lots of dirty water.

"Sackie!" he heard someone desperately whispering his name.

He turned to look around him and saw that it was Sergeant-Major Gonpue and Takpoh Duo taking cover behind a tree. He grabbed his gun and crept to them.

"We have to get out of here," hissed Gonpue. "We need to find our way to Weala without using the Bong Mines route to get to Gbarnga for reinforcement."

"Yes," Sackie agreed, his eyes red, and full of tears. "I think the only way is to head up north along the river and make our way through the bushes to connect to the Bong Range."

"And where it may take us?" inquired Sergeant-Major Gonpue.

"If we are lucky," Sackie sighed and took a deep breath. "We can enter Weala on the west by passing through the old Slocum Mission School. The Mountain range extends that far."

The three of them remained hiding until it was dark. The opposing forces had captured the entire town, and some of the town's people were sought out for questioning. Major Saydee and his men had now crossed into Haindii from the Dobli Island, and were aiding in the search for the remnants of the main rebel fighters. Sackie Dirty Water left Gonpue and Duo briefly and returned to them in his full traditional hunting gear, the one his maternal grandfather wore whenever he took him to hunt at night.

He no longer had the AK-47 he was using. An old but well-oiled hunting single barrel gun was hanging on his shoulder and a hunting bag made of the same country cloth hung on the other shoulder. A headlight, attached to a band made of animal hide, bedecked with cowrie shells was on his head. He was dressed in a black country cloth suit, encrusted with small snail shells with the trousers reaching his kneel.

"It's time to leave now," he told them in a sad and nostalgic tone, as the thought of abandoning Haindii came to him.

The three of them, with Sackie Dirty Water leading, managed to find their way through the bushes up to where the enemy had their artillery pieces to avoid checkpoints mounted on the main road and some suspecting paths out of the town. At a certain point, a safe distance away from a particular check point, Sackie pointed to a direction across the road into the bush. Sergeant-Major Gonpue crossed and then Takpoh Duo followed.

"H-A-L-T," Abraham Dukely, one of the enemy fighters manning the checkpoint, who was returning from defecating in the nearby bush called, when he spotted Sackie docking, while crossing the road to join Sergeant-Major Gonpue and Takpor Duo.

"If your prick is longer than my prick, you will move one more step," Dukely said, in a heavily accented English at the same time advancing his weapon, when Sackie Dirty Water attempted to run.

"Who the fuck are you?!" demanded Dukely, as he approached the strange looking figure dressed in traditional hunting clothes, from behind.

"What?" he asked again when Sackie Dirty Water muttered something in Kpelle. "I am your grandfather's ghost," he repeated loudly when the youthful enemy fighter was about to shoot.

Sackie Dirty Water swiftly hauled out a long knife from a sheath made of animal pelts that hung across his chest and sliced Dukely's throat in a single turn. Dukely uttered a sharp whimpering sound and dropped his weapon. He held his throat with both hands as blood oozed out between his fingers and rolled down his chest.

He convulsed and was making frantic effort to scream the word: "enemy . . ." But his voice was barely heard. In a few minutes, he was lying in the middle of the road, dead. Sackie Dirty Water skipped into the bush and joined Sergeant-Major Gonpue and Takpoh Duo who were anxiously waiting for him.

The three men walked, sometimes docking and taking cover along a path that headed northwards to old man Kpellemou's farm. With Sackie Dirty Water in the forefront, the fighters started walking very cautiously, keeping in mind that if they continued, they would be heading north east which would take them away from the St. Paul River.

The river was the shortest way to their destination, or else they would spend days walking in the thick bush. Then they turn in the left direction, leaving the path and heading down another one leading to the river. Though in the bush they were not too far away from the town. They could hear shots being fired into the air and the voices of victorious enemy fighters, singing jubilantly.

In spite of the euphoria of the enemy's victory, the town was still tense. People were being rounded up and interrogated, which led to the arrests of some remnants of the defeated forces, who had disarmed themselves and joined the civilian population. G2-officer Michael Saye was pointed out, and arrested. He was tie-bayed, flogged and interrogated. Tongor, the strong fighter who held the defensive perimeter at the south of the town for some time was also arrested. He was dragged to the enemy's G2-Quarter. But he died along the way due to a fractured rib cage from enemy shrapnel.

His assistant, Disco Rebel body was disfigured beyond recognition when he stood in the way of the projectile of an enemy RPG, while demonstrating a maneuver that went wrong. A maneuver that once startled an artillery unit of the Senegalese contingent of ECOMOG soldiers, forcing them to retreat when they were responding to an attack on their positions somewhere near Division 26, in Margibi County, during the Octopus Invasion.

The opposing rebel group had set up their temporary G2 headquarter at the Town Palaver Hut and they were using adjacent houses as holding cells. Gbarto who was also brought in by Cpl. Bryant was being questioned, but kept muttering something in his dialect.

Sackie Dirty Water heart started pounding, when he heard a loud cry that echoed through the night and recognized that it was Gbarto's Voice. It was somewhat similar to the yelling and wailing Semou made when he had led the group of fighters towards the enemy. But this one was slightly different. Gbarto was being tortured in an effort to disclose the location of Sackie Dirty Water. He was the only one who knew the shortcut to Weala and the fighters wanted to set up a base in Salala in order to attack the city of Gbarnga. Salala, just after Weala, is located just a few miles from Gbarnga city.

"They are torturing our men," cried Takpor Duo.

"That's Gbarto's voice. He is undergoing severe pain," Sackie Dirty Water said, and clung to a tree and began to cry for his friend.

Gbarto was using the devil's code, a special language he and Semou devised while they were in bush school, he thought; it was meant to warn him to get away as fast as he could, if he was still alive. Sackie was convinced that maybe they were torturing Gbato to reveal his whereabouts. He suspected they were looking for him for his vast knowledge of the terrain. Gbato's voice became louder and chilly as he continued to recite the Devil's Code signifying that he was in a state of delirium and at the point of death.

Sergent-Major Gonpue and Takpoh patted Sackie on his back to console him. The Bush Dog squad leader took a few deep breaths, convulsed for some time and fought to regain his composure. After that, he resumed leading Sergeant-Major Gonpue and Takpoh Duo along the path that headed down the river. He was sure that there would be no enemy patrol on that side, because they would have left the town further behind them.

The path they were on was a zig-zag trail that sometimes snaked its way up a small cliff where the St. Paul River could be seen about 10 feet below. The trail continues into the bush, leaving the river at its rear, and then it curves all the way down a bamboo swamp with a tiny watercourse that runs into the St. Paul River. Sackie hoped they'd find old man Labalah Flomo's canoe and use it to ferry them up stream.

Labalah Flomo was a meticulous Canoe man that paddled the Haindii belt of the St. Paul for years. He had a wife and a daughter and he was famous for his ability to navigate dangerous parts of the river and most times, rescuing fellow canoe men, especially during the raining season, when the water was over full and the current was high.

People attributed this to the kind of self-made canoes he used. Some said he used a special kind of wood to craft his canoes and he was never willing to share the secret of his unique craftsmanship with anyone. Labalah Flomo was envied by other canoe builders in the entire town.

Then, on his daughter's fifteenth birthday, while old man Flomo and his family were returning home from their new farm, the impossible happened. For the first time ever, his canoe capsized. Fortunately, he managed to turn the canoe back on its keel. He urged his wife and daughter, both good swimmers, to hold on as they were fighting against the current to remain afloat.

When he had regained control of the canoe and started paddling to rescue his family, Flomo suddenly saw a mysterious creature pulling his family underneath the water and they instantly disappeared. He made frantic efforts to rescue them by plunging deep into the water, diving into the direction where they had been taken, but his beloved wife and precious daughter had suddenly disappeared without any trace.

Since then, he had not been himself. He could not explain what it was that he saw that pulled his wife and daughter under the water. People speculated that he may have sacrificed his family to what they said was the river god to further enhance the mastery of navigating the waters of Haindii.

Because of this, he was mostly on his farm and avoided Haindii itself. Moreover, he could no longer paddle up and down the St. Paul as he continued to moan about the loss of his wife and daughter. He was discovered dead one day, on his farm which few believed it was due to depression while many maintained that it was due to guilt.

Sackie Dirty Water used to visit him whenever he passed this way from hunting and he would see the old man sitting by his canoe, looking very transfixed, gazing for hours in the direction of the river. He seldom responds whenever he is greeted. To Sackie, the once famous canoe man was locked up in an inextricably futile hope that one day his wife and daughter will return to him.

For months, he had not frequented the old man's place especially when he died. He was hopeful that he would find the canoe probably in a fairly good condition. They finally entered Labalah Flomo's village, after walking for thirty minutes. Satisfied that they were a good distance away from Haindii, he turned on the hunting light on his forehead and hurried to the spot where he always saw the old man's canoe. He cursed in his dialect when he found the canoe to be in a bad shape, and was impossible to use. Termite had borrowed into the wood causing tiny holes on the sides of the hull. To make matters worse, the floor was eaten up by rodents.

"We can't take our chances with this canoe," he informed the Sergeant-Major and his deputy who looked very disappointed. "The current in these parts of the river is dangerously rough. We need to keep moving on this trail," he continued. "There are other farming villages further up the river and most of them are owned by canoe men."

Sergent-Major Gonpue was contemplating on asking whether it was safe to rest for the night. They were extremely exhausted. Unfortunately, they were startled by the sound of light automatic rifle fire and the sequential launching of RPGs. Soon there were footsteps fast approaching their way.

Sackie, sensing that some captured rebel fighters may have escaped and were being pursued, swiftly turned off the light and whispered to Gonpue and Duo to follow him. He hurriedly led them to another direction north east of the village, anticipating that whosoever that was being pursued would be tempted to jump into an old swamp rice plot with few piassava trees few yards from the dilapidated farm kitchen to hide. And the arm men in pursuit would surround it and shoot and launch rounds of RPG into it.

Sackie Dirty Water and his two comrades were some safe distance away from the farm village when they heard someone and another person jump into the swamp rice plot and were sloughing through the muddy water in search for a place to hide. Just as Sackie expected, they could hear some arm men giving instructions to surround the plot and started shooting and launching the RPGs.

Chunks of mud and slices of branches of piassava trees filled the air as the arm men from the opposing rebel forces fired bullets and RPG rounds into the swarm rice plot. This continued for about ten minutes, until there was a sharp cry and then another. The two men who jumped into the plot were hit and would eventually die. Satisfied that the escapees they were pursuing might me dead after firing for another ten minutes, they stopped and waited to see whether there was going to be some movements, but there was none, except for the bodies of the men they were pursuing.

"Attention, gentlemen," one of the fighters by the name of Foday, said, suddenly alerting the rest. "I saw a hunting light turned off, just before we got here and there were feet sound of people running in this direction."

"Maybe it was a lightning bug," suggested Khaley Karhn, another fighter, one of the two with the RPG.

"If it was, we would have seen many of them flying around," insisted Foday.

"Then let's smoke the area you say they ran," suggested Gbaou Blayee, another fighter, who looked very confident and battle tested, changing the magazine and advancing his LAR.

The group of fighters, about fifteen in number, formed a straight line as they turned towards the north east side of the village. They pointed their guns at a small hill of tall grass and scattered rubber trees. At Gbaou's Command, they started launching the RPG in such a way that the blast from the warhead will have a devastating effect on every square inch of the areas where they thought whosoever ran, was hiding.

Sackie Dirty Water, Sergeant-Major Gonpue and Takpoh Duo were hiding behind a huge brown sedimentary rock lying flat on their stomachs. As the warheads tore through the branches of trees and blasted, dirt, leaves, sticks and wood shards clouded the air. The tip of the sedimentary rock was struck. The blast chopped off a large fragment and scattered it into plumes of dust particles, raining down on them. Some of the hot red shrapnels from the blast ignited the piles of dry leaves and sticks, setting them ablaze.

The launching of the rockets stopped after a few minutes. The three besieged rebel fighters immediately began to crawl from behind what was left of the rock. But their assailants switched to firing the Light Automatic Rifles, emptying magazines after Magazine. With the thunderous sound of the LAR fire muffing their movements, they managed to crawl for some twenty minutes and got up to run when it was safe.

Sackie switched on his headlight to see where they were running. It was north of where they were hiding. They continued running and docking northwards with Sackie who was ahead, being mindful not to drift too far away from the St. Paul. Unnoticeably, they reached a valley and started sliding down.

Gbaou and his men had stopped firing and decided to wait until dawn, to start the search for whosoever was hiding up the hill. It had now passed midnight and the bush was very dark. Just before chasing the enemy fighters that escaped, there had been word to search for a certain individual with incredible knowledge of the bushes of this part of Bong County.

Apprehending him will be a great advantage, as their strategy is to eventually surround and pester Gbarnga from all sides in a bid to hasten the compliance of the leader of the main rebel group. Any attempt to comb the area in anticipation that the fellow in question could be whoever was hiding in there, would be foolhardy. They would continue in the morning when more of their men joined them.

The three fighters slid down the valley for some time, bumping into trees and dead wood, but not causing them injuries. They were prevented from sliding further down when they landed on a big log that lay horizontally on the ground. They rested on it for a few minutes and examined themselves for any injuries. They also checked their weapons and they were intact.

Sackie Dirty Water brightened the light a bit and looked further down the valley. From their position, he calculated that getting down to the bottom will not be too long. The slope was not too steep and so they will have to walk all the way down and use the trees to balance themselves and to sometimes rest.

He switched off the headlight when he had memorized the places, they will have to pass to get to the bottom. This was something he learned from his maternal grandfather. Keeping the light on was dangerous and it could expose their location, making them easy targets.

It took them about an hour to reach the bottom of the valley. After briefly resting on some granite rocks with flat surfaces, they cautiously surveyed the place. Sackie could not turn on his head light to avoid being spotted from up the valley. There were no trees at the bottom except for the big rocks and if they were spotted, there would be no cover from rockets and bullets raining down on them.

They had walked westwards towards the direction of the St. Paul for some time when Sackie became very attentive to the sound of running water in the distance ahead. It took them a few minutes to reach where the sound was coming from and soon they realized that they were standing on top of a huge rock partially buried in the soil that formed a wall of a cliff.

To their left was a small running water flowing out of a rock. Few feet below them was what looked like a lake about the size of two-football fields. Further west at the edge of this water log was a fast-running creek that fed into it. But the creek headed further west in the direction of the St. Paul.

This place seemed strange to Sackie Dirty Water. He could not recall roaming this part of the forest on the numerous hunting expeditions he and his maternal grandfather made or alone when the old man was no more. What he now remembered was what the old man, Kpakolo Leynumah always told him when he was introduced to the art of hunting.

"These jungles hold many surprises, but never let them frighten you," he would say, and further narrated, "It was these many surprises that led to the expulsion of the Gola from this area."

The Bush Dog squad leader felt relieved, when it occurred to him that he was the only Haindii's native that discovered the place. Nobody from Haindii or the surrounding farming villages along the banks of the St. Paul River had talked about such a place. As a kid who was always with Kpakolo Lehnumah, his grandfather, whenever he visited his friends, and listened to some of their conversations, there had been no accounts which descriptions matched this part of the forest.

The old man died at a very old age and on his dying bed he told Sackie that he would join his ancestors as a happy man as he had successfully transferred his knowledge unto him. Reflecting on these memories, a deep sense of loyalty to the old man suddenly took hold of him. He was not going to let Kpakolo Lehnumah down.

He then assured Sergeant-Major Gonpue and Takpoh Duo that it was safe for them to pass the night. They were going to continue their journey at dawn.

"Rest is a weapon," the Sergeant-Major consented. Then he turned to his deputy, "Remember what the Supreme Commander told us when he visited the training base? To rest is a weapon. He said he read it in a book."

Just before dawn, Sackie Dirty Water was awakened to the songs of the early morning birds. Overnight, the three of them had descended the cliff through layers of rocks serving as natural stairs. At the bottom they found some hollow crevices into the rocks that looked like caves which they selected for a perfect place to rest for the night.

Before that, Sackie briefly observed the terrain and figured out a possible escape route, in the event of a sudden attack from the enemies. It was decided that he would get up early to do a quick sweep of the area in search of the best possible route that would take them to a village where they would find a canoe to ferry them upstream.

Sackie grabbed his hunting gear and started off. It was still dark. The sunlight was not yet visible in the sky and so he had to turn on his head light. As he got out of the crevice where he slept, stepping and sometimes jumping on the rocks along his way, freshwater crabs ran and hid themselves between and under the rocks.

A sheen of beam ran across his face, when it occurred to him that finding food was not going to be a problem. He came across a path covered by the cascading branches of low bush. Surprised that he did not see it while he observed the terrain at night, he raised his shoulders and made a face, telling himself that it was not a big deal, after all.

He scooped under the low bush and made his way on the path. He continued walking carefully on the cleaned path, and after covering some distances, Sackie would mark a spot sometimes on the trunks of the young trees or on the ground in such a way that no one would notice. He repeated this until he reached an area where the path was bordered on both sides of a large marsh.

Remaining expressionless, but slightly raising his eyebrow in astonishment, he stopped for a while and observed the area. The path no longer ran under the low bush. The area ahead was a clearing extending for some acres with another low bush at the far end.

Satisfied with what he saw, he resumed walking on the path which was now little higher than the one he left behind because it somehow formed part of a heap that made up the edge of the marsh. As he took his time taking careful steps, he was startled by rustlings and disturbances in the water, but was relieved; they were caused by giant frogs leaping from the grass into the water. He became more cautious. Such terrain was fertile grounds for large snakes that prey on the frogs. So, he readjusted his head light as the sun was gradually lightening the gray sky. Then he hauled out his long hunting knife.

Sackie continued along this path for some time and reached the end of the marsh. The low bush was now right before him, and he needed to find another path that would take him west towards the St. Paul River. He observed that to the left of the low bush, the area a few meters ahead looked like the fine olive-green vegetation that grows along the edge of shallow creeks, thus raising his suspicion that a running creek may not be far.

Canoe men or fishermen always keep their water crafts in such creeks and it is possible that he would find a canoe there. He was trying to make his way to the creek by using his long hunting knife to clear the path when something caught his attention.

The branches of the trees of the low bush looked like they were trimmed in the shape of a cone, and the ground underneath was clean like someone wanted to nurture cocoa seedlings. If so, it meant that a village was nearby. Delighted, he abandoned the search for the creek and scooped to enter into the low bush.

Observing the place, Sackie Dirty Water was suddenly bewildered. To the far corner were small structures made of sticks planted in circles with palm thatches around them. They looked like outside bath rooms. He walked past the structures, never bordering to look inside and reached to where he saw something like a door made of reef trunks. Without any hesitation, Sackie Dirty Water opened the door and to his astonishment, he was standing before a village.

It seemed abandoned. There were about six huts, dubbed with fine white clay, and roofed with palm thatches. There were few palm trees, and the ground was covered with white clay. Sackie could see some abandoned winnowing fans, funnels, mortar and pestles and several calabashes lying about. There were fishing nets, and farming materials scattered around.

He was happy to find canoe paddles lying against a hut. He also noticed that in the middle of the village was a palaver hut decorated like a shrine. In the middle was a beautifully carved sculpture. Sackie hurried towards it to take a closer look. When he got closer, he was suddenly plunged into fear. His head started to swing and his heart began to beat rapidly, almost causing him to collapse.

Sackie stood shivering. He was terrified to the extent that his vision was getting blurry. But he began to regain his composure and to focus on how to process the realization of the eerie discovery he had made. The small voice in his heart was reminding him of what his grandfather, old man Kpakolo Laynumah had told him. "The jungle is full of surprises, but don't let them frighten you."

With his hunting gun pointed forward he cocked it and drew it closer to the sculpture. Briefly taking his eyes off the sculpture, he scanned the palaver hut. There were six benches made of sticks, arranged in an arc before the sculpture, making the shrine to look like it was some kind of theater. He took a look again at the strange thing and was very determined to figure out what it was.

The sculpture was a crocodile with a human head and feet. It was carved with red wood and was emblazoned with fine red and black tread with black beads hanging on them. Sackie was looking at the god of the water witch. He had discovered centuries of hidden secrets. He was sure of this, because he had listened to many stories of the water witch.

They were a secret colt responsible for the perceived drowning of countless number of persons mainly women and children. The six huts indicated that there were only six of them in Haindii and this village was their secret abode.

The Gola were the first to practice this kind of tradition in order to prevent the Kpelle from venturing into their land. But the Kpelle somehow discovered the secret and used it to harass the Gola from their fishing villages.

During the many wars between the two tribes, the Gola used the secret of the water witch to target the families of the strongest warriors of their opponents. Losing one's family especially, before one's very eyes, has a devastating psychological effect on a person's well being. Many of the strongest Kpelle warriors whose families disappeared under water without any trace, were eventually killed in battle, due to weariness and lack of focus.

The Gola always had the upper hand in these circumstances, but not until the Kpelle learned about it and used it militarily. Special groups of warriors, especially the good swimmers, the ones who built the monkey bridges across rivers, were trained in the knowledge and they formed part of the special warrior Navy Seals. They would emerge from under the water, sneak in on the Gola and attack and destroy their fishing villages.

Subsequently, the Gola could no longer venture into the river to fish and to also venture into the forest to farm for fear of being ambushed and killed by Kpelle warriors. After some time, they felt threatened and were forced to decapitate, and gave up their land.

After the war, the Water Witch became an Occult practiced by some Kpelle people. Probably, its members were former Navy seals warriors. But as competition for owning the best fertile land for farming ensued, the families of rival tribesmen were targeted and that continued even up to present times.

As a kid, Sackie witnessed occasions of many women and children going missing in the St. Paul River and were never seen again. This led to serious conflicts between families pointing accusing fingers at each other.

He remembered a particular incident that almost led to a tribal war between the Kpelle of Haindii and a group of Lorma people from Bong Mines. As tension between both tribes intensified, the Bong Mines Police Department had to deploy a task force to put the situation under control.

This happened when Yanwolo, a young and talented canoe man who ferried people across the river from Haindii to the shores of Gbarpolu, was blamed for the drowning of a little girl when his canoe capsized. He was among a few of the canoe men that crossed the river by making their way around the southern tip of Dobli Island.

Market women loved this hour and a half course, order than the one that will land them first on the Island. There, they will have to find manpower to haul their goods to the other side of the banks, then, sometimes wait for hours to find another canoe to cross to the Gbarpolu side. This was expensive and time consuming.

Most often, before Yanwolo ferries his clients, especially when it included a child, he practiced a ritual of dropping a red penny into the water.

Korpo Pewee, a renowned market woman who traded along the entire route between Kakata, Bong Mines and Gbarpolou was one of his best customers. Her husband was a man named Guzzeh Pewee who was a Deputy Chief Foreman of the Bong Mining Company for the unskilled and semi-skilled Laborers. They had three children, two boys and a girl named Yassah.

Guzzeh Pewee's job was to interview and recommend laborers to the chief contractor for possible hire. And, many of them were from Haindii. One of his functions was to monitor their behaviors, especially drinking on the job. This was a safety measure to prevent accidents, because they were mostly assigned up the mountain where the heavy-duty equipment were operated. He recommended wage cuts for first offense, and the uncompromising deputy foreman immediately terminated contracts of second time violators.

One day, as the Bopolu market day was fast approaching, Yanwolo had ferried Korpo and most of her goods across the river, and had come back to get the rest and Korpo's six years old daughter, Yassah who was also travelling with her mother. He could not carry the little girl and her mother on the first trip, because the goods Korpo was carrying across the river were too many and the canoe could not take them all at once.

Just before passing the southern tip of the island his canoe suddenly began to rattle in a violent manner. Perturbed by the unexpected occurrence, he struggled to steady the bow at the same time calling for help, when he realized that this did not seem normal. The canoe started spinning and little Yassah began to scream, calling her mother's name.

Some canoe men from the island heard the little girl screaming and quickly jumped into their canoes to help Yanwolo, but the current started to carry him downstream and then his canoe capsized after a violent spin of the water. He was however rescued with strenuous efforts by his fellow canoe men, but the six-year-old girl disappeared under the water.

The news reached Haindii and Bong Mines like a wildfire. The entire Fuamah District was embroiled with speculations and conspiracy theories. One explained how the young canoe man was involved, especially, when it became known that he did not drop the penny into the water before letting Yassah into the Canoe.

Some even said that he did drop a coin but it was not the usual red penny, and this was interpreted as a signal to the water witch. This led to the rounding up and subsequent flogging of some people in the middle of the town. Fortunately for Yanwolo, he was released when the canoe men who rescued him gave their accounts of what they saw, maintaining that the young canoe man had almost drowned in an attempt to rescue little Yassah.

Guzzeh Pewee, not willing to buy into that, and with the urging from Koikoi Pewee, his relative, gathered some of the male members of his family to go to Haindii to apprehend Yanwolo to compel him to confess the names of persons involved in the mysterious disappearance of his daughter.

Yassah's father chartered ten single cabin Toyota Stout Pickup trucks, loaded them with his male relatives and machetes, to transport them to Haindii. The news reached the town and in no time, some Haindii youth, calling themselves friends of Yanwolo, quickly organized themselves.

Just before reaching Haindii, the convoy was halted when huge logs were seen lying across the road ahead of it, and later at the rear, thus barricading the entire convoy. Immediately the friends of Yanwolo came running out of the rubber bushes bordering both sides of the road and surrounded the convoy. They asked everyone out, one by one.

The men, a total of thirty, including Koikoi Pewee, were led, single file, to a secret place in the bush and held for several hours. No one laid hands on any of them as it was by tradition that a Kpelle man should never waste the blood of a Lorma man or vice versa. With the involvement of both tribal chiefs, Koikoi Pewee and the others were rescued by the Task Force of the Bong Mines Police Detachment.

After the incident, Guzzeh Pewee was no longer the same person he was. Laborers with links to Haindii were heavily prejudiced. He refused to recommend many of them for contract or for permanent employment. The chief foreman learned of this and warned him, but he persisted. When it became imminent that he was going to be asked to resign, he called for early retirement. Guzzeh later established his rubber farm somewhere along the road that leads to Todee from the Bong Mines main checkpoint on Bong-Mines-kakata Road.

In spite of all the troubles he faced after the drowning and subsequent disappearance of his daughter, Guzzeh Pewee never gave up figuring out the mystery behind it. One of his findings suggested that it was due to his wife, Korpo's negligence; that day she had hurried across the river to meet a man by the name of Sekou "Beard-Beard", the owner of many of the Toyota Stout Pickup trucks that hauled goods from the Gbarpolu side of the waterfront to the town center, and as far as Bomi Hills using the Swen-Mecca route.

He learned that she and this man were having an affair. She had left her daughter behind on Haindii side, and had gone across to meet him at a village on the Gbarpolu side. He also learned that Sekou "Beard-Beard" had the habit of keeping Korpo for long hours whenever they met at that village.

With this new information, Guzzeh Pewee confronted his wife, Korpo about this, but she vehemently denied having an affair with Sekou Beard-Beard.

"The same people who are telling you these lies are hiding the truth from you. You made lots of enemies of the workers from Haindii when you had that job with the company. And they used Yassah's death to get to you. To hurt you the same way you hurt them," she told her husband, instead.

One day, just before the civil war, a Toyota Stout pickup truck drove on Guzzeh Pewee's farm to pick up a large pile of cup lumps and dried latex to take to the weighing station somewhere along Division 45 road, behind Kakata.

"Are you the Sekou Beard-Beard that owns the pick-ups that run from the waterfront at the Gbarpolu side of the St. Paul to Bomi Hills?" the former Deputy chief foreman suddenly asked when he heard one of the Car Boys mention the name.

"Yes, boss man. I am the one you chattered to come pick up your rubber," answered the short and fat man with a huge belly.

"So, you are the one who was behind my wife, Korpo. For your business my daughter died," Guzzeh Pewee suddenly screamed and grabbed Sekou Beard-Beard by his neck and started to choke him.

"Boss man, leave my neck. I did not come here for trouble," cried the transport business man at the same time fighting to free his neck from Pewee's grip.

There was a brief scuffle. Before the two car boys and some of the farm workers could rush to the scene to stop them, Guzzeh Pewee uttered a sharp cry when he was head-butted under his right cheek, turning his right eye blood-red and around it to swell. The impact swung his head backward, causing him to stagger and fall to the ground on his buttock. In no time he got up and ran into his farm house.

"He's going for his hunting gun," screamed one of Guzzeh's workers.

In no time Sekou Beard-Beard raced for his pick-up truck, swung the driver's door open, and jumped inside. He ignited the engine, and spun the truck into a U-turn. The car disappeared in a cloud of dust, almost dragging one of the car boys.

Since then, Mr. Pewee and his wife continue to live together on the rubber farm. But he vowed to never sleep with her. Sometimes they quarreled, fought and other family members would intervene. This continued up to the time of the Civil War.

Sackie Dirty Water became inquisitive as he reflected on these incidents. Sometimes women disappeared when they went to lay baskets or fishing in the nearby streams or shallow creeks that ran into the river. There was a case about a beautiful girl who was about to be given to a man for marriage, after he was able to win her over from her parents.

But there was another man who was also competing for her but did not succeed. He was very boastful and was absolutely sure of winning over this girl. When he failed, he became a laughing stock among his peers, whenever they drank palm wine at the town's main palm wine kitchen.

One day, this girl, after watching her clothes at an area upstream where only women go to wash their clothes and take bath in the water, something snatched her under the water and she was never seen again.

Seeing this village with huts, fishing nets and farm materials, the disappearances began to make sense to Sackie, and so he decided to look around. First, he scanned the vicinity of the village hoping to spot graves but he could not make out any. He was dealing with a very secretive cult and so he may not have any idea where and how they bury the dead.

He abandoned that idea and instead, entered one of the huts after stepping the only bamboo door open and calling anybody who could have been in there to come out or he will shoot inside. While standing between the doorway and turning on his light, because it was dark inside, he was startled to see, first a crocodile skin hanging on the wall above a bamboo bed with a lantern sitting on a small stool made of a nicely chopped off tree trunk. A corpse, almost completely decayed, was lying on the strew mattress and partially wrapped up in a white country cloth with black linings.

Sackie muttered something in his dialect and ran outside. What got him more perplexed were three human remains lying on the floor beside the bed. They looked like kids. Sackie stood outside breathing heavily. Tears ran down his eyes as he contemplated on how many people were abducted and had died, buried and graves will never be found. The last incident occurred two years before the civil war started, and the persons responsible for this village may have left in a hurry, probably for fear that rebel fighters patrolling the bushes might discover and kill them.

He had seen enough; there was no need to examine the other huts, and he needed to stop poking around too much or else he might fall into a trap. People who keep deep secrets like these do all they can to maintain them, even if they are not around.

He took a path that led to the back of the village and he was astonished to see that it was bordered by a very large creek. He looked around and was finally happy to see some canoes and paddles still intact. He observed that they were all old canoes and have not been used for a long period of time. The villagers may have gotten away on foot or may have used new canoes.

He examined all of them carefully. Some of the speculations attributed to the water-witches were that they planted holes in the canoes of their targets and pasted them with a kind of tree latex that quickly dissolved in water. Many canoe men have experienced water entering their canoe at high tide.

Sackie Dirty Water inspected all and was satisfied with one. He pushed it properly into the water and in no time, he started paddling towards the direction of the St. Paul.

Day has now fully broken. The Bush Dog leader had paddled for some time and became more elated when he recognized the same olive-green vegetation he spotted at the left of the cone-shaped low bush that led to the village of the water witches. He was sure that the water would lead him to the greater St. Paul. And when that was achieved, he would turn left and head downstream until he reached the estuary where he left Sergeant-Major Gonpue and his deputy.

Then, they would paddle back up stream with hope to get a glimpse of the distant Bong Range.

He kept reminding himself that he will never disclose what he saw to them. It would be to his conviction that he will never do so.

The strength of any tribe is the display of its success as well as maintaining the secrets of its woes.

Nonetheless he told himself that such secrets will not be kept hidden forever. Maybe this will be exposed after the war, as justice for those who were abducted and the pains bore by their families will have to one way or another be dispensed. For now, he has lost his beloved town, lost some good friends and relatives to strangers and he needs to do whatever it takes to regain it.

Sackie kept on a steady course downstream, surprised that the current was rather rough than the crossing at Haindii, no wonder why the water-witches choose these parts of the river to establish their secret abode. As he paddled and then drifted, he kept his eyes on the floor of the canoe to make sure that there were no leaks. Drifting for about 40 minutes, he had now covered some distances, and was increasingly getting satisfied that the canoe he was riding was not bewitched.

He finally reached the estuary and managed to turn left, paddling for some time until the cliff where they descended was insight. He navigated his way into the running creek and entered the water log. As he found a place suitable to land the canoe, he spotted the Sergeant-Major and his deputy docking for cover. Sackie allowed himself to be more visible so that they should recognize him. When they were satisfied that it was Sackie, they came out of their cover and ran to help him land the canoe.

"I have never been worried," said Takpoh, helping to haul the canoe on shore.

"I have never been scared," Sackie responded, disembarking.

"Scared? Were there any problems?" inquired Sergeant-Major Gonpue.

"Yes," responded Sackie, taking a deep breath and reminding himself about the commitment he made. "Losing my friends and my town, I have never been scared."

"We will get it back," Takpoh assured him. "Let's just pray we get to Gbarnga."

"Yes. But we must first find something to eat. There's a rough ride ahead of us and we need to build strength as we will be paddling for hours," Sackie said.

He then took from his hunting bag some of the large frogs he caught while walking through the marsh. He also took out a pot, a pan and a box of matches. Sergeant-Major Gonpue and Takpoh Duo stared at the Bush Dog leader with admiration.

"Will you guys also have some crabs?" Sackie asked, expecting them to be surprised.

"Crabs!" the Sergeant-Major raised his eyebrows.

"Yeah, crabs," Sackie Dirty Water answered. "We slept under these little water mechanics."

Sergeant-Major Gonpue laughed when he heard the word Water Mechanics. That was the name they called crabs when they were on training base. The small brownish-red back fresh water crabs were usually found under rocks along streams and ravines when they are not in their holes, and the young commandos liked to eat them a lot. For a moment he began to reflect on how he and a group of fighters attempted to survive on crabs in the mangrove swamps of Monrovia during the Octopus's Invasion.

A large group of them had infiltrated the Barnersville area at the north west of Monrovia through the township of Louisiana, two days before the attack. ECOMOG immediately sent a patrol, when some residents reported seeing men looking like rebel fighters lurking in the surrounding bushes. The sightings were confirmed, but the West African Force Monitoring Group pretended like there was no rebel activity in the area.

On the day of the invasion, just before dawn, when the first rocket was fired, signaling to rebel units positioned at strategic locations at the outskirts of the capital, that the attack had begun, a unit of the pro-interim government militia and some ECOMOG soldiers had condomed the entire area, thus putting Sergeant-Major Gonpue and his men in a circle.

Overwhelmed with such a surprise and becoming apprehensive that all along they did not know they had been encircled, many of the fighters climbed the surrounding tall trees within the perimeters of where they were confined, to try to scout out a possible route to reconnect with their comrades already positioned on New Georgia side, a couple of kilometers south of their position. But they were gunned down like birds by snipers of the pro-Interim Government Militia.

Sergeant-Major Gonpue and his surviving men, hemmed in on all sides, detected a gap in the defensive lines of a squad of the enemy to their left. They exploited that opportunity and concentrated all their fire power in that direction. After a fierce battle, they managed to bulldoze their way out of their confinement until they reached the Dry Rice Market junction.

They attempted to march through Barnersville Estate to connect New Georgia from the West, but were prevented by ECOMOG and the Pro-interim Government Militia suppressing them with heavy fire from their right. This eventually forced them to turn towards Banersville Junction Road.

At Banersville Junction, Sergeant-Major Gonpue's group, now down to a quarter, but still a sizable number, made another attempt to join their comrades at the New Georgia Estate area by marching down south to New Georgia Junction. Unfortunately, they were again halted by another unit of the Pro-Interim Government Militia led by a Lieutenant named Booker Ray, a formal Liberian Armed Forces officer.

The E-die 90 conscript, recruited at the onset of the 1990 civil war was generally known by his men as 'bullet shadow' for his tactics in which he and few of his men would first engage the enemy face to face and then they would pretend to retreat. The enemy pursuing them would be lured into an ambush and his snipers would take them out one by one. He held the rebels at St. Michael Catholic School Junction for an hour, until they were forced back to Barnesville Junction.

Back at the Barnesville Junction, they were also squeezed in by a unit of ECOMOG soldiers advancing from Stephen Tolbert Estate side. Becoming increasingly enveloped, especially with the appearance of ECOMOG fighters jets flying overhead, Gonpue and his group were left with no alternative but to take the Kesselly Boulevard Road, east of the Barnesville Junction and ran all the way towards the distant Mangrove Swamps for cover from the fighter jets.

Midway on the boulevard, they were further harassed by Booker Ray's men who they noticed were creeping behind them in a Liberian Armed Forces style known as zig-zag formation.

At that moment a bomb was dropped from an ECOMOG fighter jet, causing heavy casualties and dislodging the surviving rebels. In the midst of the disarray, Lt. Booker Ray and dozens of his men, who had taken a by-pass by way of Dark Forest Community to the right, suddenly emerged from between some houses and the small market, with heavy and sustained fire, further increasing the number of casualties and splitting the group.

Half of what was left of the fighters were cut off from the rest when Booker Ray and his men had created a buffer zone by forming defensive lines across the road, thus pushing the remaining half in which Sergeant-Major Gonpue was part, further into the mangrove swamps. The other half, beguiled by the indecision of penetrating the defensive lines before them or disrupting the zig zag formation at their rear, remained in that circle and fired aimlessly at the fighter jets which would sometimes swoop down low towards them. At the same time, some of them were firing towards Booker Ray's positions. Soon they ran out of ammunition, thus enabling their opponents to quickly close in on them.

A second ECOMOG fighter jet made another dive and dropped a bomb when Sergeant-Major Gonpue and what was left of his group were making their way for the mangrove swamp right at the end of the Boulevard. There was a huge explosion leaving many of the fighters dead.

Gonpue and some of his men somehow managed to survive the blast and hurried into the mangrove swamp, cradling their way out of the mud until they reached a field of low grass and small water logs.

Their number had suddenly decreased to 15 from a battle group of 300 gorillas. The same fighter jet was still circling overhead, making some acrobatic swoops as it flew over the field, discharging its guns. Seven of Gonpue's men lay dead when the bullets from the fighter jet riddled the field.

Now with only eight fighters remaining, the Sergeant-Major was forced to push deeper into the swamp to take advantage of the cover under the mangrove trees. Fortunately, it was the dry season. The tide had receded, and in some parts of the swamp, the water level was visible at the roots of the mangrove trees.

Gonpue and his men slouched their way into the water, sometimes scooping very low under the low branches until they were able to find a perfect place to dock for cover. There were three fighter jets now hovering overhead, displaying their usual stunts of swooping very low as the thunderous roar of their engines was causing a great deal of discomfort for the fighters hiding beneath the mangroves.

Agbameleah Dahn, one of the fighters docking under a cluster of Mangrove trees, became very weary of the roaring engines of the fighter jets, whenever they swooped low. As the jets swayed, he would climb up the branches, positioned himself and take an aim with his Ak-47 in an attempt to down one of the planes. Agbamaleah was trying to take a shot at an approaching jet, when another one suddenly appeared at his rear, discharging several caliber rounds and tearing him apart as his body parts scattered into the water.

Another fighter was also hit. Some of the rounds tore through the branches and pierced his chest cavity. The young fighter was hopeless as he looked down and saw his almost lifeless heart beating out of his opened chest. The lad soon fell forward, dying painfully as his body sunk into the cold muddy water.

Gonpue and the rest, now down to six, remained under their cover as the jets continued to hover overhead. It was fast approaching the late evening hours. The fighter jets had been reduced to one, probably because they suspected that the rebels in the mangrove swamp posed no serious threat. The last fighter jet had retired to base, giving small relief to Gonpue and his remaining men.

They were hoping to leave the swamp to make their way back to kesselly Boulevard under the cover of darkness but soon started receiving artillery fire from that end, forcing them to abandon that plan.

The fighters remained hiding in the swamp as the night seeped in and gradually, the tide began to rise. They had to find their way through the water to get to a dry ground which they had earlier discovered, but it was impossible to get there when the jets were flying overhead. So, they waited until it was fully dark. Then, they took careful steps into the water which was sometimes between waists and knee high. Before they took a step, they would use their gun butts or nuzzles to test the softness of the ground beneath their feet to avoid sinking into layers of deep mud.

Sometimes they would dock and wait for the occasional firing of artillery from the direction of Booker Ray's men. Then, they would resume as soon as the dark swamp brightened, when the flight path of projectiles lit the sky. Taking the lead, Sergeant-Major Gonpue finally reached the dry ground. A junior commando by the name of Dorlea was the next, followed by three other fighters.

Suddenly Cooper Kerlea, who was the last and was still making his way started screaming when something grabbed his left ankle and started pulling him into the water. Gonpue and Dorlea immediately jumped into the water and started pulling him by both hands. Cooper cried with agony when he felt his heel bitten off when his comrades pulled him with a very decisive jerk.

While the others were helping him out of the water, Gonpue had pulled his legs out to inspect the affected area when a large crocodile, about 6 feet, leaped out of the water and charged at him. Because he scooped over while looking at Cooper's legs, the ferocious reptile was aiming for his head but he was quick to tilt it backward a little and instead, the animal missed but gashed the left side of his face. Gonpue yelled when the crocodile teeth tore through the front of the camouflaged vest he was wearing. It landed back into the water pulling the Sergeant-Major with it.

There was a tussle in the water between Gonpue and the crocodile that could not let go of his vest. It was pulling him under the water. The other fighters froze with shock and helplessly looked on as Gonpue struggled with the merciless reptile. The water splashed on their faces as Gonpue fought to free himself from the animal.

The Sergeant-Major managed to reach for his bayonet on his side and started stabbing the animal all over its head. It finally left him when he managed to gouge out the eyes and it when dashing aimlessly into the deeper waters, a safe distance from the men. Sergeant-Major Gonpue made his way out of the water, petrified, but grateful that he was able to free himself from the vicious attack of the crocodile.

Cooper Kerlea was now groaning from the pain of the crocodile's bite. His entire left heel was bitten off along with the part of the rubber sanders he was wearing. His comrades had to tie the wound to stop the bleeding, but the cloth used to cover the wound was already soaked with blood.

The Sergeant-Major cleaned his own wound and tied it from his forehead down to his check with a bandage he got from his cargo pocket of the military trousers he was wearing.

"We have to spend the night on something high," he told his men at the same time looking around. "Or else the crocodile will attack us if we fall asleep here."

Dorlea and the two other fighters who were not wounded walked to a low bush a few yards from where they stood shivering, and cut some sticks and bush robes to build a scaffold. They covered it with leaves and branches until it was soft enough to lie down on.

Copper Kerlea was helped on it, and then the others climbed on the scar fork. They lie on the scaffold all night looking at the gray sky and listening to occasional rustlings in the grass below them and splashes in the water, telling them that the crocs were around and agitated by the taste of human blood.

It was dawn and the sun was gradually appearing in the sky. For about four hours now, the occasional firing of artillery had stopped. In the distance ahead of them, the horns of cars occasionally blurted, indicating the beginning of the early morning traffic, and that downtown Monrovia was not far. Cooper Kerlea had survived the night, but he was still whimpering from his wound. The left side of Sergeant-Major Gonpue's face has swollen, under the bandage.

Hungry, thirsty and exhausted, Gonpue was thinking of something to eat when he noticed some fresh river crabs coming out of the water and crawling into the grass covering the dry ground. He signaled to Dorlea and the two other fighters who were not wounded to catch them while the other fighter positioned himself on the lookout for the crocs. The two fighters were using their bayonets to bow the back of the crabs when suddenly the firing of artillery resumed from the direction of Booker Ray's men. Then a fighter jet was soon spotted hovering high in the sky.

On the scaffold, there was no way for them to take cover. Furthermore, one of them was severely wounded and the aggressive crocs in the water made it impossible to venture further deep into the swamp. And the fighter jet began to dive towards them.

"We will have to surrender," suggested Dorlea, who had abandoned catching the crabs, and ran to Sergeant-Major Gonpue.

With tears running down his eyes, Gonpue agreed. Dorlea quickly wrapped the muzzle of his AK-47 with a white T-shirt and started waving it above his head. The jet flew past them twice and then it took a vertical soar high in the sky as Dorlea kept waving the white T-shirt above his head.

Flight Lieutenant Eric Esien, the young Ghanian fighter pilot of the ECOMOG jet had radioed the command-and-control center that there were some enemy fighters trapped in the mangrove swamp and wanting to surrender. It took about an hour and some minutes when two small boats with ECOMOG Soldiers inside came speeding from the direction of the Montserrado River and entered the water where Gonpue and his men were trapped.

Dorlea saw the boats from a distance and started calling for help. The rest of them except Cooper Kerlea who was increasingly groaning of his wound, quickly removed the magazines from their weapons and joined Dorlea, also calling for help.

Lieutenant Mamadouba Bangura, the ECOMOG officer that led the soldiers in the boats, holding a microphone in one hand and a cigarette in the other, waited for the fighter jet to circle directly over the fighters and then spoke into the microphone.

"This is ECOMOG," he said, his English, heavily accented with Guinean French. "Leave your weapons and knives on the ground and come closer to the boat one by one. We will not harm you"

"Please come closer. There are crocodiles in the water," Dorlea yelled back at them, and pointed to Cooper Kerlea. "It attacked two of us last night."

"Oh voilà, mon ami," the ECOMOG officer said, after one of his men had whispered something to him. "They will not arm you. The sound of the boat engine had scared them away."

Sergeant-Major Gonpue and his men hesitated.

"Come now, my friend," Lt. Bangura said, becoming agitated and nervously puffing on his cigarette. "If you do not come to us now, the pilot up there will think you are out for tricks and will drop his bomb on you."

The boats landed with Gonpue and his men at the Slipway side of the Montserrado River. A crowd had gathered to see the rebels who were trapped in the swamp, jeering and booing at them. They were taken to a holding center at the ECOMOG base and Cooper Kerlea was treated for his injuries sustained from the crocodile bite.

At the holding center, Gonpue met some of his men who were cut off on Kesselly Boulevard, thus assuring himself that he did the right thing to surrender to ECOMOG. Later that day, more fighters were brought in by Lieutenant Booker Ray and his men.

Gonpue saw that he was a light skinned young man who looked the opposite of the kind of brave soldier he was. Booker Appleton Ray who preferred to be called Booker Ray grew up with his mother in the Johnsonville belt. As a kid, people always took advantage of him because of his somewhat soft looks, but he would surprise them as he would turn out to be very tough. He was a staunch supporter of the president.

In January 1990 he voluntarily showed up to join the army, when in December, 1989 the news broke up of a rebel incursion at the Liberian -Ivorian border. The recruiting officer attempted to send him back home, but he and some of his friends that went along with him, caused a serious commotion, threatening to appear on the State's Television Station to inform the government that the recruiting officer was a rebel collaborator. Their actions forced a senior officer present to allow them to be recruited.

His first combat experience was when the Liberian Army was sent to repel an attack when White Plains, an area situated on the St. Paul River, north west of Monrovia that hosts the city water supply, was invaded by the independent rebel faction. They were beaten back in the first attempt to dislodge the rebels. The commander who led the government soldiers' counter attack, Capt. T. Quiah Garlo was a private of the first Infantry Battalion, who participated in the attack that drove dissident forces from the Liberian National Television and Radio Station, during the abortive invasion of 1985.

Captain Garlo allowed his troops to drive right into the enemy ambush resulting in heavy casualty. One of the American Army issued GMG KKCW G. I. trucks with almost a company inside were blown off. He and the rest of the soldiers were forced to retreat to a certain location along the Dixville Vicinity and set up roadblocks and a buffer zone.

Booker Ray, then a Private First Class who had just turned 20, blamed his commander for cowardice. He, out of disregard of instruction from his superiors, managed to convince some of the men in his unit to sneak in on the enemy, surprising and at the same time continued to harass them which sometimes led to a see-saw battle.

He was recalled for acts of indiscipline to his superior officers. And was then reassigned at the Executive mansion. But he had to ask for an excuse for a week when his mother became sick and he had to accompany her to Sierra Leone. To his mother's urging, he had to abandon the army. There, they remained until the president was captured and killed. But for fear that he would cross into Liberia to avenge the death of the president, his mother took him to Guinea. While in Guinea, he met a fellow claiming to be an official of the Interim Government who encouraged him to join a pro-Interim Government Milia that was being organized.

Gonpue and the others remained under detention for most part of the Octopus invasion. When Monrovia and other parts of coaster Liberia were cleared of the main rebel faction, they were turned over to the Interim government. They underwent a quick disarmament demobilization and rehabilitation program until family members were allowed to sign for them. Sergeant-Major Gonpue was signed for by someone who was sent by CO Alfred Mentee, under the pretense of a relative.

Now sitting on a rock finishing the crab soup prepared by Sackie Dirty Water, he was thinking about the men who were rescued along with him from the mangrove swamp. Dorlea had remained in Monrovia to the urging of some relatives and was in the petty trader business at Paynesville Red Light Market. Cooper Kerlea was amputated to the feet, and the last time he heard about him, he was somewhere in Nimba county. The last three guys were killed when the Liberian National Police were responding to an arm robbery attack in Sugar Hill Community, west of Paynesville City, outside Monrovia.

Rubbing the scar on his face, when he had finished with the crab soup, he began to wonder how the attack on Haindii was planned and the offensive style of the enemy forces. From the way it was coordinated, it appeared like Lieutenant Booker Ray was part of the planning, but he disabused that from his thoughts. He did not hear the enemy fighters mention his name during the attack. The names he heard were Cpl. Charles Bryant and Sargant Joseph Chebeour.

Sackie Dirty Water and Tapkor Duo had also finished eating and were packaging the leftovers to take along with them. Sackie anticipated two-or three-days canoe ride upstream to connect to the bushes that will lead them to the Bong Range, and another two days or more to get them to Weala. So, they would need more food and water.

They boiled enough of the water they got from the water log and filled them in some containers Sackie Dirty Water found at the village of the water witch. The Bush Dog commander hoped to remember the route that will take them down the mountain range into the old Tenera ('Makindo') oil palm farm of Slocum Mission School. There, they will use the unpaved road that will take them to Jennita, along Weala-Gbargba Highway.

The journey began, when the sun was fully in the sky. Its descending rays brightened the waters of the St. Paul, making it appeared like it was covered with sheets of gold. As the sun got hotter, the water was warm. The current was a mixture of calm and aggression with a deceivingly quiet surface, except for the countless undulations of ripples and the sound they made.

The vegetation on both sides of the banks appeared to be stable as there wasn't much wind to sway the branches of trees. The aroma of floating dead water weeds, sticks and leaves filled the air above the water thus, awarding it its unique identity.

Sackie Dirty Water, Sergeant-Major Gonpue and Takpor Duo had ridden for about two hours, keeping the canoe on a steady course. The three of them took turns to paddle. When the current was high, where it required more skills to navigate through the rough current that often disrupted the speed of the canoe, for his knowledge of the river, Sackie Dirty Water would paddle. Sergeant-Major Gonpue and his deputy would take terms when the current was gentle.

To Gonpue's suggestion, the canoe was positioned in the middle of the water where the river was wide, hoping to gain an angle of incidence as the sun was shining overhead. If they were spotted and shot at, they would not be hit-a trick he learned from Major Jacob Saydee during the Dobli Island attack.

After switching terms with Tapkor Duo, Sackie Dirty Water sat at the bow to rest. He was thinking about Haindii and wondering what may be happening now. The town has fallen and most possibly will be deserted by most of the inhabitants who may be on their farms. He reasoned that they will only return to the town when it is liberated.

Should they reach Gbarnga, it was possible to lead some troops along this way, and engage the enemy fighters from the north-west. There would also be forces coming by way of Weala and passing through Popota and turning right, leaving Bong Mines on the left to eventually put the enemy into a huge circle and hem them on all sides.

Bong Mines lingered on his mind for some time. He was also wondering what has become of the mining town. It was obvious that it was a target or maybe it was now under attack. If so, for a successful counter attack, the Weala-Popota Road will be the best route to take. This will enable them to creep in on the enemy right under their nose, and conduct a simultaneous attack. They would be overstretched and busy defending both Haindii and Bong Mines at the same time.

Sackie began to reflect on his days as a kid, growing up in Bong Mines. Not only was he frequented at the Dirty Water area where he almost drowned or the Bong Town supermarket where he sold his cold-water fish at the entrance, he also visited the Bong Town Horse Club.

He was fascinated whenever he saw the German people, mainly their kids, riding on horse backs. To him, the animals looked a bit smaller than how they appeared on Television. He liked to stare at the brown ones, especially those with the white or creamlike strips on the forehead, when they were in their stalls. Sometimes he would loiter around the stable until the horse club was about to close for the day and old man Koboi Kollie, the Stable keeper or the local boys who worked with him would send him away.

Koboi Kollie was in charge of supervising the stable boys to clean the stable, rid it of horse dung, and also bathe the horses. They would put the horse dung in 100 lb. rice bags and sell them for large sums of money to mostly the company's female staff or wives of male staff who use them as manure in their flower gardens. He would charge the white staff or their wives more than what he would charge the Liberian staff.

The stable keeper had an extreme love for money. The stable boys often complained about being cheated, whenever they sold horse dung, except one of the stable boys by the name of Dolo, who always supported Koboi Kollie's action.

Sackie often overheard the rest of the stable boys saying that Dolo's loyalty was predicated on the extra cash Koboi Kollie gave him as compensation for being his eyes and ears at the House Club. Sackie did not like the old man for these things.

Local vegetable gardeners who grew and supplied fresh and succulent ones to the people that sell them in front of Bong Town Supermarket often come to the Horse Club to buy the manure, but Koboi Kollie will refuse to sell to them because they could not afford the high prices he charged. Even if they begged him to help clean the stalls for a little of the manure, he and Dolo would vehemently refuse, with the stable keeper telling them that it is a matter of the club's policy that non staff are prohibited from working in the stable and that the manure will not be enough due to high demand from the company's employees who were given first preference.

Sometimes this would result into a commotion until the Horse Club Manager, a German named Mr. Friedrich would intervene and the gardeners would be given some of the manure. One thing Sackie thought was odd was old man Kollie, and his boys, after bathing the horses would also bathe with the same shampoo that was used to bathe them. To him, it was a very sick and stupid idea to bathe with the same liquid soap that was used to bathe the animals. He did not think Mr. Friedrich could do that.

He pitied the brown horses when Lee Gbamou, one of the stable boys, told him that the German people like brown horse meat, when Sackie once asked him what happened to them when they die. Gbamou explained how the red meat that looks like the big sausages sold in the supermarket are made of horse meat, mainly the brown ones. Sackie believed him because he always saw the German people coming out of the supermarket with those big red meat in plastic bags.

One day he became annoyed when a little girl who sold boiled groundnuts for her mother visited the house club. She was also from Nyenen and she had only gone there when she saw him. She followed him, with the bucket of ground nuts on her head, into the stable to look at the horses and soon both of them started staring at a brown one.

She was frightened when the horse suddenly neigh and she mistakenly threw the medium size rubber dish pan full of the ground nuts into the stall. She stood crying and watching the horse eat almost all the ground nuts. Old man Koboi Kollie came rushing into the stable, scrolling the little girl and shoving her outside even as she pleaded with him that her mother will kill her, if she did not report the money for the grand nuts the horse had eaten. Knowing the kind of mother she has, Sackie tried to add his voice, pleading on her behalf, but he was also shunned and asked to leave the stable and never to come back again.

"You kids want to put me in trouble?" raged old man Kollie. "Who told you that the horse can eat boiled ground peas with the hull still on them? Do you want the hull to choke and kill the animal? And you know your poor parents, even if they work 100 years will not be able to pay for the dead animal."

The little girl resisted leaving the House Club without her money. Koboi Kollie ordered Dolo to drag her out of the stable. He immediately started pulling and shoving the little girl all the way out of the Horse Club. The girl fought and cried bitterly as Sackie pitied her and helplessly watched how she was mistreated. Her mother will never understand that it was a horse that ate more than half of the boiled ground pea. In fact, she was going to ask what business she had at the Horse Club rather than selling at the supermarket or at Bong Town School?

Later that day, the girl was severely flogged and was given little food for a week. Sackie hated old man Koboi Kollie more for putting the interest of a mere animal over a poor and innocent little girl.

After that incident, every now and then, he would sneak into the stable when no one was looking and would use his slingshot with an iron ore pellet in the pouch to aim at the horses. When the animals whined and made a lot of noise at the same time jumping about into their stalls, he would quickly get away upon hearing the footsteps of old man Kollie or the stable boys rushing into the stable.

This day, he sneaked in again. He hauled out his catapult from the back of the waist of the short pants he was wearing, inserted an iron ore pellet into the pouch, stretched the rubber bands until it passed his chest, and released it. One of the horses chirped with a very high pitch, and whined when the pellet hit the bone above its right eye. All the other horses started whining and making an attempt to jump out of their stalls.

Not quite satisfied, he inserted another pellet, this time a bigger one, into the pouch and stretched it. Just then Dolo rushed in, and started shouting and calling to the others when he saw that Sackie was about to take an aim at a horse.

"You wicked little boy. So, you are the one who has been hurting the animals, right? We will carry you to the Mine Guards' office today and lock you up for good," foamed Dolo.

Sackie turned the slingshot towards him and shot, aiming for Dolo's chest, but the right-hand man of Koiboi Kollie dodged, dropping to the ground and at the same time uttering a frightened and sharp cry when the iron ore pellet smashed against one of the planks that barricaded the horses' stalls and cracked it. Next, Sackie was out of there when he heard old man Kollie and the other stable boys running into the stable.

Koboi Kollie was trying to calm the injured horse. But it gave him a back kick which sent him crashing on the concrete wall of the back of the stall.

"Catch that boy. Catch that boy!" old man Kollie sat on the floor, crying.

By then Sackie had raced past the vicinity of Club Hill, leaving it on his left and headed down Rice Farm, another vicinity of Bong Town at the south eastern end. He crossed the plots where the swamp rice were planted and entered the bush of rubber trees. He continued south wards along a path that snaked through the bush, stepping and crushing the dried rubber seeds that littered the path. He came out on Bong Mines-Kakata Road, at the intersection of J.D.K Baker Episcopal Mission School.

He crossed the road, raced up to the schools' campus to a relative on his mother's side who was called Nathaniel who worked in the school's maintenance department. When Nathaniel saw him, he knew that his little relative had gotten in some sort of trouble, and while he was still at work, he told him to wait for him at his farm, not very far from the campus.

Anticipating that Koboi Kollie would use the Mine Guards to track him down in Nyenen, if he went home right away, Sackie stayed with Nathaniel for two weeks. During these times, he would help Nathaniel set his traps on his farm that was not far from the train tracks that ran a few meters from the west to the south of the campus. He would also help him pack the fire wood in the store room of the School's Kitchen, behind the Dining Hall. Part of Nathaniel's work was to provide fire wood for the school.

He was a jovial and muscular man who kept a shining black afro haircut. He would fell the old rubber trees on the school's land, chop them into logs of about 3 feet long and split them into firewood with one swing of his axe. Many of the students enjoyed watching him doing this.

The traps also caught groundhogs and possums. Nathaniel's wife would prepare hot pepper stew, whenever there was a catch, and brought them to the dining hall on Saturday evenings to sell them to the students. When it was time for Sackie to go back to his parents, who later knew of his whereabouts when Nathaniel informed them, he took him to Varney Town Market, bought him some clothes and took him back home.

It took a little while before Sackie resumed roaming Bong Town, but he no longer sauntered around the Horse Club for fear of being caught by Dolo or Koboi Kollie. He gathered that the Stable keeper had not fully recovered from the horse's kick. His main focus was now the Club House and its vicinity, especially around the football field, the tennis court or the swimming pool, where he often watched and enjoyed, from the wire fence that separated the pool from the football field, German and some Liberian staff or their older kids, jumping, bouncing and somersaulting from the high dive board into the pool. He also liked to watch the kids playing in the small pool.

Sometimes he would venture around the Golf Club to watch the Germans playing golf. Whenever the golfers arrived, he often observed with disdain, how local lads scrambled and competed to be their caddies, hoping to be given tips for the service. Sometimes, fighting would break up, and the golfer for whom they competed and quarreled, would get frustrated and eventually demand service from no one. Sackie later appreciated, with pride, how one day, the caddies were able to organize themselves to elect a leader and set their own rules.

He remembered once when he was forced to be a caddie. It was around Christmas when a German couple accompanied their son, who looked to be in his early teens to the Golf Club. In these festive times the golf course was usually busy with golfers and their caddies. The couple and their son were looking for a caddie and then Torstein, their son, saw Sackie sitting quietly on the visitors bench. Thinking that the couples were about to engage the bench, Sackie got up to leave when Torstein called him.

"What's your name," he asked in heavily accented English.

"Sackie," he responded, almost mimicking the German lad, and struggling not to laugh at his accent.

"Oh! Sackie! I want you to help me carry my golf bag. I will pay you plenty dollars."

"No. It is very heavy."

"Ok. No problem, Sackie. Just drag it on the ground."

Before Sackie could say a word, Torstein grabbed a club and gestured to the local minor to follow him to the Teeing ground. Surprised, Sackie watched the strange white boy closely, as he dragged the golf bag behind him.

Torstein was slim with chocolate-like spots all over his skin. For his age, he had a large, pointed and elongated Adam's apple.

They stopped briefly and then continued after his mother called him and spoke something in German. This startled Sackie, because the verbal exchanges between the mother and son were harsh; it appeared like Torstein was being strongly warned.

They reached some golfers and their caddies. Sackie stopped, thinking that was where Torstein was going to start, but the German teen passed and headed toward the course which was mostly isolated.

"No, Sackie. Not here. Follow me. I will give you plenty of dollars," he said, pointing his golf club in the direction of the last golf course, far from the rest.

Sackie stood, looking around for some time. The other golfers were busy playing. He watched how one of them hit a golf ball with a swing of his club. The others cheered and watched its long flight. When it landed, immediately a caddie ran towards the direction to mark the spot.

Again, Torstein called his attention, this time, a bit irritated, and Sackie immediately followed. They walked past the second course which was also occupied with golfers and their caddies, and then they reached the last course, and got to the tee box after a few minutes' walk. There were no golfers and caddies. Satisfied, Torstein gestured to Sackie to put the golf bag down. He asked Sackie to look into the bag for a pin and a golf ball. The innocent minor looked in, rummaged through the things in the bag and got out a pin and then a neon green ball.

"No. Sackie. This is too stupid. A green ball on a lawn?" Torstein screamed, ceasing the ball from Sackie and repeatedly knocked it on his head.

"Give me a white ball, Sackie," he handed back the neon green ball. "We will be able to see the white ball on the lawn."

Sackie rubbed the part of his head where Torstein knocked the ball for some time at the same time looking around to see whether someone was watching.

"What do you mean by lawn?" he muttered in Kpelle, then he looked into the bag and got out the white ball. Torstein asked him to put the ball down so he could take his first shot. But the Nyenen kid, who realized, with a glee, what the German was trying to tell him, when he saw the ball was clearly visible on the green field, suddenly uttered a sharp cry, when Torstein hit his knuckles with the golf club.

"No, Sackie. Very stupid again," he scooped over and said, his face suddenly turning red with rage. "You must first insert the ball into the tee box, not outside of the tee box."

Sackie again looked around him at the same time rubbing his knuckles. The pain was more than the one he felt on his head. He has now understood the hash exchanges between the temper tantrum kid, and his mother.

She and her husband were having coffee and lost in a deep conversation with some people at the Golf Club veranda, reserved for recreation. Sackie wiped a little droplet of tears from his eyes, and as Torstein again demanded, Sackie positioned the ball at the right spot. After that, Torstein asked him to take a few steps away from the spot.

Torstein looked around to see whether he was being watched, but no one was watching. He then positioned his club, adjusting it right next to the ball as his face brightened with an ominous glee. After two test swings, he lifted his head towards the location where he would take his shot, at the same time stretching his neck to see beyond Sackie who was standing a few meters in front of him.

Balancing himself, he took the shot. Sackie yelled and again cursed in his dialect, when the ball hit his right sheen, causing him to sit on the ground rubbing it, and crying. He got up and ran down the course, but the German Kid ran after him.

"Sackie. Come back here. It was a mistake. Come get some dollars," Torstein said, grabbing the now sorrowful looking kid's hand, when he had caught up with him, and shoved a dollar bill in it, and then another.

Sackie hesitated for a while and held the money. Torstein then gestured and he headed back to the teeing ground. Sackie followed, but kept a safe distance. He was wondering how troubled this German kid might be to enjoy inflicting pain on others. No wonder why his mother had the hard exchange with him when he asked him to be his caddie. Sackie also wondered how many kids like him will suffer from Torstein's thirst to inflict pain on others. They reached the teeing ground and were near a flagstick. To Sackie's surprise,

Torstein handed him the club he was using and got another one from the golf bag.

"Sackie. We can play together. I will show you how to play golf, and I will give you more dollars."

Sackie nodded. Torstein smiled and then took a ball from the side pocket of the white polo shorts he was wearing and set it on the tee hole. He told Sackie to step further ahead of him, and ordered him to stop when he had reached the right distance he wanted him to be. Again, Torstein adjusted his club, braced himself and then looked at Sackie who appeared not to be following.

"Sackie. Just watch this," he said and took his next shot.

Sackie saw the ball fast approaching and was aiming for his forehead. But he dodged it, taking a quick dive to the ground as the ball flew and entered a nearby bush.

"Very good. Very good, Sackie" Torstein mused, at the same time putting his club between his legs and clapping. "Go and get the ball and come take your shot."

The German kid watched with amusement when Sackie got up and ran towards the direction the ball landed. He chuckled, shook his head and then said something in German.

"These people never learned," he repeated it in English, struggling to hold back a laugh to avoid giving the innocent looking kid a hint of what was going on.

"Torstein," Sackie came out of the bush and called, mimicking the German accent. "The ball has stocked in the sand."

"No, Sackie. Very Stupid. The ball can't get stock in the sand."

"No. Torstein. I am not stupid now. Come and see for yourself."

The German suddenly became agitated and cursed in his language. His hyper-behavior was now at full swing. Next, he went racing towards Sackie, who saw him coming and ran back into the bush. Torstein reached the spot where Sackie ran. His tantrum was now beyond proportion, and in full rage, when he did not see him.

His face had gotten pink red, and the hair on his head stood. What he was thinking now is to slam the club on the poor local kid's head, and hit it again, until he falls to the ground, unconscious. Then he would hurry to his parents to complain of a headache and needed to be rushed home. He would never care what will happen to the stupid and poor kid, since in fact no one cares for a local kid, whose parents may not be working for the company.

"Sackie. You have made me mad. Where are you?" he roared when he entered the bush.

"Torstein," Sackie suddenly came from behind him. "A ball doesn't stick in the sand. Very stupid."

The German kid yelled when Sackie landed the club with all his might on Torstein's left kneecap.

"Get this hard lesson, Torstein," raged Sackie, scooping over the German kid who had fallen to the ground holding his knees screaming. He landed the club again on the other knee cap. "Not everyone can be stupid more than once."

As Torstein rolled on the ground crying, his brown hair covered with dry leaves and stems and at the same time soiling his white T-shirt and pants, Sackie gave him a kick in his buttocks and next, he was out of there.

He found his way around the other bushes to avoid exiting the course at the main entrance gate. In a couple of minutes, he was out of Bong Town and back in Nyenen. This time he didn't need to hide, since no one would be looking for him. The hash exchange between Torstein and his mother suggested that his parents were aware of their son's habit. Sackie remained in Nyenen for about two weeks before he started visiting Bong Town again.

It was once during the St. Martin's Day celebration where both the German and Liberian kindergarten and first grade Students of Bong Town School will gather at the school's campus during the late evening hours, dressed in their St. Martin Day customs, holding lanterns which they themselves built of colorful posters or pumpkins with either a small colorful light bulb, or in the case of the one made of pumpkins, a candle. The students were usually accompanied by their parents or their older siblings to watch the procession of the kids, holding their lanterns attached to sticks and singing St. Martin's Day songs.

This colorful possession always attracted even the children who lived outside of Bong Town. They would flock in from the various communities in Bong Mines. They would walk on the side of the road and follow the kids as they toured some of the streets of Bong Town and back at the school where bonfires are made and roasted ducks were served.

Sickie had never missed this ceremony, and it was at this one, after the incident with Torstein when he spotted him with both of his knees in cast, using a pair of clutches and was walking next to a little girl who he assumed might be his sister.

He had slowed down his steps in anticipation of how he would get away, if he was spotted. In that moment, his eyes caught Torstein who immediately called to his mother who was walking alongside the little girl and pointed at Sackie. Sackie was about to run away but he noticed that the woman turned to her son and said something harsh. Sackie smiled and continued to follow the St. Martin's Day procession, but at a safe distance.

A year later, while on his way to the supermarket to sell some cold-water fish he caught from dirty water, he suddenly jumped in the grass along the side of the road when a group of German kids sped past him on their motorbikes. He gasped, watching them breath-takingly laying into a deep curve without falling and maneuvering between cars. He was surprised to see Torstein among them.

That same day, he was hoping to meet Mr. Proud, a Liberian senior staff member who once worked in the Central Office, in the Accounting Department. He always brought fish from Sackie whenever he went to the supermarket. This interaction had been going on for years when Sackie was much smaller.

Mr. Proud was a prominent and well-known man all-over Bong Mines. He was a member of the Masonic craft and the number two man at the Kelekuta Lodge, along the road between Nyenen and Varney Town. What he was really known for, mainly by those who lived outside of Bong Town was that he was gay and a pedophile. Parents often warned their young boys to avoid him. This became widespread when it was rumored that he sodomized the 12 years old son of a fellow staff member and workmate.

Sackie did not mind what people said about his regular customer, because Mr. Proud had never molested him. The July 26 Independent's Day Celebration was fast approaching, and Sackie needed some money to buy his toy gun. It was habitual among the kids that lived outside Bong Town to play war games in the woods of rubber trees. They will organize themselves into groups and the persons with the finest toy guns were often chosen as group leaders or commanders.

Sackie always wanted to be a commander and so he wanted the best gun.

He was now 12 years old. His body was expanding; his shoulders were getting broad, and the muscles in his arms and legs were forming. His hips were also getting large. Sometimes people will joke that it was due to the dirty water he swallowed, when he was sinking in the mud.

After the incident, the company had cordoned off that area with a wire fence to prevent local kids from roaming that dangerous part of the concession area. Sackie and friends had managed to use pliers to cut through the wires to go fishing, but they were always chased by patrolling Mine Guards. This made fishing difficult and this did not allow them the chance to get a good catch.

It was one of those days where he only managed to catch two sizable catfish, when he and two other friends were chased, almost got caught and got separated. Later at the supermarket, he met Mr. Proud who bought them a dollar each.

"You are becoming a very handsome man now," said Mr. Proud, looking at Sackie in an enticing manner, as the kid walked him to his Volkswagen.

Not saying a word, because he was thinking on how he will get the balance money for the toy guns he wanted, he gave Mr. Proud the catfish. The toy gun he saw at the Varney Town Market cost $2.50. It was a toy rifle made in China. When fired, sparkles of flames are emitted in its red synthetic plastic nozzle that makes it appear like it was discharging fire, especially when shooting it at night.

He did not only need the balance 50 cents to buy the rifle, he also needed additional $2.00 to buy a Cowboy revolver with the holster and the gun belt with the bullets in the loops. Acquiring these two toy guns was his way of imitating his two favorite heroes, Vick Monroe of "Combat" and Otis E. Young of "The Outcasts" which were two television series, shown on ELTV, the Liberian National Television Station in the 70s and 80s.

The toy rifle symbolized his admiration and imitation of actor Vick Morrow, as squad leader, leading his men deep behind German territories, in his full military gear in the World War II action series. As for the cowboy revolver, it was his way of paying homage to the African American actor in the 1960 television Western, "The Outcasts". It was the first television series he watched, when his father, through a credit union scheme organized by a group of BMC laborers, purchased a 12-inch Black and White Sharp TV. He liked the way Young, as Jemal David wore his revolver in its holster around his waist.

"I know you want money to buy more things for the 26th, right?" inquired Mr. Proud, looking at Sackie who stood playing with the two silver dollar coins in his hand. "Let me take you to my house. I got some work for you to do."

"Will you pay me?" Sackie asked eagerly.

"You will have enough to buy many things," Mr. Proud assured the kid.

Sackie got into his Volkswagen Beetle and they drove to Mr. Proud's house, an isolated apartment in the vicinity of Club Hill. Getting down from the car, Sackie observed that it was one of those apartments at the southern edge of Club Hill, bordered by a valley that runs all the way to the creek that divides Nyenen from Bong Town.

Mr. Proud carried the things he bought from the supermarket inside his house while Sackie stood in the yard looking around, a little bit surprised that he did not know Mr. Proud lived not far from Nyenen. From the Nyenen side, he always saw these isolated houses, and thought only German people were living there.

He remembered that a German man, who kept a very large boa constrictor in a glass cage once lived in one of the houses. When he was much smaller, Sackie and friends used to cross into Bong Town from that end, climbed the valley and entered the German man's yard to look at the snake. Sometimes he would see a living hen or rooster inside the cage, but would marvel at the fact that the snake would appear like it was always sleeping and never bordered. He had always wanted to see a boa constrictor feeding to compare to what he heard people say it fed, but he was never lucky.

"Come inside, boy," Mr. Proud came out and called him.

Sackie hesitated a little, and then followed Proud into the house. Mr. Proud ushered him into his living room and asked him to freely sit in any of his beautifully decorated chairs. He then went into his ice box, as Sackie's eyes swept the living room. He got out a bottle of icy cold water, poured it in a glass he got from his hanging glass cabinet and gave it to his young visitor. Sackie took a glug, but made a face in reaction to the coldness of the water on his teeth.

"I am so happy to have you visiting me," Mr. Proud said, smiling. "Young kids your age are afraid of me because of what people tell them. But you are different."

"They say you are a society man who does bad things to young boys," Sackie said, his tone rather stern and full of concern.

"No," Mr. Proud responded, laughing. "I do good things for young people, if they make me happy."

He stood in front of Sackie who remained sitting and expressionless. He observed that the boy's eyes were focused directly at the front of his trousers, prompting Mr. Proud to deduce that the kid might be thinking of the risk of being hurt depending on the size of what was in his pants. He smiled with this thought and unzipped his pants.

"Young man. This is what will make me happy to do whatsoever you want me to do for you. It will not hurt you. I will send you to America and your life will change."

"Ahh," gasped Sackie, his mouth opened in bewilderment, as Mr. Proud stood before him, pants down and dangling his penis.

"It will not hurt you," Mr. Proud said, getting closer, and suddenly reaching for his pocket. "Here. Take this $20.00."

Sackie, who was inching against the chair as Mr. Proud got closer to him, took the money. Sensing that the kid no longer looked spooked and did not seem afraid, he gave him another five dollars and Sackie quickly grabbed it. Now having $25.00, his face suddenly brightened.

"All I want you to do for me is to take off your trousers and turn around. I will use Vicks so you will not feel pain at all. Just few minutes you will be going home with $25.00. I will give you another $20.00 if no one hears about this."

Sackie got up and first put the money in the back pocket of his trousers. His eyes were now fixed on Mr. Proud's penis which was now fully erected while his hand remained in his pocket, with his fingers pressing on the $25.00. Out of a sudden Sackie uttered something in kpelle and took out a small knife, about three inches long, and charged at Mr. Proud in an attempt to slice his penis, but the older man was quick to block it with his hand. The shape blade gashed the back of his palm, cutting some of the veins, causing Mr.

Proud to yell. Sackie ran past him and dashed out of the house by way of the back yard and went sliding down the valley.

Mr. Proud attempted to run after him, but he was bleeding severely from the cut, so he rushed into his bath room for his first aid kit. Sackie always kept that knife whenever he went fishing to dig out tiny earthworms to use as bait.

Again, he stayed away from Bong Town for about two weeks. He did not tell anyone. He finally bought the two toy guns, eventually earned his commander role at the war games and kept the balance money in a safe place. He did not hear anything about Mr. Proud or see him until one day the Masonic craft were parading. He had gone to watch it, but soon became afraid, when the society men kept staring at him, while he stood on the side of the road. He told his mother about it, and brought the balance money as proof. She contacted two Justices of the peace lawyers named Cllr. Mulbah Supui and his associate, Cllr. Galakpa Ricks.

The two attorneys suspected that the kid's allegation seemed to be true, when they visited Mr. Proud and noticed his hand was heavily wrapped in bondage. They later asked Sackie's mother to take her son out of town as a precautionary measure until they determine whether to press charges on the Bong Mining Company Senior staff or pursue out of court settlement, since in fact no physical damage was done to the boy.

Sackie was sent to Haindii and stayed there for some time. He came back to Bong Mines when he heard Mr. Proud had retired and had moved to Monrovia. After a few months, Bong Mines was awakened, one early morning to the death news of Mr. Proud. Rumor had it that he died a very broke man, while awaiting a term of court on a sodomy lawsuit. The case had taken its toll on him, causing him to spend all his retirement money on lawyers.

Sackie had since remained in Bong Mines and continued his elementary schooling at the Zaweata's Elementary and Junior High School in Benuma, right outside of Varney Town. He remained in Zaweata until 6th grade, shortly before the civil war.

Joining the 1990 revolution did not come as a surprise for those who saw the kid growing up. This was not only because of his love for the war games and his quest to always play the role of the commander. His student militancy role was a trait to also consider.

One of his best days in school was the National Flag Day parade ceremony, which was held every year on August 24. Two weeks before the main day, all the schools in Bong Mines will assemble either at Bong Range United (BRU) park, a mini football stadium, or the Catholic School football field to rehearse.

This was usually, each school day, after recess. And, because students often boycotted this, special students' units, called MPs, were organized to prevent this. The MPs were charged with the responsibility to make sure all students participate in the practice and to keep the formation lines in order. On the day of the parade, they will ensure that bystanders do not intrude into the procession, and that students don't leave the lines.

These responsibilities were meant to be handled lightly, but they were often abused. The MPs used this opportunity to settle scores with other students they may have personal problems with or, they may not just like. And this often led to flogging and dragging, especially when they were resisted by fellow students.

Sackie himself was once mal-handled, during a Flag Day Parade when his company, composed of the 4th grade class, had left him behind after they had marched through the main streets of Bong Mines. He was taking his own time to catch up, but was forced to rejoin his unit, when he was suddenly kicked on his right heel by a MP who was wearing the iron-toe boots miners wore. The sharp and excruciating pain from the iron nose of the booth lingered for a while even after the parade. From that day he vowed to be an MP.

He became a member of the MP, the year he was in the 6th grade. He was about sixteen years old and he had grown huge and muscular. Usually, one has to be in either 9th or 12th grade to be eligible to be a member of the MP corp. It was during the last week of the preparation, when all the schools were practicing at BRU Park, when Sackie organized a group of six graders from his school as MPs.

The Assistant Country Superintendent for Administration was present to ensure that the drill and ceremony was well planned and organized, as the New County Superintendent will be visiting Bong Mines on the main day. Everyone was surprised to see a new MP group marching toward the eye-right lines during the pass in review.

The group, about sixty in numbers, all of them about the same height and size, with Sackie leading the parade, marched with their hands swinging and taking steps in the standard military drill formation with boldness and determination at the same time singing:

"MP corp's coming; Boe reckeh, boe reckeh, boe reckeh. Sackie our leader Boe reckeh, boe reckeh, boe reckeh. Sackie Dirty Water Boe reckeh, boe reckeh, boe reckeh."

At the eyes-right line, Sackie halted his group with the 'Unit Halt' command. He then commanded the right face which his group expertly demonstrated, and faced the Asst. Superintendent and the Bong Mines Flag Day Parade committee. He immediately shouted the 'Preserve Arms' command and his group saluted with perfect uniformity to the cheering crowds of students and onlookers.

The news of a new MP corps comprising of Zaweata School six graders spread among the student community like wildfire, prompting Bangalee Conneh, of the 9th grade, the commander of the MP Brigade of the school to invite Sackie and some of his cohorts to a meeting on the school's campus. After serious arguments and commotion, an uneasy agreement was reached.

On the main day, Sackie and his MP corps were fully attired with the usual MP outfit of Red T-shirts and blue jean trousers, except that the jeans trousers were shot pants, because they were six graders. Only the long pants were reserved for the 9th and 12th graders, which was one of the agreements reached at the meeting.

Every one of them were wearing the booths that employers of Bong Mines wore up the mine, which was easy to get because most of the children that attended Zaweata School parents were ordinary staff or laborers. The role of this new unit was to ensure that the elementary students of all the parading schools were tidy, punctual, and to drill in orderly fashion, since in fact, there was huge enrollment in elementary schools that year.

On the main day, all schools were assembled at BRU Park with their students standing in their respective line formations from the early morning hours up to the afternoon. There was a heavy downpour of rain. The parade did not start early because the Booker T. Washington Institute (BWI) Marching Band and the new superintendent had not yet arrived.

It had passed mid-day. The sun first started appearing slowly and then it was up, shining in the sky, and striking the already drenched students, drying their drill outfits and uniforms on them. Many students were now exhausted and thirsty and were given permission to leave the lines to buy cold water and Kool-Aid sold in plastic bags by kids who were not in school.

At certain times, they were permitted to sit on the ground but remained in their respective formations. It was approaching the late afternoon hours when suddenly there was the sound of the marching band from the direction of John Hill. The bus, bringing BWI Marching Band, was soaring up the hill, when it sounded the signal of its arrival. Everyone began to cheer and jubilate, as soon as the bus turned left, towards BRU Park.

It did not take long when there was another roar to the sound of sirens, suggesting that the County Superintendent and his delegation had finally arrived. When the delegates were all seated at the stadium, the Sergeant-Major, student Josiah Doe of Borbor Nyuma High School commenced the ceremony upon the order of student, Theophilus Crayton of Zaweata School, the colonel and commander of the Senior Staff line.

Sergeant-Major Doe drilled through the process of ensuring proper line formation, roll call, preparing for inspection, in which the superintendent and delegates marched between the line formations and then finally, the Pass-in-Review. After the schools have given their eye-rights in front of the superintendent and delegates, the parade proceeded towards the principal streets of Bong Mines.

By this time, many students have gotten too exhausted and thirsty. The sales of coldwater and Kool-Aid sellers continued to increase with students leaving the lines scrambling to buy them. Emptied plastic bags littered the field of BRU Park and along the streets, as the parade progressed. MPs were heavily engaged, chasing students, especially the ones who were leaving the lines, and attempting to flee the parade. They were pursued, apprehended and brought back on their respective lines or were forced to catch up with their respective units. The MPs were also making sure that bystanders and onlookers and parents who were accompanying their kids, especially the ones in elementary school, did not intrude into the lines.

Cynia Myers, the daughter of Bong Mines Magistrate, Cllr. Charles Q. Myers had gotten very exhausted and was taking her own time walking behind her company. She was in the six grade and was a student of Bong Town School. It was her very first Flag Day Parade. Her parents moved to Bong Mines from Monrovia at the beginning of the year when her father was transferred as the Magistrate. She was aggressive and many of her schoolmates complained about this. Some said it was because her father did not hesitate to send any one to jail, no matter who it was.

Sackie noticed that there was a group of people gathered along the road and were obstructing the parade. Deducing that it may be as a result of a commotion, which his boys were finding it difficult to handle, he hurriedly rushed to the scene.

To his utmost surprise, he met his classmate, Ezekiel Dalamou, also an MP sitting on the ground, bleeding from his forehead and holding it. Dalamou was trying to force Cynia Myers back on her line when she hit him on the head with a stick, she found along the road to lain unto when she had gotten tied marching. Sackie immediately raced after her.

"Look you are not better than the other students that are on the line, okay," he said, when he had reached her, and grabbed her by the callard of her uniform blouse.

"Take your filthy hands off me," she lashed at him, at the same time trying to pull herself away from him.

Sackie seized the stick from her, beat on her legs with it, and violently shoved her until she caught up with her unit that was far ahead. She burst up into tears and was weeping bitterly as Sackie marched along with her ensuring that she marched along with her class.

Three times, she buckled and fell to the ground, but the elementary MP commander jerked her up, and ran with her, until she re-joined her unit. She later got body aches after the parade and was unable to move both arms and legs. She was taken to the hospital where she remained in the therapeutic section for almost two weeks, missing her classes.

Around the end of November of that year, Magistrate Myers, who was not in the country at the time, had returned and learned of what happened to his daughter. He informed the police about this and soon they planned to search and arrest Sackie. Learning about this, Sackie immediately headed for Haindii to his grandfather, soon after he completed his final semester exam. He remained in Haindii with Kpakolo Laynumah, until the civil war started. When the war intensified, especially when Gbarnga was overrun, Magistrate Myers fled to Monrovia.

These memories helped Sackie to peddle more when it was his time. They had gone far, at the end of the first day. As evening approached, they paddled to an area of the river at the right side of the banks, where the vegetation cascaded over parts of the edge of the water, forming a perfect shade and cover, and suitable to rest for the night. They ate some of the hastily smoked frogs they prepared at the water log where they began their journey and drank some of the boiled water. Sackie Dirty Water was the first to keep guard as Sergeant-Major Gonpue and Takpor Due slept.

Then, they continued to navigate upstream on the second day, surprised by the vigor they had been exhibiting in paddling the canoe, sometimes overcoming some of the toughest currents without much problems. At the end of the first day's journey, the food and water they took along with them had not finished, which so far had proven the Bush Dog commander's calculations correct, that they were going to last for at least three days until they reached to the place where they will have to leave the water and get into the forest, map out the trail to the part of the Bong Range where they will cross over to the Slocum Mission side. By then, what was left of the crabs, which they have so far not yet eaten, since they take a longer time to sour and spoil than the hastily smoked frogs, would be relished.

While in the forest, they will hunt for animals, as the journey on foot progresses. Unlike the water logs, where they had to boil the water for safe drinking, finding safe drinking ones in the bush was not going to be a problem. The topography of the terrain they were headed was bedecked with highlands and mountains which are the sources of very cold running water, safe for drinking.

It was approaching the evening hours of day two. As they paddled on, Sackie was careful not to miss any detail of where they will have to navigate and land the canoe at the right location, east of them to commence the journey on foot. He had never paddled this side of the St. Paul, but he had on many occasions listened to his grandfather, Kpakolo Laynumah tell the story about an attempt made by some brave warriors to navigate these parts of the river.

Their plan was to head for the region further northwest, which is president day Lofa County when there was an SOS call for help to defend that region against the French. It was during the reign of Samori Touré, when the Mandinka Empire was at war with the French who were rapidly encroaching into West African Territory.

He forged an alliance with Zubah Keleko, a very powerful Lorma warrior King, who controlled that region all the way to present day Guinea border to allow his mercenaries access to the present-day Liberian Coast to trade with Western traders for arms to help sustain his campaign. But the Faama was eventually captured in the forest of present-day Liberia thus, giving the French the opportunity to concentrate their forces at the northwestern border of president day Liberia and Guinea, putting it under threat of invasion. Zubah Keleko had used his trusted messengers known as the 'Kolubahs' to spread the message to all the related tribes strewed in the mid-south of this imminent threat to their ancestral lands.

In Solidarity to their nephews from the northwest, the Kpelle, including those of present day Fuamah District, assembled their warriors for an all-out war with the French. The ones from Haindii belt, reasoned that in order to get there on time, the best way was to navigate the St. Paul River.

A band of warriors with hundreds of canoes left Haindii and the Dobli Islands and headed upstream. After three days of paddling, they reached a beautiful scenery with many waterways. Fascinated, some of them abandoned the mission and wandered off into this paradise, and since then, nothing was heard of them.

However, a sizable number of them mustered the courage to continue the journey upstream, when they thought they found the right course to take them directly to Zubah Keleko. After many years, Zubah Keleko, aided by the tribes that came from as far as present day Gbarnga, managed to contain the French advances, which was followed by an uneasy truce. Only one warrior returned to Haindii, and he was Moie Laynumah, the father of Kpakolo Laynumah.

Moie Laynumah told his son, Kpakolo, of what they encountered and how he thought he may have sighted a chain of strange high lands further north east of this strange and beautiful scenery that appears to extend towards Weala or beyond. When the Bong Range was discovered and explored with the coming of the Bong Mining Company, it was then that the account of Moie Laynumah was confirmed.

Unfortunately, he did not live long enough after his return to Haindii as kpakolo Lehnumah had narrated. He was killed in a battle defending Haindii from a Gola onslaught to reclaim their land. They were taking advantage of the fact that the Kpelle had lost most of their best warriors, following the expedition.

Sackie was certain to not miss one key detail as the account was handed down to him. The scenery so described can only be spotted at the early morning hours of the rising sun when the rays hit the surface of the water giving it a magnificently glamorous color making the surface to appear like it glitters tons of gold from the river bed. The same can be seen to the right of the river where the vegetation illuminates similar appearances on the branches of trees from the distance, immediately after the twilight.

He reasoned that the best way to arrive at this place is the early morning hours to ensure that they did not miss it, or else they will peddle further north and might probably enter the terrain of Lofa County. Now that it was the second day and night was approaching, there was going to be no rest or little of it.

They had navigated a few hours into the night. Sackie was sitting at the bow with his head light on, providing a clear view as Takpoh Duo paddled. At first the moon was up, its reflection illuminating the surface of the water. But it soon disappeared into the sky and the surface became dark. As Sackie beamed his headlight on the surface, they could see ahead of them.

The water was quiet. The only sound was the paddle slicing its surface and the ripples hitting the hull of the canoe. There was also the humming and flipping of tiny winged insects, hovering over the water and circling around the beam. But the bushes along the banks were alive with the cries of insects and animals.

Occasionally, a fish or two would leap out of the water for the tiny insects and back in. A sizable one suddenly leapt and landed on Sergeant-Major Gonpue's lap. He almost flipped over board in a brief struggle to contain the fish as it fought to release itself from his grip.

"Never underestimate the antics of some of these fishes," Sackie warned, when he had helped to neutralize the fish by pulling it from the Sergeant-Major's hands, flipping it on the floor of the canoe and hitting it almost lightly on the head with the butt of his hunting gun. "Many inexperienced fisher men have fallen overboard, trying to catch a leaping fish like that."

An hour or two after the incident with the fish, lightning suddenly flashed through the sky followed by thunder and then a heavy downpour of rain. It was Sackie's turn to peddle, and as he did, Sergeant-Major Gonpue and Takpoh Duo were busy throwing water out of the canoe. It began to pour down ferociously and the current was getting rough and impeding the speed of the canoe.

Sackie knew that it would be futile to continue and so he managed to navigate his way close to the banks and landed, where it was suitable to get out of the canoe with ease. They struggle to pull most of the canoe on the dry ground to prevent it from being swept into the river by the increasingly flooding banks. Then they ran and sought shelter under some growth.

The bushes along the banks were now quiet, except the sound of water droplets hitting the branches and the ground, and the roaring flow of the river. Sackie prayed that the rain should not last, because they must complete the night to enter the third day to be able to see the twilight and the early morning sun rise. He however assured himself that if the rain did not stop soon, they would have to wait for one whole day to pick up from where they stopped.

Fortunately, the rain subsided. They anxiously waited for a few minutes until it finally stopped. It did not take long, they hurried to haul the canoe back into the water. After making sure they left none of their belongings behind, they huddled back inside and continued the journey. Not very long they were back on course as Sackie steered the canoe in the middle of the night.

As they continued, the forest at both banks of the river began to spring to life again, with the chirps of insects and animals who all went silent during the heavy downpour. Sackie continued with the paddling until the current had subsided and then turned the paddle over to Sergeant-Major Gonpue.

He again knelt at the bow, with his shoulders above the gunwale, and his head light on. The sky began to brighten again with the reappearance of the moon, when they had continued the steady course for an hour. Not quite long they reached an area where the river got a bit narrow and they could clearly make up the vegetation on both sides of the banks.

It could have been a perfect place to rest, for a while, mainly under where the branches cascaded over potion of the edge of the river, but the rain had taken most of their time which had put them in a desperate position to hurry against time to meet the early morning twilight and sunrise.

This part of the river was eerie and extended for some nautical miles. There was no sound of the cries of insects and animals, contrary to what they had been hearing when paddling at night. So, they needed to increase the paddling to sail faster out of such a place as it was a perfect place for the enemy to set their ambush.

Takpor Duo who was now paddling was making frantic effort to pad faster at the same time quietly, to avoid being noticed, if enemy fighters were positioned under the outgrowth. Sackie Dirty Water and Sergeant-Major Gonpue advanced their weapons as each pointed this gun at both sides of the banks. Very tense, they reached mid-way of the narrowest part without any problem. After some time, and sensing no danger, Sackie looked at the Sergeant-Major and then at Takpor Duo and made a face of assurance that there is no enemy activity on this side of the river banks.

Just then something screamed, suddenly startling the three of them. Sackie Dirty Water immediately focused his light in the direction of the scream, at the same time pointing his hunting gun in aiming position. There was another scream of higher pitch and then it continued. Also, there were violent rustlings in the branches of a tree that was partially cascading over the edge of the water to their right.

Sackie beamed his hunting light and saw that it was a small monkey hanging on to a branch, screaming. The frightened primate was caught by a large rock python with a portion of its tail coiled around the monkey's legs. The head and the rest of the snake's body was swinging around the branches, trying to find a way to go for the monkey's head. Unfortunately, it was being harassed by another monkey who seemed to be the mother, and probably, the one making the loudest screams.

"No! Do not shoot!" suddenly hissed Sackie, when Sergeant-Major Gonpue was about to shoot the snake. "Jungle rule # one. Never interfere with the matters of animals. Also, you can never tell when the enemy is around."

The three of them watched, when several times the python would make an attempt to go for the monkey's head, but the mother monkey would scream at it and would pull some of the smaller branches of the tree to itself and release them. The branches would slap the python's head, and the leaves would cover the snake's face, distorting its vision, causing it to jerk its head backwards.

The snake, with a portion of its tail still coiled around the smaller monkey legs, would swing in another direction and make another attempt, but again the mother monkey would repeat the same thing. While making another attempt, Sackie beamed his headlight and the python head was caught in the reflection, blurring its vision. It tilted upward and suddenly froze, putting its head within Sackie's firing range.

The mother monkey immediately focused on Sackie, screaming but in a different pitch, which Sackie interpreted as a plea to shoot the predator. As the canoe slowly drifted away from the scene, the mother monkey would scream louder and violently shake the branches, with its eyes on the gun as a sign for Sackie Dirty Water to take the shot, but he didn't, even as he wrapped his index finger around the trigger.

'Never interfere with matters of animals in the jungle,' Sackie Dirty Water could hear the small frail voice of Kpakolo Lehnumah in his ear. In this situation you only have to shoot, if it was your hunting dog in danger.

With the reflection of the head light gradually ebbing away from the snake's eyes as the canoe had drifted further away from the scene, the python regained its vision and quickly went for the little monkey's head in one swing. Before the mother monkey could focus back on its young, the python, now with the little monkey's head in its mouth, released itself from the branches and landed at the edge of the water in one splash. The mother monkey quickly descended the cascaded branches and was hovering over the spot where the python had landed with the young one, by wrapping its tail around a branch to keep it suspended.

The distressed primate continued to scream as it remained suspended and at the same time hovering in a desperate attempt to distract the python from having its meal, but it was not good enough to stress the reptile.

The monkey suddenly stopped screaming and climbed back on the branches. It began to leap from branches to branches in the direction of the canoe at the same time shaking them violently. Concerned by the behavior of the strange monkey, Sackie focused his head light in the direction of the violent shakes of the branches and his eyes caught the monkey's. The expression from the primate's eyes told him that it was disappointed in him. It would have even preferred to be shot, then allowing it to live and helplessly watch the cowardly reptile crush the skull of its young with its jaw.

As the reflection of the head light faded, Sackie could still see the expression in the monkey's eyes. He became quiet for some time, and almost wanted to cry. When he and his friends used to go sneaking into the German man's yard at Club Hill to see the boa constrictor in the glass cage, he never felt sorry for the chicken he used to see inside the cage. They would even shout and knock on the glass to awaken the snake so they could see it swallow the chicken, but he now felt very guilty as the expression in the monkey's eyes gnawed at his conscience.

"You did the right thing," Takpor Duo said, adjusting himself closer to the middle of the bow when he had shifted term with Sergeant-Major Gonpue. "If you were going to shoot the snake, we were going to be spotted if there were enemies around."

By now, they had left the narrow part of the river and were now in the wide-open course. Sackie Dirty Water felt a bit relieved as they were no longer paddling closed to the banks.

It was long past midnight which he could tell from his experience as a hunter. The kinds of insects and animals that were crying in the now distant vegetation along the banks, suggested to him that in a couple of hours, they were nearing dawn. When he informed the Sergeant-Major and his deputy, they again exerted energy to ensure that they did not rest until dawn.

He was now faced with two options depending on the efficiency of their navigation. They either meet the early morning twilight and the sun or they are met by them. The good thing he sensed was, the twilight and the early morning sun will take a time interval of 15 to 30 minutes before the twilight disappears and the sun ascends beyond the clouds. Either way, he was confident to be at the spot, before this happened.

Finally, it was dawn. The canoe was slowly drifting and the three of them were seated up right in the hall, sleeping. They had somehow dozed off due to exhaustion, probably not for long, when they took terms paddling for hours in rapid rhythms to be at the right spot at the right time for the twilight and the early morning sun.

Luckily for them, the current was gentle, and the canoe was maintaining a steady course upstream. Early morning birds in the trees on both sides of the river banks began to chirp. Schools of king fishers were hovering over the surface of the water and making dives for the early morning catch. Sackie was suddenly awakened to the sound of a splash when a kingfisher made a dive. The catch was too large for its beak, causing the fish to slip off and landed next to the side of the canoe where Sackie was. It was the sound and the flash of water on his face that woke him up.

Sackie Dirty Water cursed in his dialect when he awoke and realized that it was already dawn. He also woke up Takpoh Duo who was in the middle, who in turn woke sergeant-Major Gonpue up.

"Ayyy God. Did we miss it?" suddenly alarmed the Sergeant-Major.

"Don't know yet," responded Sackie Dirty Water, looking at the horizon to his right. "But we might know any moment from now."

"Look!" suddenly shouted Takpor Duo, Pointing at a tiny glow in the sky from the East.

"Might be the sun coming up. Which means we missed the twilight," Sackie said.

"Oh God. We were lucky. We made it," exclaimed the Sergeant-Major, suddenly jumping to his feet in an awkward manner that rocked the canoe.

Sackie slowly rose to his feet with his eyes sparkling with excitement. The rapidly rising early morning sun cast its magnificent rays over the vegetation to his right, giving the branches and leaves of the trees a gold-like color. After a few minutes it descended on the surface of the water, with the similar gold like reflection almost blinding them. Sackie tried to look at the beautiful skylines and saw many colorful birds circling above the treetops in a joyous fashion.

"We sail right through there," he said, almost in a hoist voice, and breathing heavily with excitement when he saw the first tributary on the right, sneaking its way into the vegetation.

The early morning sun was becoming more visible as the canoe slowly entered the tributary and continued eastwards with the flow of the smaller river. Sackie was making sure that they continued on a north eastern course to avoid navigating in circles thus, preventing a similar fate of the brave warriors from Haindii.

As they gently paddled on, mesmerized by the splendor of the surrounding vegetation, colorful butterflies hovered about the branches of trees on both sides of the banks. Sackie noticed that these hundreds of different spices suddenly flew in a formation of the shape of a cone and soared at a high altitude above the tree lines just then the sun was fully visible and was disappearing into the clouds. The insects finally broke the cone-shape formation and swooped down on the branches like a phantom of fighter jets, landing on the leaves just in time the sun had totally disappeared into the cloud.

"Is this place really a part of Liberia?" mused Takpor Duo, marveling at how the branches were covered with butterflies, making the trees appear like huge flower orchards.

"Yeah," admitted Sergeant-Major Gonpue. "This is the beautiful country we are destroying."

Sackie remained expressionless in the mist of the euphoria. He was adamant to refuse being a part of those that are destroying his country. He was only defending his historic town and its people from intruders. But a surge of emotionally charged admittance ran through his spine. If all the fighters from the different warring factions ever come to this place and see what they were seeing, they would immediately drop their arms, and embrace each other for the beautiful country they have.

He was confident that this place has such powers, and It was not going to be the first time this had happened. It was going to be of similar fate to some brave men of war, who once ventured in these lands, in response to a call to defend a cause, but they were conjured to the wonders of the sceneries, and abandoned their cause. The power of this place held them back and they never returned to their land, except one courageous man.

As they continued along this tributary, Sackie wondered what may have happened to the men that decided to make this place their home. Did they later continue the expedition to join Zubah Keleko or they just got sucked up in the mystery of the elegance of this place? The Bush Dog commander reminded himself to remain focused; just like his great grandfather Moie Leynumah, he would return to Haindii and partake in its liberation.

He had already passed some tests. They had passed some other water channels, and beautiful creeks outlying much more wonders which was difficult to just let go without exploring. Some of them branched off westwards towards St. Paul while others curved their way south east of their position. But he was determined to direct the course north east wards, to where he believes was the direction of the Bong Range.

"We will continue on this course. We might probably see a cliff or a high ground where we can climb and get a better view to carve out our trail to the Bong Range," he said, looking at the two pairs of eager eyes.

About two hours of steadily sailing and fighting all the temptations to wander off course, a cliff suddenly appeared in sight. Jubilantly, they hastened towards it. Midway towards the cliff, the river turned westwards, and appeared like it headed back towards St. Paul. They were perturbed at first, but they were soon spirited with the cliff still in sight.

So, they continued with the flow for about a few knots, until it again turned right, parallel to the St. Paul, separated by a stretch of land, its edge, adorned with a variety of species of water lilies. Bees were humming overhead and were descending on the beautiful flowers. They kept gliding for some time, with Sackie making sure that the cliff continued to be in sight, until they entered what looked like a lake.

The cliff was now to their right, seen above the low vegetation that formed an arc around the lake. They saw the mouth of a little brook at the far right of the lake, which they assumed may lead them all the way down to the cliff. Sackie was sure of this because the waters of the brook were in the form of rapids with grey-like pebbles partially protruding out of the water. They are signs that a cliff may be nearby.

Sergeant-Major Gonpue and Sackie switched terms and the Bush Dog commander gently navigated the canoe into the brook. They followed the flow downstream for about a few minutes, carefully avoiding collusion with the rocks, until they soon realized that they were at the foot of the cliff. Sackie maneuvered the canoe between the rocks and landed it at the edge of the cliff.

The three of them got out of the canoe and stepped on dry ground in broad daylight for the first time in more than 48 hours. They could highly stand straight. Their skins and faces looked white and wrinkly for continual exposure to moisture. At Sackie's urging, they walked around to allow the blood to freely flow down their spines to their legs.

After that, Sackie sat on a rock and looked toward the direction of Haindii. He was proud of himself. Only an experienced canoeist could have made such a perilous journey.

"Gentlemen," he said, wiping a tear that was forming in the corners of his eyes with his middle finger, and then looked up the cliff. "Let's get our things and try to make our way up this cliff."

The three men, with Sackie Dirty Water ahead, wandered around the foot of the cliff to their left, until they discovered the best way to climb up. It took them about an hour to ascend to the first layer, where the land was flat and covered with moor and beautiful trees.

Further up seemed easy to climb. Sackie thought it was a good idea to ascend as high as they could to get a better view to scout the land below. They discovered a natural path to their right, and walked through. In about an hour they were at the top, overlooking the land below.

They could see what they assumed was the St. Paul River, extending to their left. The beautiful scenery with creeks, dotted lakes and brooks were to their right. To the northwest were undulating high lands covered with forests. Further beyond the highlands were a more elevated one in the form of a chain appearing in the midst of the fog.

"That may be the Bong Range," Sackie pointed toward the direction and said, his face beaming with joy.

"Really?" whispered Sergeant-Major Gonpue, not believing his eyes.

"Yes. As you can just see with your naked eyes. It is the only highland above the others that stretches for miles," Sackie explained.

"We could have had a better view with the binoculars," the Sergeant-Major turned to Takphor Duo and said, at the same time feeling disappointed in himself for losing the spying glass during the attack on Dobli Island.

Sackie studied the jungle beneath the cliff to figure out where they will create their trail to take them all the way to the Bong Range. There were small rivers and creeks that seemed to be running out of the highlands, but different from the complex water systems like the wonder land to their right. This was going to be the best place to calve their trail.

"We will take that direction," he said, pointing his finger. "We might cross small rivers or creeks on rafters."

"Will it lead us straight to the mountain?" asked Takpor Duo.

"The Bong Range extends miles to the north east of Bong Mines. This direction will take us right into the middle. The other side is the west of Weala. When we reach the range, we will find a pass to cross to the other side."

"So, when do we leave?" asked the Sergeant-Major.

"When can we decide?" Sackie Dirty Water also asked, looking up at the sky. "We got less than an hour before night."

"Then we need to make our camp here for the night, find food, eat, get rest, and build our strength for the early morning journey," said Sergeant-Major Gonpue.

"I think so," agreed Takpor Duo, looking around him to figure out the best place to camp.

"Let's descend a bit. There is running water further down to our right. I saw it on our way up with prints of animal huffs on the ground," Sackie Dirty Water informed them.

The three of them descended the higher part of the cliff and found the running water that was flowing from a crevice in a rock. They followed it all the way down to where they realized that at some point, it cascaded midway over a steep rock and fell into what looked like a waterfall pool.

"These lands hold many wonders," marveled Sackie.

"We have a beautiful country," concurred Sergeant-Major Gonpue.

"Well, let me make history to be the first person to swim in this pool," Takpor Duo said, laying his Ak-47 rifle against a rock and taking off his clothes. After that he plunged into the pool.

"We'll camp right ahead of us," Sackie turned to the Sergeant-Major and pointed in the direction, a few meters ahead of them, where there were huge trees that provided perfect shade from the sun ray. "Let me follow the trail of these animals huffs and see whether I can kill one of them for food. Hope you still got the fish you caught last night?"

Takpor Duo left the fountain pool, feeling refreshed. He gathered his clothes, put them on, then grabbed his weapon and joined Sergeant-Major Gonpue to set up their camp. He chose one of the few trees a few meters from the fountain pool as the spot he will rest for the night, while Sergeant-Major Gonpue chose one of the trees behind him. After that, they went searching for firewood.

Sackie Dirty Water was out wandering in other parts of the cliff scouting and at the same time tracing the hoof prints of the animals he suspected to be wild goats. 45 minutes later, Sergeant-Major Gonpue was cleaning the big river fish, and Takpor Duo was building a fire. They suddenly heard a gunshot, and almost sprang for their rifles lying against the trees next to them, but they realized that the shot fired was coming from the Bush Dog commander's hunting gun.

The fish was sliced into potions enough for three of them and was put in a pot on the fire. They were preparing what they called GI soup. Suddenly they heard the bush shaking from their rear. Demonstrating the 'Be prepared' mode they learned on the training base, they got hold of their rifles and pointed it in the direction of where the sound of someone approaching was coming from. They were aware that Sackie Dirty Water had gone about roaming the terrain, but they were at war, the enemy was just two days away, and they couldn't take chances.

"At ease, comrades," Sackie said. Moments later, he came out into the clearing with a big wild goat across his shoulders. "I got a kill."

"That is a black backed duiker," announced Sergeant-Major Gonpue.

Sackie was helped with the animal when he had gotten close to them. He was then offered his potion of the GI soup which he ate. After that, he re-built the fire as the other two butchered and skinned the animal. A stick was inserted into the mouth and was shoved through the opened stomach and came out through the anus.

They laid the stick, now with the meat on it, on two folk-like sticks they inserted into the ground, next to the fire and began to roast the meat.

"I hope the higher ups in Gbarnga will listen to our suggestions on how we will plan the attack to take back Haindii and possibly, Bong Mines," Sackie Dirty Water suddenly opened a discussion while they continued to roast the meat, barbecued style.

"Only CO. Alfred Mentee can push our case, if he is still alive," stated Sergeant-Major Gonpue.

"So, what will be the best plan for this attack?" interjected Takpoh Duo, throwing a few dry sticks into the cracking fire.

"Simple," began Sackie Dirty Water. "First we can ferry fighters along the St. Paul. The river splits at a certain point at the border of Bong and Lower Lofa Counties. One extends deep into Lofa, where it crosses into Guinea while the other flows along the border of Lower Lofa and Bong and enters Guinea through Jawa, which is in Bong. Men can be ferried from the Bong end all the way to Haindii. And incase Bong Mines has fallen, another group of our fighters can take Weala-Popota Road, while another can branch off around the mountain and enter Bong Town through the dirty water area. That's where I got my 'Dirty Water' name. But as for the St. Paul River route, there may be a small problem."

"What problem?" asked the Sergeant-Major, slowly rolling the meat over the fire to roast the other side.

"How can we make sure to never arrive at this spot before the twilight and the early morning sun? lest the fighters are distracted by the wonders of this place, and abandon the mission."

"Well," sighed Takpoh Duo, looking around. "We make sure to sail in such a way that we don't have to see the twilight and early morning sun, until we pass by this place."

"Makes sense," Sergeant-Major Gonpue agreed. "My worry is only if we don't find CO. Mentee alive."

The three of them looked a bit apprehensive at first, but when Sackie signaled that the meat was ready, each got his knife and chopped off a piece.

It was now getting dark and as usual, Sackie would do a final sweep of the terrain. He grabbed his hunting gun when it was completely dark and resumed his patrols. His plan was to tour the place for some time, hoping to discover some details of the cliff he may have missed, and then head back up the highest point to view the land below.

With the moon shining in the sky, he would be able to clearly make up the small rivers and creeks in the distant jungle below. Takpoh Duo was throwing some dry stick into the fire to keep it alive for warmth while Sergeant-Major Gonpue had walked to the fountain pool to swim under the moonlight.

As the night slowly progressed, the temperature was mild and welcoming with the breeze blowing from the direction of the distant St. Paul below and its tributaries, carrying along with it a nice fragrance. The atmosphere was conducive, creating a perfect place to have a good night's rest, and get prepared for the next day's journey.

The elegant outgrowth was not alive with the cries of wild animals, rodents, and the high-pitched chirps of insects, that reminds one of spending the night in the jungle, like what the three escapees experienced in the bushes that covered the banks of the St. Paul. They could hear only the cries of crickets beneath the species of ferns and other palm plants that adorn the cliff.

With the roasted wild goat almost half eaten, the fire on which it was roasted appeared like it was dying down, but the velocity of the wind kept the flames steady and the firewood glowing.

Sergeant-Major Gonpue and Takpor Duo were sitting, with legs spread and their backs lying against the trees, sleeping. Their weapons were across their chests with their index fingers on the triggers. Sackie Dirty Water returned from his usual night patrol, and had woken up Takpor Duo. It was the junior commando's time to serve guard, while Gonpue remained far as sleep.

Sackie offered his head light to Takphor Duo when he woke up, but the junior commando refused, gesturing through his body language that it wouldn't be necessary. Since he joined the revolution, and participated in many night raids, he had never used a head light or night goggles. He had always depended on his naked eyes and a little moonlight, as it was now the case.

He stood with his gun in his hands at the same time looking around, planning where to make his rounds. He will first walk to the waterfall pool to listen to the flow for some time. He likes to hear the mesmerizing sound it makes when the water from up the rock falls into the pool. Then he will ascend the highest part of the cliff, view the forest below, and do some walking around, bearing in mind to stay close to their campsite to not get lost into the wonders of this place.

Before he started, he pulled out his knife from his side and sliced off a forelimb of the roasted black backed duiker meat and wrapped it in a fresh and wide leaf he had earlier chopped off from a tree branch. At the pool, he filled a small water container with the running water from the rock, held it up above his mouth and took a long and refreshing drink. After that he listened to the sound of the water descending into the pool for a while. Satisfied, he then headed up the highest part of the cliff where the three of them had earlier climbed to view the forest below.

He could see the reflection of the tree lines in the midst of the moon light extending all the way beneath him, including the direction of the Bong Range. He enjoyed the view for some time while sitting on a rock, eating the meat and drinking the water from the small water container. After eating all the flesh from around the bone, he tossed it down the cliff. Suddenly feeling full and sleepy, he decided to do some minor patrols to observe more of the beautiful scene under the moonlight with the hope that the excitement would kill the sleep brewing in his eyes. He got up and descended, to check on his comrades.

When he had passed the waterfall pool and looked straight ahead of him to where Sackie Dirty Water and Sergeant-Major Gonpue were sleeping, strangely, the fire was completely off, and the remaining meat was gone. He had gotten closer when his heart suddenly leapt with fear when he saw that Sergeant-Major Gonpue was braced up on the tree, with his hands tied backwards to the trunk, and a man was rubbing something like a chalk mixed with herb on his face at the same time reciting a strange incantation.

His T-shirt was torn wide open from the neck down to the hem, and Takphor Duo could also see that Gonpue's chest, all the way down to his abdomen, was rubbed with the chalk. His body shivered with fear as he struggled to compose himself, when he noticed that Sackie Dirty Water, who was a tree behind, was tied in similar way with the country cloth vest he was wearing, shredded.

Their weapons were lying on their feet and it seemed that a charm was used to conjure them while they were lost deep in sleep. It appeared they did not know all this was happening to them. Extremely terrified, Takphor Duo advanced his Ak-47 rifle and took a few steps closer, with his legs shivering and almost buckling under him.

"Who the fuck are you?" he demanded, his usual raspy voice suddenly getting hoist with fear.

The man paid no attention, but continued rubbing Sergeant-Major Gonpue with the chalk. And when he had finished, he circled around the Sergeant-Major and Sackie Dirty Water three times each, taking giant and drunken strides and reciting his incantation more audibly.

After that, he walked a few meters away from them and scooped over and pulled a ram's horn, bedecked with cowrie shells and feathers from the ground. Spell-bond, Takpor Duo watched the strange fellow while his index finger quivered on the trigger. From the day he joined the revolution, this was the first time he was hesitant to shoot.

"Oh my God! What's happening?!" Sergeant-Major Gonpue suddenly woke up, bewildered when the strange fellow had poured out a black dust from the horn and blew it in his face.

"Who are you? What do you want?" he demanded, as he fought to break loose from the strong vines.

Takpor Duo fired twice, when the fellow was now walking towards Sackie Dirty Water with the black dust in his palm and the ram horn squeezed under his right arm. The bullets, like red flames, hissed past Sergeant-Major Gonpue at close proximity and hit the fellow, one on his right shoulder blade and the other on the back of his head. But they were extinguished when they touched his skin and fell to the ground.

Again, paying no attention, the strange fellow reached Sackie and blew the dust in his face, waking him up immediately.

"He's got Zaykay!" cried Sergeant-Major Gonpue.

Right away, Takpor Duo inserted the nozzle of his Ak-47 into the ground and recited something in Gio, an antidote to neutralize anyone with a bullet proof body. He fired twice into the ground, with dirt flashing in his face, and then pointed the gun at the fellow. He fired at the same time yelling, until an entire magazine was emptied on the strange fellow. Unfortunately, the bullets, travelling like swans of flames of red pellets ricocheted off the stranger, doused, and fell to the ground one after the other.

Horrified, while he struggled to break free from the vines that bind him to the tree trunk after unsuccessful attempts, Sackie Dirty Water looked at the strange fellow, who was still standing before him.

He was a huge and muscular man with large arms. His eyes were large and red, and his head was striped clean as it shone under the moon-light. He had no clothes on, except a country cloth wrapped around his buttocks and private like a pair of shorts. He was dark in complexion, though covered with the yellow-like chalk mixed with herbs.

"Gbeh-vay?" Sackie managed to ask.

The man did not answer, but the expression on his face told Sackie that his intention was to ravage them. The fellow turned and faced Takpoh Duo who was replacing the cartridge he had emptied on him. He again inserted the nozzle of his Ak-47 into the ground, this time fired thrice, as more dirt covered his face. Then he pointed the gun at the man and started another round of shooting, yelling and cursing in his dialect.

Again, the bullets extinguished upon hitting the man and dropped to the ground. Breathing heavily when he had emptied the magazine and it did not kill the man, he made a split-second decision and charged at him with a swing of his gun butt on the man's head in an attempt to split it open.

He had seen this happen, during the attack on the First Infantry Battalion during the early part of the civil war. A Liberian government army major who was posing serious resistance to their advances by standing in the way of their bullets because they could not penetrate his body was eventually captured and killed when a hammer was used to burst his head open.

The Ak-47 butt landed on the man's head, but it bounced off. Takpor Duo hit it again, this time with all his might, but it again bounced off. The man grabbed the gun on the third attempt, pulled it from the junior commando's hands, after a brief tussle, and hit his side with the gun butt.

The impact from the force smashed Takpor Duo on a nearby tree, thus fracturing his ribs. Seeing this, Sergeant-Major Gonpue and Sackie Dirty Water immediately exerted more efforts to break free from the vine binding them to the tree, causing the strong robes to tear into the flesh around their wrists and upper arms.

They were yelling and crying for themselves and for Takpor Duo who was lying on the ground, breathing little by little, at the same time coughing out blood. The man walked to him, pulled him from the ground and began to tie him to the tree with the same vines.

"What have we done?!" cried Sackie, when Takpor Duo altered a sharp cry when the man hauled his arms around the tree to tie them, causing his injured ribs to stretch.

When the fellow had tied Takpor Duo to the tree, the same way he did his comrades, he took a sharp machete that was lying near the ram horn, and walked back to Takpor Duo. He grabbed the camouflage vest he was wearing and began to tear it peace by peace. The Junior commando, who had gotten weak and dizzy caused by his fractured ribs, emitted excruciating shrieks whenever the sharp blade of the machete tore into his flesh.

"Why treat me like this?" lamented Takpor Duo, coughing out blood, with his head wrung, and his cheek resting on his chest. "I have taken no innocent life since I joined the revolution. I was only fighting for my country."

The man suddenly stopped and began to convulse, like he was reacting to a high fever. Then he stopped and looked at the three men for a while, his scarlet eyes shining through the dark. He took the same yellow-like chalk mixed with herbs from under his country cloth shorts, stood before Takpor Duo, and examined him with his roving eyes.

After that, he rubbed a portion of the chalk into his palms, and started rubbing it all over the junior commando's body beginning with his head, as he resumed reciting the strange incantation. When he had finished, he again took the giant zigzag strides three times around the junior commando, raising his voice, and continuing with the strange incantation.

"Ay God. I only joined the revolution to protect my family," Takpor Duo continued to lament, reeling from the pain from his fractured ribs. "Government forces raided my village in 1990. Some of my family members were killed while others ran into the bush and were never seen up to this day. But I have never killed innocent people."

The man suddenly turned his giant drunken strides towards Sackie Dirty Water and circled around him three times. At the completion of the third one, he stopped and faced the Bush Dog commander. Exhausted from fighting to break loose from the robes, Sackie made an effort to tilt his head to look in the eyes of this strange man.

"What did we do?" he asked, but again, the man did not answer. "Then let us go," he then demanded, deducing from the stranger's face that indeed, they did nothing.

"We did nothing," cried the Sergeant-Major, he himself also exhausted from trying to loosen himself from the strong vine holding him tight to the tree.

The man suddenly convulsed again, this time, more violently then the first. He circled around the three of them once and took his giant drunken strides towards the waterfall pool, circled around a corner, surprising the three domed men that all along the man had been lurking near the pool. He passed a tree near an outgrowth and disappeared into the dark.

In no time, he reappeared before the three men with what was left of the roasted duiker meat in his hand, raising it so they could see that they did something wrong.

The fellow took his zig-zag strides towards Sackie again, and scooped over, reaching for the rubber sanders he was wearing and took from the bottom a chunk of dirt. Then he stood up facing Sackie, and threw the dirt in his face, causing some of the sand to enter his eyes.

To Sackie, this was a sign that the man had sealed their judgment for trespassing on these lands, and for also wreaking havoc on its denizens, especially when he became agitated and threw the half-eaten roasted meat before them.

He again resumed his giant strides, circling around them.

"It was never our intention," shouted Sackie. "For the past three days, we have been on a mission from Haindii to Gbarnga. We thought these routes to be the shortest, by way of the St. Paul River. I only killed the animal for food."

Upon hearing this, the man looked at Sackie, and started convulsing again, this time, contorting his face, and violently storming his feet to the ground, like he was emotionally reacting to an affliction. Sackie heart leapt, when he understood this to mean that his explanation was vehemently rejected. No one finds this place without prying the twilight, he thought. These lands are sacred and they have trampled on it, which is an abomination to this strange man and they were going to account for their actions.

The strange man circled around them again and hurriedly took his giant strides to where he had disappeared into the dark and appeared before them again. This time he had a large bag made of animals' skin. He rummaged through the things inside and got out three large calabashes split in half at the center, but fused together.

He removed each half and turned them over. Reddish clayish material fell to the ground, when he gently stroked the back of the calabashes. He formed the materials into the shape of an earth mound of about

2 feet high with a circumference of 5 feet. A hollow was formed at the base of the mound, facing him.

Then he searched into the bag again and got out two cutlasses and laid them on the ground. He also took from the bag three logs of about 3 feet long and used one of the cutlasses to split them into pieces of wood, whose inner part looked orange-yellow. He placed them into the hollow of the base of the mound.

The man got two long air sacs made of pelt with a handle at one end and what looked like a wooden curvature at the other end. He bore two holes into the right and left sides of the mound and inserted each of the air sacs into them. Smaller holes were also inserted all over the mound making it possible for anyone standing a few meters away to see inside.

He got some chaffs, formed them into a ball in his hands and placed it between the wood in the mound. Two small stones that looked like granite were then taken from the bag. The man rubbed them together close to the chaffs for some time, until they sparkled and the chaff ball ignited a tiny glow of fire. When it began to increase, he got a small wooden stool out of the bag and sat on it, facing the built-up of fire in the mound.

Sitting on the stool, he gently drew an air sac up above his armpit and back down on the side of his feet, at the same time drawing the other one up to similar height and down again. Light gray plumes of smoke bellowed out of the holes as the fire in the mound started to blaze.

Sackie Dirty Water and Sergeant-Major Gonpue could see the fire through the holes which started with its usual saffron nature and then it later changed to an orange-yellow color because the next culprits were all men. The man observed it for some time. Then put the two cutlasses into the furnace, and began to blow the fire with the air sacs.

In a few minutes the two metals turned red and later turned orange-yellow like the fire itself. Seeing this Sackie realized that the man might be a blacksmith, and an extremely weird one.

The man took one of the cutlasses from the furnace when it had gotten extremely hot to the extent that droplets of the liquid metal were dropping to the ground and igniting the dry leaves and stalks into flames. Raising the molted cutlass in the air, the man looked up at the sky and recited something in his dialect.

Then he resumed his drunken strides, first around the mound furnace. After a couple of strides, he continued in like manner towards Takpor Duo, who had now gotten weary of the pain caused by his fractured ribs. He was about to faint.

He held the junior commando by his cheek, tilting it up to give him the chance to look in his eyes. Then he recited the words of the verdict's code in Kpelle in a high pitch melodious tender.

> "Your innocence is betrayed by your woe;
> and your woe is the source of your fear:
> for the radiance of the steel to consume your flesh;
> for the abomination you have brought upon yourself."

"What are you saying?" asked Tarkpor Duo, with a faint voice.

"Sackie. What is he saying?" cried Sergeant-Major Gonpue, terrified.

"Oh God!" Scakie swallowed at the same time, convulsing, and weeping. "He's going to have us roasted like we did the duiker."

"Why are you doing this?!" screamed Sergeant-Major Gonpue, crying bitterly. "We are freedom fighters defending these lands from enemies that attacked us from Sierra Leone and Guinea. We are just on our way to Gbargba for re-enforcement. If you kill us, how will we defend Liberia? You hear me? How will we defend this place?"

The man tried the molten steel on himself, first, on his head and then his face as he repeatedly recited the code. But nothing happened to him. At his first attempt on Tarkpor Duo's head, his hair and skin burned instantly, exposing his bare skull. He pressed and slid the hot cutlass down the left side of his face taking his left ear and flesh. What remained was the jaw bones, and teeth.

Sackie Dirty Water and Sergeant-Major Gonpue, both crying like hell, could smell their comrade's burned hair, flesh and cartilage. Takpor Duo's voice was the loudest in the midst of the excruciating pain. Still pressing the hot steel, the man continued to drag it down the left side of Takpor Duo's neck, burning it all the way to his neck bone. The junior commando was in severe pain.

The man suddenly turned towards the blazing furnace mound. He raised the cutlass in the air and studied it. It was covered with thick black steams of burned skin and flesh. He shouted in an ominously but triumphant tone when he turned to look at Takpor Duo, and saw that he was dead.

He again convulsed in his usual fever-like seizure manner, and made his drunken strides to the furnace. He sat on the stool, put the cutlass back in the fire, and took the other one. Then got up and headed straight for Sergeant-Major Gonpue.

The battle group commander had increased his efforts to loosen himself from the vines. But the robes have torn deep into the flesh around his wrists to the extent that his bones were showing. Trying not to end up scourged like Takpor Duo, when he saw the man coming to him, he suddenly reverted to knocking his head backwards on the tree trunk, splattering blood, flowing from the back of his neck, down on the tree bark.

The Sergeant-Major was now hazed, and in the state of delirium when the man appeared before him. "Please chop off my head," he said, but the man held the cutlass up in the sky and recited the verdict's code, again. The code of 'innocence and guilt.

After this, he slapped and pressed the hot metal on Sergeant-Major Gonpue's left shoulder, and dragged it all the way down. It burned the upper part of his armpit and his entire left hand, turning them into fresh skeletons. Eric Gonpue screamed as his voice echoed through the cliff and down the forest.

Next was his left leg, from the thigh region to the knee cap and down to his foot. He also repeated this on the right leg and similar parts.

"You crazy swine," Sackie Dirty Water cursed, becoming infuriated when the man had pulled down Sergeant-Major Gonpue's jean trousers, exposing his genitals.

The man pressed the hot steaming cutlass horizontally on his lower abdomen, which charred its way into the Sergeant-Major's torso, consuming his genitals. He continued until his abdomen burst open with the lower part of his large intestine pouring out. Feces were dropping on the ground.

The battle group commander continued to scream in anguish. He looked at his burned arms and legs, and was petrified to see his skeletons, while he was still alive, and how badly his abdomen was burst open. His large intestine continued to pour out, still dropping feces as the foul smell filled the air. Then he made an effort to look the man in the eyes.

"Our country is invaded," he wept, reeling in pain. "How can we defend it when you treat some of its best fighters like this?"

The man looked up and raised the hot blood-stained cutlass into the air and shouted in another triumphant tone when Sergeant-Major Gonpue died.

He took his drunken strides back to the furnace and put the cutlass back into it. He again worked the air sacs and the blaze increased. Sackie could feel the radiance from the furnace striking him as the man aggressively blew the fire.

Still hazy, he made an effort to lift up his head and saw the orange-yellow flames of the fire through the tiny holes. The man took out one of the cutlasses and raised it above his head to examine it. The orange-yellow hot molten from the extremely hot metal dropped on him and rolled from his head, and then down his cheeks. But it doused and appeared like sweat on his skin.

This was extraordinary, Sackie thought. The fire from a furnace is usually yellow-red, but not orange-yellow. Any metal placed inside is also hot and yellowish-red, but not this furnace and the metal he was looking at.

The man pulled the two cutlasses and suddenly sprang to his feet. Sackie saw that he was taking his drunken strides towards him. He was next.

Faced with the reality that he was going to succumb to the hash ordeal like his two comrades, he reflected on the meaning of his life and all the things that happened in the past two days. Was he destined to die like this in the middle of the jungle he had learned about and mastered? Has he ever envisaged facing a strange ordeal? What was the meaning of discovering and encountering these strange things? A strange fear took hold of him, and then it was the voice of Kpakolo Leynumah, 'these jungles hold many secrets, but never allow them to frighten you.'

Reciting the ordeal's verdict code, the man now stood before Sackie. 'These jungles hold many secrets, but never allow them to frighten you," instead, Kpakolo Laynumah's voice again rang in his grandson's ear.

The man had finished reciting the code and had tried the hot cutlasses on himself with nothing happening to him.

As he now brought the cutlass closer to Sackie's chest, the Bush Dog commander winced and squeezed his eyes when he felt the heat. But suddenly, he saw the mother's monkey's face. The disappointed mother monkey's face, sternly staring at him when he had failed to take the shot to rescue its young from the python.

The defiant eyes of the primate, he now realized, told him that with all the screaming and shaking of the branches, it had accepted the predator-prey predicament. And as he looked at it with his hunting gun in his hands, the monkey had also accepted the hunter and the hunted predicament; it was ready to die as well, and to Sackie it was the strangest thing he had ever seen.

He reflected once when it was reported that elephants were wreaking havoc in the nearby bushes of some towns and villages in Gbarpolu county, destroying farms and properties and sometimes human lives. This prompted the residents in the affected areas and their surroundings to flee for their safety. For months, the people were afraid to go to their farms, and it was already in the planting season.

Through the Ministry of Internal Affairs and the Forestry Development Agency (FDA), traditional hunters in that area and across the river to Haindii were summoned to help bring the situation under control by driving the giant pests far away from human habitats, deep into the forest. Or else, there would be fatalities or severe famine. Kpakolo Lynumah took Sackie, then in his early teens along with him.

It took the hunters about two months in the forest, applying every traditional means to drive away the elephants. They first beat drums and shot in the air to scare them away. Next, they planted beehives in their tracks to deter the animals from returning back.

One day, Sackie, his grandfather and a group of hunters, came across an abandoned farm. They had patrolled the forest all day long, and decided to stop and to have dinner and rest. Sackie spotted some banana trees, and had gone to pluck some juicy ripe ones.

He was startled when suddenly a monkey screamed, almost like an infant, and disappeared into the branches taking giant leaps from one tree to another. The animal saw him and then his hunting gun on his shoulder. But the one he encountered, the night before, did not back down from expressing its disappointment in him, even in the midst of danger when a hunting gun was pointing at it.

Sackie now understood the purpose of all of this. He will no longer plead or cry for mercy. He will accept his predicament; the victim-perpetrator predicament. If it was his fate to end up being scourged on a stick, and can do nothing about it, he will accept it.

He suddenly felt a surge of bravery taking hold of him. He felt himself gaining the courage to open his eyes and looked the strange man straight in his face as he violently slapped one of the hot orange-yellow cutlasses on his naked chest, and landed the other one on his foreface.

He firmly pressed them against his skin. But Sackie courageously held on to his breath as he made every effort to not give in to the pain and scream. He slowly closed his eyes in anticipation of accepting his fate, as the strange black smith performed the Sassaywoo on him.

CHAPTER 4

Tonolah Wuamah slowly opened his eyes when the sun ray struck his face. He realized that it was day but was suddenly grappled with fear when he thought he was dead, or was actually dead. The last time he remembered he had left Nathaniel Kpaingba's Farm and came paddling in this direction, where he discovered this river cliff and a waterfall pool. He also discovered a horrific scene of human remains tied to the trees which looked like the victims were scourged in some kind of ordeal.

Then he was approached by a huge figure that emerged from the dark. He remembered running, and also remembered being pursued, and while trying to climb the high rock, he slipped and fell. Next, the figure was standing over him. From there on, he was conscious of nothing, until now.

Whosoever it was, may have sealed his fate like those of the skeletons tied to the trees. Maybe he was now his own ghost about to roam the land for some time, before being called to the final abode of the spirits, prepared by the maker of all things, as this was widely his traditional belief.

In the setting in which he grew up, it is believed, sometimes people died and they didn't immediately realize that they died and would continue to roam the material world, until people they knew unexpectedly bumped into them and would flee from them. Or, only when the dead realized that they no longer have physical contact with the material world. Many times, the people, especially women who see someone who is supposed to be dead, will exclaim 'you're supposed to be dead!' and those who see them will sometimes wail, and scream about seeing a ghost.

He remembered an instance, where almost a whole town was giving accounts of seeing the ghost of a popular village dancer who died of mysterious circumstances, and was buried. This person continued to appear to a number of the town's people, some of whom were on their way from their farms. This instilled fear in the entire community until the chief and the elders sent for the traditional spiritualists who were mainly women to appease the dead.

The spiritualists found out that this dancer was murdered, and vowed that his spirit will remain restless and roam the land, until he was accorded justice. When the mystery of the murder was solved by the traditional spiritualists, prompting the apprehensions and subsequent confessions of the culprits, the ghost of the young town's dancer ceased to roam the land and never appeared to the town's people again. Remembering this story, Wuamah was afraid that a similar occurrence was happening to him.

As he lay on the ground, face up, he rolled his eyes to look around him. He could not feel anything and was unable to move, thus adding to his suspicion that he was dead, and his remains were also strapped to a tree. But he needed to be sure of this, and so he tried to lift up his head to look in the direction of the gruesome scene and check whether his body, burned to the bone, was also tied to a tree.

When he did, he felt a sharp pain at the back of his head, making him remember what was the cause, and that it was when the back of his head hit against a rock when he slid down the high rise. And because of the pain, he was a bit relieved that he may not be dead, and he may not be his own ghost, since spirits don't feel pain.

However, he still needed concrete proof to confirm this belief of the ghost's theory that was well etched in his tradition. He attempted to look ahead of him to see for himself, but he could not, for fear of seeing his condemned body with charred flesh and bones.

He again made another attempt by first taking a deep breath and preparing himself for the best or the worst. With a renewed energy, he lifted his head, ignoring the sharp pain and looked to the direction of the dreaded scene. He was elated when he did not see his remains tied to a trunk.

"O Gala. E mama," he crooned in Kpelle, thanking God for still being alive.

Wuamah remained on the ground trying to move his hands and legs. He felt another dose of relief running through his spine when he clawed his fingers and could feel dirt in his hand. if he was a ghost, his fingers could have passed through the dirt with ease, which would mean a disconnection from the material world.

He suddenly rose to his feet, and staggered towards the waterfall pool. He cupped both palms and dipped it in the water and flashed it on his face. After that, he repeated some and put some in his mouth. He worked the water in his jaws to rinse it, and then spat it out. Then he looked up at the high rise, and again at the gruesome scene.

Suddenly, he was concerned about why he was still alive. Maybe the ordeal only works when the victim is alive, and he was unconscious when he fell, and maybe the bogeyman was unable to resuscitate him.

Fear again gripped Wuamah, now that he was conscious which would make him an easy victim, and the boogeyman was probably lurking behind one of the trees waiting for the right moment to perform his evil ordeal. In no time he was up on the high rise, climbing with all his might, ignoring the pain at the back of his head and his body aches. In a few minutes he made it to the top.

Remembering where he landed his canoe, and left it, he raced in that direction and started sliding down the slope, bumping against trees and rocks, never caring for the pain until he landed at the bottom.

Fortunately, he found his canoe still intact. He sighed with great relief and wasted no time to hurry towards it. He mounted the canoe, scrambled the paddle, and was out of the edge of the cliff in one giant stroke. He opted to maintain a swift and steady course southward, with the cliff behind him.

Wuamah assumed that the canoe may have drifted this way, probably for an hour or two while he was sleeping. When he had almost managed to maneuver out of the rapids, he suddenly turned and looked behind to make sure that he was not followed.

Satisfied, he turned, looking ahead, stroking the paddle as the canoe gained speed and moved through the water. Before he noticed a rock ahead, and to maneuver his way around it, the canoe collided with it.

It flew into the air, landed back into the water and capsized. Displeased with himself, Wuamah cursed when he also landed into the water with a gigantic splash and watched his canoe turn upside down, partially submerged and it began to drift with the current back toward the direction of the cliff.

Remembering what to do as an expert canoe man, he gained his composure, and first ensured that he did not attempt to land his feet on the river bed to determine how deep it was or else heading back up for the surface would take some time. And if the water is too deep, it might cause a seizure for holding his breath for long under water.

With the paddle firmly under his arm to use as a weapon in case something or someone tried to pull him under, he swam towards the canoe. But seeing that it was drifting his way, and throwing only an arm as he swam, while the paddle was under his other arm, would quickly make him tired.

To preserve energy, he managed to somehow remain steadily afloat against the mild, but sometimes rough current as he maintained a frog-styled vertical position by gently gliding his legs and his free hand. He remained so for some time, until the canoe got closer and made the distance short to swim to it.

He reached the canoe, and rested on the partially submerged keel for a while, and at the same time figuring out how to flip it over. Wuamah took a dive underneath, and when he was inside, he clanged the paddle to his teeth and raised one side of the canoe above the water level. He shoved the raised side hard until it flipped over.

He then took the paddle from his mouth and threw it in the canoe, now floating on its keel. After that, he held on to the starboard on the right side, angling himself until he was sure he was in the middle to balance the craft.

After two attempts, he grabbed the far side of the starboard on the left and thrust himself upward to re-enter the canoe. Now seated, he sloshed out the remaining water with a cupped hand. When most were out, he looked back again at the direction of the cliff, and then continued paddling south ward.

Unsuspectedly two and a half hours later, Wuamah was now navigating through familiar terrain. Convinced that no one was following him, he lay on his back, resting his head on the stern as the canoe slowly drifted. The early morning sun was almost disappearing into the clouds as the remnants of its rays were still visible on the surface of the water and the glamourous vegetation along the banks.

When he had rested for a few minutes, he got up and gently glided out of the tributary and entered a smaller one to his left. Tears ran down his eyes as he thought about Maila, and what he encountered up the cliff the night before. Someone in the bushes had committed a horrific crime, and the thought of it, made him feel sick in his stomach. Moreover, flashes from the gruesome scene and the stench of skeletons and burned human remains, made him want to vomit as the canoe rocked to the motion of the ripples.

As he paddled on, he remembered the earth-mount furnace with the aches from the special wood to heat whatsoever metal that was used to scourge the victims to death. He remembered quite well that Sengbeh the black smith sometimes used it. In the old days, his great grandfather made a discovery of iron ore deposits up Mount Zaweah, a part of the mountain chain of Bong Range. To smelt the ore, he invented a special wood that produces immense heat and that craft was passed down to his sons, and the ones after them.

"So, all these years Sengbeh had been in this bush waiting to kill people like that?" Wuamah asked himself, and started to cry.

Then he also remembered the story his late father told him about Sengbeh Gbelema and why he behaved the way he did when he walked out of the meeting the day the elders decided to allow Representative Barclay to explore their land.

During the conflict with Gbokai Lamine, Sengbeh's great grandfather was the architect in manufacturing the weapons the Jokorlleh used to defeat and drive the Gola out of their land. After the war, he was the one that encouraged Kerlulah Maila to establish the town, and the two men lived as brothers.

Many years after the Gola were defeated, they once more rose up against the Kpelle in hope to regain their lost land. As the time seemed right, when all the strong and brave warriors from Kpelle Land responded to their nephew, Chief Zubah Keleko's call to help him fight off the French from encroaching on that part of president day Lofa County, the Gola, who became emboldened with the courage and tenacity of a new and powerful chief, used this as an opportunity to launch an all-out war against the Kpelle, pillaging every village, town and settlement from Hendii all the way to Maila and beyond.

Lamine Gangama was a grandson of Gbokai Lamine. He was just an infant, still feeding on breast milk and was on his mother's back when a band of Kpelle worriers discovered and attacked a large Gola settlement, which for many years was used by Gbokai Lamine's men to launch incursions to harass the Kpelle after he was driven from the territory of Maila.

The kid's father, with an arrow pierced in his back below the right armpit, managed to rescue the mother and her child by putting them into a canoe and hauling it into the river. He watched until it drifted down stream and was out of sight before he joined his father in the fierce battle in which both of them were killed. The canoe with the mother and child drifted for some days until it was discovered by some Gola fishermen along the St. Paul, around present day Todee District belt.

Lamine Gangama grew up to be very strong, brave and determined. He was in his teens when he took his mother and ventured further southwards on the St. Paul to present day Banjor, Virginia, where he lived amongst the Dei people. He and his mother stayed there for many years, fishing at the mouth of the river where it enters into the Atlantic Ocean.

As a young adult, he traded with Portuguese merchants who ventured along the coast in search of Malaquetta paper, and sometimes served as their trapper. It was the first time he saw a musket and learned how to fire it.

Years later, Lamine Gangama, now a full-grown man, immensely huge, well-built and an imposing physique, became famous amongst the Dei, most notably, with the coming of the settlers from across the Atlantic Ocean. When conflict with these strangers over land erupted which soon led to war, he was part of Dei warriors and their allied Vai and Mamba tribes that participated in many fierce battles intended to drive the settlers into the Atlantic Ocean.

But to his displeasure, the tribes soon made peace with the settlers, and their chiefdoms were gradually becoming municipalize, as more settlers were encouraged to settle within the confines of these chieftaincies, prompting the extension of control from the main settler's authority at Cape Montserrado.

He became a fugitive when he was condemned by the tribal chiefs who were once hustle to the settlers when they received complaints from their authorities that Gangama had organized a group of equally disgruntled Dei and Gola men who were constantly launching raids into the new settlements of present-day Virginia, Clay Ashland, and Arthington, killing the men and abducting women and children. They would set the settlements ablaze in a move to scare and drive them out. Sometimes they concocted plots and assassinated elders and chiefs who were sympathetic to the settlers.

There were many stories told about him as he became very elusive, due to his vast knowledge of the surrounding forests in Dei-Gola Land to search parties organized to have him and his bandits apprehended. Because of the horrible things he did, and the stories told about them, his mother, who was now aging, was summoned by the chiefs on several occasions to try to see whether she was in contact with her son. If so, to encourage him to abandon his senseless struggle.

But a few days after she was informed that she would appear before the settler's authority at Cape Montserrado, she was found dead in a nearby swamp along the river banks where she often went to lay her fishing baskets. The chiefs and elders ruled that it was due to drowning while people said she killed herself to be relieved of the embarrassment caused by the denigrating behavior of her son.

In these times, Lamine Gangama became more vicious in his raids, blaming the settlers and their collaborating chiefs for the death of his mother who did not have any part to play in his struggle. As he wreaked more havoc, many of the settlements in Dey-Gola land were razed, and burned to the ground. Settlers' militia patrols were ambushed and large caches of arms and ammunition were seized, which he used to train his group of bandits.

However, he was forced to retreat far north, beyond Todee, when a joint search party of both settlers and friendly tribes was organized and led by a settler named Benjamin Horace, an explorer who also possessed great knowledge of both the coastal belt and the jungles in the hinterland. The fugitive was hunted down and was almost apprehended, when he ran out of animations. Most of his bandits were either killed or captured. Also, some of the abducted women and children were rescued.

Lamine Gangama and remnants of his bandits wandered along the banks of the St. Paul until he bumped into some of his kinsmen who welcomed him when he told them, giving vivid accounts narrated to him by his mother about his lineage to Gbokai Lamine.

He saw first-hand the plight of his people, who have since lived in constant fear of their Kpelle rivals. He himself hated the Kpelle for their suspected treachery for failing to show up for the many battles with the settlers. When the Kpelle, especially those that occupied the nearby vicinity north west of what is now the Township of Careysburg, were approached by the Dei, Mamba, and Vai tribes about their plan to attack the settlers, they concerted, but they did not always show up for these battles.

Full of vengeance, he began to organize his people and started preparing them for war. Within a few years, Lamine Gangama was leading a campaign to liberate their Land, when the opportunity came.

When Hendii and the surrounding Kpelle settlements were eventually overrun by the vicious Lamine Gangama, Kekaula Maila, who was now very old, and his people were one day taken by surprise when they were attacked from the east.

Frightened by the thunderous sound of the muskets fired by Gangama and his men, he and some of his people, mainly the elderly, women and children retreated to his secret hideout, squeezed to a tiny area along the St. Paul and leaving a band of warriors to defend Maila.

Helplessly confined in this area, he received constant feedback from the battle that the Gola had taken Maila, and were setting it ablaze. Tears ran down his eyes as he was given accounts of the destruction of decades of what he had built.

When Kerkulah Maila was nowhere to be found, Lamine Gangama sent word, demanding the chief 's head in exchange for the lives of his people. He was given three days to come out of his hide outs, and when he had rejected the demand to the urging of some of his bravest warriors, the time elapsed and Lamine Gangama beheaded some of the people he had captured, and repeated this each day after the deadline.

As Kerkulah Maila contemplated on finally surrendering, he hated himself for underestimating the Gola, when Gbokai Lamine was finally defeated and killed. Fearing for the continual loss of life of his people, he finally gave in to the demand and sent word to the Gola champion that he would surrender the next day.

On the morning of that day, the people were crying and whining around him, with the women and children falling at his feet and holding onto them, when he was about to be escorted to Lamine Gangama to be executed. But there was a large explosion, and a sudden burst of musket fire and the sound of distant clashes of machetes and spears, followed by the familiar battle cries of Kpelle Warriors.

This continued for almost the whole day, until a group of Maila warriors came running to the chief, at the same time rejoicing that the Gola had now abandoned the town to the firepower of the Kpelle who had similar weapons, and they were now on the run.

Kerkula Maila could not believe his eyes, when he saw his friend and brother Sengbeh Gbelema, who had returned from the war with the French after many months, along with a large group of warriors with the strange weapons in their hands.

Later that day, Gangama and his men, who could not fathom how the Kpelle managed to acquire the musket they were using, scattered into the bushes and were being pursued. Many of them were killed or captured, but he again became a fugitive and remained so for weeks until he was trapped, pinned down and finally killed by a band of Kpelle worriers led by Tokpa 'Toto" Kolleh, a short, stocky and equally persistent and vicious warrior, who was a confidant of Sengbeh Gbelema.

The battle hardened, Toto Kolleh as he was commonly called, fought side by side with the black smith during the campaign against the French. He continued to pursue the Gola until they were driven back to the present day Todee area. Sensing an imminent attack on Todee, the Gola forged an uneasy truce, and Toto Kolleh was ordered to abandon his campaign which he reluctantly did.

At a ceremony marking the celebration of the final victory of the people of Maila, Chief Kerkulah Maila, along with his council of elders made a park with Sengbeh Geblema and Tokpa 'Toto' Kolleh that the wonders of Maila must always be protected and that its beautiful scenery will only be explored and improved with the consent of three of them, or their children. But Toto Kolleh later left Maila to join another group of his kinsmen who were waging a campaign against the Bassa people around the area of present day Bolola, north east of the present-day city of Kakata.

"The Park made between Kerkulah Maila and the black smith remained enforced and their children respected and maintained it long after they died," Klemani Wuamah, narrated to his son, Tonola. "My father told me that Sengbeh's father used to discuss with Chief Lomeh's father about how Maila can be like Bong Town. He was among the first laborers recruited to brush the site to the mountain and where Bong Town was built. Sometimes when they were resting, the white people used to display pictures to them about how their country looks like. And seeing that Maila has similar features, that was how the idea came to him.

Sengbeh was born when his father was very old. And people said the baby was sickly and used to cry until one day a zoe advised that he must be named after his great grandfather, Sengbeh Gbelema. And strangely afterwards, the child stopped crying and suddenly became well.

Like his fathers before him, he inherited the black smith craft with a great degree of proficiency. He even learned how to manufacture firearms, a knowledge that was handed down to him, from his great grandfather who learned it from a certain Lorma and powerful black smith, named Guowola Acquoi, during the campaign against the French. But in the 1970s, it was abolished by the Liberian government. Sengbeh also inherited his ancestors' gifts with herbs.

Growing up, he refused to play with other kids and seldom spoke. But he would gaze for hours at the wonders of our land, and would refuse to eat. In his early teens, he would wander into the bush for days, taking stock of the natural features.

As an adolescent he was fully aware that his ancestors had certain decision-making rights regarding Maila. For this reason, he would act hustle to anyone farming, hunting, or setting traps near the town's beautiful vegetation. One evening, a couple was returning from their farm, when they found Mullah Tarte, an animal trapper and the brother of Grualee Tarte tied to a tree.

He was almost at the point of death, when the couple rescued him. After he was given food and water, and came to himself, Mulbah Tartee explained how he had gone into the bush to inspect his traps he set the evening before, when he met Sengbeh destroying them. He grabbed the boy by his hands and attempted to bring him to his father to complain to him. To his surprise, he was overpowered and tied to the tree.

Sengbeh warned him strongly that if his traps were going to catch an animal, he was going to throw branches of gravel ants on him to eat up his flesh to the bone. When the then young black smith was asked why he did it, he neither confirmed nor denied it. That day he walked out of his father's yard and stayed three days in the bush when his father tried to talk to him about his behavior."

Wuamah could hear the voice of his late father echoing in his ears, as the narrative continued to flow through his memory.

"When Gorpue gave birth to Barclay's son," Klemani Wuamah continued. "Sengbeh was the only one amongst us that did not go to the chief compound to celebrate the new birth."

"Laypay ka, Sengbeh?" the child's grandmother asked, "what's the matter, Sengbeh?" early one morning when she spotted him in the dark staring at the infant on her back. She had gone to her outside kitchen to make hot water for the chief.

Though he said nothing, his gaze meant something, sensed the child's grandmother. He stood for a while and then walked away, deep into the dark."

"Sengbeh will do something bad when Boima returns to Maila," Wuamah's heart pounded, saying this to himself. "I wonder why he did not kill me?"

Then he reflects on his father's narration on how two weeks after the incident with Mulbah Tartee, Sengbeh's father, was found dead on his farm. The body of the old man was smashed, lying under a huge tree that accidentally fell on him while chopping it down. His mother continued to live in the town even after he unceremoniously left. She survived the civil war, but she was lonely. When she had gotten old and could no longer go to her garden, Ma-mye would encourage him to help her with her garden. In 2006, she died in her hut on the night the town's people were celebrating the inauguration of the first post-war president.

Calming himself, Wuamah decided against landing the canoe to where he got it the day before, because that part of the bush was a little far away from the town and it was going to be risky-one could never tell whether the black smith might be lurking there, waiting for him. So, he veered off the small tributary in which he was paddling and entered a creek to his left that runs all the way to a nearby swamp at the outskirts of the town. At the creek, he would wait until it got dark before entering the town.

He did not want to be seen walking and reeling with body aches, moreover with his spooked face would raise concern, prompting the town's people to ask what happened to him. Of course, he will not want to be mute as it will only lead to suspicion.

The only explanation that will make sense to them will be the story of the black smith. The older folks knew that he did not abandon Maila at his own volition, but was due to a decision taken by the chief and the elders that did not go down well with him. Announcing that Sengbeh Gbelema was in the bushes of Maila strapping people to trees and burning them to their skeletons will only instill fear and possibly a mass exodus from the town.

It was late in the afternoon, Wuamah had reached the place and landed the canoe at the edge of the creek, where the branches of the reefs cascaded over the shadow water and provided a perfect shade. it would not take long to get dark, and so he rested for a while in the canoe.

He suddenly began to think about his mother and his cousin, Flomo. He knew that Mamaye would be worried. Though he sometimes did not return home the same day, whenever he left his house, it had never taken two days. He also knew that Chief Lomeh would go check on him. It would be unusual, because both men were together the day before, and the young chief should have known if he was not going to return home.

That was the part he was afraid would make her extremely worried, especially when little Flomo would have laid before her all the different possibilities that something may or may not have happened to him.

The wet clothes on him were now dried as the sun was hot all afternoon. He got out of the canoe and looked around him, but he soon started feeling pains all over his body when he got up and made an attempt to walk along the path that would lead him to Maila. The pain was so severe and so he took his time walking.

Wamah managed to trek along the path, holding his left side and dragging his feet, and sometimes hopping as the pain in his legs and entire body wore on. He realized that, had it been the time he landed in the water, when the canoe collided with a rock and capsized, it was going to be difficult to swim. Maybe he could have drowned. He thanked God in his heart that it did not happen.

It was now completely dark when he finally entered the town from the north side, and was happy that the few persons who passed by him greeted without noticing anything. His only concern was passing by Gotolo's house.

He was a young man and popular among the girls, and knew everything about everyone. Most of the young men in the town avoided having conversation with Gotolo or when he was around for fear of hearing what was discussed in confidentiality, in public. His house was strategically located on the main road where everyone likes to pass.

Gotolo would sit in front of his house all night until he was sure everyone had gone to bed, and would do the same thing early in the morning. When the moon was not up, especially during the rainy season, he would sit outside with his torchlight and would flash it in the face of any one emerging out of the dark.

"Oh! I am sorry! I thought you were someone I am expecting," would be his reason when the person raised an issue. But his actual intention was to know who it was at that time of the night, and who was accompanying the person, especially when it was a man and a woman.

"Hey. Who's walking over there like Wuamah? How are you doing?" a voice called from the dark as Wamah circled around Goloto's house. He turned and saw that it was him, just as he had expected.

"I am good," responded Wuamah, struggling to forge a calm voice and his normal way of walking.

"Ok. But you don't sound too good, and you haven't passed this way for a while, especially at this time of the night."

"And you are not the town's cop, right?"

"Well," sighed Gotolo. "I am not the town's cop, but I saw you pass by my house and you were looking to see whether I was home. So, I thought you came to see me."

"I have never visited you, Gotolo. Even when we were friends," Wuamah said. "Remember that I told you to stay away from me, right?"

"Right," Goloto admitted, gesturing a plea as he attempted to get closer to Wuamah. "But I have told you that I am sorry . . ."

"Then let it remain so," warned Wuamah, interrupting him and then continued trekking towards the Chief's compound.

Gotolo stood, his arm akimbo with strings of remorse running across his face as he watched his friend leave.

Since the incident with Korto, a girl who once lived in Maila, Wuamah had vowed to never forgive Gotolo. All the young men in Maila wanted Korto, and she would agree to everyone that proposed to her. And just how each man would later discover that she did not admit to having an affair with the other men, and was cheating on him, right away that man would end the relationship. As a result, she was the talk of all the young men and women.

One day there was an argument amongst the young girls about how the men in Maila can behave like dogs; every one of them, knowing that Korto was having an affair with the others, would still make advances at her. Only Wuamah they held in high esteem for being the only man that had paid no attention to Korto.

"Wuamah does not even make advances at women in this town." observed Lela, one of the girls in the group. "I suspect his manhood may not be active."

"Who told you so?!" exclaimed Gotolo, stretching his eyes and cupping his hands around his mouth in astonishment. "My friend has a very active manhood. In fact, it was Korto who showed Wuamah woman business and the two of them are serious lovers."

"Ayy Gotolo," crooned, Laymah, another girl. "How did you get to know that one again?"

"Oh! Look at this girl," Gotolo said and then laughed. "One day I was coming from inspecting my palm wine tree, near the creek before reaching the path that leads down to the river. It was late in the evening when I saw his canoe at the edge. I heard some giggling, and then I recognized Korto's voice. When I looked, I saw a lapper flipped out of the low bush into the air, and then trousers, a blouse, a bra and a T-shirt, and a head tie. Next, I heard 'Yeah, just like that-do it harder, Wuamah'.

After that I heard a loud groan and total silence. So, to make sure it was them, I waited at the road that leads to where Mulbah Tarte used to live and pretended like I was looking for something. Not too long, they walked past me, and I saw the same trousers, and t-shirt on Wuamah and the same lapper and head tie on Korto. I greeted them, but only Korto answered me. Wuamah had his face in the air, pretending like it was just a coincidence to be walking in the same direction with Korto."

The girls laughed upon hearing this as Gotolo continued to explain the many instances he saw them together; Korto had ended all her relationships and was only focused on Wuamah. He also narrated an instance where he once spied on them at a different location in the bush, when after undressing themselves, Wamah asked Korto to get on top of him and ferociously work herself up and down. When she did as he commanded, with her large breasts digging in his face, Wuamah cried out loud with her name.

Gotolo told the group how Korto asked him how come he got such an idea when in fact, he did not know anything about woman business prior to their affair and Wuamah explained how years ago, a woman used to do the same to his uncle, and he wanted to know why his uncle always screamed.

When Wuamah got to know about this, he confronted Gotolo. He tried to explain the reason he did it. The girls were not only saying they held him in high esteem, some of them were questioning his manhood, and he wanted to prove them wrong. Wuamah did not believe him, and he blamed him for not covering his deeds as a friend even if Wuamah did not know Gotolo knew about them. What he expected was Gotolo to tell him what the girls in the town thought about him. For this reason, Korto left the town and had since resided in Salala.

Wuamah made his way to the chief quarter and saw the young chief sitting on a bench in front of his house. He appeared like he was about to go out. Upon seeing Wuamah trekking towards him, he immediately jumped from the bench and ran to him.

"Wuamah," he called, holding his shoulder to prevent him from falling, when Wuamah's feet buckled. "What happened?!" I was just about to go to your house."

"Where is the old chief? We must see your father now?" Wuamah demanded, instead and began to cry.

Very concerned and confused, the young chief knew that he would not get any explanation from his friend, until he saw the old chief. So, he helped Wuamah to walk, bracing him, by holding his shoulders and accompanied him into the chief quarter.

Entering, Chief Peter Lomeh helped Wuamah lie down on a bench and hurried into his father's house. After 30 minutes, he came back outside. Wuamah was now feeling more pain. His head was hurting severely and he began to shiver. He helped him up from the bench and carried him into the old chief's house. They entered and met him lying on his bed. When he noticed that his son and Wuamah had entered the room, he got up.

"Greetings, Chief." Wuamah spoke, as he took his time to sit on a stool opposite the old chief's bed. The old man nodded and became attentive. "We have a serious problem. Sengbeh Gbelema is in the forest of Maila and he is bent on bringing harm to us."

"Why do you think so?" asked the young chief, upon seeing that his father's face had brightened with concern.

Wuamah took his time to narrate his encounter up the cliff as he cringed, telling them about the discovery of human remains of persons he believed to be fighters from the main rebel faction during the civil war, tied to the trees and burned to their skeletons with their rusty guns lying by their feet. He also mentioned the furnace, and the orange-green aches that no one but Sengbeh Gbelema possesses. The old chief remained expressionless when Wuamah had finished.

He looked up into the ceiling for a while and lie back on his bed. But the young chief looked very worried when the thought of J. Boima Barclay Jr. ran in his mind. The day before they spoke on the phone, Barclay confirmed that he's due in Liberia within a month and a half. After the call, Chief Lomeh had to stay in Varney Town for a day because he had to send word by a young man named Varney Yasiah to Koikoi Pewee "Siegie," who, he was told, was somewhere in a village along the Bong Mines-Monrovia rail road where telephone could not reach, of the important message from Hon. Barclay. He had to wait for Yesiah to return with the response from Siegie.

He thought about this for a while, got up and stood by his father's bed side. "Papa," he said, "What can we do about this when your grandson will be here in a few days?"

CHAPTER 5

MONROVIA AT NOON, IN mid 2008. A city, still enmeshed in the aftermath of the drama of the first post-war general and presidential elections, which brought the first female African President to power. It preceded a runoff in the first round, which was participated by more than 20 presidential candidates. Her party came second in the first round, to a new grassroot political party, led by Liberia's only internationally acclaimed soccer accolade.

The period after the final results were announced and up to a week before the inauguration of the new president was very tense. There were sustained agitations and protests by this new grass root political party, which commanded about 61% of the post-war youth, on grounds that having won the first round with a huge margin, it was not possible to lose the runoff, and so the process was fraudulent.

The country again was at a standstill, as uncertainty loomed as to what will happen next, evident by the popularity of the candidate of this new youth base grassroot party, in which a sizable amount were ex-combatants of almost all the warring factions with memories of the brutal civil war still fresh on their minds. What was more threatening was these ex-combatants went through a fairly effective disarmament, demobilization and rehabilitation process, barely two years before the elections.

Moreover, was the size, prowess, and resilience of this grass root party, and the ability of its many executives, which comprised mainly of students and formal students of the state-run university, of which some of them were student militants and leaders with years of cadre training and practices in the advocacies of social justice to organize rallies geared to expressing their disagreement with the results. One such demonstration against the result was a protest march that covered a distance of about 2.5 miles from its headquarters located in the enclave of Congo Town to the United States Embassy, near Monrovia.

The newly elected president herself, a veteran of the advocacies of social justice, was credited for challenging two immediate past presidents, both of whom were military dictators. She was well positioned to counter the claim that there was fraud. Also, her party possessed some of the country's brilliant youth, some of whom with similar state-run university base student militancy and leadership, encrusted with advocacy skills.

Furthermore, to her advantage, was a highly recognized international academic success and her years of working in international circles and the impact she made. As the tension built, the international community, including the United States, the United Nations (UN), the African Union (AU) and the Economic Community of West African states (ECOWAS), out of which ECOMOG was founded to intervene in the civil war, were all on edge, as the two political forces, in their agitations laid claims and counter-claims, as to the results of the run-off election.

What was more at stake was the billions of dollars spent to broker peace and the conduct of the elections that risked becoming a total waste of time, effort and resources, should these agitations slip the country back into another round of the civil conflict.

Fortunately, what led to a sudden zig from an agitation on both sides of equal potential that could have led the country back to the senseless carnage of more deaths and destruction to a mere, but however heated agitations of intellectual clashes with a great degree of effrontery between both supporters, was when the candidate of the new grassroots political party finally accepted the results, which according to the soccer legend, was in the name of peace and agreed to work with the new government, if given the chance.

What was now witnessed, was a display of the brilliance of arguments and counter arguments along the street's corners of Monrovia, which was not until the end of the civil war, was only seen on the state's university campuses. One main area where such intellectualism was displayed, was at what was known as 'Attaya Centers' where these youthful agitators, meanly the unemployed would organize these debates, and soon such centers and the activities thereof, were spread to the other communities in and around Monrovia, and other cities and major towns throughout the country.

Also were the proliferations of the print and electronic media, imbued with the emergence of new youthful political pundits, expressing their views both as radio talk show hosts or guests and newspapers columnists. The entire county through the eyes of what was now taking place in Monrovia, as the new government was gradually establishing itself was the reintroduction of a Governance Economic Management Assistance Program known as GEMAP, comprising of international experts with a broader role to help the new government manage its day-to-day economic activities, the result of which was bringing credibility to the new regime's plan to attract foreign direct investment.

These were the observations of Sam Olu Wilson, a Liberian who had returned from the United States, two years after the new president was inaugurated. He was driving over the Gabriel Tucker Bridge, which is commonly known as the 'New Bridge' that connects

Bushrod Island, an enclave West of Monrovia to the main business district of central Monrovia.

Cruising from Vai Town in his white double cabin Ford pickup truck, a commercial district on the Bushrod Island, and then over the historic Providence Island where the settlers first landed, he was looking down at the historic Montserrado River and at the faces of pedestrians commuting to and from Vai Town, walking on both sides of the bridge. What he could see from the many faces were the mixture of anxiety, hope, disappointment, uncertainty, etc.

His brakes squelched, when he suddenly held them, when two motorcyclists cut in front of him, with one almost ripping off his view mirror on the passenger side. He was a bit disappointed in himself for not yet getting used to driving in post-war Monrovia traffic, almost 7 months since he returned home. The transportation system had changed with the plethora of commercial motor cycles known as 'Pen-pen', ridden by youthful lads without any formal training in traffic rules.

He slowly released the brake paddles and gently accelerated to the vicious blurting of horns at his rear, temporarily halting a huge column of traffic coming from Via Town. He was returning from Brewerville from visiting the Lott Carey Baptist Mission School, his alma mattha. Since his return to the country, he had not visited Lott Carey, as it was commonly called. And when he did, earlier in the morning, he was full of childhood memories.

Driving by the school building, he got a bit confused and was feeling disappointed. At first, he recognized the old school building, in which he sat in classes for many years, from elementary to Senior high, but a new one that was erected next to an old dilapidated building.

Fortunately, he was later able to recognize the dilapidated one to be the old school building, and remembered that it was damaged during the civil war, when a rocket landed into it. To his disgust, what he was looking at was what was left of a school building, which in his view, was the epitome of an unimaginable academic excellence, out of which some of the best brains and high-quality characters were nurtured, was still bearing the scars of a senseless civil war.

For a moment, he cried bitterly over his steering, when he drove around the boys' dormitory, and saw that it was in total ruins. How can a place he always described as the embryo in which the better man in him was nurtured, be in such a state?

Sam and his parents left Liberia for the United States when he was in his early teens at the height of the civil war around the time when the main rebel group overran the city of Kakata, some 72 kilometers north of Monrovia. His father was a senior staff at the American Embassy who worked there for many years. This gave his family the leverage to seek asylum in that country.

He studied environmental science and geology at the University of Connecticut, where he met J. Boima Barclay Jr. who was also studying in similar fields. But before attending the University, he earned an Associate Degree in Criminal Investigation. As both were from the same country, and were the only sons of their parents, they became very close, even up to graduate school. But Sam, a lover of wrestling from his days in Liberia as a kid who never missed wrestling matches shown on ELTV, from the late 70s to the late 80s, soon found his calling in mixed martial arts (MMA). Through his girlfriend, a Brazilian he met in college, whose uncle ran a gym, he signed in and trained for several hours each day and everyone saw that he was going to be a very good mixed martial artist.

After a few years of training and becoming top in a tournament organized by the gym commission of Boston, he was spotted by a man named Jake Debois, a promoter of the sport. Through Debois, he was signed to the State Valley MMA Development in Florida, where he began his developmental activities fighting in the light heavyweight division.

He scored a major achievement when he defeated the American Carlos Greene in the third round, having been dominated in the first two rounds. He also went on to defeat three more dangerous opponents, thus placing him among the top ten spots that earned him the name Sam 'The Black Dragon' Wilson. Almost a year later, he worked his way through this level and landed as the number two contender, which put him face to face with Nicholas Vasquez, the number one contender.

Vasquez was a very dangerous kick boxing champion, and a silver medalist at the Olympics, when he represented his native Dominican Republic. What shocked the entire network of promotions in Florida was when he took less than 3 minutes to decimate Vasquez in the first round by a combination of flying knees and vicious elbow smashes on both sides of his jaw, sending the silver medalist to the floor and remaining there until the referee ruled it a technical knockout.

Sam's next match was to face Daniel Ortiz, the Brazilian Bull, known as the master of all submission moves. Weighting 205lb, he was very effective in Brazilian Jiu Jitsu, Kick-boxing, Muay Thai, and wrestling. Credited with 20 fights, he won all in the first rounds with TKOs while Sam 'The Black Dragon' Wilson, weighing 190 lb, was credited with 15 fights, winning 8 in the first rounds with TKOs, 4 also with TKOs, but in the second rounds and the balance 3 with unanimous decisions at the end of the rounds.

In the last 3 fights, having being dominated and severely beating in the first two rounds, and several times breaking free from his opponents' submission attempts and gaining impressive scores with his vicious elbow smashes and subsequent take downs and ground pounding in the last rounds, he spectacularly made comebacks to win the judges favor. Defeating Ortiz would earn him his debut at the Ultimate Fighting Championship (UFC) which would make him the first Liberian to ascend to that level of MMA.

Sam saw this as a glorious opportunity for him to lift his country's flag in another sport that was rapidly gaining recognition next to professional wrestling in the United States. Liberia at the time was engulfed into a civil war where all the news coming from the country was negative. The only positive one at the time, was that of the soccer legend winning the Would Best, European Best, and African Best soccer player, all at once. As Sam prepared himself for the fight, he drew his mental strength on the accomplishments of his fellow country man. He watched all his soccer matches over and over and listened to his interviews about his rough upbringing and how he made it to the top of his calling.

As he trained harder for the fight, which date had not yet been announced by the Florida Commission on the Sports, he had mastered to counter all the finishing and submission moves of Daniel Ortiz. Watching Ortiz's previous fights, he observed that the Brazilian Bull won his fights with a particular move best suited for the kind of opponents he fought. If his opponent's strength was in kick boxing, Ortiz would deny that opponent from using his legs by inflicting injuries on them through his powerful and effective inside leg kicks.

For a wrestler, he will take you to the ground and apply his most vicious submission move, the Anaconda Neck Choke in which he will wrap his muscular and powerful legs around his opponent's torso at the same time wrapping his arms around the opponent's neck and squeezed them simultaneously until the opponent tapped out or in most times, the opponent would faint before the referee put a halt to the fight. That was the only move Sam anticipated countering, when he discussed this with his trainer.

There were two things to do to counter the onslaught of the Brazilian Bull. The first, which the 'Black Dragon' had mastered was to control the amount of oxygen that would be sucked out of his muscles doing the fight, anticipating that Ortiz will use the advantage of his heavier weight to wrestle him to the ground. This is because, attempting to break free from a take down by a strong opponent, usually requires lots of energy, and when used, all the oxygen is often sucked out of one's muscles which quickly leads to exhaustion against an opponent like Ortiz, in seconds. There will be none left to build the strength needed to break free from the Anaconda Neck Choke.

The next was how to break free from a Neck Choke. And what he and the trainer agreed to do was to practice breaking free from the ferocious coils of a python. An arrangement was made with a man who was licensed by the Wildlife and Fish Service to trap and catch pythons to have Sam train with the animals. But in such a practice, one has to abide by a standing rule, and that is, never attempt to practice with the reptiles alone for one's own safety and the safety of the animals.

Taking into account his weight at 190lb and that of his opponent's 205lb, it was decided that he train with the smaller Burmese python which weighed 200lb with a length of 21 feet.

He would be drenched in pig blood to entice the animal which will coil its body around his, from his feet to his neck, except for his hands with hope for the animal to attempt to squeeze and suffocate him to death. He would then use his hands to break himself free from the coils and the choke of the reptile. Sam was successful with the first trials. Then he moved on to the middle size ones which weigh around 300lb. One afternoon, barely two weeks to the fight after the date was announced, Sam went for his last scheduled training with the animals and met no one. He called his coach and his two trainers but none of them picked up their phones. So, he decided to train with the animal himself, a particular 300lb one he had been training with. But he later realized that it was not the identical one, even though it had similar color patterns like the one he had been training with, when the animal coiled around him, almost strangulating him to death. In the struggle between him and the animal, he managed to get hold of a sharp object lying nearby on the floor, and pierced the animal on its head, and plucked its tiny eyes out before he was able to break himself free from its grip.

When he reported the incident to the animal trapper, Donald Whiteman, the trapper told him that the animal was a 300lb and 23 feet female breeding about 200 eggs in its stomach, and that such ones are extremely aggressive as it had not fed for more than the required days. He said the animal must have been placed there mistakenly by one of his staff.

Whiteman asked him to pray that the Fish and Wildlife commission does not get to hear about this, after he helped the frightened MMA fighter dispose of the dead snake. Later that night, Sam received a call from a woman who identified herself as an animal safety agent from the Fish and Wildlife Commission, who had learned of his actions and threatened to report it to the police, since he had broken the safety rule. But she urged him to talk to someone in the Florida MMA Developmental Board, to find a way forward out of his serious predicament.

The next morning, he met a man at the MMA commission who told him in his face to backoff out of the fight with Ortiz on grounds of medical reasons. But what Sam got to know later from Dubois was that it was a conspiracy by the MMA Florida board, dominated by Latino-Americans, who saw that he was a threat to one of their own, Daniel Ortiz.

Moreover, Sam was from a country that most fans in the MMA barely knew, and that the UFC would be happy with a fighter like Ortiz appearing in the Octagon.

Sam became so frustrated when he realized that it was indeed the work of a syndicate when he tried to call his Brazilian girlfriend who could no longer pick up her phone. She even changed her phone number and her address. For fear that she would press charges for harassment, he abandoned that, left Florida and returned to Boston.

Ortiz went on to fight the Polish immigrant Arnold Sadoski who he destroyed in the second round with an arm bar, dislocating his shoulder. Sam cried as he watched the fight on ESPN. His hope of becoming the first Liberian to fight in the Octagon was squashed. A year and a half later, Dubois informed him about an ongoing investigation by the State Commission on the sports that the Florida MMA commission was involved in match fixing, conspiracy and blackmailing, emanating from a case in the heavyweight Division. It follows when the American of Cameroonian descent, Kelvin 'The Power Puncher' Kabirou was denied competing with Dany Alvarez an American of Latino descent.

It had been discovered that Kabirou at 215lb was going to destroy Alvarez at 225lb with his heavy punches. But 'The Power Puncher' was denied when his medical report revealed that he was unfit to fight thus, allowing the next on the roster, Steve Garrison to fight Alvarez. This resulted in the death of Garrison who was indeed the unfit one. It was now obvious that 'The Black Dragon' was to retain his number one contender spot after the investigation, but such investigation could take almost two and a half years or more.

As the investigation progressed slowly, Sam became anxious. Dubois advised that in order to quell his anxiety he needed to leave the United States. It was then that his friend, Boima Barclay told him about his plans for Liberia, now that the war was over and a democratic election was held and a new government was in place. Sam agreed to a partnership and decided to leave for Liberia ahead of his friend. He had left the New Bridge and turned right on Ashmun street, leaving the communities of Slipway and Crown Hill to his left and later at his rear.

As he soared up Ashmun Street, passing by the old dilapidated E. J. Roy Building, he tried to reconstruct the battle of Crown Hill he learned in school. The settlers were probably positioned up the Hill, overlooking Slipway and Providence Island. With Vai Town to the west, the Vai warriors may have come from that end with hundreds of canoes crossing the Montserrado River charting battle cries. Also, were the Dei who may have paddled to the south of the providence Island for what is present day water street also known as waterside. The Mamba may have used the present day Sinkor belt with one group passing through what is now the Jallah Town Community, while another group of them may have taken the route around what is present day Capitol Hill. The probable motive was to encircle the settlers and push them all the way down to what is now South Beach.

As the battle raged and the settlers now probably cornered, as some of them who may have been staying on the providence Island, and the Sinkor belt were forced to move to what is now central Monrovia, it was then that the old lady saved the day by igniting a cannon with a single drop of the aches from her smoking pipe. He could imagine the warriors, with fear and confusion to the terrible sound of the big gun, abandoning the vicious attack and running away as many of them were dropping dead or wounded.

Sam used to listen to some Intellectuals suggesting that Matilda Newport, the old lady who is believed to have ignited the cannon which dislodged the allied tribes on that fateful day, may not have existed. In fact, some argued that the entire narrative written by H. Doris Banks Henries, a Liberian historian and educator, was a myth. But none of them had written a book outlining the facts as to what really happened on that day.

These thoughts clouded his mind, as he drove past the Centennial Pavilion when his Black Berry suddenly rang.

"Hello," he answered, taking the phone lying by the emergency gear and pressing the ok button at the same time keeping his eyes on the road on the watch out for 'pen-pen' riders.

"Yeah, this is Orlando," a voice sounded through the speakers. "The Broker."

"Oh, year Orlando. I am driving to you now."

"Okay, I will be waiting in front of the Ministry of Commence."

"Okay, but we will be dealing with LBDI Bank now, not EcoBank. Got it?"

"Yes, Papay," Orlando answered at the other end of the line.

"Hey-hey-hey-hey. Don't call me Papay," Sam protested "Just call me Sam, okay?"

"Okay," Orlando responded after a brief silence.

"Okay, bye."

"Bye."

Sam was now driving past College of West Africa (CWA) High School, surprised that there was not much traffic ahead of him while accelerating down the hill. Orlando was the custom broker he contracted to clear all the survey equipment and a small engine propelled boat that Boima Barclay had sent. He will be in Monrovia in a few days and from there, they will go to Bong Mines.

Like his father, Sam did not like to be called 'papay' which is interpreted as a good for nothing old man. In post war Liberia, 'papay' means someone who is older, a boss, and a chief which commands great respect. Sam observed that it is now being used widely for such a connotation. He could not understand why a man, almost his age, or, possibly older than him, can choose to call him 'papay'.

Before reaching the National Fire Service Headquarters, his phone blurted again. He looked and recognized the number and allowed it to ring until he found a place to park, opposite the Ministry of Commence.

"Hello," he spoke into the phone when he pressed the redial button after it stopped ranging.

"Yes. Hello," crooned a voice in a somewhat melodious tone. "This is Valarie; the girl whose phone was jerked yesterday. When I later call my number, you answered and left this number to call you today"

"Yes, I did, because your phone battery ran dead. So, I gave you my number to call me."

"Okay, Thank you very much," Valerie said excitedly. "I highly appreciate it. How can I get it?"

"You tell me where to find you."

"Oh ok. I am presently on the Old Road at 'In-Town Parking Restaurant.'"

"I 'll find that place." Sam assured her.

"Okay. Thanks again," Valerie said. "Just remember to look for the 'In-Town Parking Restaurant' when you get to Old Road—Monrovia Parking Station."

"Okay, Valerie. I am in town during a small run around. So . . . let's say I will be there in two hours. You will need to reset your stopwatch."

Valeria laughed at the end of the line and Sam could see that she trusted that he would return her phone.

It was on Sunday, the day before, while driving from town and had reached Sinkor. He had passed Monrovia City Hall when he saw this girl standing in front what was once Royal Air Maroc Monrovia Office.

She was dressed in an African lapper suit, with a nice head-tie of similar color, standing on the sidewalk holding a small purse in one hand and a little girl also dressed in an African dress in the other hand. Apparently, they were coming from church. With her purse in her hand, she was waving at every taxi cap that passed by, to stop.

She resembled a childhood friend during his days at Lott Carey. So, he was trying to leave the middle lane he was on for the last one to his right, to stop and offer her a lift. Before engaging the lane, he had to slow down to wait for a white Toyota Land Cruiser Jeep he caught from his rear-view mirror.

As soon as the jeep passed by him a 'pen-pen' with the rider and a guy sitting behind, suddenly sped past him on the same lane, and headed straight to the girl. It came too close to her and the little girl like it was going to run them over. She immediately pulled the little girl and skipped backwards. Just In that moment, the other guy at the back jerked her purse and the motorcycle sped off.

Sam immediately followed them, instead of stopping for the girl who had covered her head with both hands shouting, crying and calling for help that her purse was stolen. The guys on the 'pen-pen' sped on and veered right on Cheeseman Avenue on 9th street and headed straight for the beach.

Sam followed them from a distance to avoid being noticed. At some point he slowed down and acted like he was turning on Payne Avenue to head for JFK Medical Center, on the 20th street side, when he sensed that the guys on the bike were trying to see whether they were being followed.

They rode into an opening that looked like a mix-shaped gate and entered the beach. As soon as they were out of sight, Sam quickly accelerated right after them, and later killed his engine so they could not hear the roar of the Eco boost V6. He parked opposite Providence Hotel, got down from his pickup and ran after them, passing through the same mix-shaped gate.

The two guys have parked the motor bike by what was left of the frame of a house taken away by sea erosion. They went walking towards the wave.

The one who jerked the lady's purse was holding it in his right hand. Sam saw that they were young boys probably in their late teens or early twenties. They sat down on a sand dome and looked towards the sea at a man who looked to be in his mid-thirties, walking out of the water after a huge wave brought him to shore. The middle height and muscular man was wearing a back skinned tight Adidas swimming shorts, stopping at his knee.

When he approached the two boys, they immediately stood up to meet him.

"Hey, Papie, Emmanuel," with his eyes fixed on the purse, he greeted them. "Got something for me."

"Yeah, Papay," Emmanuel, the bike rider responded scratching his head nervously "The hustle is hard today. But we managed to jerk a lady's purse."

"Let me have it, quick," frowning, the man demanded.

He horridly unzipped the purse.

Suddenly raising his eyebrows, he hauled out a Nokia 3310. He rummaged inside the purse with his fingers, touching some earrings, a ring, some lipsticks, a few eyebrow pencils and then a paper carefully folded and squeezed at the bottom. He quickly pulled it out, and unfolded the paper, while Papie and Emmanuel watched with eagerness.

Folded with the paper was a US$100 bill, two US$50.00 bills and two hundred Liberian dollars bills.

"So. Is this all you guys brought today?" he asked, struggling to hide the smile on his face.

"Yes, Chief Morris," Emmanuel answered, his voice quivering with nervousness. "The hustle is getting tough now. The people are getting smarter."

"What do you mean?" barked Morris. "You guys need to go back on the hustle or else I will not pay you."

"They won't be doing that again," interrupted Sam, who had been observing them the whole while. "You need to return the phone and the money. They are not yours."

"But who the fuck is this?" Morris alarmed, stretching his eyes on the two boys who looked confused at the same time walking towards Sam. "You led him here?"

"Morris or whatever they call you. You need to hand the purse with all the items inside over to me now," Sam again demanded, also walking towards Morris.

They stood a few yards apart, steering each other in the face on the sunny beach. As Sam stood with his hands folded, Morris pumped himself, causing the muscles around his neck, chest and arms to swell, making him appear bigger, tough and dangerous.

His eyes were roving all over Sam. Then they focused on the thick gold chain around his neck, and the Rolex Oyster Gold plated watch he was wearing, when they glittered in his face due to the reflection from the sun. He took a step closer to Sam, his eyes sparkling with the luster of this golden opportunity that has easily presented itself. Now running through his head was to subdue the guy, and seize the valuables, glittering in his face.

"Give me the Rolex and the gold chain around your neck now," he demanded, and then looked to Emmanuel and Papie and instructed,

"Dig out the cutlasses buried in the sand right before you and let's naked this stupid fool."

"I mean now," he shouted, stretching the veins on his neck and further pumping his muscles, when the two boys hesitated.

Emmanuel remained motionless, but Papie immediately dug the nose of the old tennis shores he was wearing in the sand in search of where the cutlasses were buried and when he felt them with the tip of his shoe, he scooped and pulled out one. He walked to Sam pointing the cutlass at him at the same time gesturing with a body language that it was best for Sam to not have followed them.

The mixed-martial artist took a few steps backwards, inching closer to the edge where the ocean waves landed and soaked the sand. Papie hurried to him, raising the cutlass in the air with one hand, while he demanded Sam to hand over the chain and the watch with his free hand, at the same time threatening to chop him, if he refuses.

As he got closer, Sam was digging the nose of his dark brown suede loafers he was wearing in the soaked sand.

"Oh! My eyes!" Suddenly, Papie screamed to the burn of the salt water mixed with wet sand, when Sam kicked the heavily soaked sand in his eyes.

In a very swift move, Sam swept Papie's two legs from under him and he went crushing to the wet ground. Papie yelled again, this time screaming when Sam stepped closed to the palm of the hand still firmly holding the cutlass. He then scooped over, grabbed his thumb and index finger and twisted them like he was going to break them. This forced Papie to let go of it.

Sam took hold of the cutlass and slapped the flat part on Papie's back.

"Oh! My People! My back!" thinking that Sam had chopped his back, Papie cried out loud, his voice reverberating above the sound of the wave descending on the beach.

He stretched and became stiff like a kid who is about to be given an injection. But he quickly sprang to his feet and ran with full speed after Sam kicked him in his buttocks and asked him to leave.

"Now Morris. This is your last chance. Hand me the purse," he said, now facing the muscular man.

Morris also stood in readiness at the same time calculating what best to do to incapacitate the guy standing before him, now that he has realized he may be a black belt holder, which was not a big deal after all.

Recently, he had decisively beaten a black belt holder at Samuel Kanyon Doe Sport Complex on a Saturday morning where students of the Liberian Martial Arts Federation have their classes. One of the Karate instructors spotted him with a set of master keys trying to force open the driver's door of a White Nissan Altima that belonged to the mother of one of the students. Kona Blackie, a two-den holder had sneaked behind him, tapped the auto thief on his shoulders and as soon as he jerked and turned, he was collared.

In the ensuing tussle, Morris gave Blackie a nasty head butt that instantly sent the Karate instructor to the ground, unconscious.

Now figuring out what to do, Morris charged at Sam, in an attempt to grab him by his rib cage, squeeze it, and give him a nasty head butt on his temple which would cause him to stagger and lose balance and then he would wrestle him to the ground. And while on top of Sam, he would bloody his face with some vicious punches.

On the contrary, he instead cried out loud, when Sam first landed an inside leg kick on the side of his left knee with the impact spreading his legs, forcing him to wobble. This gave Sam the opportunity to drive a low flying knee in his testes. In no time Morris received another powerful leg kick on the left side of his face when he had scooped, holding his genitals. The leg kick sent him to the ground, as blood ran from the left side of his mouth and nose.

"You made a mistake, Morris, by depending on your muscles," teased Sam, when Morris made an attempt to get up, but staggered and fell back to the ground just in time a wave landed and rolled over him. He managed to struggle to get on his knees, coughing out blood when some of the salt water entered his mouth.

"You were stupid to think that I would have followed your boys here without knowing how to defend myself," Sam said, shaking his head and walking pass him.

He looked at Emmanuel who had taken the purse from the ground when Morris dropped it. As Sam approached him, he threw it at his feet and attempted to run away, but Sam told him to stop.

"I don't want to go to jail," pleaded Emmanuel. "Morris always forced us to steal from people."

"I know." Same agreed. "I am sure he won't bother you guys again. Come follow me with your bike. Don't be afraid."

Brushing that incidence off his mind, Sam looked ahead of him and saw Orlando, the customs broker crossing the road from the First United Methodist Church side, but it appeared like he did not see his ford pick-up truck, so, he put down the windshield on the driver's side and blew his horn, at the same time waving his hand to call his attention. He continued and it seemed the broker did not notice this. Becoming embarrassed to the constant blurting of his horn, a habit not common in the United States, he jumped out of the car, slammed the door and went running after Orlando.

"Hey Orlando. Here I am," Sam called. "You don't know my car again?"

"Sorry," the broker apologized, as he approached Sam, extending his hands for a handshake. "It'd been two weeks since we last met and it was at night."

Both men shook hands, and then they walked back to the Ford pick-up truck. While sitting in the car, Orlando took out a set of documents from his backpack and showed them to Sam. He received them and began flipping through the pages.

"These are the IPDs," Orlando informed him. "The Input Permit Declarations. So, your partner must make sure that all the items he listed in the parking list you give me the other day must match the items in the container, or else we will pay a huge penalty for false declaration."

"Yes, he is aware. So, what we will do now is to go to LBDI to open an account there."

"Why did you switch to LBDI?"

"Because we want to promote our own Liberian bank. So, he will be transferring our money into the account we will open."

"Okay. From here I am taking the IPDs to the Ministry of Finance customs department for assessment so we can know the total duty to pay."

"And, as you told me the other day, we will need a Manager's Cheque to pay the duty fee at the Central Bank of Liberia?"

"Yes," Orlando said. "Since your partner will be transferring the money at LBDI, we can obtain one form there."

"Okay. Just accompany me to go and open the account now. Then you can go to the Ministry of Finance. Time is not in our favor."

"Okay," Orlando agreed. "But if we are going to open the account today, we will need at least two passport size pictures of yours".

"Well. I don't have them."

"Some guys under Education Ministry can take passport size pictures."

After taking and receiving the passport size pictures, Sam and Orlando went to the bank and spent close to 30 minutes to complete the process to open an account. Both of them left the bank together, and parted ways.

Now Sam, looking left and right, was crossing Randall and Ashmun Streets intersection, on foot, heading back to his Ford Pick-up truck. His next stop was to see Valerie on Sinkor Old Road. Not very long, he was driving up Ashmun Street towards Global Bank. Passing the Bank, he soared further up, until he reached Cathedral High School and turned left and later drove past UBA Bank and crossed upper Broad Street at the Sacred Heart Cathedral, joining Robert's Street briefly, before turning left on Carey Street.

He continued, descending Carey Street at the back of Trinity Cathedral, crossing Newport Street intersection. He passed by the back of the Ministry of Finance, crossed the intersection of Mechlin and Carey Streets, and slowed down opposite the National Civil Service Agency, due to heavy traffic. While waiting for the traffic to ease, he looked across the road at an Attaya spot on the sidewalk to his left. There were groups of young men gathered and were in a heated debate. He listened keenly and tried to get a gist of what was the center of discussion. As usual, it was a general street debate pertaining to the state of the economy in post-election Liberia and the new government's ability to deliver to the Liberia people.

He also listened to some of the young men vehemently debunking the others who claimed that the new government will deliver. The argument was heated with one group accusing the new government of corruption, nepotism, and cronyism, while the other group denounced the allegations and defended the government's Poverty Reduction Strategy, claiming it is the best that no government in the past 150 years has delivered. Sam listened with amusement. Before the war, this could not happen.

He could remember quite well when the main rebel group had overrun Kakata in 1990, when they had returned to campus, after Easter break. The Lott Carey administration had asked all parents whose kids were boarding students to to come and get them home due to the growing escalation of the war. With normal academic activities disrupted, Sam and a friend usually visited Roxy Cinema on Broad Street to play Nintendo.

One day, while trying to find their way back home, it was unusually difficult to get a taxi for Garnerville where he lived. It was about 2pm and a 6pm curfew imposed by the government was in place. He and his friend decided to walk to Vai Town by way of the new bridge, hoping to get a taxi or a bus to take them to Garnerville.

The streets of central Monrovia looked very tense. People were hurrying from one part of downtown Monrovia to another. They were at Broad and Johnson Streets intersection and were about to turn left to head down the bridge when they saw a huge group of people matching down Crown Hill.

"Monkey, monkey come down," they chanted a popular anti-government slogan, meaning that the president, who they were referring to as a monkey, must step down.

The large crowd had reached Eurobank, the glass building when shots were fired. The crowd dispersed and people started running heather scatter. Sam could see waves of people sliding and rolling down Slipway, while some were hit by vehicles trying to get away.

He and his friend also started running down to the bridge. It was crowded with people and lined up with vehicles stuck in the traffic, including what was known as the old bridge that connected Waterside and Vai Town. Some of the people were jumping out of cars and running.

Just before reaching the bridge at the right side of the sidewalk, a group of people, running down from Johnson Street were getting out of the way when a white 33 seater Coaster bus, jammed packed with passengers, screaming, when the brakes gave up. It went speeding down, hitting cars and some pedestrians along the way.

To avoid hitting more cars, the driver managed to maneuver to his right. The front right and back tires climbed on the sidewalk to the screams of pedestrians as they rolled over their feet. The driver was dodging some steel poles that hoisted billboards, almost flipping the bus over, when the front right and back tires lifted in the air.

A lady with a baby managed to jump through the back-seat window, but was dragged down, towards the slipway field. Sam could hear the baby crying. Three other persons forced their way past the car boy and jumped through the bus's sliding glass door, seriously injuring themselves, when they landed on the ground. One of them was trampled on by a wave of people running behind the bus.

As it headed towards the Slipway field intersection where a large group was running and forcing their way into the sidewalk of the bridge, the driver dodged them to avoid a heavy human casualty and went zig-zagging his way right into the river. Sam saw a group of people running after the bus and jumping into the water to rescue the people trapped inside.

By now he and his friend were at the middle of the bridge, forcing their way forward among the huge crowd. Luckily for them, they were able to reach home safely by walking all the way to Chocolate City, an enclave of Garnersville. He later learned from a neighbor friend of his mother that the crowd had gathered to protest against the government, when it was reported that the independent rebel faction had attacked Mount Coffee Hydroelectric Dam at White plains, about 6 kilometers northwest of Monrovia, and there were fierce battle between the rebels and government forces.

The next day, there was an explosion and the county's power and water supplies were shutdown. Sam's parents were briefly relocated at Mamba Point near the United States Embassy where they stayed for a week before they left the country by way of the Roberts International Airport, about 69 km, east of Monrovia. Few months later, the airport was attacked.

The traffic had eased a bit and as he was driving slowly, he looked through the window to his right, and witnessed another heated debate on the Civil Service Agency (CSA) Building side, while everyone else, including police officers and uniformed security personnel were moving about on their normal businesses. He told himself that the country has changed. People were expressing themselves without fear of retribution.

He ruled out the notion that this was only because of the presence of 10 thousand United Nation peace keeping soldiers and police in that, by the time they shall have left, the aura of free speech and freedom of expression would be well grounded and would continue.

What he envisioned and worried about was that this could have an adverse infect in the long run; with the pace in which these civil liberties were moving, subsequent governments will have to grapple with the fact that it is the new culture of the day, and it would be very difficult to control, even within the ambit of the law. He foresaw that exercising these civil liberties would lead to constant protests, which could scare investors away and stall much needed reconstruction and development.

By way of Camp Johnson Road, Sam had left central Monrovia and had passed the Executive Mansion. It was his second time driving past the Mansion since he returned home. As a kid, he was always overwhelmed with a strange fear whenever he passed by it. This was because he listened to lots of stories of rituals performed in the mansion. Now as an adult, he was surprised that that strange fear was still there, but not like the way it used to be when he was a kid, believing that some of these stories were not true.

In about 20 minutes, due to small traffic, he had reached the old road junction, now referred to as the president's junction. He turned left and accelerated all the way up to the elbow before turning right and passed by the old Grassroot Cinema, putting the commercial hub of Old Road Joe Bar Market ahead of him.

It took a little time to reach Old Road-Monrovia packing station due to occasional traffic. Taxis were lined up on both sides of the road waiting to get full. It was after mid-day and the habitual traffic congestion at such time of the day, has soared. A long queue of private vehicles, yellow taxis caps and other private cars, which were used as commercial cars were coming from Monrovia. The ones that were transiting through Old Road for ELWA Junction or Paynesville

Red-light, or vice versa, were depositing and picking up commuters who scrambled for to hop in. Car Loaders, mainly unemployed men, announced the destinations in sometimes melodious tone, offering, in many cases the unwanted service of finding and helping passengers to board the taxis.

Pen-pens sped up and down the road, with some branching off Gaye Town Road, with sometimes up to three persons, some of whom are pupils, sitting behind the moto bike rider. Schools have just ended for the day, and Joe Bar Market was emblazoned with the uniforms of the different schools in the area, with Haywood Mission, Open Bible and Christ the King Catholic School the most.

Sam found a place and parked. He got out of the car, swung his computer bag across his shoulders and went strolling towards a chain of buildings on his left, looking for the one with the 'In town Parking Restaurant' painted at the front.

As Sam made his way between the parked vehicles and the front of the chain of buildings comprising mainly small shops, looking for 'Intown Parking Restaurant' he could see money exchangers with huge quantiles of Liberian dollars in all denominations neatly arranged and placed on small box-like tables or booths, used as their forex bureau.

He remembered the two times Boima visited Liberia, he told him how he was trailed to see money exchangers displaying these mountains of local currencies and was fascinated that all the time he stayed in the country, he never heard they were arm rubbed, given the fact that the country was awash with hidden arms. Across the road were fruit peddlers selling in front of Shanzu Supermarket as customers trooped in and out. Sam found the place and entered.

It was a small restaurant and a bar with varieties of drinks on the shelf. A big freezer was at the back of the counter that made up the bar. The tables were neatly arranged with the chairs and were beautifully decorated. There were fans up the ceiling and the wall was painted with a nice strawberry red paint and bedecked with beautifully carved dark brown African sculptures.

The restaurant was half full of customers, sitting, eating and drinking as background music echoed through some speakers and tutors at the corners of the wall. Sam looked around him to find a vacant table, and saw one at the back, where he noticed an air condition hinging on the wall, functioning. He headed straight for it and took his seat.

"Good afternoon," a polite and soft-spoken voice drew his attention when he had settled down and was unzipping his computer bag. "Are you ordering?"

"Valarie?" he asked, instead, lifting his head and looking in the face that bore so much resemblance to his former school mate.

"Yes," she responded politely, struggling to hide her concern.

"I am Sam. I brought your purse," he said smiling and reached into his computer bag, took out the purse and handed it over to her.

"Oh! You the Sam Guy?" she exclaimed with an uncontrollable laughter, covering her face briefly with her hands. Taking the purse from Sam, she continued in the same mood. "But you said to be here in two hours."

"Sorry I lied. I didn't want you to think that I was fooling around." Sam said, looking Valarie in the face as she stood over him and did not know what to say.

"I . . . I don't know how to thank you," she managed to say.

"Yeah, but you might want to check whether everything is inside."

"Okay," Valarie agreed, taking a seat next to him and looking into the purse.

"Actually, I don't know how to appreciate you," she said, after examining her purse and was satisfied that all her items including cash were inside. "You are a nice man, and looked like you are not based here in Liberia."

"Yes. You are correct, but thanks. I am here now."

"How did you get it from those useless thieves?"

"I was just lucky," he sighed. "I was driving from town when I saw you and the little girl standing on the road looking very tired and trying to catch a taxi cap. You looked like someone I know and so I decided to stop for you. Just then, the guys on the motorbike sped past me and jerked your purse and so I sped after them and got it back."

"And you have to go through all that?"

"Yeah, I hated seeing a pretty girl like you distressed."

"You really mean that?" Valarie asked, laughing. And then looked back at the counter. "Let me offer you something to drink. And if you won't mind, I prepared you something to eat."

He agreed to having only water, but she insisted on preparing something for him. He asked for the menu. Valarie looked around and saw one on a vacant table, went for it and brought it to him. Sam took it and read the list of food and drinks, but he did not see the kind of dish he would like to eat.

As a mixed martial artist, he takes his diet very seriously, especially when keeping himself fit. When he was training for the match with Daniel Ortiz, he had managed to control the amount of oxygen leaving his muscles by eating certain kinds of food. When he returned to Liberia, he made sure he ate a lot of vegetables with fish and some meat and very little rice as a supplement to the diet he ate back in the states.

"I don't see anything in your menu that's good for my health, Valarie," he said, trying to be apologetic.

"What do you eat?" she asked, feeling a bit disappointed. "Feel free to tell me so I can prepare a nice dish for you."

"Vegetables with fish or meat," he told her, after hesitating.

"Are you diabetic?"

"No. But I try not to be."

He made a list of things to buy and handed it to her. He wanted to pay for it but she refused. She will pay for them and insisted when he did not agree to that. After what looked like a jovial argument with lots of laughter, he finally gave in and waited at the table, doing some work on his lab tap.

Valarie went to get the things. She came back with a woman and introduced her to Sam.

"Veronica Sackor," she said. "Valerie's big sister. Thanks for getting back her stolen purse."

"Nice to meet you. And thank God I was right on the spot when her pursed was jerked."

"Nowadays, it's hard to find such kindness in Liberia. The war has destroyed everything. You look like you are just returning back home, right?"

"Yeah, I am back home on business, and I am waiting for my partner, Boima, who will be returning to Liberia soon."

They both talked as Veronica asked more questions which he did not hesitate to answer, though he did not provide details for some of them. Valarie had gone to the kitchen through a glass panel door next to the counter to prepare the dish for Sam.

More people were entering the restaurant and placing their orders while other customers were eating and drinking, amidst the clattering of spoons, folks and plates. The tempo of the background music had changed when some songs of the mid-eighties filtered through the speakers. Two customers, a girl and her friend who had just entered and placed their orders, suddenly chirped in a nostalgic mood as the music, 'Girl You Know It's True' by Mili Venlili played.

Veronica and Sam were lost in their conversation when Valarie interrupted them by announcing that the dish she had prepared for him was ready. He nodded appreciatively, as she sat the plates on the table. She turned to leave but her sister told her to sit by Sam, instead. When Valarie took her seat opposite Sam, Veronica left for the kitchen.

"Humm. Tastes good," Sam said as Valarie watched him eating. "Guess What? I have found a new place to eat. I will bring my partner Boima here when he comes."

"That will be nice," Valarie responded. "Sometimes if you don't have the chance to come, you can send someone for your food."

"That will be a good idea."

They continued conversing for some time while Sam ate. The background music continued to play some R&B oldies and goodies. Raymond Usher's 'You Get It Back' crooned through the speakers and was influencing the way the conversation was going.

"The girl who was standing by me when my purse was jerked is my 6 years old daughter, Promise," she told Sam, surprised that she was a bit open, since her last relationship ended in disaster.

"Where's her father?" he asked, and waited for her response, before helping himself with a slice of fresh tomato with his folk.

Seeing how he suddenly became attentive, Valerie smiled.

"Well. I don't know. The last time I heard, he was in South Korea, playing football."

"Sorry to hear that," he said and then continued with the fresh tomato and more.

Valerie laughed when Sam made a face to suggest that it was the answer he wanted to hear.

She met promise father when he came to Liberia during the period of the many interim governments. He told her he was playing soccer somewhere in Asia and was back home on vacation. She was little and inexperienced and thought he was the best person in her life.

Valerie was 10 years old when the civil war started. Her father, Gabriel Sackor was a high-ranking government official and a staunch supporter of the President at the time of the conflict. He was part of a government delegation that was sent to Abuja, Nigeria to attend a peace dialogue organized by the then Nigerian president, who was trying to mediate between the main rebel group and the Liberia government.

But he was amongst the few who had to return back to Liberia to his wife and two daughters, Veronica who was 18 and Valarie, when most members of the delegation remained. By the time he returned, all the roads out of Monrovia were blocked as the fighting between rebel fighters and government forces inched closer to the city.

When Mount Barclay, approximately 24 km outside of Monrovia was attacked by rebels, which resulted into heavy fighting for days as the government forces were making efforts to repel the attack, Gabriel Sackor received word that the president had asked him to relocate his family to the old Budget Bureau community, near the executive mansion.

One morning when the fighting had gotten closer to the Omega Tower community, in the city of Paynesville, a group of government soldiers in a convoy of three military jeeps sped into their yard. The head of the group, 2nd Lt. Anthony Geeplay, informed Mr. Sackor that the president had sent for him and his family. They were quickly bundled in one of the vehicles, leaving behind their belongings they were trying to gather, when a young Corporal interrupted Mr. Sackor and 2nd Lt. Geeplay who were standing on the side having a conversation, informing them that the communication exchanges from is walkie talkie suggested that the situation around the Paynesville City belt was becoming more fluid and that they should leave immediately.

While approaching Duport Road Junction, the convoy was ambushed by unknown men, with some of them wearing military uniforms. All the soldiers in the convoy were killed, but the Sackors miraculously survived and ran all the way back to Police Academy Junction. They met a group of civilians coming from the Paynesville Red light area toting their belongings. Mr. Sackor informed the group that they were ambushed at the Duport Road Junction by unknown men when he was asked why they were returning from that direction.

A man in the group from Paynesville Red-light who identified himself as an intelligence officer advised that they should take the road passing through the Police Academy to connect to SKD Boulevard to the west and then turn left and head towards Tubman Boulevard which will put them directly behind government forces defensive lines, he learned that had been established at ELWA Junction.

Everyone in the group agreed, including the Sackors, and so they took that route. Approaching the Police Academy, Mr. Sackor called his family together and whispered to them that he will be walking far ahead of them because too many people were recognizing him and should in case he fell in the wrong hands, they would not be caught together-no one knows who was who. So, the girls walked alongside their mother while he walked ahead.

The group walked for about 45 minutes until they got to the end of the road. Ahead of them, was a mangrove swamp that separated the end of the road from SKD boulevard. They met three young boys coming from the swamp with fishing lines attached to bamboo sticks hanging on their shoulders like rifles. They were holding in their hands some sizable cold-water fish attached together by a vine that ran through their gills.

The boys, demanding ransom, offered to show them the safest way to cross, and get to the SKD Boulevard side. When a bargain was made, including buying their fish, the group was led into the swamp by a trail that zig-zag its way into the mangrove.

Valerie recounted how small crabs ran into their holes and into the water when they reached the edge. She could also hear splashes in the water when they were led into the swamp, taking careful steps walking through thick mud and sometimes hard ground. She became afraid when she overheard a man saying that the splashes were crocodiles dashing into the water.

They continued walking through the water for some time. At one point the level reached chest high for the men, women and children at average height. Some men were compelled to carry their children on their shoulders. They finally managed to cross to the SKD Boulevard side. There, Valarie saw her father from the distance waiting, and checking to make sure that they had crossed safely.

The group rested along the side of the laterite road for some time, before moving towards Tubman Boulevard. Out of a sudden, everyone became alert and began to run, when there were gunshots and explosions from their rear. A large group of people with some soldiers among them came running from the direction of 72nd, saying that the barracks there were under attack. Valarie, Veronica and their mother ran along with the large group, all the way to the SKD Boulevard junction.

They met a large group of government troops, screening the people. But they could not find their father. Feeling relieved that they were in government-controlled areas, the two girls were looking for him among the group of people. Again, there was a barrage of rocket fire, this time from the direction of ELWA Junction and shells were landing all over the place causing everyone to run heather scatter, again.

Valerie and Veronica were running back to their mother when someone stepped on one of the rubber slippers she was wearing, causing her to stumble and fall. She couldn't remember how long she remained on the ground, but managed to get back on her feet, very lucky that she did not experience much stampede. She continued to run to where she remembered they left their mother, but she did not find her mother and Veronica.

The rockets were raining down and government soldiers were docking for cover. Men, women, and children were running in all directions and many of them were dropping to the ground with some of them remaining there, injured and groaning. Valarie stood, looking around crying for her mother and sister.

She was suddenly whisked by a young girl who looked to be in her mid-teens who she recognized to be a neighbor named Agnes. They managed to cross the road and ran up the hill towards the TB Annex building and made their way all the way to Bishop Michael Francis Road at the back of the annex and remained at Kpelle Town Community.

They stayed there for a month as government forces tried to prevent the main rebel forces from capturing ELWA Junction. After some time, they were rescued by some government soldiers when the rebels were beaten back. Agnes and Valarie were then taken to Central Monrovia and every effort to locate her sister and mother was futile.

When Valarie asked whether Agnes saw her father, she told her that she witnessed how some soldiers from the group that ran from 72nd Barracks recognized him and were trying to look for her mother and Veronica, but in that moment every one scattered and went in separate directions when a rocket landed. She said she saw him and the soldiers running after some civilians who were running towards 72nd, trying to warn the group that that area was not safe. Her father was running far ahead of the soldiers, calling after his wife, thinking that she and his daughters were also part of the group.

Agnes and Valarie remained in Monrovia through the first phase of the civil war until the coming of ECOMOG. They later moved on the Old Road, after the death of the president for fear of retribution by his supporters who were threatening to burn down the capital city.

On the Old Road, they met a former neighbor, a man named John Dayugar who was part of a Smythe Road Community team organizing the distribution of relief services from the Red Cross. Dayugar told them that he saw Veronica and her mother bundled onboard a ship that was heading for Lagos. He described how her mother said she was not leaving until Valarie was found. He saw how she fainted while protesting hysterically that she was not going to leave her young daughter behind, and that will only happen when she is convinced that her daughter had died.

That same day, there was heavy fighting around the Freeport of Monrovia between the government forces, the main rebel group and the independent rebel faction. Bullets, rockets, and missiles were flying all over. An Army officer who knew her husband was urging Mrs. Sackor to leave, promising to locate Valarie. She only agreed to board the ship when a man recognized her and told her that Valarie was safe and how he saw her and Agnes running towards the TB Annex, the day SKD Boulevard was attacked and later remembered seeing them in central Monrovia.

The next couple of years Agnes and Valarie continued to live together on the Old Road, making their living by barbecuing in front of an entertainment center at the Old Road Joe Bar Market. When the first interim government was formed and some level of calm and normalcy were restored in Monrovia, the two girls enrolled at the Haywood Mission School, following the re-opening of schools. Valarie enrolled in the 8th grade while Agnes, in the 12th grade.

She was 16 in the 11th grade when she met Jeremy Doe, Promise's father. She got to know him through Anthony Keselle, a schoolmate and close friend who was commonly called 'Kerzo'. With both Kerzo's and Agnes urging, Valarie agreed to a relationship with Jeremy Doe.

The Asia based Liberian footballer was a great help to her as the relationship progressed. He paid her tuition fees and took care of her other expenses. To the dislike of Agnes, who thought that she was still in high school, she moved in with Jeremy Doe at an apartment he rented somewhere in Gaye Town, Old Road. While they were together, Jeremy Doe returned to base and came back once. Valarie was just promoted to the 12th grade when she got pregnant, and at the same time Jeremy Doe was returning back to South Korea.

Before leaving, he left her with some money to take care of herself and the unborn child, and that was the last time she saw him.

Things soon became tough when the money ran out. Rent was overdue and the landlady was frequently knocking on her door. Unlike the first time he left, it was difficult to hear from Jeremy Doe. All the numbers he left with her either rang endlessly or were not operational, whenever she called. When the time was approaching to have the baby, with Kezo's urging, she moved back to Agnes.

Valerie explained how in the midst of all the challenges, Promise was born. With Agnes and sometimes Kezo's help, she struggled to take care of the baby. She however managed to complete high school, including taking the West African Examination Council (WAEC) and passed.

Promise was three years old when she met Victor Karr, a warehouse manager for an international NGO. He was looking for an apartment to rent on the Old Road when someone recommended 'Kezo', who would help find one with ease but with a commission. Kerzo made a living by helping to find apartments for people.

Victor Karr had gone to look for him at Agnes' and Valarie's apartment when he met both of them. Kezo helped him to find the kind of apartment he wanted and Victor was impressed. Soon Victor and Valarie started having a conversation and then they fell into a relationship.

Kerzo inwardly did not like this as Victor Karr was very aggressive and jealous. He used his huge and imposing physique to intimidate others. Moreover, he drank heavily and when drunk, he discussed his past relationships and all the women he had slept with in the open. Because he made a little extra cash for the job he did, he had respect for no one.

Also, because he did not complete high school and was making money, he scorned those who were struggling in college. To him it was a waste of time to go through the odorous journey from elementary, through Junior high, high school and college, just to earn a decent living while he did not need to go through all of that. Since he was taking good care of Valarie and Promise, Kerzo did not make his dissatisfaction known to her and Agnes.

Valarie narrated how the relationship started smoothly. Victor Karr, with all the aggression, seemed nice after all. He bought her a taxi to help with food and her other expenses. He even sent her to learn computer science at a nearby computer school, which she was reluctant to attend because her focus was attending the University of Liberia. But he managed to convince her that it will enable her to get a job faster, and start to earn money on her own and then, if she still wants, she can go to college.

In these times, all of Valerie's beautiful features gradually appeared; her fair complexion shone, her hair became brownish gold like her mothers', Victoria Dumbar Sackor. Her face became round and charming. With a height of 5 feet 11 inches, her body formed a perfect and enticing curve and soon her friends started calling her Miss Liberia, including Kerzo who always joked that if she had not had Promise, she could have contested and possibly won the prestigious Miss Liberia beauty pageant.

Promise was 4 years and was attending a preparatory school at Old Road Grass Root Cinema Community. Sometimes when the taxi was in the garage undergoing repairs, Valarie would walk Promise on the road to find a taxi to take her to school. Most times, she was offered a lift by men who wanted to be-friend her.

One strange thing about Victor was, he did not allow Valerie to live with him. He only sent for her and Promise on weekends, more especially when he was in town as most of his work was in the counties. Most of the men that befriended Valarie always visited her against her will. She always informed them that she was in a serious relationship, but they did not listen. It was then that Victor Karr started getting jealous and inferior when told by friends that most of the men after Valarie were mostly educated and working in government or were from the United States.

He became uneasy and more aggressive and at times involved into fist fights with some of these men. He even started accusing her falsely for cheating on him and at times beating on her. As he felt more insecure, he would make love to her anyhow, and whenever he was drunk and angry, he would discuss it with his friends in the open. He would talk about how he had spent his money on her and he would make sure to get all of it out of her to the extent that if she chooses to leave him, no other man will enjoy her.

Othello Gbah, Uriah Gaye and Alvin Choloplay were three of his friends he hung out with, whenever he was in town. Uriah, who lived not far from Valarie, would give him details of all her activities while he was away. Then, they would strode to her yard, and Victor Karr would send for drinks and they would drink, talk, tell jokes and laugh.

And when he had gotten intoxicated, he would boast of his job, his money and the size of his penis and that no other man would be able to satisfy Valarie besides him. There would be lighters and other drunken talks about the women he slept with at his job site, most especially the white women.

Sometimes he and Agnes would fuss. He once shoved and swung Kerzo to the ground for trying to prevent him from beating on Valerie, when he learned of a frequent visit of an elderly man called Mr. Edwards. Mr. Edwards had told Valerie that he knew her father and for that reason, he always stopped by to see how she and her daughter were doing.

Valerie later noticed that Mr. Edward suddenly stopped visiting. She met him once, driving towards Chugbor Community, west of Gaye Town, while she and Promise were returning from visiting a friend around Eleven Rollers Football Field. She waved him to stop and when he did, she asked why he stopped visiting her.

Mr. Edwards looked at her and Promise for a while, shook his head, and invited them in his car. After parking on the side of the road, and struggling to concealed his anger and disappointment, he explained how Victor visited him at his office and explained how she was of no use, and if he, Mr. Edwards was thinking about a relationship, he was going to regret it because no man can satisfy her-only him.

Tears rolled down her eyes as Mr. Edwards recounted, sometimes with traces of jealousy in his tone, all what Victor told him about her including how he was the first person to sodomize her.

Valarie was angry and at the same time surprised. She had thought that Mr. Edwards, who she saw as a father would have come to her and give her some advice, but he chose to stay away from her only because he was jealous and thinking of having a relationship with her. She wiped her tears, thanked him for all the things he had been doing for her, but encouraged him to continue to stay away from her;

she was of no use to him, since he did not pity her situation, but was rather disappointed with her because he had intentions and Victor had told him about his sexual exploits with her.

From that day, she vowed to end the relationship with Victor. He at first took it to be a joke and boasted to his friends that she would come back begging him after a week and that her punishment would be to give him a blow job three times a day for an entire weekend.

But Valerie was determined. Three weeks have passed. She was managing with the small money she kept into an account Kerzo advised and pressured her to open at First International Bank (FIB). She did not bother when Victor came for the now aging taxi, thinking that it would compel her to run back to beg him.

Fortunately, Agnes, played the American Diversity Visa (DV) and won and eventually traveled to the United States. After some time, she started sending small support to her friend and Promise. Through a friend, Valerie found a church and became a dedicated member, promising herself that the next time she falls into any relationship is the time she is about to get married.

A year later, she had just finished her evening prayers in her room, and just as she came on her porch, a jeep sped into the yard and stopped. Getting out was her sister Veronica who she immediately recognized. The two sisters, who had not seen each other for about 16 years, ran and hugged, crying in each other's arms, bitterly. They cried about everything. Their father who had not been seen since the war, and their mother who was in Lagos and refused to come to Liberia, blaming the Liberian people for killing her husband.

That night she and Veronica talked a lot. She introduced Promise to her aunty. Later, Kerzo came and he was also introduced. Valerie called Agnes and was able to get her. Veronica, who also remembered her before the war, thanked her a lot for her sister. She stayed with Valerie for two weeks and returned to Lagos, promising to return in a years' time and take her and Promise to see their mother.

Veronica did exactly when Valarie and Promise visited Lagos. Victoria Dumbar Sackor was happy to see her daughter and granddaughter. To Valerie, her mother looked the same, except for small wrinkles on her face, suggesting that she was aging. But she was happy to see her mother. She stayed in Lagos for some time and returned to Liberia because she did not really like the place.

Few months after her return, Victor Karr started visiting her. He was surprised to see that she and promise were doing good. With the help of her mother and Veronica, she opened a small shop, selling women's hair and cosmetics from Nigeria. Later, Agnes started sending barrels from the United States also full of cosmetics.

"I have realized my mistakes, Valerie, for the way I treated you," he told her. "I missed you a whole lot, and I want us to get back together again."

"Well," breathed Valerie, not surprised when he apologized to her. "I accept your apologies, but I am not thinking about having any relationship now. I am focusing on my spiritual life. I have a business to run, and at the same time concentrating on my remainder in mathematics at the University of Liberia, this coming semester."

"Valarie," Victor said, his voice quivering with an urgent plea. "I realized that I have been very foolish. I wasted my money on liquor and women. But now I am building my own house somewhere on the Roberts Field Highway. I can put it in your name and if you like you and Promise can move in. I promise that all will be ok. I am a changed man now. Trust me."

"That's very nice of you, Victor. But the day I fall into a relationship with anybody again, it will be the person I will marry. And it cannot be you. We can be friends and you are welcomed to my place anytime to see Promise. You took care of her, and I cannot be ungrateful for that."

That day, Victor left the shop with his head wrung, and was very sad. But he still visited her at the shop, whenever he was in town, and sometimes at home.

The restaurant was almost emptied by the time she had finished explaining her past to Sam who sat listening. He did not talk much about himself.

"You really look like my school mate," he told Valerie, after staring at her for a while. "I visited her once when the war was getting near Monrovia, but since then I never saw her or heard of her again."

That night they stayed long talking about other things, until both of them were the only ones in the restaurant. It had passed 11 pm and Sam told her it was time for him to leave, but waited for her to close the restaurant. When she tried to find a bike to take her home, he asked to drop her off somewhere safe and close to where she lives, if she felt uncomfortable with that. she agreed.

The next couple of days, Sam visited the restaurant and as was arranged, Valarie would bring him his food and he would eat and do some work on his lap tap. Sometimes he would leave sooner, but most times he would wait until the restaurant was closed and would drop her to the safe spot.

But other times, when he did not have the chance to go to the restaurant, he would send Emmanuel to pick up his food. He decided to personally rehabilitate the kid and it was progressing well.

During the wars of 2003 that forced the President out of the country, Emmanuel Tarwo briefly affiliated with the rebel group that fought the government militia west of Monrovia. He was then living in New Kru Town when the rebels captured the Freeport of Monrovia. He had ventured there to look for food when he met one of the commanders who was a friend of his mother. Throughout that brief period of fighting, Emmanuel, then 12 years old, was with this commander and he saw some of the hideous crimes committed on both sides.

One Saturday evening while at the restaurant, Valarie had brought Sam's food and he was about to eat when Kerzo came in. She had not seen him for a while, especially when Sam started coming around, and so she was excited to see him.

"Kerzo," she called to him. "You are hard to find these few days. Welcome, my brother,"

"Ay this my sister. Always looking beautiful," he said and went to her, smiling and slightly taking his eyes off her to focus on the strange man sitting next to her. She got up to meet him and they embraced.

"I was having some problems. Someone took me to the police station for my own money business."

"Why?"

"I found an apartment for this foolish girl who refused to pay my commission. When I pressed her for my money, she lied that I stole her phone, and so she took me to the Zone 3 police depot. But it was proven that she lied on me. A boy in her house found the phone somewhere in her bedroom. And I made her pay all my money."

"Humm. Next time please let me know of such things," she said and turned to Sam. "Please meet Sam, a friend."

Sam got up and both of them shook hands. "As you heard, Sam."

"Yeah, likewise, Kerzo."

"I heard a lot about you," Sam said.

"Yeah, big brother," Kerzo responded. "You're most welcome, on first sight."

"On first sight?" Valerie interrupted, suddenly becoming suspicious. "What'd you mean on first sight?"

"Oh, Valerie! My very first time meeting this brother, my heart is clear," he answered, looking straight in her eyes.

Valerie stood looking at Kerzo and did not know what to say. He looked back at her with the expression on his face that he meant what he said. Since the incident with Victor Karr, he had not been opened to any man who came around her. Even when she once introduced to him the head of the music ministry of her church, Clar Wesseh, a young and resourceful man in his late twenties.

He often visited her for Bible studies and they would pray together. Kerzo began to welcome him when he met Faith, his young wife. It was Faith who introduced Valarie to their church. They met and became friends when she once visited her at the shop to buy some hair products.

"Kerzo. You can sit and join us, and drink anything on me," Sam interrupted, gesturing a seat to Kerzo as Valarie gazed, speechlessly at him.

Kerzo pulled out a chair and sat opposite Sam while Valarie sat next to him. He looked back and called to the waitress at the counter, ordering a bottle of tonic.

"Is it always like that when people don't pay their commission whenever you find a place for them?" Sam asked Kezo.

"Yes, especially these so-called big town girls around here, but the men always paid. But there are some female clients who respect themselves."

As Kerzo spoke, Sam observed that at some moments he would look sorrowful, like he was worried about something, but spoke with boldness and determination. He was small in the body and slightly hops on his left leg. Sam noticed this when Kesselle entered the restaurant.

"I say Salome. Please bring me a bottle of tonic," Kezo called the bartender and ordered, as the three of them talked.

The conversation continued until it was late in the evening. After drinking an additional bottle of tonic, Kezo switched to drinking stout. The restaurant was getting empty when, out of a sudden, a group of guys entered, Joking and laughing. They were Victor Karr, Othello Gbah, Uriah Gaye, Alvin Choloplay and two other guys. They approached the counter, demanding some drinks when Victor Karr hauled out his wallet from his back pocket and pulled out a US$50.00 bill and laid it on the counter.

"Where is Veronica," he asked, interrupting the Waitress who was trying to record their orders.

"She'd already left," Salome, the waitress answered.

"How about Miss born again, Valarie?"

"She's sitting right behind you," responded Salome who then turned to open the freezer to get the bottles of Club Beer, Heineken, and stout, Alvin, Othello, Uriah and the two other guys had ordered.

His features immediately changed, when he turned and looked behind him, and saw Valerie, Kerzo and this strange guy sitting at the last table at the back, talking. Sam had shown Valeria something on his laptop screen and said something that made her laugh and she jokingly poked his nose and pulled his left ear.

Victor's heart leapt, causing painful burns on the left side of his chest. He had never seen Valarie so involved with someone, especially when he started visiting her again, in his efforts to win her back. Flirting with this guy meant that a relationship was brewing. Is this the dude she will marry? The thought of it further raised his heartbeat.

Now he realized that he had been a fool to think that because she accepted his apologies and told him they could be casual friends, things were going to eventually work out. He should have known from the onset; the way she had controlled the extent their friendship would go. She kept a certain distance; she asked him for nothing. She did not walk with him or ride in his car, and whenever he visited her, she kept the conversation casual. She had always managed to prevent talking about the time they spent together, whenever he tried to bring up such a topic.

He had thought doing all that meant Valarie was observing him, and so he kept on convincing her that he had changed, hoping that she would finally give in.

When Veronica finally moved to Liberia, he talked to her about this.

"For what she told me you did, my sister needs time to reflect, and to follow her own heart," Veronica told him.

"All is left with God," Clar Wesseh once told him, when he brought the issue to him, because he saw Clar as her spiritual brother. "So, just continue to demonstrate that you are a changed man, now."

Taken aback, and discouraged, he stood looking, while Valerie paid no attention to him. She was talking to Sam and Kerzo. Her right-hand man seemed to be in support of the strange fellow. Biting his lips with rage, Victor watched Kesselle, now a traitor, drinking his stout and didn't even care to recognize him.

"Hi, Valarie," his voice audible and quivering, he managed to greet her.

"Oh! hello, Victor," she responded, only when Sam gestured that someone was speaking to her, just when she was saying something to him.

Victor said nothing else and joined his friends at the counter. From watching the drama, they turned to their drinks. He called for a large bottle of Club Beer, which Salome brought. He felt it with his hand and was satisfied that it was icy cold. Then he nodded with an approval that she must uncap it. When she did, he put the bottle to his mouth, tilted his head towards the ceiling and took a long drink with deep grunts as the liquor flushed down his throat. He did not stop until the bottle was emptied, and slammed it on the counter, startling Salome and his friends.

"Take it easy, Victor," cautioned Alvin Choloplay.

"What the fuck you mean, my man?" he grunted. "What do you think is happening? Let's drink or you can just leave."

Alvin remained sitting and said nothing, as Victor ordered another bottle and took another gulp.

"That's Victor," Valerie informed Sam.

"Is there going to be a problem?" he asked.

"Common, Sam," she sighed. "I can't tell when last I have worried about any problem."

"Ok, Miss Julia Roberts. So, we should just mind our own business," Sam said, at the same time rubbing her shoulders in a bite to assure her.

"Juliah Roberts?" she asked, frowning and at the same time struggling to suppress a smile.

"Yeah, remember that movie, 'Pretty Woman'?"

"You're funny," she said and then burst up into laughter.

At the counter, Victor had finished his fourth bottle, and was getting intoxicated. His friends were taking their time drinking and were having low conversations as each would occasionally spy Valerie and continue mummering.

Sam left his table, after asking Valerie to show him the restroom. Victor turned and watched Sam walking pass them to go into the restroom. He saw a handsome and tall fellow wearing an expensive looking Calvin Klein army green collared T-shirt with a University of Connecticut logo on the left breast and short Dickies Khaki pants with an expensive brown suede loafer on his feet.

Othello, Uriah, Alvin and the two other guys with them also turned to look and kept staring at him. Full of envy and jealousy, Victor turned to focus on his drink.

"Hi gentlemen," Sam spoke, when he passed by the counter and entered through a small door, labeled 'Toilet' to the left.

"Yeah," Alvin Choloplay responded.

"Cholo," Victor said, calling Alvin by how he is commonly called. "Are you forced to respond? Why do you guys always feel inferior to these guys?"

"My man," Alvin responded, feeling a bite agitated. "The man greeted and I did not see anything wrong to respond."

"You see," Victor suddenly roared, slamming his fist on the counter, rattling the bottles and jumping from the stool he was sitting on. "Some of you can behave like some of these stupid girls who can fall in for these guys from America. Most of them don't come with anything. They wasted all their lives in the states, partying and nothing they get to show, when they come back home."

"You remember that girl at 'Christ Temple of Healing Church on 12th Street?" Uriah interrupted.

"Yeah, where that foolish girl who used to lead the praise and worship, attended," suddenly recounted Victor. "There was this guy, Teah Blamo, who used to play for the Junior Professional soccer team. He was in love with her and told her about this. She said she was born again and told him that if he is serious, they should first date, until the spirit of God leads them to marry, and so he agreed.

For her business he joined the church and became a dedicated member. But right after the 2003 war, a guy came from the states on some kind of high grid, and she jumped behind him. That guy used that girl all kinds of ways, mehn-she who was keeping herself untouched for years.

My man Blamo became frustrated; he started performing poorly on the field until Junior Professional dropped him. And since that guy traveled back to the states, almost three years now, he has not yet come back to her, or has sent for her. I am even told that the guy changed his address and phone number."

"They say the church took her from the praise and worship team for fornicating and she had to leave for shame and disgrace," Uriah added and then took a drink of the small bottle of Club Beer, before him.

"Yes. That's exactly what's about to happen to that useless fool over there," Victor continued, pointing to where Valeria was sitting. "Some of these guys just come here to fool these stupid girls. They have nothing. They just come and find some place to eat with their laptops in their hands and use that very place as an office on pretense. My man, let's leave this derm place, mehn. I don't know why I am worried about someone who I am tired of using like a dog. There are better girls out there. I don't know what I was thinking to have come here in the first place."

Victor finished the sixth bottle of the Club Beer he was drinking, slammed it on the counter and stormed out of the restaurant, almost bumping into Sam who slightly skipped out of his way when he was returning from the restroom. Uriah Gaye and Othello Gbah ran after him while Alvin Choloply and the two other guys stayed behind to finish their drinks.

Sam joined Valerie and Kerzo at the table. Her eyes were on him and appealing, trying to tell him to be calm and to downplay what had happened. She saw how Victor intentionally meant to hit him. He sat by her side stroking the left side of her cheek to assure her that he was not deterred by Victor's action.

Kerzo had finished his second bottle of stout, when his phone suddenly buzzed. He grabbed it from the table, and immediately got up. Spinning his right index finger in a circle, meaning that he will be back, he hurried outside to answer the call.

Sam and Valerie sat quietly while he opened a bottle of mineral water and took a drink. "I am good," he said when he caught her eyes, still appealing to him. "I will wait until you close for the day. And I will drop you home."

Suddenly there was a noise outside. Victor's voice was heard shouting with rage. Then they heard Kesselle's voice. Valarie immediately got up. Sam got up too, but she gestured to him to stay. She did not want him to get involved, if it was a comoton between Kezo and Victor, as it seemed. Reluctantly, he sat down.

When she came outside, she saw Kerzo jammed to the wall as Victor held him by his collar with both hands. He had slightly lifted him up against the wall to the extent that Kerzo was partially resting on his toes. Alvin Choloplay and the two other guys had also come out of the restaurant and were among some passers-by who were trying to separate Victor and Kerzo. Remaining calm, Valerie managed to make her way through the crowd to talk to Victor.

"You are damn ungrateful," Victor roared at Kesselle. "Is it today that you don't want to speak to me? You think I care the fuck about Valerie? You damn ungrateful fool."

"You need to grow up, my man," responded Kerzo. "There's no point in venting your frustration like this."

"Oh!" Victor roared again, pulling Kerzo towards him and slamming him against the wall. "Are you listening to the nonsense you are telling me? You think I'm frustrated over that piece of shit you call sister?"

"Victor. What is the meaning of this?" tapping him on his shoulder, Valerie tried to call his attention. "This is not necessary."

"Get your fucking hands off me," Victor said, suddenly leaving Kerzo and turning to her.

"This is not necessary. This is my place of business and you are disturbing my customers," she tried to explain.

"Don't tell me that bullshit," raged Victor, attempting to rush on her to hit her, but he was prevented by Alvin Choloplay and the two other guys who came along with them.

"Is it now that you have a business?" Victor continued to roar at the same time fighting to break free from the grip of Alvin and the two other guys. "Where were you when you had nothing and I used to fuck you anyhow-anywhere, just to feed you and your daughter? I was trying to make you look like a woman again since no man can take you for real, then you want to pretend like you are holy. You're just a useless and stupid girl."

Valerie remained calmed and said nothing as Victor ranted on. His friends were still restraining him from attacking her and were trying to get him out of there as more people were coming around. Kesselle came close to her and held her by both shoulders and escorted her back inside the restaurant. At the entrance they met Sam.

He was about to walk past them, but Valerie held him by his hands and gently pulled him back inside. After a brief hesitation, he went back to his seat. Valerie and Kerzo followed and sat down. His face was expressionless while he sipped on his mineral water. Trying to avoid Valerie's eyes, he turned to his laptop.

The commotion outside had subsided, except for mummering and arguments of those who were around. Valerie adjusted her chair closer to Sam who still kept his head into his laptop. She pulled it away from him and closed the lid.

"Olu," she said, now catching his attention when she called him by his middle name for the first time. "You are way above that to get into confrontation with a low thinking guy like Victor. That's how I see him."

"I am good," he sighed and forced a smile at the same time looking at his watch. "When are you going to close for the night?"

"Let's wait a little."

Salome had finished parking the emptied bottles and had washed the glasses and told them she was leaving. Kerzo also asked to leave. Sam asked him to wait so he could drop him, but he declaimed-he was going to catch a bike home.

Sam watched as Kerzo went limping to the door, quite different from the way he first entered the restaurant. He suspected Victor injured his already disabled leg when he was jacked up. Sam was not happy with this.

"A fragment from a blast pierced his left knee while fleeing when the rebels attacked the James Springs Payne airfield during the 1990 civil war. He and his family used to live around the Keyhole Community, not far from where they had the military camp," she explained.

Sam nodded and gently squeezed her right shoulder.

"Shall we leave now?" he asked her, looking her directly in her face with the suspicion that she intended to delay a little, until she was sure that Victor had left and was not lurking around to attack him.

Sam got up and put his laptop in his bag and zipped it. "Valerie. It's late now and we certainly need to leave. Your young daughter may be missing you now," he insisted.

She suddenly got up, very worried. She hesitated for some minutes and before leaving, she first did some last-minute checks of the restaurant ensuring that all the lights were off and the freezer and other accessories were unplugged.

Sam waited for her outside of the entrance door. And when she was through, she locked the Iron door, told the watchman who had been waiting outside, good night, and walked closely beside Sam while he led her to his Ford pick-up truck. That night, he drove her home, passing by the spot where she had always told him to stop her and walked her to her door steps. When she entered, he got back in his car and left.

Before going home, he passed by the restaurant to check on the watchman. When he finally reached the compound where he lived, his phone rang while driving through the gate. He looked and saw that it was Valerie, and he knew why she was calling him.

"Are you home now?" she asked, her voice full of concern and worries.

"Yes. Just arrived," he responded, struggling to park the pickup in front of his apartment at the same time talking on the phone.

"Thank God," she said with relief. "Good night."

The next day he visited the restaurant at lunch time. After eating, he sat and waited.

"This was another delicious plate. Thanks," he said, when she joined him. "I have a busy schedule this week. And I will not be coming for lunch. But I will come late to drop you home."

The following day Sam called her to let her know that he will send Emmanuel for his food, and that he will later stop by to drop her home.

"Don't bother, Sam. Veronica will stay at the restaurant late. Both of us will be going home together," she told him.

When she hung out, she began to feel guilty because he lied to him. She did not want him at the restaurant that day, because she heard that Victor had promised to attack him anywhere he saw him. Someone told him that Sam made a nasty statement against him the night he collared Kerzo.

Throughout that week, they talked on the phone and texted each other, but they did not see each other much.

On the following Saturday evening at about 11 pm, Sam, Kerzo, and Emmanuel were sitting in the Ford pick-up truck, parked on the side of the road at the Polotori Junction, slightly opposite Zone three Police Deport in Congo Town. The car was facing the direction of Total Petroleum Filling Station. Not quite long, at a distance ahead of them, Victor Karr, Othello Gbah, Uriah Gaye and Alvin Choloplay came out of Musu's Sport Entertainment Center.

They crossed the road to the side of Novaphone building and strolled towards Polotori Community in their usual jokes and laughters, and talking about the pool games they came from playing.

Sam immediately ignited the engine and drove slowly towards them. They reached the Palm Beach Motel sign board and took the little road to their left that led to the beach, a few meters from the rented apartment where Victor had just moved. He then parked the car and got down, telling Kerzo and Emmanuel to wait. They will join him later.

"Victor," he called, walking behind them with bold strides.

"Yeah, who is it?" The entire group turned when Victor asked.

"Sam. Valerie's friend." He answered, flipping back the hood of the skin tight Nike T-shirt of the biking outfit he was wearing to allow Victor and his friends to recognize him.

"Who?" Victor inquired, surprised that it was strange; all the men he had frightened away from Valerie have never dared to confront him, more especially alone, and at such times of the night, when people were not around.

"You heard me," Sam said, speaking firmly in his American accent. He took a few steps closer and then stood before him. "I came to warn you to stop the shit you did the other night to Valerie. She's been done with you a long time now and you need to live with that. This must be the very last time you repeat that bullshit, especially when I am around. I mean this, dude."

"What the fuck is this?" enraged, Victor asked, with his hands spread apart like a lawyer pleading his case in a courtroom, at the same time looking at his friends like he was expecting answers. "What'd the fuck do I care when she's fucking you now? Or it is that the sex she's giving you has turned your head to venture out here this time of the night to tell me this bullshit, when in fact I have been planning to flog your ass for the nonsense I heard you said about me that night?

In fact, what pleasure are you getting so much from that useless bitch who I laid anytime I wanted and anywhere for years to encourage you to stand before me?"

"I meant it when I said this should be your last saying cribs about her," Sam said at the same time he moved towards Victor and gave him a swift and low outside leg kick on his ankles. It swept his both legs and sent him to the ground on his buttocks with a huge impact.

"He's attacking Victor. The man came to fight for woman business!" alarmed Uriah Gaye.

"Oh! so you came to fight me for that piece of shit between her legs that I can even draw for you right now?" stunned, and increasingly enraged, Victor sprang from the ground and asked.

"You will soon realize that I came purposely to rid you of all the things you've been saying about Valerie. They will end here tonight," responded Sam, readying himself as Victor, with his both fists drawn, started circling around him like a boxer.

"Gentlemen we can settle this peacefully," Alvin, who sensed Victor was going to be no match for Sam, from the way he saw his friend's feet swept from under him, stood in front of Sam and said, while Uriah, and Othello looked on, also stunned and very worried for their friend.

Convinced that he was swept off his feet, unaware and was not deterred by that, Victor solved Alvin out of his way and rushed to Sam. He landed a heavy punch in his opponent's face. But he was stunned again as the mixed martial arts athlete did not seem bothered by that. He threw another in his stomach, but it bounced off the muscle linings that made up Sam's abdomen.

"Come on, Victor," taunted Sam as he reframed from throwing punches and reverted to circling around him, boxing style again. "Is this all your big mouth can offer?"

Struggling to compose himself to ward off the panic that was gradually gripping him, Victor again charged at Sam in an attempt to grab him by the wrist, and to first give him a nasty head butt to startle him and make him lose balance, and then try to use his bigger body and strength to wrestle Sam to the ground. But he was caught mid-way with a powerful Muay Thai style straight foot jab, forcefully preventing a closed distance between him and Victor as the kick sent Victor crashing on the trunk of a mango tree that stood nearby.

The impact was so severe that it made a sound like his vertebrae columns were splintered. Victor certainly became disoriented. Pretending to ignore the severe pain from his aching back, he managed to pull himself away from the tree, wobbling as he struggled to balance himself in disbelief that a guy, who appear innocent looking and soft, Valerie's boyfriend for that matter, was disgracing him in front of his friends.

His feature immediately changed to total embarrassment when he saw Kerzo and this kid he did not know, emerged from the dark and stood behind Sam, with their hands folded. But he soon remembered seeing the kid several times lurking around, whenever he went to play pool at night. He panicked again, realizing that the kid had been monitoring his movements since the night of the incident at the restaurant.

His friends rushed to him to prevent him from continuing the fight, when they saw that he was still wobbling and he was struggling to balance himself to prepare for another charge at Sam. But Victor scrolled them, yelling that they should get out of his way. Sam stood, his arms now folded and shook his head.

Victor moved forward, still struggling to brace himself, as his back arched. Then he scooped over and charged with a dive, aiming for Sam's legs to grab and pull them to knock him down, but he was met with a low flying knee into his mouth, ripping his lips, and splattering blood.

This time he uttered a sharp cry when another knee kick landed into his chest. Not quite done with him yet, Sam forced his arms under Victor's armpits and pulled them upwards until his two elbows touched, at the same time forcing Victor's head between his legs. Everyone yelled, putting their hands on their hands, including

Kesselle, when Sam executed Tribble H's pedigree, crushing Victor's face on the ground when he brought him down.

As Victor lay groaning and convulsing, Sam then grabbed him by his collar and pulled him to his feet.

"You think you can wrestle me?" he said, looking at his already broken nose and bloody face at the same time, shaking him violently. "So, who's the stupid one now? To want to flog someone you barely know? You were lucky I did not crush your face on the hard ground or else I was going to break your neck."

"Big brother, we beg you. It's enough now," pleaded Alvin, trembling with fear for his friend while Uriah and Othello Gbah looked on with appealing eyes.

"Call me Sam," he said. "And this was just a small warm up for Victor. The next time he addresses Valerie the manner he did, I will attack him right there and it will be worse than what I did tonight. And this should be a lesson to him. No one knows what the next man is capable of."

"Yeah, Sam. We will make sure he never does that again."

"You guys got to talk to your man," added Kerzo "He needs to grow up, like I told him the other night. I was rushing outside to answer a call, only to attack me because he said he spoke to me and I did not answer."

"And that was just very stupid, my man," Sam said, again shaking Victor violently while holding him by his collard. "What did you gain by attacking a handicap?"

Victor tried lazily to free himself from Sam, but he was pulled closer and given an elbow smash in his face. He uttered a loud cry as his voice echoed through the dark and between the houses.

"Cholo. You guys are standing here allowing this guy to hurt me like this for woman business," he began to cry bitterly as a flow of blood from a cut above his left eye brow caused by the impact of the elbow smash, drained down his face. "Please run right here to Zone 3 and call the police."

"If you like you can call the entire police force. This is my country, too. But I will beat you anytime you talk about Valerie like that. Remember she has a daughter. And I believe that kid still takes you as her father. What will she think about you when she grows up, especially the way you always address her mother?"

Sam again pulled him closer and attempted to give him another elbow smash, but Alvin, Othello, Uriah, even Kerzo continued to beg on his behalf. Helplessly, and groaning with severe pain, Victor stood jacked up, at the same time complaining to his friends for doing nothing as Sam was inflicting injuries on him for woman business. Why haven't they gone to the deport to call the police.

With continual pleading from Kezo, Sam released Victor. He was helped by his friends as they walked him home. Sam, Kerzo and Emmanuel then walked to the Ford Pick-up truck and drove towards the German Embassy, after a U-turn.

Sunday, the next day, Valerie was at her Church, the Tabernacle of Fire, located behind Royal Air Maroc former office on 8th street, Sinkor. The service had just started, usually with the Praise and Worship team taking the stage, leading spiritually filled captivating praise songs as the entire congregation sang alone, clapping, jumping around and dancing.

Clar Wesseh and his Music Department were energized as they played the instruments with great proficiency while he was on the keyboard, playing at the same time directing the flow of the music to the admiration of his wife, Jugbeh, who stood next to Valerie.

Pastor Adolphus Solomon, the head Pastor, was jumping from one corner of the platform to another, shouting 'Hallelujah' in a spirit filled frenzy, and waving his white handkerchief. Mother Amie Solomon, his wife and the rest of the Deacons and Deaconesses were at their respective seats on the platform, jubilating and celebrating the Lord.

Usually, Valerie would also be part of the fray, jumping, dancing and praising God for getting her out of all what she had been through, but instead she remained standing by her seat at the front row, reluctantly clapping, with Promise standing by her also clapping, until Sister Abigail, the Sunday school teacher came for her.

Throughout the week, she only saw Sam twice when he went to the restaurant to have lunch. She observed that he was not talking much or calling, or responding to her text messages when she refused to allow him to drop her home. She sensed that he knew she was preventing him from having any confrontation with Victor. Her ex-boyfriend was very rude and did not have any manners and shame. She did not want a decent man like him to be mixed up in a street fight with Victor.

The brute, as she regarded him, had been telling people that he was planning to beat Sam anywhere he saw him. What worried her, she called the whole of Saturday, but Sam did not answer. She even sent him text messages but he did not reply, either. She tried Kerzo's number to ask whether he can locate where Sam lives so he should take her there, but he was not also answering his phone.

With all of this, she began to blame herself for getting too used to him. Since she left Victor, she has always kept a certain distance from men, in order to put the issue of having another relationship behind her. This has since freed her from the burden and distraction of having to pre-occupy her mind of thinking about someone, again.

Because Sam was different and seemed very nice and well-mannered, she now finds herself always wondering about him. Though she knew that he likes her, he had never prioritized the issue of having an affair with her, almost a month since they met. For this reason, she felt secured with his style of friendship, which had gotten her too used to him too soon, and it was now starting to play on her.

Odell Masalley, the head of the Praise and Worship Team introduced the favorite praise song, 'We Will Praise Thee Forever Hosanna', after a spectacular interlude of a melodious display of the instruments by Clar Wesseh and Team. Valerie, still not responding actively, quietly sang along, looking up at the ceiling and closed her eyes with her hands open and partially raised.

A familiar perfume certainly filtered through her nostrils. She immediately opened her eyes and looked to her left to where the scent was coming from, and saw Sam, standing by her clapping his hands and Dancing.

"Good morning, pretty girl," he greeted.

"Sam!" she exclaimed, but rather in a low and astonishing voice. "Welcome."

"Thanks. I am glad to be in the house of the Lord, looking for my beautiful friend," he responded and this made Valerie laugh, especially the way he was dancing.

"I guess it's Sam," Jugbeh nudged her on her side and whispered.

"Yeah, he took me by surprise."

Sam pretended like he was not following the little gees between the two friends as he continued to dance along with the music, his eyes on the platform and at the same time occasionally scanning the congregation. Odell Masselley had introduced a worship song 'Jehovah Is Your Name'.

Valerie was now into her usual worshiping mood, raising her hands and singing along. Sam observed from the corner of his eyes, she was sharing tears. She had attempted to take her bag from her seat to get her handkerchief, but he gently shoved a pink and beautifully designed one in her hand.

"Thank you," she whispered when she used it to wipe her tears, appreciating the nice smell of the perfume on the handkerchief.

Pastor Solomon was observing keenly from the platform.

After the service, Valerie introduced Sam to Clarr Wesseh and his wife. Then the pastor and mother Amie Solomon, who thanked him for visiting their church and that he was welcomed any time. He was also introduced to some of her church members who, also thanked him for visiting their Church and appreciated him for his boldness especially when he told the congregation during the part of the service in which first time visitors introduce themselves, that it was because of Valerie he was visiting, though she had not yet invited him.

After having some conversations with the Wessehs, Pastor Solomon and his wife and a couple of other members, she went to get Promise from the Sunday school. Sam, who had been waiting for them in a silver Nissan Maxima 3.5 SE Sedan, waved them over, when he saw them looking for where he was parked. First, he opened the back door and gestured to Promise to get in. Then he did likewise to the front passenger door for Valerie.

"I am taking you both to see my place," he said as he ignited the V-8 engine.

"Really?" she asked, very much surprised.

"Yep," he responded. "I prepared something to eat, but you and Promise will want to first take the running stomach medicines I got for you."

"There you go again," she said, laughing, and then turned to look at Promise sitting quietly at the back seat. "Promise. This is Sam. You always hear Aunty Veronica and I talk about him."

"Hi Uncle Sam," certainly chirped the kid, coming forward and squeezing herself between the space of the driver and the front seats. "Heard a lot about you, about how you brought Mamie's phone back to her."

"Oh yeah, thanks. I finally got to meet you. What a great day."

"Mamie says you are nice. And thanks too."

"Yeah, that's correct, Promise. Mamie's pretty and nice to me, too."

Promise and her mother caught each other's eyes and both smiled. Valerie rubbed her daughter's head and turned to Sam. As he drove, she kept staring at him, wondering. This was a man who was not talking much to her these few days and was not answering her calls. But out of a sudden, there seems to be a change of heart; he surprised her by visiting her church unannounced and had invited her and Promise to his house.

She now realized that she had been wrong for blaming herself, after all, for getting close to him too soon. Maybe he was vexed because he knew she was lying to him when she said Veronica was staying at the restaurant late and they would go home together when he had offered to take her home, the next day after the incident with Victor. Maybe it was his way of expressing his dissatisfaction.

"Mamie, can I borrow your phone to complete the game I was playing?" Promise asked, interrupting her mother's thoughts, and without hesitation she handed her the phone, but with an expression on her face, warning Promise that the battery was getting low.

She turned to Sam and both caught each other's eyes. Promise had now eased herself from between the space of the driver and front seats, and was now huddled at the back seat, and was deep into her mother's phone. Several times Sam would catch Valerie's eyes on him whenever he took them off the road. Sensing her thoughts, he began to whistle.

"What's that song?" she asked, smiling. "Sounds familiar."

"Oh yeah. You are supposed to know it. It's this song by Simply Red- 'If You Don't Know Me by Now'."

"Heard it," Valerie burst into laughter. "And I will never-never know you, right?"

"Right," Sam answered, and then another laughter.

By now they have passed VAMOMA Junction and were around the President's. Sam sped past it and took the unpaved road to his right after he passed Lone Star MTM and cruised down the dirt road that stretches towards the beach. He turned and stopped at a moron gate and honked his horn. Not quite long Emmanuel opened the gate and Sam drove in and parked in front of his apartment.

Valerie observed that it was a compound of five houses. The yard was paved and adorned with good landscaping. There were two big palaver huts made of concrete and zinc roof at the north and the south of the yard, and Sam's apartment was at the south. He got down from the car and ushered them into his apartment.

"Valerie. This is where I live. It's a rented three bedrooms apartment for my Partner Boima and I. He's due here next week and we will be spending most of our time in Bong Mines where we will be implementing our projects."

"It's a nice place, Sam," she mused, at the same time looking around.

"Thanks, and feel at home," he acknowledged, and turned to Promise. "Do you want to watch some cartoons while Mamie and I fix your food?"

Sam and Valerie set a dinner table for two in the palaver hut outside to give Promise the chance to watch her cartoons as she was busy flipping through channels when Sam showed her how to use the remote control of the 64 inches Panasonic Television.

Sam had prepared some mixed vegetable sauce with rice.

"You did not take my calls the whole of yesterday. Why?" Valerie asked, serving him his plate of fresh vegetables salad with tomato, and lettuce and steaks of grilled cassava fish.

"We were very busy, trying to set something straight," he responded, pouring a Fonterra red wine in his glass.

"What were you setting straight, Sam?" Frowning, she persisted.

"To avoid being like Mr. Edwards and others," he answered. "Kesselle and Emmanuel had to help me in the process.

I guess you called Kesselle too and he did not answer. In fact, I am expecting him here today."

"You mean Kerzo knows this place?" she asked, becoming surprised again.

"Yes. And he works for me now. Throughout last week he was busy with Orlando, our broker, to help clear our containers from the port. He was very much instrumental in finding a place to rent to store the items in the containers."

"That is very nice of you, Sam," she said with great relief. "You are also nice to the people around me. Thanks. But you mentioned Mr. Edwards."

"Yes, I did. Victor scared him and others away from you, but I could not allow you to scare me away from him in the name of preventing him from harming me. So, I worked out a plan and beat the hell out of him last night for the nonsense he said to you the other night. It was not a street fight, though. I had Emmanuel monitor the places he frequented. And I made sure he was with his three friends and was not drunk before I confronted him in his own community. I heard he was looking for me to beat, right?"

"You beat Victor?!" she exclaimed. "I did not think you could do that."

"So, how did you think I got your phone back? I followed those pikings that jerked your purse all the way to their criminal dent. There I met their leader and beat him to get it back to you. Asked Emmanuel. He was the one ridding the bike when your purse was jerked. I followed them and bloodied one Morris I met. He's a huge guy and a bad criminal, and even stronger than Victor."

"You mean Emmanuel who is here with you?!" Valerie stretched her eyes.

"Yes, Valerie," Sam said, trying to calm her down. "He explained to me how he was forced by this Morris guy who sent him to steal from people in the street, and I felt sorry for him and decided to help him. You can see that he will not steal from anyone again. And I beg you to forgive him."

Just then there was the sound of a bike outside the gate, and soon someone was knocking. Emmanuel who was sitting on the porch ran toward it and asked who it was. After hearing the response from a familiar voice, he opened the smaller gate and Kerzo passed through and entered the yard with a computer bag across his chest. He looked to his right and saw Sam and Valerie sitting in the palaver hut, eating. Sam waved him over.

"Anthony Kesselle," Valerie called, as he approached them.

"Yes, my beautiful sister in the whole wide world. How are you doing?" he responded, entering the palaver hut and taking his seat next to her.

"Just got better, after knowing the reason why you and your Boss man, Sam were not picking up my calls yesterday."

"Oh yeah, he told you what he did to Victor last night, right?"

"And you were right there. And you know that brute. What if he was going to take something and hurt Sam with it?

And hurt you too?"

"How was that going to happen?" asked Kerzo, smiling and shaking his head. "If you were there, you were not going to be saying that."

"Mama. You got a call. Its Aunty Veronica," certainly Promise came outside holding her mother's phone, and spoke.

Valerie excused herself and hurried to answer it. She and her sister talked for some time as she kept looking at Sam like they were talking about him. Kerzo had opened the computer bag he brought along with him and was showing Sam some papers.

"Veronica just told me Victor called, telling her how you almost killed him. He even told her how I am in danger. You are far more jealous and you can kill for woman business," Valerie interrupted them at the same time laughing.

"Then you be the judge, Valerie," responded Sam. "I went to warn him, but he put up a fight. The bottom line is, he will never say anything like the nonsense he was saying to you again. At least he knows what I am capable of."

"Uncle Sam. Is this you?" Promise suddenly joined them with an album she had gotten from under the tinted class living room table, pointing to a particular photo of someone who looked exactly like Sam in his youth. He was dressed in a karate outfit holding a trophy in his hands with some people standing behind him.

"That's me, Promise," he admitted, his eyes on Valerie who also looked at him, very much amazed. "That was the night I won my state's high school karate championship."

Valerie could not hold back her astonishment.

"I noticed you and Victor have one thing in common," he said.

"And what's that?" Valerie asked, suddenly frowning.

"Because I look too soft, both of you thought I am not capable of acting street-like."

"Not that, Sam," Valerie smiled. "I was not prepared to see you get hurt."

CHAPTER 6

THE HOSTESSES WERE SERVING dinner about an hour after take-off from Casablanca International Airport for the 4 hours 25 minutes flight to Monrovia. The economy class was full to capacity with Liberians and foreigners, traveling from the United States, Europe and Asia. Most of the Liberians on the Royal Air Maroc were traveling from the United States and returning home for visit while the foreigners, mostly Lebanese businessmen, were either returning to the country from business trips or from seeing friends and family back home. Others on the flight were Americans, and Europeans, and other Africans on holidays or were expatriates sent by their respective organizations to work in Liberia.

J. Boima Barclay, Jr. was seated at the 29th row in Economy Class C of the cabin at the far-left window at the rear of the plane, just before the lavatory and kitchen compartments. He always preferred this part of the Cabin, because it was shorter to go to the lavatory, instead of taking the long walk through the aisle, a thing he hated to do on flights.

The beautiful Moroccan flight attendant had wheeled the trolley to the row where he sat, and was asking the two passengers before him, a European lady who sounded German from her accent and a Bangladeshi man, what they would prefer to be served with.

"Est-ce-que vous avez du vin rouge?" Boima asked, trying to remember his high school French, when the hostess approached him.

"Si," she answered with a gentle smile, and continued in heavily accented English. "We do have some red wine, both in medium size and large bottles, sir."

"Okay. Two of the medium size ones will do."

"Are you also eating anything?" she inquired, while serving him two medium size bottles of Cavalier red wine. "We have hors d'ouvreur, gourmet salad, cheese, pastries and fresh fruits."

"Oh! Thanks. I will prefer some fresh fruits. I dined heavily in New York, hours ago," Boima replied, again smiling and wondering whether the beautiful flight attendant was a Moroccan of French descent.

He pulled the food tray from the seatback, and sat the two bottles, and a glass in the cup compartments, and then the plastic bowl of fresh fruits, close to the bottles. Boima tried to relax himself when he had taken his first sip of the wine while he listened to the sound of the avionics of the Boeing 737, at high altitude.

For a while he kept his mind busy, figuring out the composition of the passengers on board the flight, and the economic benefit to the country. The Librarians from the diaspora, the other Africans, the Americans, Europeans, and Lebanese Business people all seem to have an inherently common desire-and it was a strong need for recreation. But the only remedy for this is when the tourism sector in Liberia is revitalized, which will generate more revenues for the country, as there will be more people visiting, thus increasing the demand for what his father always referred to as the ultimate relaxation.

He mused that Maila, with all its beautiful features will be a hub for such endeavors, possibly surpassing the Sapo National Park, and he was determined to make that a reality.

Amid the chattering on board, the voices of his fellow country men and women were the loudest. He could hear some of their conversations which were mostly about a little row at the terminal, just before boarding the plane. Some of the Liberians were complaining that the flight attendants were discriminating among the passengers; they were only allowing the Liberians with American passports, the Americans, Europeans and the Lebanese businessmen to carry their overnight bags on board while they told them to leave theirs for the cargo area, because the overnight compartments of the plane were full.

Boima remembered how a group of them gave him a hard look, when the flight attendant inspected his ticket and passport before ushering him on board the flight with his overnight bag. He felt privileged, lucky, and envied for carrying an American passport for which he had always appreciated his father and his step mother.

As a child born in wed-lock to a rural girl with junior high school education, his step mother could have refused his adoption into their family as a legitimate Barclay and it could have prevented him from traveling to the United States and probably, he would have been in the same position or even worse than his fellow countrymen who were not happy with the preferential treatment he was given.

He always thought about his mother even as a kid when he traveled to America. He remembered how beautiful she was, with enticing hips and legs forming an attractive and seductive shape that no man could easily resist. Growing up, he often asked himself why his father, years ago, on his campaign trail in Fuamah District, when he was running as representative, could not control himself for wooing a town chief's daughter? But as he grew older, he reflected on his own experience. He understood why the old representative was hypnotized in having an affair with the woman outside his marriage that eventually brought him into this world.

"I could not resist the beauty of your mother when she came to let me know that my hot water was ready the night I slept in the town of Mahwah while on my campaign trail," his father once told him.

When the civil war was waging, Representative Barclay at times felt lonely when he had not gotten word from home of the whereabouts of Esther Gorpue Lomeh. She blamed him for abandoning her, after he had adopted his son. She could no longer see him like before, and sometimes the representative had to sneak her son to Maila to see her for fear of his wife.

Mrs. Barclay agreed to accept the child, with a vow from her husband that he must put an end to the relationship. She had no son, only two older girls who were off to grad school by the time their step brother was born, and so she took to him and was always reluctant to allow his father take him to Bong Mines.

Esther felt she was deprived of her son and when she confronted old chief Lomeh, her father about what will become of her, after her son was taken from her, she did not like the response she received. Old chief Lomeh, longing for his grandson to be taken abroad, was reluctant to confront Representative Barclay about this. And when the representative, under pressure from his wife, stopped seeing her, unlike the time he did when he rented a place for them in Sugar Hill, a community in Nyenen, when she was pregnant and up to the time she delivered, one day, out of frustration, she left Maila.

Shortly before leaving the states, his father visited him and had his son promise him to look for his mother when he got to Liberia. Boima promised his father and vowed to do so and also ensured that he would mitigate between his mother, his step mother and the old representative.

The old man gave him some money and lots of things for Esther and promised to support any arrangement, if he finds her and if she wishes to travel to the United State.

To Boima, that wasn't going to be a problem, since he was also an American citizen and it was his right to take his mother to the states for a visit, except one thing he had to do. And that was to convince his fiancé, who would be his wife by the time he found his mother and subsequently ready to take her to the states.

He took out a brown envelope from the breast pocket of the gray lightweight summer sports blazer he was wearing, opened it and gently took out a picture of he and his mother, taken when he was about eight years old. He stared at it for a while after taking another sip of the Cavalier red wine and then closed his eyes in reaction to flashes of memories of the woman he had not seen or heard from, for years.

He planned to show it to her which would earn him a proud son who had kept the memories of his mother for many years. Lately, just before leaving the states he confided to Diana Rice, his fiancée, that his biological mother is somewhere in Liberia and part of his trip is to find her. He had only brought this out, because they have finally planned to get married, after four years of being together and so he needed to make sure that she knows everything about him.

The resourceful African American business executive, whose paternal grandfather is white and conservative, did not first react to this, until a week later she called him and asked how was it possible that his father could have a child in wed-lock, as she had always known Mrs. Barclay to be his biological mother.

"Where I am from, such things, though not morally accepted, happen," he explained over the phone.

"How does such a thing happen, but morally unacceptable? And why should it have happened in the first place?" she demanded to know. "Remember we have just agreed to spend the rest of our lives together. So, I need a clear head here."

"That's why I am telling you now, hon."

"So, how and why was that possible?" she persisted, exhibiting her conservative upbringing.

"Baby," he managed to say, in his usual claimed but stern voice. "Where I am from, a son does not question his father's sexual resume, especially when his father is still alive. Please. Can that one just clear your head for Christ sake?"

Boima met the beautiful Idol in grad school, when he was working on his second Masters, this time in Community Development, a discipline his father encouraged him to do as an added advantage in executing the Maila Project. She had entered the library to research a paper she was writing on the African business climate and its impact on American direct investment. She had sat next to this handsome and very quiet looking guy, and after a brief conversation, she was surprised that he was born in Africa, more especially Liberia, where a civil war was raging.

She asked him some questions about the continent and then his country. After that, they became friends and they soon started liking each other. She spent her entire upbringing with her conservative grandfather, and for this reason, Diana lived within a confined community of like minds which made Boima sometimes wonder whether she at times forgets that she's black, and even in love with someone like him with a somewhat dysfunctional family background.

"Is she your mother?" inquired the Bangladeshi, sitting next to him.

"Yes, she is," he answered with a faint smile. "Wanna take a look?"

"No. That's ok," said the Bangladeshi. "Are you returning home for a visit or business?"

"I would say both, but with more emphasis on the business part."

"I am visiting your country on business, mainly in the area of rice production. I represent an agricultural firm that engages in the mass production of rice. We did some studies with the Interim government, and we want to share our findings with this new government. And if they are interested, we can get into an agreement of rice production and export them out of Liberia."

"Sounds good to me," Boima said, having managed to get a gist of what the Bangladeshi was saying, due to the heavily accented English he spoke. "But I am into Tourism. It's a long project to explore an unnoticed tourism hub, and develop the little town where it's located. That's where my mother's from. But maybe we will be able to identify some acres, fertile for growing rice. My mother's tribe has been practicing the growing of rice for centuries."

"That will be very good," mused the Bangladeshi, reaching for his call card in the breast pocket of his coat and handing it to Boima.

"This is my address in the states and my partner's contact in Liberia," Boima explained as he, in return, gave his call card to the Bangladeshi, after writing Sam's contact number at the back.

They both shook hands and nodded at each other. "I suspect you don't drink or else we were going to have a toss and drink to this," Boima joked and they both laughed.

Boima continued to sip his wine, but briefly paused to listen when the Pilot announced through the speakers that there would be turbulence ahead and that all passengers should fasten their seat belts as the ride would be bumpy. After following the instructions, he completed the first bottle of Cavalier red wine and turned on the monitor at the seatback to check on the flight time.

They had flown some 2 and 1/2 hours, and they had an hour and a half to reach Monrovia. He flipped to the map and saw from the graphic display on the screen that they had flown over south western Mali not quite long and were now flying over Guinea. The turbulence could probably mean that they would shortly fly over the Futa Jallon, where strong atmospheric winds are thought to hover directly over the plateau.

About an hour after the turbulence, he observed from the screen that they were steadily descending from high altitudes, which told him that they were now in Liberia's air space. When the map on the monitor confirmed this, he looked through the window but saw darkness. It was in the late evening hours and that they were flying over northern rural Liberia.

Then he felt his ears ringing like they were going to lock, suggesting to him that they were descending further from high altitudes. He did not always like this and had not gotten used to this part of the flight when the plane was descending. This often causes a reaction to the ears like when one has taken quinine pills.

He remembered once when he and Diana visited China and were on a Hainan Airlines flight from Beijing to the port city of Dalian to honor an invitation from Diana's friend and associate, a New York based Chinese model, to attend an annual international fashion fair. As the gigantic plane descended from high altitudes coupled with the heavy sound of the avionics, minutes before landing, Boima's ears began to ring like they were going to bust, and it was worse than all the other flights they had taken from New York to Brussels to Istanbul and then to Beijing.

Remembering what he heard people say what the heavy artillery men in the military do, whenever they are firing the big guns, he opened his mouth so wide that it made Diana upset.

"Hey baby. You look odd doing that. This is unseen and you are drawing unnecessarily inquisitive eyes on you," she told him.

Even at their 40 storey Conrad Hotel suite, Boima's ears continue to ring. It was compounded by a headache, while watching the late evening news on CGTN when it was reported that a missile fired from North Korea flew over Japan at the exact time, just before they landed at the Dalian Zhoushuizi International Airport. Through their 38th floor window overlooking the East Harbor, he looked towards the direction of Japan which is not far from that part of China, and created a mental picture of the radius of their flight path, which to him was considerably close to the Hwasong-15 missile flight path.

"Jesus," he whispered, at the same time shivering with fear, imagining the catastrophe if the missile had malfunctioned and headed their way.

"You can't be serious, James," returning from the shower wrapped in a towel, Diana had said. "Remember this is China. And we were flying far away from that missile."

The voice of the pilot quacked through the speakers again, informing the passengers that they would be landing at the Roberts International Airport in a few minutes and that everyone must fasten their seat belts. As usual, silence filled the entire flight deck as the different landing sounds of the jet engine roared. Boima looked down through his window again and saw nothing but darkness.

Of course, he understood. He was back home and there was hope, and he hoped that now the war has ended, and democratic elections were held, the country is poised to begin its reconstruction process. And he was proud that he will be one of those who will be contributing to this in the private sector.

He felt the plane angling towards the runway after a swoop and then they were descending fast. His heart leapt to the screeching of the tires, almost thinking that they glided over portholes on the runway if there were any, when the Boeing 737 finally touchdown.

It sped on the runway for a few seconds and it began to slow down. As the roaring of the engine suddenly increased, it stopped briefly. After some time, it taxied to where the passengers would disembark and finally stopped. Again, the Pilot voice was heard over the speakers thanking everyone for flying with Royal Air Maroc.

Boima was surprised that the airport buses were already waiting to ferry passengers to the terminal when he had left the cabin and was descending the mobile stairway. The last time he visited Liberia, it took the buses about 20 minutes to arrive. He was impressed that they had to deplane using a mobile stairway, unlike the ordinary stairway that was used, then.

With their overnight bags in their hands, he and the Bangladeshi while chatting, joined other passengers to board one of the buses which took them to the terminal. There they went through immigration and then baggage claim, and finally customs. Boima followed the long queue through the narrow steel gate to get outside of the terminal, closely followed behind by an airport attendant wheeling his luggage. After two and a half years, since his last visit, he felt the warm breeze of Liberia blew his face as he stood outside scanning the crowd, who had gathered to receive their guests.

"Ladies and gentlemen, we will now welcome to the ring, weighing 190lb, from Liberia, West Africa, Sam 'The Black Dragon' Wilson," Sam, who was explaining something to Valerie who he brought along to receive Boima recognized the voice and turned.

"Hey. The love of Corporate America's promising top-notch business executive," Sam exclaimed upon seeing Boima and rushed with his arms open to embrace him. "Welcome back home, brother."

"Hey thanks, mehn," Boima responded as they embraced each other. "Hey bro. I am making no mistakes. For the looks of things in Florida, they are going to nail some sons of batches and you will get your first contender slot back. But hell no. Hope our project will be well on course before that happens."

Both of them burst up laughing and embraced each other again.

"Hey Dude. Let me guess," Boima suddenly crooned. "That's Valerie, right?"

"Yeah, you guess right, bro?" Sam answered, turning to look at Valerie who was standing behind and smiling. "Valerie. This is Boima."

"Hey Valerie," Boima said when he approached her and opened his arms to hug her. "Miss Liberia in your own right. I'm happy to meet you."

"Me too," Valerie said laughing while walking to him, also opening her arms. "Welcome to Liberia."

They embraced and held each other for a while as Sam and the airport attendant who was carrying Boima's luggage stood looking. Sam then told him to follow them to the Ford Pick-up truck with the luggage, which he did. Boima and Valerie walked behind, holding hands and talking and laughing. He took his blazer and put it around her and kissed her on her left jaw, thanking her for his friend and brother.

The luggage was loaded on the back of the Ford with Kerzo who had also come along, to help. He was also introduced to Boima as Valerie's brother, and Boima greeted and appreciated him. Sam gave the airport attendant a tip and then they were on their way to Monrovia, while the karate champion drove. Boima was in the front passenger seat and Valerie was in the back. Kerzo insisted on remaining at the cabin to protect the luggage.

"Hey dude," Boima said. "I almost forgot. I got a Cavalier, this time. You might need it for the road."

Sam received it from him. This was what they did as friends. Whenever one of them traveled, that person would bring back a bottle of red wine that was offered on the plane. They said this is the way they appreciated the number of trips they made, successfully. Whenever they were returning from a trip together, they would deplane with a bottle each and would drink it at the terminal.

Diana had always told them that was the weirdest thing she had ever seen. Valerie laughed when they explained this to her. Sam unscrewed the cap and took a drink. He passed it over to Valerie who refused, but Boima encouraged her and said it is their tradition and she was part of it now.

"How's Diana?" Sam asked after he had taken another drink, careful not to take his eyes off the road as they were around Armbush Curve.

"You know her, Sam," Boima sighed. "She's cool. She wanted to clear her head to come to terms with why Elizabeth Barclay is not my biological mother. And I just told her point blank that in Liberia, where I'm from, a son does not go inquiring about all the draws his father had pulled down, instead of his wife's."

"Diana, Diana," Sam laughed. "And the wedding?"

"She said it will still go on. But we have not yet concluded on a date. At least her heart is clear about that. Remember what I told you? We spent a week in New York visiting places and making me to promise her not to end up like my father by having a child out of wedlock."

"Oh boy. She has gotten too attached to you. Guess who and I will be standing with you?"

"Well, let's keep that as a surprise for Diana," Boima suggested, instead and looked back and winked his eyes at Valerie.

"So, how's the schedule like, this week?" he asked, changing the topic as Sam drove in the middle of the night on the dark Rebert's Field-Monrovia Highway, the powerful headlights of the Ford Pick-up truck bright enough to clearly see ahead of him.

"Beginning tonight we are having a light welcome refreshment for you at the compound. Your uncle, the young chief and his friend came from Maila to welcome you, and there will be a couple of friends we casually know from the states. One lives in the same compound with us. Some of them work with the new government. Then we rest on Sunday. Monday, we visit David Lakay, the contractor who we supposed to negotiate with to rehabilitate the road to Maila.

The broker informed me that on Monday evening he would have cleared the last container and so Tuesday we will be inspecting all the things. So far nothing really for Wednesday and Thursday. Friday morning, we leave for Bong Mines."

"Sounds good. But Wednesday we will have a meeting with this Bangladeshi I met on board the flight. He says he represents a company that deals with rice production, and I told him we might be able to secure acres of fertile land in Maila, if he's interested. But the meeting will be held if only he calls us. Thank God Uncle Peter Lumeh and Wuamah are here. They could also attend the meeting.

Then, after that, we can take Valerie out on a ladies' night."

"Find with me," Sam agreed and turned to Valerie. "Are we good?"

"Why not, Sam?" she agreed, rather shyly. "I can't remember when last I was taken out on a lady's night. And you boys have afforded me the honor. WOW!"

"It will be good. We will have a good time," Boima assured her.

"Valerie. I think the Club Beer in the cooler is cold by now," Sam informed her.

Some fifteen minutes later, they were now on Tower Hill, as Sam had engaged the engine to full throttle, souring up the hill at the same time drinking the club beer while they told jokes and laughed.

Ahead of him was a trailer he could make up from the orange siren glowing on top of it. When he gained distance, he realized that it was carrying tons of planks and the DAF truck was struggling to climb the hill. The sound of the engine could tell that it was straining.

The truck would jerk, when the engine coughed and thick black smoke would pour out of the exhaust pipe and fill the air, blurring the vision of any driver souring up the hill from its rear.

"Are you thinking what I am thinking?" Sam asked, briefly turning to Boima and fixing his eyes back on the road.

"Yeah, looks like it's going to fail, and we left a long queue behind. And not every car has the powerful lights like this pick-up. Remember we asked for it to be designed like this," Boima said.

"Okay, bro. Let's do what we do best. I will drive past him and you tell the driver to park off the road now, or else, people will die tonight."

"Hey," Boima shouted above his voice at the trailer's driver who fortunately had his window glass down, at the same time Sam was husking his horn repeatedly. "The trailer is going to fail and there will be disaster when you roll back down. There are people driving behind you. You hear me. There's a long queue of convoys driving behind you."

The driver slowly drove the trailer on the side of the road. The three car boys sitting on top of the piles of planks, jumped down with large square planks in their hands, and quickly shoved them underneath the tires just when the trailer engine finally stopped and was about to roll back down the hill. Sam turned further on his left, leaving the main road and then gave a swift U-turn, facing the direction of Smell No Taste, and stopped.

With the headlights remaining on, he and Boima got down, telling Valerie to stay calm as apprehension grew on her face. They hurried to the back of the pickup, and pulled out the bed cover from beneath the truck. They told Kerzo to unbolt the tools and accessories boxes to get out some reflective road signs. And when he did, two of the signs were given to Kerzo and one of the car boys with the instruction to run up the hill and erect them on the right side of the road, few meters from the broken-down DAF truck to enable drivers coming from the direction of Monrovia to see them.

Kerzo came back and stayed with Valerie who was alone in the pick-up truck, while Sam and Boima raced down the road with the other reflective road signs. Few meters from where the trailer was parked, they erected the signs on the left side of the road to enable the drivers in the convoys of cars ferrying people from the airport to see the danger ahead of them and slow down.

In a few minutes, a white Range Rover, speeding up the hill, from the direction of Smell No Taste, slowed down just before reaching the crest, when the driver saw the reflective signs with the inscriptions and symbol that danger was ahead. It then slowly drove past the trailer it could see clearly with the help of the headlights of the Ford pick-up truck, and then sped off, after it had completely passed the danger.

Other cars came speeding and did likewise. As Sam and Boima, including the trailer driver and his carboys watched, the drivers of 10 cars observed the danger, slowed down, passed the truck and then continued.

Satisfied that all the cars have passed, the grateful trailer driver thanked Sam and Boima, and told them that he will move the truck from the spot as it still posed danger. Sam, Boima and Kerzo watched as the driver ignited the engine and as he accelerated, the car boys would shove the planks under the tires to prevent it from rolling back if the engine failed. They repeated this, until the truck had almost climbed the hill. Sam and Boima, before leaving the scene, gave the car boys the reflective signs when they were satisfied with the driver. Then they warned him strongly to repeat what they had demonstrated to avoid cars running into them and causing accidents.

It took them about 45 minutes to reach the compound. The guys who Sam had asked to join him to welcome Boima were already seated in the palaver hut, drinking and talking when the Ford pick-up truck entered the yard. Sam, Boima and Valerie got down and walked to them while Kerzo, Emmanuel and the compound security guard helped to carry the luggage in their apartment. The three guys and a girl greeted them.

"Gentlemen and Lady," Sam said. "This is my friend, brother and partner, James Boima Barclay Jr. who I told you about and had just returned to the country."

"Welcome home, bro," Dr. Lasana Dukuly, one of the guys, the government official Sam talked about, got up and embraced Boima.

"Thanks brother. But I know you. Sam and I were at your graduation party in Philly when you obtained your doctorate. A doctorate degree in Hydrocarbons? You made your country Proud. Congratulations."

"O really?!" exclaimed Dukuly.

"Sure. But you did not see us," Sam interjected "We left after you made your speech, and when you introduced the girl, you said you were going to marry."

"Oh, wow. You guys were really there."

The other two guys, Patrick Gibson, and George Tamba, including the girl who was sitting next to Dr. Lasana Dukuly, introduced themselves and also embraced Boima. George was an employee of the National Oil Company of Liberia (NOCAL) while Dr. Dukuly was the third person in command and Patrick worked in the office of the Minister of Finance. The girl, Kemah, was Dukuly's girlfriend. While they sat talking, Kerzo came and whispered in Sam's ears who also whispered to Boima. He then informed the group that Boima's uncle and another person from his grandfather's town were waiting for them in their apartment and they will rejoin them after a brief meeting.

"Go ahead brother. We got all night," noted George Tamba.

"Valerie. You and Kemah can now begin with the barbecued," said the young Hydrocarbon specialist.

"Oh Sure. I just need a second."

Sam, Boima and Valerie entered the apartment and met Chief Lomeh, Wuamah and Jugbeh, who Valerie had invited to help her with the barbecue, in the living room. Valerie and Jugbeh embraced and then she introduced her to Boima and after a brief chat, the girls joined Kemah to help prepare the barbecue.

Boima and his uncle, Chief Lomeh hugged each other, and then Wuamah. He introduced them to Sam, as his friend, brother and partner on the Maila Project. They also embraced him and welcomed him to Maila any time. As their son Boima is his friend and brother, so Maila is also his home.

"So, how's grandfather?" Boima asked, when they all sat down.

"Like I told you the other time you called, he had always been indoors since he and the elders handed the chieftaincy over to me. Until lately, when he heard about your coming, he has since been spirited," responded Peter Lomeh.

"My dad told me to look for my mother, and I will be doing that at the same time on the Maila Project."

"We will join you in the search for my sister. After the war, word came that she was in a village near Weala. Wuamah and I went there to search for her, but the people in the village where she was staying told us that she was no longer there," explained the young Chief.

"One person that we may have always forgotten to ask is Gotolo. They were close friends and I believe he might know something. Gotolo always knows everything about everybody in Maila," interjected Wuamah.

"And we also have a problem, nephew," alerted Chief Lumeh, his countenance suddenly changing "We believe that Sengbeh Gbelema, the black smith, is back, and wants to sabotage our project."

"He's in the surrounding forests of Maila, and we have reasons to believe that he may have committed evil and he is bent on committing more, if we commence the project. We informed the old chief, your grandfather, but he told us to wait till you come," added Wuamah.

"That's not going to stop us. We will open that beautiful scenery to the outside world and we will build Maila. My father told me about that black smith. How he refused to allow Maila to be explored based on some historic park between his ancestor and ours. We are not going to be bothered by that, so long my grandfather and the elders have given us their blessings.

Look Uncle Lomah. We are in the 21st century. It's time tradition should give way to development. This black smith may have a problem with my dad, but not with me. I will never allow that. My mother was born in Maila, so am I."

"Look whosoever this guy is, we will apprehend him and turn him over to the authorities, if he does anything stupid. The war is over now, and we have a constituted government. This black smith needs to get that clear. No one is going to take laws into his or her own hands anymore. That time has passed," interjected Sam.

"Uncle Lomeh. Wuamah. Let's just enjoy ourselves tonight, and contemplate on the success of our town, okay?" Boima said. "When we get there, we will handle that."

Chief Lomah and Wuamah looked at each other for a while and then nodded. To their surprise, Boima and his friend were not afraid. No matter what, they were determined to go ahead with the project. They realized that the old chief was right, when he said to wait for his grandson.

He knew that his grandson is not someone that can be made to back down, easily. The night after the dispute with Sengbeh Gbelema, he told himself that he was right to encourage the old representative to adopt his son and carry him abroad.

As a seed of Maila, through his daughter, Esther, Boima has all traditional bindings to Maila. And because of his western orientation, he will not be tied down by any sacrilegious traditional prohibition. He had always wished his daughter could understand this.

"So, uncles," reading their thoughts, Boima smiled. "I brought you guys some American gin. You might want to help yourselves with them while I join my friends outside, okay? Our friend Valerie will bring you some food."

"And if you get sleepy, Kesselle will show you your room," added Sam.

"Hey Champ. What's about Dukuly and that girl, sitting next to him?" Boima asked, calling Sam by the name he called him whenever he was in the ring, while they were on the porch and were about to rejoin the guys at the palaver hut.

"She's his girlfriend. The dude's in love but I think he doesn't want to admit it."

"Really?"

"Sure, Bro. He still doesn't accept that he can fall in love with someone else, more so than his wife. One morning I heard him yelling in his apartment and I thought someone broke in and was attacking him. When I rushed there, I saw him quarreling with the girl about making up his bed, and cleaning up the house. He took it as she was trying to win him over and make him forget about his wife.

He explained how he told her several times that he was married, and they are just helping each other. He said he was aware of the ploy of some girls in this country. They will do everything to snatch husbands away from their wives, as soon as they notice that that husband is nice to them. And it starts by doing what she did, and next thing, they will take something of the man like a picture of him or his under clothes to carry to Guinea or Mali to have him charmed.

And because of this, he always reminds her of her limits, even though he invites her every evening to spend the night. I told him that maybe she was just trying to show that she appreciates him. But he told her to leave and never to come back; the relationship was over. But a week later, when Patrick told him that she started hanging out with some dude also in the government, he one day drove to her house and brought her back. She's almost staying with him now."

"And her limit has extended?" Boima laughed. "Well, he's a smart dude; top of his class and probably the only hydrocarbon nerd the country can boast of. The only one we had before him; Dr. Eric Newland died three years ago, remember that?"

"Yeah, with all of that, he's socially weak," Sam admitted and both of them descended the porch, laughing as they walked to the palaver hut to rejoin the group.

"Sorry, guys," Boima apologized when he and Sam rejoined the group and took their seats. "The tete-a-tete with my uncle was a little longer than expected, because there were issues we needed to address, before they leave for Bong Mines early tomorrow morning."

"Issues surrounding land are often carefully discussed with our traditional people," added Sam.

"It's no big deal, buddy. We got all night," Dukuly said, spreading his hands over the table. "This is how the table looks, guys. We got Jack Daniels, large and small bottles of Club Beer and Heineken, some wine and Baileys."

"I'll do with the Obequa over there," Sam said, getting up and stretching his hand for the Obequa bottle across the table."

"I'll continue with the Club Beer," stated Boima. "Never had these for more than four years."

"Yeah, speaking of Bong Mines," Patrick interjected, after taking a long drink of Heineken. "My little brother who works at the Ministry of Planning told me about some city directories they are currently developing for the cities along the highway corridor from Paynesville to Sanniquelle. While doing the one for Kakata, he said he was surprised that most of the towns, creeks and swamps along the Kakata-Bong Mines Road have Gola names but they are occupied by the Kpelle."

"Well. I think your little brother shouldn't be surprised, because the most possible reason could be as the result of war between the two tribes. The Kpelle just conquered the land, drove the other tribe out, but retained the names," offered Boima.

"Professor Wilton Sankawolo tried to give a picture of that in" Why Nobody Knows When He Will "Die", and "The Rain and The Night," Sam interjected.

"Certainly," Dukuly came in, after he took a sip of his Lime Juice since he was the only one who wasn't drinking alcohol.

"I remembered that an issue was raised by one Liberian Professor, Dr. Kennedy Golafalee. He taught Anthropology at one University in the Midwest. It was during the height of the civil war when he said one of Liberia's problems was that lands were taken from weak tribes by stronger tribes and so there's a need for land reparation. And guess what? His comments sparked public outcry among Liberians. Some said the professor had learned too much and he was confused."

"Yeah, I heard something like that," acknowledged Boima. "Because of the lashes he received, the old prof has since distanced himself from the Liberian community. He doesn't attend Liberian functions anymore. Says we are a strange kind of people."

There was a sudden outburst of laughter. Soon the barbecue was ready. Valerie, Jugbeh and Kemah wheeled a charcoal barbecue grill of steaming chop pork, spare ribs, stakes, chicken, fish, and some barbecue sauce mixed with vegetables from the back of Dukuly's apartment to the right of the palaver hut and announced that everyone should get up and serve themselves.

One after the other, they all got up, and walked to the barbecue grill. Valerie took some of them and carried them to Chief Lomeh and Wuamah. After Boima, Sam, Dukuly, Patrick, and George had served themselves, Boima looked around. Seeing Kerzo and Emmanuel sitting on the porch, he gestured to them to also serve themselves.

"So, how's the oil company doing, Doc.?" Boima, munching on a well-seasoned and grilled cassava fish, asked Dukuly.

"Well, for starters," Dukuly began, after sipping on a glass full of Eva non alcoholic wine. "We are currently working on the new petroleum law to set the stage for negotiating with some big oil companies to explore some of our oil blocks."

"And we are sure of striking oil, right?" asked Sam.

"We may, because we are in the Gulf of Guinea and situated at the most strategic part, where it is believed the stock pile of reserves are," responded the young hydrocarbon specialist.

"Unfortunately, our opposition says it's a mirage," George said, as he chewed on a chopped pork steak.

"Obviously they would," chuckled Sam. "That's one reason we had the civil crisis. For people to say at will, even though there's a danger ahead for subsequent governments."

"Even the Dems have said nothing good about President Bush as the unemployment rate has dropped to 4.4% from 6.3%. Oppositions are the same all over the world. Just that back in the states, it's a little more refined," added Boima.

"Yes, but this Opposition?" stressed George, accidentally knocking and spilling the half full bottle of the Club Beer he was drinking on the table. "Is full of a bunch of emptied headed guys. I can never join such a party."

"But back in the states you support the Dems, right?" asked Sam.

"Right," Patrick answered.

"But yet and still they advocate for one of the sickest things contrary to nature," Boima offered.

"And that's guy rights," Sam interjected "How about that?"

"And I guess after the next 6 or 12 years you will not praise the next government when you have now become an opposition," stated Boima.

There was silence in the palaver hut. George Tamba got up and went to the barbecue grill for some spare ribs. The young hydrocarbon specialist remained sitting and eating and drinking his Eva non alcoholic wine. Sam's eyes were fixed on Valerie who was busy with the barbecue while Jubgeh stood by her repeatedly looking at her watch. George came back and joined the group, but his continuance showed that he still wanted to argue and was contemplating on a rebuttal to Boima's statement.

"Gentlemen, gentlemen. Let's respect the sanctity of this gathering," sensing that, Dukuly got up and said, holding his glass in his hand. "I would like to welcome our brother, J. Boima Barclay Jr. back home and I wish him and his partner, my own man Sam, all the best in whatever they will be doing in Liberia. A toss."

It was now midnight. The guys were still under the palaver hut drinking and eating. Jugbeh said she was leaving and Valerie asked Sam to drop her. Young chief Lomeh and Wuamah had also eaten and drank, and went to bed when they felt sleepy. Sam and Valerie dropped Jubgeh to her house located at Rotto Town, Airfield shortcut, and had returned. It was about half past 1am when they returned. Dr. Dukuly and Boima were still under the palaver hut talking. After a few discussions, the young hydrocarbon specialist felt sleepy and left to join Kemah who had left earlier.

"Valerie. The room is there when you are sleepy. Sam and I will be out all night," Sam told her, when Boima, who received a call and said it was Diana, excused himself and walked out to answer it.

"Thank you, Sam," she responded. "But you said nothing when I told you, one of Dukuly's friend, Patrick slipped a call card in my hand."

"You're a pretty girl, Valerie," Sam crooned, smiling. "You know some guys will not admire a woman unless they see a man treating her special."

"But what is he taking me for? Like some street girl you just brought here?"

"You want Sam to confront him about this?" asked Boima who joined them when he had finished talking to Diana. "Sam only reacts when some dude takes advantage of you. That's where he gets so vicious. And you wouldn't want that."

Sam smiled as Valerie, from her expression, reflected on the issue with Victor. Since that time, he had stopped coming to the restaurant, and she believed he had learned how to behave himself. She smiled back when she caught Sam's eyes. Kerzo, who had helped to wheel the barbecue grill back to Dr. Dukuly's house, told them he was leaving, and then left when the bike that brought him returned.

"Let me share something I learned from Sam with you, Valerie," Boima said, taking a small bottle of Club Beer from the cooler, removing the cap with his teeth, and taking a long drink. "He taught me to be tolerant with women. It was because of this, a woman, an idol in her own right, is in love with me. I was able to tolerate her. And it has paid off.

Sam once had a Brazilian girlfriend named Amanda. They met in a strip club where she worked. We were attending the same university.

But back in Brazil, her family has ties with a powerful gang whose network extends to the States. Through this same network, she migrated to America, when she was in her early teens. And because of this, she was indebted to them. She was to pay tithes to them for life and this was affecting her wages. When she met Sam, he later discovered her predicament and confronted the head of the gang about this.

Apart from being a gangster, this guy was also a very dangerous karate fighter, very skilled in their kind of karate called Brazilian Jiu jitsu. Knowing that Sam was also a martial artist, he arranged a meeting with Sam and the girl in Charlotte, North Corallina, and I went along with them. At that meeting, this guy challenged Sam to a fight, and if he wins, Sam and the girl will be working for him forever. But if Sam beats him, he and the girl will go free.

More frightening, he said the fight will take place on that very day. Guess what? Sam agreed. And the fight took place. Two minutes into the fight, Sam beat him mercilessly, including some of his gangs who interfered in solidarity with their gang leader. While he was on the ground half conscious, Sam handed him the agreement paper to sign, but his other gangsters held us at gunpoint. Fortunately for us, we had earlier informed a Liberian friend of ours whose name is Arthur Willie. He came to our rescue with a group of crazy North Corallina boys.

The Brazilians were overpowered and the gang leader was forced to sign and stamp the agreement. But that girl later betrayed Sam."

"She was part of the scheme that set me up, and cost me my denial into the UFC," Sam added.

"You didn't tell me all this, Sam," Valerie said.

"I wanted you to hear it from Boima. I didn't want to beat my own drum."

"So, Valerie," Boima came in. "Sam trusts you so he will not bother about Patrick secretly asking you out. I guess that was why he slipped the call card in your hand. I dare if he ever takes advantage of you. You don't want to see how my brother will react."

"I already know him for that," Valerie admitted, laughing. "He recently taught my ex who refused to get over the fact that our relationship had ended years ago, a hard lesson."

"She didn't think I could do that, Boima," teased Sam.

"Yeah, because Victor is very rude and you don't look like someone who knows how to fight."

They stayed under the palaver hut joking, laughing and having some more drinks until it was after 2 in the morning. Valerie said she was sleepy and went to get some rest, when she had unsuccessfully encouraged Sam and Boima to go inside and also have some rest. The two friends stayed outside until 3 in the morning. Then they went back into the apartment, sat in the living room and watched the early morning news on CNN. They again talked, but in a very low tone to avoid disturbing Valerie, Chief Lumah and Wamah who were asleep. By 4 am, they were sound asleep, with the television still on.

The next day Boima, Sam, his uncle, Chief Lumeh and Wuamah were guests to David Lakay, the road construction engineer, to discuss a contract to recondition the road that leads to Maila, from Bong Mines Popota Road. He was recommended to Boima by the old representee who knew his father, a retired road construction engineer, well known in Fuamah district.

When Mr. Barclay was representative, both men worked on the feeder roads that connected towns and villages. The last time the road to Maila was rehabilitated was in 1989 when the old representative and Alan Ziptter were given the green light to explore the wonders of Maila. Since then, it had spoiled, became narrow and inaccessible to small vehicles. Only motor bikes, and 4 wheeled jeeps and pick-up trucks can manage to drive on it.

Tick grass had grown in the middle, making the once almost all-weather dirt road look like a trail of two paths lying parallel to each other. Miraculously, some of the log bridges constructed by the old representative were mostly intact, except for a few of them that were damaged. Until recently, with the news of the coming of Boima, they were replaced and re-enforced.

"Firstly, the road has to be assessed for its actual length and the condition before we apply the standardized formula to estimate the cost of rehabilitation or construction," David Lakay, the construction engineer said, in the meeting.

"Well, from the diagram my father prepared long ago, says it is about 6km from the main road from Bong Mines to Popota," Boima pointed, handing the map to the road construction engineer.

"Then we have something to start with," Lakay said, studying the map, and then took a notepad and started calculating something.

After that, he got from behind his desk, led his guests to his work room, and told his secretary to get a flipchart to replace it with the old one on the stand. As Boima, Sam, Chief Lumah, and Tonolah Wuamah sat attentively, he demonstrated the formula on the flip chart.

"Okay. This is how it works," he began, clearing his throat. "For what I see, the road to your town will require these basic needs; widening, graveling to fill at points of possible flooding, compacting of course with laterite, culverts to bridge the small streams and creeks as I see indicated on the map, and informational signage.

Now this is how it is calculated as per FAO (USA) Standards; for clearing, widening and culverting, the cost is US$ 3,555.00 per kilometer. At 6 kilometers, it will cost US$ 21,330.00. For graveling, it is US$ 6,550.00 per 10KM, so it will be 6,550.00 times 6, divided by 10 which will be US$3,930.00. So, for the clearing, widening, culverting and then graveling, it costs US$25,260.00. Now for the informational signage, it's US$ 2,000.00 at one end. So, if we add this figure to the US$ 25,320.00, we will get a total of US$27,260.00."

"How about building the boat ramp? Remember we discussed that too?" inquired Sam.

"Oh yeah," David Lakay responded eagerly, as his guests seemed not to be bothered about the cost. "Through a friend of mine, we were able to put together some designs."

The slim and dark completion road construction engineer excused himself and ran into his office. After a few minutes, he hurried back to the conference room with a mamillar folder in his hands. His secretary had asked the guests what to offer, and they all said only water will do. Lakay then shared with them some designs of boat ramps and mini docks made of timber.

"Luckily, the timber we will be using can be found in the forest near your town. So, the average cost of a simple boat ramp is US$6,000.00. This includes felling the trees, hauling them to the site, and sawing the logs into planks of various sizes."

"So, we are talking about a total cost of thirty-three thousand dollars" Boima turned to Sam, his uncle and Wuamah and said to them. "Just to get the road to the town and to build the place where the boat will be. Remember we will be exploring the waterways to know where each one of them leads. At least we will spare Wuamah the burden of memorizing where to navigate and never get lost."

There was laughter in the room and then the meeting was concluded. Lakay's construction company will pre-finance the work, while Boima and his partner agreed to wire half of the amount in the company's account in two weeks, and the other half to be paid when the job is completed and evaluated.

David Lakay also agreed that he will get his road construction team to the area in two days to do emergency work so as to ease Boima's trip from Popota Road to Maila. Chief Lomeh and Wuamah agreed to leave the next day, to wait for Lakay in Bong Mines.

"How's your old man?" Boima asked David, when the young construction engineer was accompanying them out of his office after the meeting. "My father got a word for him."

"Oh, my father Robert Lakay? He's retired now and lives in his own town along Kakata-Bong Mines Road. It is called Lakay Town."

"My father told me your father was the one given the contract to pave the Kakata-Bong Mines Highway in the late 80s. He was ready to start, but the war came."

"That's correct," admitted the younger Lakay. "We were all little then. And I can say they are proud of us, now we are stepping in their shoes. But the matter of fact is, this government is currently negotiating with the Chinese to have the highway finally paved."

"And you hope to be subcontracted?" Sam asked, smiling.

"Well," Lakay sighed. "It depends whether the government will want to promote a Liberian construction firm, like what you guys are trying to do."

"Well maybe they would," thought Boima.

"Okay guys, we'll meet in Bong Mines," Lakay said when his guests were leaving.

On Tuesday, the next day Orlando, assisted by Kerzo, had cleared the last container, and was trucked to the ranted parking yard. It contained a white 2003 4WD Range Rover, a boat propeller engine, a water pumping machine, and some other navigation aids such as markers and buoys that will be used to determine where a tributary, a creek or a stream leads and how to navigate them without getting lost.

Later that afternoon, they had lunch at 'Intown Parking Restaurant' where Valerie and her sister who met Boima for the first time, the day before, prepared a nice dish. Veronica felt so proud with the way Sam and his friend had shown the level of respect to her little sister. After lunch, Boima, Sam, Kerzo and Orlando went back to the parking yard to continue checking the items they will need to take to Maila.

On Wednesday at noon, they held a lunch meeting with the Bangladeshi national, at Mona Lisa in Sinkor, and it was fruitful. Chief Lomeh was excited, though he needed to brief his father and consult the town's elders, seeing that it was a good idea to grow rice for production on Maila soil. But the meeting was generally focused on fostering more commitments and mutual understanding on both sides that the land can be secured and be used for such purposes.

The rice production company executive had said that if the land is provided, testing will be done to determine whether the production can reach export level. Later that night, Valerie was taken out for the 'ladies' night' to 'Classic Touch' in Congo Town and they had a good time.

That night, she cried on Sam's shoulder when both of them were dancing the slow dance as the popular live band, the 'Exodus' played 'Suddenly' by Billy Ocean. She could not hold back her sobs as life recently has had a new meaning to her. She had never been taken out on a lady's night by two well intentioned friends.

She closed her eyes when she listened to the part of the song that says, 'Each day, I pray this love affair would last forever . . .'

When the song ended, Sam walked her back to their tables at the elevated VIP platform, rubbing her shoulder indicating that he knew and also felt what she had been going through and to assure her that all will be fine. She took a sip of the Savannah Dry she was taking her time to drink. It had been very long, she had not tasted alcohol.

Then the Exodus Band, noted for its playing of old school music, mainly of the 80s, played 'She's Fresh' by Kool and the Gang.

Immediately, Sam and Boima got up and ran to the stage, startling the other attendees.

They asked for the band manager and when he introduced himself to them, they asked to sing the song along with the band; they have special persons in their lives to dedicate the night and the music to. Though the band manager did not ask for anything in return, Boima gave him a twenty dollars bill.

"Well ladies and gentlemen of the house," taking the microphone, Sam addressed the group of attendees. "My brother and I will like to apologize for interrupting the band, but we could not allow this music to play without dedicating it as we sing with this fabulous band to two special persons in our lives and as we do this, you can join us to sing this song to all the special persons in your lives.

For me the special person I am dedicating this song to is the beautiful lady at the back with the red blouse and white trousers, Miss Valerie Sackor. Will you please stand."

Valerie could not hold her gaps when she stood up, very surprised. Next thing, she was sobbing and tears rolled down her eyes. All she heard herself saying was 'thank you ever so much. I 'll never forget this night.'

The attendees were still clapping when she sat down. Sam then signaled to Boima who took the microphone from the stand before him. He nodded in approval when Sam took his phone and dialed Diana's number on a video call. When she answered, her voice, sounding like she was still in bed as it was early in the morning in New York, Boima brought the Mic close to his mouth.

"Ladies and gentlemen. My special person I am dedicating this song to is Miss. Diana Rice, the most Exquisite American Idol. The woman of substance who has stood by me no matter what. I love you. And one thing I am confident will happen is that, pretty soon, you're gonna be called Mrs. Barclay. Okay guys let the music play."

The band started the song and Sam sang the first stanza, and after both of them sang the chorus. Sam shot the live video from the phone as Boima sang the second verse to the disbelief of Diana who was watching. She had never gotten so surprised.

Also, Valerie kept clapping, jumping and cheering as both sang the chorus for the second time. After the music, Sam slipped a twenty dollars bill in the band manager's hand. As they were descending the stage, the attendees clapped and cheered the two friends who in return, nodded and thanked everyone and the band. As they neared where they were sitting, Valerie got up, ran and hugged both of them. Then she hugged Sam for a long while before going back to her seat.

The rest of the night went on well, amidst all the fun. There were other guys who got on the stage to dedicate special songs to the special ladies in their lives as more clipping and cheers continued throughout the night.

They stayed out until 3am. Back at the compound, Valarie and Sam were in the Living room. Boima had gone into the bathroom to take a shower.

"Did you have a great time?" Sam asked her, noticing that she was quiet.

"Yes, I did. But you will soon be off to Bong Mines and I don't know whether I will cope with the fact that I am going to miss you."

"We will be over there for about two weeks, Valerie. If it is not for Promise school and all that stuff, I was going to take you along. And also, you got to prepare for your reminder, right?"

"The remainder is still far, and Promise aunty is here. Sam, you have not yet gotten it. I have never felt the way I am feeling since I met you. You have spoiled me by treating me too nice, so short a time. You can't just leave me here alone."

"If I were you. I will let her come with us, buddy," Boima who had just entered the living room, cut in.

"Okay," Sam sighed, taking her hands. "I 'll talk to Veronica, Okay. Can I see that pretty face, smiling?"

Friday morning, after having breakfast, they drove to the parking yard and arranged all the things they needed to take to Maila. In the next 30 minutes, the two-car convoy had driven past ELWA Junction and were heading to Red Light Market. Boima was leading the convoy, driving the Range Rover, while Sam, with Valerie sitting by him in the front passenger seat of the Ford Pick-up truck, followed behind.

The Ford was heavily loaded at the back with all the things they needed, and were neatly covered with a gray tarpaulin, including the small boat, also parked with things, attached to a carrier that was attached to the back bumper of the pick-up truck. They spent some time in the heavily congested traffic at Red-light market, taking close to 40 minutes to reach the United States Trading Company (USTC) locally called Coca Cola Factory, from Victory Chapel Church. The traffic had gotten static, before reaching Parker Paint Junction to the cluster of moto bikes, pedestrians, taxis, transport buses and trailer trucks refusing to give each other the right away.

What was more frustrating was when the traffic had dragged them to the middle of the intersection, when suddenly a kid, walking along the right side of the road selling bundles of black plastic bags uttered a nasty curse, an invective directed at the mother of a taxi driver whose right view merroir hit the kid's hands because he was walking closed to the road. Boima, whose car was slowly driving behind the taxi, heard the kid and gaped in horror at the profanity coming out of the boy's mouth. And the taxi driver, instead of parking off the road, suddenly stopped, jumped out of his car and ran after the kid. Soon there was a commotion with a group of passers-by running to the scene, and adding to the already static traffic.

However, police finally arrived and after several painstaking efforts lasting for about 35 minutes, they arrested the situation and the traffic was allowed to move a bit faster than what it was. As Boima slowly drove past Soul Clinic Junction, it had occurred to him how grievous the social problems of Liberia are, after the civil war. There should be some sort of a court to bring perpetrators of the civil war to justice.

It took some 15 minutes to reach Mount Barclay, and then another 8 minutes, Careysburg. They were at 15 Gate after some 12 deep curves. And Boima, as a kid riding with his father, whenever they were going to Bong Mines, wondered why there were too many curves from Careysburg to 15 Gate.

He also remembered a particular curve, upon reaching Todee Junction, and how the old representative used to refer to it as 'moto car graveyard', due to the many accidents and fatalities that occurred at that spot. After another 30 minutes, they passed Morison Farm to their left. Next was the bridge over the Du River, and then Booker Washington Institute (BWI) on the hill at the far right.

Right after the crest of BWI hill, they slowed down, and drove slowly behind a long queue of vehicles, approaching the police checkpoint. After the fifth car, a White Land Cruiser Jeep with an NGO license plate was allowed to cross the pass, then, the convoy of Sam and Boima was the next.

"Where are you carrying all of these things?" asked a police officer whose badge at the tip of his uniformed breast pocket, read 'Sgt. Aaron Garteh'.

"We're taking them to our farm, somewhere behind Bong Mines," answered Boima. "We are Liberians returning home to invest."

The fat and dark in completion police officer nodded, and then walked to Sam. After a brief inspection with his eyes, he walked back to Boima.

"Yeah, carry on. We need many of you guys to come back home to fix this country."

Boima casually saluted him, and kept nodding when another officer, wearing a gray T-shirt with the police logo etched on the upper left breast, dropped down the robe, which was used as a gate, allowing the convey to drive through.

Not long after, they were driving along the main street of Kakata which is the Monrovia-Gbarnga Highway. As usual, Kak City, as it was called, was busy, as Boima remembered. He and the old representative, traveling back and forth from Monrovia to Bong Mines on many occasions, passed through this city.

Also, his mother, Mrs. Barclay, on every first Sunday, after church, would take him along, when she visited the Chenoway family who had their farm on the Kakata-Bong Mines Road, just 3km from the city. And whenever she asked him whether he missed Bong Mines, he would shake his head no, because his father took him there to see his mother whenever his wife was away.

As they slowly drove past Monrovia Parking Station, attracting the attention of curious onlookers who for years had not seen a boat being pulled by a car, what was considered central Kakata looked much the same. The main street was strewn with petty traders on both sides of the road. The only strange things were billboards and signs of the branches of the different banks operating in Liberia at almost every intersection they drove past.

There were also signs and billboards of the sub offices of governments ministries and agencies, and the two leading telecommunication companies in the country. Also, symbols and directions, portraying the proliferation of guest houses, motels and entertainment centers adorned street junctions. There were more stores and commercial activities had extended from the main road with tee shops owned by Fula business men at almost every street corner.

But the city was largely remembered for its DNA, a trait Boima remembered as a kid viewing the pedestrians, whenever he and his father drove through the city. And it was the ubiquitous sale of boiled eggs by mostly children, who tote them in carts on their heads or between their forearms. 'Hot boiled eggs here. Hot boiled eyes here,' they would announce. But now they are sold in transparent plastic buckets.

Boima and convoy turned left after driving past the old Shell Gas Station to their left and headed down the dirt road in the direction of Bong Mines. They passed the old Miss Moore Mission, and then the intersection of the Kakata correction center. In about 7 minutes, they passed Chenoway Farm.

Boima slowed down and felt a bit nostalgic, looking first at the sign board on the road, and then the farm with the same old structures. After covering a distance of about a mile and a half, they reached an area where the road passes through a hill that formed a border on both sides.

Lakay Town, built by the retired road construction engineer, Robert Lakay, and named after him was situated on top of the border on the right side of the road. They reached a junction with a sign board planted on the right that read 'welcome to Lakay Town' and turned right. They drove in for about a few seconds and then turned left, up a hill and reached what looked like a square surrounded by small houses built of dirt bricks and plastered with cement. There they made a stop, and waited in the cars.

A man, upon seeing the cars, walked to them.

"The old man is expecting you," he said and gestured to them to follow him.

They got down from the cars, and followed the man who led them to a clearing at the back of a big house made of cement. Robert Lakay was sitting under a palaver hut made of mud bricks and a zinc roofed roof. With him were two Chinese men wearing yellow reflective safety vests and white helmets, seated around a table full of yellow folders.

"Welcome to my little town, Barclay Jr. and friends," greeted the old man who immediately recognized Boima, and got up from his seat to receive his guests. "I have been expecting you when my son, on his way to Bong Mines two days ago, stopped by and told me you were coming."

"Thank you, Mr. Lakay," Boima said, and then gestured to Sam and Valerie. "Please meet my associates."

Mr. Lakay shook Sam and Valerie's hands and then led them into the Palaver hut. They took seats already arranged for them, and waited as the retired road construction engineer briefly chatted with the two Chinese who then left afterwards.

"They are engineers from the construction company the government and the Chinese company who has taken over Bong Mines are negotiating with, to pave the Kakata-Bong Mines Highway. They came to seek my expert opinion. Remember I was contracted by the then government and Bong Mining Company to pave this road," he said, taking his seat. "Had it not been for the war, that road could have been completed long ago and next, your father and I were going to be concentrating on opening up the entire western Fuamah District front to connect to the rest of Bong. Now the only accessible road to get to the rest of Bong is this route and the Kakata-Gbarnga Highway. And Kakata is in Margibi County."

"That's why my father sent me to you. He has completed the assessment you both worked on before the war and had asked me to bring it for your opinion," Boima informed the retired engineer, and got from his computer bag a document sealed up in a green plastic folder.

"Oh thanks." The old man said, taking the folder from Boima and opening it. After inspecting what looked like a series of diagrams, he continued. "That's exactly what we planned. Linking Fuamah to the rest of Bong County in two ways. First, by paving the road that passes through Popota to Wheala and then a bye pass to connect to Salala. I will study it and give my opinion. You can get it back from me before you go back to the states."

They sat with the old man for some time, talking, when he offered them drinks.

"Such a plan will need the blessing of a good representative; a representative with lobbying power to persuade the government to carry on the two major road projects to open up the entire Fuamah District, including the construction of the bridge over the St. Paul River to connect Gbarpolu County through Hendii," Robert Lakay lectured them.

"The bridge was going to bring great relief to the people who will use it to get to Gbarpolou then to cross the river in a canoe," Boima said.

"Perfect."

"I remembered my father always talked about it. But I was surprised that you could recognize me," Boima said, after a brief thought.

"Yes. I knew your biological mother, from the time she got pregnant for you up to the time she gave birth."

"Do you have any idea where she may be now?" Boima asked.

"No," answered the old man. "Throughout the war, I remained on this farm helping many displaced persons from Hendii, Bong Mines and the affected villages along the road. But I did not see your mother during these times, and I had not heard death news about her."

Sad, Boima thanked Robert Lakay and told him that they were about to continue their journey.

From the town, they got back on the main road to Bong Mines and after covering some distances, they got to the checkpoint. On the left was a dirt road that led to Todee. After they were asked a few questions by the joint security minding the checkpoint, followed by a brief inspection of the vehicles and the boat, the gate was dropped down for them and they continued their journey.

The next 13 minutes they were at St. Mark's Mission, JDK Baker Episcopal School junction, just before entering the community of Nyenen. From Maila Elementary School, Boima continued his primary education at the school from kindergarten to third grade before he went to live with his father in Monrovia.

He slowed down and parked on the left side of the road, and had anticipated driving on the campus, but the road from the junction to the school looked impossible to drive on; it was covered with tall grass, and trees due to years of abandonment. Only a path that snaked its way up to the campus was visible. The school was shut down in the late-eighties, and has since been uninhabited.

Boima got down from the Range Rover, walked to Sam and Valerie and told them they were already in Bong Mines and he wanted to take a brief look at the place where he spent the early part of his primary education. The couples agreed to walk with him.

With Boima ahead, they threaded on the path covered with cascading sawgrass reaching to their knees, but causing no scratches on their skins. Thanks to the jeans trousers they were wearing. Unfortunately, tiny grass seeds, which the JDK Baker students used to refer to as 'homework grass' because they stock on their socks and anklets, and it took painstaking efforts to remove.

Boima remembered how his mother used to tell him never to walk in the grass on campus, and whenever he forgot and did, she would make him remove all the tiny seeds from his socks, and it took an annoying and painstaking effort to do. They reached what was the basketball court to their left which Boima could only recognize by the rust eaten steel poles that held the board and the rim. Then they reached the boy's dormitory to their right.

The campus was bushy and Boima was surprised that he could still remember the place. The dilapidated school building, which once hosted the chapel, in which he was baptized and the principal's office stood before them. To the left, partially surrounded by bushes was the frame of what was left of the principal's residence and the adjoining apartment where the priest that oversaw the school was lodged whenever he was visiting the campus, from Monrovia.

Boima remembered the very bulky Rector who would drive on the campus in his white single cabin Peugeot 504 pickup truck, and how during his stay, some of the big male students would be selected to help him with some renovation works.

He also remembered where his classroom was, which was situated at the left side of the building, facing the principal and the priest residence. He remembered Mrs. Williams, his 1st and 2nd grade teacher, and how when it was test time, she would warn them not to spy and if they did, the bats in the ceiling would make lots of noise. There was a large colony of bats up in the ceiling in the school building.

"This was a day and boarding school," he muttered as he struggled to suppress the hysterical emotion that was brewing inside him.

As a day student, he remembered his mother walking him to school every morning. They would walk from Sugar Hill, located on the left side of Nyenen when coming from the direction of Kakata and they would take light strides along the main road that passed through Nyenen. They would enter the campus by way of a small road on the right, that passed by Bong Playhouse, the cinema.

Sometimes Gotolo would bring him whenever he was spending time. He suddenly began to sob when he could no longer control his hysterical emotion. Sam and Valerie padded him on the back and told him that he had seen enough and it was best that they left. But he appealed for a little more time to take some pictures.

It was about 1:30 pm and they still had time to reach Varney Town where his uncle, the young chief, and David Lakay were waiting to receive them. They would spend the day in Bong Mines and then early the next morning, they would head for Maila.

"You guys looked good together," Boima said, smiling at Sam and Valerie at the same time snapping them with a small camera that hung around his neck, after he had taken some pictures, including what was the teachers' apartments, and the junior high building to the right of the school building.

He was unable to walk all the way to the back of the main school building to take pictures of what was the football field, the dining hall and the girls' dormitory which, at the far right, lie in ruins and covered with thick bush.

"Thanks, dude," Sam said. "We gotta get going now."

I'll lead," Valerie offered, and led the two friends all the way back to the main road, not aware that Boima was taking her pictures.

Entering Nyenen, they drove through the hill borders on both sides of the road which was considered the beginning of the community, and then passed by the Bong Mines Cinema to their left.

The once bustling Nyenen, adorned with stores, shops, and waiter markets that lined up on both sides of the road amidst a mini but rich market that comprised of commodities of almost all varieties, also on both sides of the road, looked deserted, gloomy and appeared to be uninhibited for ages. Boima felt the first pinch of the effect of the civil war on rural Liberia. The little town was a commercial hub in lower Bong County, which usually turned into a shopping blizzard whenever it was payday.

Apart from the Volkswagen Beetles driven by Bong Mining Company staff that were often parked on the side of the road, heavily and dangerously loaded Toyota Hilux and Stout Pickup trucks, coming from the direction of Varney Town or beyond or from the direction of Kakata would stop at Nyenen to drop off passengers and offloaded different varieties of goods.

There would be the constant honking of horns, most especially from the high speeding BMC buses, coming from the direction of Varney Town, heading to the turning point opposite JDK Baker Episcopal School Junction to drop and pick-up Bong Mines workers.

Boima remembered the Gbatu and the Gio Devils that often performed in front of stores mostly owned by Lebanese, Fula or Mandingo Merchants, and an encounter he had with one, when he and a little girl of about 12 years old, who once lived with his mother, had gone to Nyenen to buy Sweets when the masquerade saw him. When he turned to run, it put up a chase after him. Boima remembered how he outran the Gbatu from Sugar Hill junction all the way to his house and under his mother's bed.

They slowly drove on, reaching Bong Town main gate to their right, and passed it. Cruising further, they passed what was Nyenen main market, which was once a football field, also on their right, and in seconds, they were driving through Keleku Town where Boima remembered the once feared masonic lodge, a small white building.

Passing by it to his left, he saw that it still remained dilapidated, since it was ransacked in the early 80s, shortly after the military coup. His mother used to tell the story of how the people dreaded that lodge for many years, due to its eeriness and secrecy, which caused them to strongly believe that was where the society people, as members of the masonic craft were called, performed many kinds of evil rituals, including human sacrifice.

During the day, most people, on their way to Varney Town never freely walked past it. They would either take the side of the road to their right when coming from the direction of Nyenen or to their left when coming from Varney Town.

At night, in order to avoid passing in front of the masonic lodge, when coming from Nyenen, many people would prefer using a bypass, by way of a trail that branched off to the left, after passing by the once popular Pink Slipper Bar. The trail passed through what was once a woods of rubber trees, where a market and the P. Lorpu Academy School were later built. It connected straight to BRU Park vicinity, leaving the Lodge and John Hill to their far right. Few months after the coup, a large group of people, led by Koikoi Pewee, ransacked the lodge and almost set it ablaze.

When they finally got to Varney Town, after ascending the famous John Hill, they met David Lakay and young Chief Lumeh standing by what was a popular gas station at the intersection of the road that led to Bong Range United (BRU) Park, waiting to receive them. Boima looked to his right and there was Botota, a part of the company's residential area once inhabited mostly by junior staff.

He tried to remember the spot at the edge of a thick wire fence that separated Botota from Varney Town, where Mrs. Mary Garnett Clinic was. She was a retired nurse who worked in the children's ward at Bong Mines Hospital. His mother always took him to her clinic whenever he was sick. And he always preferred being taken there because she seldom gave injections and whenever she did, it didn't hurt.

"Welcome to Bong Mines, Mr. Barclay," greeted the young road construction engineer walking to the Range Rover. "This is how our once beautiful town looks like now."

"Well Yes," sighed Boima, getting down from the jeep. "Thanks." Seeing his uncle, Chief Lumeh also walking to him, he embraced him for a while. "Uncle. We are here," he said.

"Okay, this is what we are going to do," David Lakay then said when Sam and Valerie joined them. "You will drive behind me to where you will be staying for the night. After resting for a while, we can drive through Bong Town and see what is left of the once small Germany."

They drove behind Lakay to a big compound in the BRU Park community. It was a guest house owned by the Lakays. As soon as they entered and parked, they were met by three attendants who welcomed them. They were helped with their luggage, and ushered to a mini suit.

Then a generator was ignited and the compound was electrified. After that, they were ushered to a lodge, where Lakay was waiting. They agreed to suspend lunch until they returned from touring Bong Town, and as Boima suggested, Sugar Hill.

But they had a couple of drinks, and a briefing from the young road construction engineer on the ongoing emergency works on the road to Maila, which started three days ago and will be finished by the end of the day. After they all drove in the Range Rover to Bong Town by using the Varney Town route, except Chief Lumeh. He told his nephew that he will walk down to Sugar Hill using the by-pass behind BRU park to wait for them there.

They drove through Varney Town market, which looked less spirited than its pre-war status, but at least better than Nyenen. They crossed the train tracks which still looked usable as Boima observed, and thanked the people in his heart for ensuring that it was protected-the rebels didn't loot it.

Then they reached what was the main bus stop where the workers, coming from or going to work, changed buses. As Sam drove and was directed by Lakay who sat in the front passenger seat while Valerie and Boima sat at the back helping themselves with some small bottles of Club Beer, they headed up the hill that led to Zaweata School. The school building was intact, and they were informed that it was now being used as a public school.

They left Zaweata and drove to Bong Mines Hospital. Boima told his friends that was where he was born. Then they drove around what was Bong Town School which they struggled to make up from a little distance to their left partly due to the bushes that now engulfed it. Lakay informed them that some of the roads were no longer accessible as they were covered with grass and bushes, and so they turned around, and got back on the road that led to the hospital from the Bong Mines main gate.

Then they turned left, passing by where the Mind Guards office was, and reached what was Club Bong Range. Directly behind the Club House, as it was commonly called, was the two-football fields; the big and the small one. And further beyond was the Swimming Pools, also the one for the adults and the one for the kids. To the left was the Tennis courts.

Like the few places they toured, the Club House and all the surrounding houses were in ruins and covered with bushes. Here again, Boima remembered how his father once took him and his mother to the restaurant. They were met by some German people, many of whom were his father's formal colleagues, when he worked for the company.

When his father introduced them to the Germans, they were offered food and drinks. Boima remembered how he ate and drank until he could no longer stand up. That night, it was his first-time drinking Club Muscatella, and since then, he had always appreciated the very appetizing and refreshing nonalcoholic beverage. And it was the last time he saw his mother. As he looked at what was the club house, and with more memories of that night clouding his mind, he closed his eyes.

"'Where are you, the most beautiful Esther Gorpue Lomeh?" he asked in a low tone.

They left the Club House, and drove to Nyenen by way of the Bong Mines main gate, where they passed the little bridge over the creek that divides Bong Town from Nyenen. Passing what was left of the main gate, they turned left, drove on for a while and reached Sugar

Hill Junction. They met Chief Lumeh and some men conversing and stopped for him.

He excused himself from the men and joined his nephew and his friends, and then they drove through the narrow road to where Esther Lumeh and her son used to live.

The house still looks the same, including the surroundings. But it was now occupied by a family Boima could not recognize. What he could still remember was a house opposite where they lived, owned by old man Lavala who was a retired laborer working with the Bong Mining Company. He had his wife, Klubol, who sold varieties of basic foodstuff, including sweets, on a very large table in front of her house. She didn't sell on Saturdays because she was a Seventh Day Adventist, and never missed service.

It was on a Saturday when she was not selling, that prompted Boima and the little girl who lived with his mother to venture to Nyenen to buy some Toffee when he was chased by the Gabtu. Surprisingly he met Klubol sitting in front of her market, selling the same assorted food Items. She looked old but was still looking strong.

"Ma Klubo!" Boima exclaimed, getting down from the Range Rover and walking to her. "Remember me? Boima. Esther Lumeh son. We used to live in that house."

"Kpo!" also exclaimed the old lady, using a common expression in her Loma dialect. "How I will not remember you," she continued, with heavily accented English. "You used to come buy candies from this very table. Sometimes you used to pull your father over here to buy them for you, whenever he came to visit you. In fact, your uncle told me you were coming to look at your old place."

Boima scooped over to embrace her while she remained sitting.

"Sorry, my Son," she said, also embracing him around the waist. "I can't get up. I am old now and my legs are heavy and hurting."

He introduced Sam, Valerie, and David Lakay to her. She greeted them and told David that she knows his father; at one time her late husband worked with him when he was contracted by the company to condition the Bong Mines-Hendii Road. And she asked how he was doing.

Remembering that she had a boy and two girls, Boima asked for them.

"They have all left me here o. My oldest daughter is in Monrovia. She is a nurse. My son is a pastor, while my youngest daughter is also a nurse. She was recently assigned at the Phebe Hospital in Gbarnga."

"That's very good," Boima said. "Have you heard about my mother?"

"Yeah," the old lady sighed, suddenly becoming serious. "Gorpue was here when the main rebel group took over Bong Mines. But she was afraid of their commanders because they were just taking people's children as their wives. She highly went out for fear of being seen, and followed. You know she's very beautiful and attractive. But when the other Rebel group attacked Bong Mines, she left with the displaced people. I later learned that she briefly stayed at the displace camp between Weala and Kakata, where Koi koi Pewee once ran. But again, for the same fear, she left. It was the last time I heard about her."

"Siegie will tell us more about this," said Chief Lumeh. "He sent word that he will be in Maila in two days."

"Well, thanks for the information, Ma Klubol. At least no one has said they heard that she has died," Boima said.

"When you get to Maila. Ask that man from her town who always visited her. He might provide more details," turning to Chief Lumeh, the old lady suggested.

"Oh yes. Gotolo," the young chief agreed.

Feeling happy and hopeful about the information provided about his mother, Boima thanked the old lady and gave her US$100.00 and told her he was about to leave and get prepared for the journey to Maila the next day. He promised to make sure to stop by and give her some money to help purchase more goods for her table market, upon his return to the states. The market table she now sat behind was not as rich as what it used to be before the war. Old lady Klubol thanked and told him that he would locate his mother.

Then they returned to Lakay guest house at Varney Town. They had dinner at 3:00pm. After that, David Lakay told them he was going to inspect the conditioning of the road and would be back late at night to accompany them the next morning to Maila.

Bright and sunny, the next morning, Boima, Sam and Valerie, with David Lakay driving ahead in his company's gray double cabin Mitsubishi pickup truck, were cruising through Benuma on the road to Hendii. They passed the Catholic Football field to their right. Boima remembered one time an older boy named Anthony Kamara, his mother's former schoolmate at JDK Barker Episcopal School, took him to witness a particular football match played on this field between two local football teams; Lofa Bridge and Azariah.

Lofa Bride, and Bong Range United were the two main soccer teams in Bong Mines, always winning the Championship. Whenever one captures the trophy, the following year, the other team will recapture it. Azariah and other smaller teams were considered the least, but that particular game, which was the final of Bong Mines soccer league, Lofa Bridge lost to Azariah 3 goals to 2, making Azariah that year, the champion team, 10 years since it was founded.

That day the field was jammed packed with spectators surrounding the perimeters of the stadiumless soccer pitch, with the fans of Lofa Bridge dominating in their green and yellow colors while Azariah fans were in their white, from top to bottom. The enthusiasm was high as supporters cheered their respective teams. But the atmosphere was tense with some of them trading jeers like hooligans. Tunny, as this older boy was commonly called, was a fan of Lofa Bridge. He had to carry Boima on his shoulders and fought his way amongst the deafening crowd to a suitable spot at the goalline of the right half of the field on his team side, so they both could get a clear view of the pitch without the spectators blocking them.

A few minutes after the game started, Boima remembered seeing a man dressed like a fetish priest running to where they stood, dingling a half brown 100lb rice bag. The bearded man with shining bushy hair opened the bag and a porcupine with black and white quills crept out. As some of the spectators watched, the man circled around the animal and shouted. "Porcupine, Porcupine. We want a goal. Lofa Bridge goal."

The large rodent immediately grunted, and chartered its teeth. Then it stamped its hind limbs on the ground and released one of its quills.

"One goal to Lofa Bridge, one goal to Lofa Bridge," the man repeatedly shouted, raising the quil and pointing it towards the goal posts of Azariah.

A few seconds afterwards, a player wearing the number 9 jersey for Lofa Bridge leapt in the air for a volley from his team mate at the far-right side of the field and landed a terrific head up into the far-left angle of the goal posts, far beyond the reach of Solomon Davis, the Azariah goalkeeper who made frantic efforts to catch the ball but they both fell into the back of the net. And there was a goal. Lofa Bridge fans erupted into cheers and celebration. Three minutes before the first half ended, there was another uproar when the same number 9 scored with a terrific ground shot that goalkeeper Solomon Davis did not see. Boima saw the same man running towards the Lofa Bridge side, now with two quills in his hands.

The second half started with the forwards of Azariah, driving into the 18-yard box of Lofa Bridge with thunderous shots, some of which missing target an inch. Goalkeeper Alphonso Dorbor was making some spectacular saves, prompting Lofa Bridge fans to cheer and jubilate. Azariah almost scored a goal when a shot hit the left post and diverted offside with the ball landing and bouncing across the goaline. With growing apprehension amongst Lofa Bridge fans, the jubilation was gradually diminishing as the forwards of Azariah, as if injected with a new vigor, continued to harass the defense of Lofa Bridge.

Perched on Tunny's shoulder, Boima could see far beyond the end of Azariah goal post, some Aladura prophet women in their white garments and red mantles tied around their waists, singing, dancing and ringing tiny bells. He later remembered hearing a spectator saying that the mother of the president of Azariah was the head prophetess of an Aladura church located somewhere around John Hill. He could also see the man with the porcupine running around the field, yelling, "No goal for Azariah. No goal for Azariah."

Lofa Bridge fans began to cheer again when a substitution was made when a player apparently in his late 20s or early 30s, wearing the number 5 jersey for Lofa Bridge entered the pitch.

"Pantoe, Pantoe. No nonsense Panto," they cheered as he briefly warm-up and entered the field.

Isaac Pantoe, a stocky and muscular Mine Guard had returned from work and had hurried to play for his team. The all white jersey he was wearing was over-stretched, exposing the outline of his chest, thigh and arm muscles. As he jogged on the field, the teeth of his Sugar Boots clattered, revealing that he was wearing iron-studs. With his presence in Lofa Bridge defense, the attacking tempo of Azariah began to slow down. Its forwards were no longer venturing into the 18-yard box, but were taking them a few inches away. Some of their shots were fortstratingly feeble with Alphonso Dorbor having a field day. Once more, Lofa Bridge forwards were mounting pressure for a third goal.

Mid-way into the second half, Boima was still clinched on Tunny's shoulders, but now at the opposite goal line which was now the Lofa Bridge side of the field. He became distracted to the cheering of a group, accompanying a slim and tall middle teen-age boy hurrying towards the substitute corner of Azariah. Two Azariah officials, with a set of jersey, a hose, and a pair of black Adidas boots with three white stripes on its sides, ran to meet the youngster. Boima watched the teenager change into the all-white jersey, as a small crowd gathered around him. When the referee halted the game and signaled his entry, the boy first waited at the entry touchline for the player he was substituting to come out, and then turned his back to the cheering of Azariah fans, revealing the number 14 on his back. He bowed, tipped his index finger on the entry touchline, signed his cross twice and jogged towards the center circle of the field.

"That Peking is from Monrovia," Boima heard a spectator saying. "They say he's a wizard dribbler."

"If he likes he can even be King Pele, but he will not stand a chance against Pantoe," another spectator said.

The first ball he was to handle was when he leapt in the air for a cross from the right corner of the field delivered by his team mate, but missed when Pantoe jumped with him and did some tackling while in the air and both of them landed on the ground, with the muscular body of the Lofa Bridge center-back all over the teen ager's frail body. Pantoe jumped to his feet and warm-up amid cheers, but the youthful stricker remained on the ground for some time until the referee ran to him and extended his hand to help him up. The second time, his teammate Christain Huff, the tactician in Azariah midfield, gave him a pass around the arc of the 18-yard box. Before he could trap the ball, and turn towards his opponent's goal, again, Pantoe was upon him in one of his no-nonse clearing of the ball from under his feet, the impact swirling gravels, dirt and dust. To avoid contact, the mask man had to skip by jumping in the air. Lofa Bridge fans were once more in a frenzy, upon seeing this.

"Peking. Pantoe will kill you," Boima heard Tunny saying.

A couple of minutes later, the teen-age striker was given a chest-high pass from deep in their half when Christain Huff saw him roaming around the center circle. The kid expertly tracked the ball and turned while still in the air, beating Pantoe who lost his balance when he attempted to race towards his opponent to engage him with a hard tackle. Next, to everyone's astonishment, the last two Lofa Bridge defenders from the left and right foot backs were dribbled when the teen-ager snaked his way between them. In split seconds, he was in the 6-yard box, one on one with Alphonso Dorbor and curved the ball under his stretched arms, when the Lofa Bridge goalkeeper thought that the Azariah sticker was going to loop the ball way above him. The fans of Azariah shouted in an unbelievable jubilation when the ball entered into the goal, making the score 2 goals to 1.

Five minutes after that goal, the equalizer came when Huff delivered a long ground pass intended for the now sensational stricker who put up a chase after the ball as it spun towards the left side of the 18-yard box. Isaac Pantoe, closely marking the player, also put up a chase after him getting close enough and, using his bigger body to outweigh him before he got the ball. Out of a sudden, the teen-age striker abruptly stopped, but picked up again in less then a second, catching the hard tackling Lofa Bridge defender off guard when he also stopped, and attempted to pick up again after his elusive opornant. In the process he tripped and fell on his belly, the impact dragging him on the gravel field, soiling the front of his yellow jersey top, and pulling down his blue shorts all the way to his thigh. By the time Pantoe got from the ground, and drew his shorts back up, the number 14 of Azariah was around the left arc of the 6-yard box. Before goalkeeper Alphanso Dorbor could come out for the cross-falling, the ball was at the back of the net, causing an avalanche of uproar from the spectators.

With the perimeters around the field now alive with Azariah supporters, as their sensational stricker from Monrovia displayed unimaginable soccer performances, the game continued until the last minute when in a one on one encounter between the now nervous Pantoe and the Azariah talisman, a foul was committed in the 6-yard box when the Lofa Bridge defender went for the player's both knee-caps in a flying double legged tackle bringing him down. The youngster was yelling and rolling and at the same time holding his knees. The referee immediately blew his whistle for a penalty.

A commotion suddenly erupted between some Azariah players, angry over Pantoe's rough tackles and some Lofa Bridge players. The whole field was now crowded with spectators of both teams, trading jabs and fists. At that point, the game came to a momentary standstill. Moreover, some players and officials of Lofa Bridge were rejecting the penalty. Boima noticed that a group of spectators and players crowded around a man, wearing a sleeveless African shirt, blue jeans trousers and a pair of brown sandals. He later got to know that he was Mr. Theophilus Nah, the match commissioner.

"The referee is right; it is a penalty," said the man who looked to be in his late 50s, his accent sounding like a Kru man, probably educated in Sierra Leone. "If Lofa Bridge refuses the penalty, we will give the trophy to Azariah."

The grumble continued for a couple of minutes, before Lofa Bridge finally accepted the penalty. The teenage striker was now sitting on the ground with his team medic wiping the blood from around spots of wound caused by Pantoe's iron studs, and dabbing them with a cotton inundated with Blue-Hydrofera. After efforts from some police task force officers, the field was finally cleared of spectators. Then the referee sounded his whistle to resume the game with Azariah about to take the penalty.

Goalkeeper Alphonso Dorbor, highly reputable as one of the best penalty savers in the league, stood between his goal posts, ready. The number 14 player walked to the ball, positioned at the penalty spot, his head down, looking at his sore knees, and stopped a few inches from the ball. The referee signaled first to the goalkeeper, then to the player, asking whether both were ready, which they nodded in the affirmative and then blew his whistle. The kick was taken. About 2ft above the ground, the ball spun towards the right corner a few inches away from Alphonso Dorbor, a position he mastered, and then he took a spectacular side dive.

"What kind of penalty this Peking kicked, so?!" an Azariah fan exclaimed, his hands on his head, when it seemed that it was going to be an easy save for Dorbor.

Lofa Bridge players and fans were now cheering, anticipating that it was going to be a save, but their goal keeper suddenly screamed, stretching his hands further. As if controlled by the wind, the ball somehow veered an inch from his hands. It hit the base of the right corner of the goal post, and rolled into the goal.

"G-o-a-l," the whole field erupted; the referee was running towards the center circle, pointing at the same time blowing his whistle. Goalkeeper Alphonso Dorbor remained flat on the ground on his belly holding the right side of his ribs.

Thrilled with excitement, Azariah fans and other spectators ran on the field. They lifted the magnificent penalty kicker in the air and carried him from one side of the field to another, jubilitatig. Boimi remembered seeing the man with the porcupine sitting on the ground, crying. Again, it took a couple of minutes to clear the field before the ball was centered. The next few minutes, it was all about stunning performances when Azariah drilled Lofa bridge around. Isaac Pantoe, now demoralized, was dribbled several times by the teen-age stricker to the cheering of the crowd. Alphonso Dorbor, complaining about his injured side, called time on himself.

A few minutes later, the game finally ended. Again, the spectators ran on the field and lifted the man of the match in the air. Lofa Bridge players were all rolling on the ground, weeping when Mr. Theophilus Nah presented the trophy to the Azariah Captain. Fighting erupted in some parts of the field between disgruntled Lofa Bridge fans and Jubiliting Azariah supporters.

Daunted, but somehow thrilled with the spectacular performance of the number 14 player of Azariah, Tunny hurried with Boima to Varney Town packing station where he left his black Coaster bike with a friend, and savely rode Boima home. All along the way people were talking about this wizard dribbler from Monrovia who later went on to play for the Liberian National soccer team, and subsequently introduced into the world stage winning FIFA highest accolades. Drawing much of his inspiration from the soccer Icon, Boima thought about his friend Sam, whose dream was to become a mixed martial arts athlete fighting in the UFC, and also winning accolades.

Passing Catholic football field, they continued for some minutes, until they branched off right, on Popota Road. They drove northwards on the dirt and sometimes hilly and rocky road bordered on both sides by a mixture of bushes and wild rubber trees. Sometimes they would see the foggy appearance of the tip of the undulations of the Bong Range in the distance ahead, and sometimes partially to their right, especially when they soared up a hill and reached its crest.

Sam marveled at how green the vegetation around them was, and couldn't imagine why people could starve in search a blessed country like Liberia.

"We got ourselves a very beautiful country with fertile soil, Valerie," he said, looking at her and focusing on the rough road again. "My father used to say our land is so fertile that even if you plant your finger in the ground, it will grow. I used to think it was an over statement. But look around you. It's all green."

"Sure," she admitted, smiling at the same time firmly holding the ceiling handle to brace herself as the Ford Pick-up truck bounced on the rough road. "And there are few people like you and Boima who are trying to make sense of it. So, you need to apology to your dad, now that you have realized what he meant."

"Yep," he nodded, staring at her and admiring how beautiful and attractive she looked wearing her silver gold Rhinestone metal steel summer glasses blending with her Viking Loc style gold silver braided hair in harmony with the complexion of her skin. More especially, she was dressed in a black skinny denim jean that perfectly showed the outline of her curved hips almost completely spreading over the front passenger seat.

"Every day your beauty gets from one level to another," he mused. "I have never been so excited."

"Eyes on the road, Olu," Valerie smirked as the Ford Pick-up truck bounced when it ran into a gutter in the middle of the road.

In about 40 minutes, they reached the junction of the road that led to Maila. They turned left and drove west, leaving Popota Road at their rear. They could see that the road had been worked on; the tall grass at the middle of the road that Chief Lumeh and Tonolah Wuamah described has been cleared. There was graveling in some parts while other parts were compacted with laterite. Also, the log bridges were re-enforced.

They covered some distances for about an hour and fifteen minutes, but the locality looked the same as the road they had just left, except for an abandoned orange farm to their left, completely immersed into the bush. There were more than three delipidated structures partially covered with bush with the tip of wooden light poles standing out among the branches.

These poles, harvested from cider trees and brought into the country by the Liberia Electricity Corporation, still looked good and usable. Incredibly, the indelible black chemical substance, pentachlorophenol, used to protect the light poles were still noticeable.

Boima could still remember this orange farm. It was planted in the early 70s by one Dominique Fasou, a Kpelle man who was married to a Russian he met while studying in the former Soviet Union. But they left after the 1980 coup.

Up to the early eighties, people from the surrounding farm villages used to pick the oranges, during the harvest season and took them to Varney Town to sell. Some of the oranges were sold in front of the supermarket at Bong Town. But when the war came, rebel fighters from Bong Mines took over the farm, and depleted it. When they were driven out by opposing rebel forces, the farm was left unattended. Eventually thick bushes took over the farm and damaged the crop.

In the next 30 minutes, they were near Maila. The yellow machines that were working on the road were parked on the side. About a kilometer later, they met Tonolah Wuamah waving them to stop.

"The people of Maila are waiting to receive you all," he said, breathing excitedly, and ran back towards the town, while the convoy slowly drove behind him.

Soon they met a group of people, including women, children and the elderly who could make it, standing on both sides of the road waving palm branches. J. Boima Barclay Jr and friends were now driving into Maila. The crowd grew larger when they entered the town. As directed by Tonolah Wuamah, the convoy drove towards the chief's compound and stopped.

Boima got down from the Range Rover, followed by Sam, Valerie and David Lakay who stood near him waving. Those who remembered Boima recognized him and started pointing their fingers at him at the same time waving and cheering.

He was astonished to see that a platform was made for them, and realized that his grandfather, the old chief and his uncle, Chief Lumeh, had planned a small ceremony for his return to Maila. The guests were then ushered to the platform and were told where to sit to the cheering and jubilations of the crowd that had gathered around the chief quarter.

Boima had thought about his grandfather and had almost asked for him when the crowd suddenly roared. The old chief, who had always been indoors for years, had come out walking towards the platform to meet his grandson who he had not seen for many years. Immediately Boima ran to him and both of them hugged each other, crying bitterly while the crowd cheered.

"Hello, hello, hello," Tonolah Wuamah called several times, shouting above his voice until the cheering and jubilations from the crowd gradually subsided. Then the old chief and his grandson took their seats next to each other. "Please let us listen to what our young chief, Peter Lumeh has to tell us. Please give us your attention."

"People of Maila," Began the young chief, walking from one end of the Platform to the other. "Today we have with us our son, grandson, nephew, and Maila's own son, James Boima Barclay Jr. He is also here with his friends, Sam who also came from America, and Valerie, the beautiful woman you see sitting by Sam. We also have with us the man who is responsible for fixing our roads, and many good things to come, Mr. David Lakay, whose father is no stranger to Fuamah District. Boima, Sam, Valerie and David Lakay stood and waved to the crowd amidst the uproar of cheering and jubilation.

"We will now call our son, Boima to say a few words to us," the young chief said, after Tonolah Wuamah had interpreted what was said to the people in Kpelle.

"Thank you very much my honorable chief and uncle," Boima said, stepping forward. "To the old chief, my grandfather, and to you the people of Maila, I am very grateful to be part of you and I am happy to be here.

Maila is my home and this is where my naval string was buried. Some of you can remember that I partly grew up here; I rolled car tires with you, I kicked ganga ball with you, I planted a garden with you, and I even fished in our waters with you. And so, I am no stranger here.

But I didn't just come to see my grandfather, my mother or my uncle or Maila who I haven't seen for many years, but I have come to implement the dreams of your old chief, our elders, and you the people of Maila. And that is to make our town the best place to live. To make Maila look more than how Bong Town used to be.

As you can see, we have started by first making sure that the road to enter Maila is in good condition. We have brought with us the necessary equipment to navigate our waters to explore our surroundings and to complete the work my father and Zeptter started many years ago. Before I leave Maila, we will make sure that our town is electrified. We will change almost all the huts to cement brick houses, likewise all the ones made of mud bricks. I am also here with my partner and his friend who you have already been introduced to and David Lakay, the engineer who will be coordinating most of the work. My people. Please let us get together and put old traditional prohibition aside and develop this potentially rich town of ours."

The people were clapping and cheering when he paused. The old chief kept nodding as the expression on his face showed that he was satisfied; the plan he and the old representative put together was working-Maila will be developed by its own son, and thank God that his grandson is as equally determined to execute the plan.

He was also proud of his own son, the young chief who had kept the communication between them and the Barclays. During the war, Peter Lumeh always made sure that he brought Malia intact, the items sent by the old representative. When the road between Kakata and Monrovia was closed, he would go to Ivory Coast to receive the items.

"But I have a very special appeal to make," Boima resumed, his continence suddenly appealing and becoming worrisome. "I have a message for my mother, Esther Gorpue Lomeh, and if any among you knows how to get this to her, please tell her, that the development of Maila will be incomplete, if she's not around to see her son implement it.

I owe her this honor as the person who brought me into this world. For the years we lived together, she infused the DNA of Maila into me, and I can say that it is because she taught me to appreciate the values of this great town and its people, that's why I devoted all my time studying how to develop this rich town. Mama, your son Boma is here, and will always be here till you come."

Boima ended with a chilly voice, remained standing for a while and walked to his seat, weeping. He firmly held onto his grandfather for some time, just before he could sit down. The old man got up and asked him to kneel before him. He then signaled to Chief Lumeh, his son, to come forward and whispered something in his ear. Then he took out a small staff made of cow tail and what looked like birds' feathers from the country clothes he was wearing, and as he stroke it gently on his grandson's head, Chief Lumeh told the cheering crowd that the old chief has given Boima the blessing to implement the development of Maila.

After that, each of the council of elders came forward and did likewise, but with their hands over his head at the same time decreeing words of blessing. Then the young chief, receiving the staff from his father, raised it high in the air and shook it violently. He struck it on Boima's head four times, and then on his back another four times.

"Upon this day before God and the people," Chief Lumeh said with a loud voice. "By the power invested in me by the council of elders and you the people of Maila, I hereby sealed this decree that our town will be explored and subsequently developed by our own son,

J. Boima Barclay Jr. He shall fulfill the dreams of the old chief, his father, his mother, and what our ancestors may have intended. May he live long as he pursues this endeavor, and may we lend him our support."

Again, there was an uproar of jubilations and cheering when Boima got to his feet and raised his right hand with a solid fist into the air. The old chief walked to him and embraced him, then Chief Lumeh, the elders and then Sam, Valerie, and David Lakay. Tonolah Wuamah also came forward and embraced Boima for a long time, and weeping for seeing that his many reveries were about to come to reality and for the joy of the occasion. They all took their seats at the platform, and immediately Tonolah announced a cultural dance performance by Maila traditional dancers.

Suddenly there sounded the beating of drums, playing of rattles (sasa), and singing of choruses. The traditional music played for a while, as the lead drummer displayed his brilliance with the split wooden drum and then the tempo changed. Entering the platform, from the left and the right, with four persons in queue from each side, were the moon-light dancers. They were all girls between the ages of 10 and 20, adorned in their traditional dance costumes comprising skits made of thatches, with their breasts covered with beautifully designed country clothes, and beads around their waists and ankles.

As the platform guest watched, the dancers portrayed the setting of an ancient traditional village during the farming season, demonstrating how women scratch the farms after the men have fallen the trees and cleared the land of stumps. Then, they display the harvesting of rice. After a spectacular dance performance, the moon-light dancers queued out of this stage, this time in one direction.

The tempo of the music changed again and the next dancers trooped on the stage. They were a group of men in warriors costumes performing the traditional ballad. The performance was captivating as the dancers demonstrated an epic depicting the founding of Maila and the war with the Gola. Sam remembered once, during his days at Lott Carey Mission School, watching similar dance performed by the then Liberia Culture Ambassadors cultural troop performing on the occasion of the school's annual cultural series festivities. The epic finally ended, and the dancers left the stage amidst cheers and jubilations.

After that, Chief Lumeh then led Boima and the platform guests to inspect the town. As Boima and the others descended the platform, they shook the hands of the men, women, children and the elderly who came to greet them. With the crowd following them, they walked to the chief quarter, then continued to the rest of the town. They passed the old black smith work kitchen and his dilapidated house, the dilapidated school building and headed towards the part of the town that Tonolah Wuamah lived.

Boima greeted his mother, when she was introduced, and then little Flomo who stood by her.

He saw and immediately recognized Gotolo when he and the group following him were now in the part of the town Gotolo lives in. Both men stared at each other for some time. Boima noticed that his mother's friend had not changed much, except for a whisker running down his cheeks and forming low strings of beard, which had started turning gray. But he still maintained his body. When Gotolo noticed from Boima's eyes that he was recognized, he came forward and greeted him.

The town's information guru looked at the young chief and his friend, Wuamah and studied the expression on their faces. He also greeted them, including Sam, Valerie and David Lakay. He was surprised Wuamah also shook his hand, and embraced him.

"Sometimes he used to walk me to school. He and my mother were very close," Boima turned to Sam and said, and then turned to Gotolo, again, still holding his hand, with his expression indicating that he wanted to ask him something.

But Wuamah, suspecting that Gotolo may not be prepared to respond to anything concerning Esther now, held Boima hand and gently squeezed it.

"I will tell you where to find him," he leaned towards him and whispered in Boima's ears.

"Okay, Mr. Barclay. I will be going back to Bong Mines to drop the operators of the yellow machines to the guest house," said David Lakay. "Also, I am expecting the people I hired to fell the trees to build the boat ramp. We will all return tomorrow morning."

"Thanks David. Your guys did a good job on the road. When you bring them tomorrow morning, we will locate a suitable place to build the ramp. Wish you a safe journey back here, again." When David left, Boima whispered to Wuamah and his uncle. "We must be careful not to show them where the wonders of Maila are, when they come tomorrow. We will tell them to fell the trees from the buses on the road to our town."

It was now getting into the early evening hours. Boima, Sam, Valerie, Chief Lomeh, and Tonolah Wuamah have all retired to the chief quarter. Sam took down a generator with some rolls of wires from the boat. Some of the town youths, mainly relatives of the Chief, assisted him to run and hoisted the wires on sticks and planted sockets and light balls on them to provide electricity to the chief compound.

It had gotten dark by the time he was finished. Then the 3.5 KVA diesel generator was ignited. The 100kW Dayton diesel generator roared for a few seconds. Then Sam flipped on a switch. Like magic, the darkness suddenly disappeared, and the chief compound and adjacent houses were lighted to the delight and jubilation of the people.

Sam brought out a Sonny musical set with a stereo system and a Philip amplifier. He connected and turned it on, playing music, beginning with the Kpelle song 'Yabalehpo', a track from David Grualee Collections. The town's children ran to the chief's quarter as the music blasted the whole town.

Next, some youth were hauling a 100lb American par-boiled rice from the back of the Ford pickup truck with gallons of red palm oil and cartons of frozen fish, chicken and ingredients. Valerie was assisted with a lapper which she tied around her waist to join some women who live in the chief's compound to prepare some food for the people who were trooping in.

Boima was in his grandfather's house, with the old chief, talking. He was opening some large suitcases, displaying some items such as clothes, shoes, sandals, slippers, canned foods and other things that his father had sent for his grandfather and the elders. As he referred to a list his father gave him, he would ask his grandfather whether a particular elder was still alive. If not, he would ask for that late elder's wife and children and when they were summoned, he would present the items to them.

The chief quarter was full of activity as people came and collected what was sent for them. After they were served with food, and ate, they lingered for a while, enjoying the music. Maila had never been alive, and had never seen such jubilation since the night J. Boima Barclay Sr won the election as representative of Fuamah District many years ago.

CHAPTER 7

THE RAILWAY FROM BONG Mines to Monrovia is encrusted with footpaths on both sides of the tracks. Sometimes they crossed the tracks and snaked their way into the surrounding bushes connecting farm villages near creeks and rivers, but at close proximity to the railroad.

Over the years some of these farm villages were transformed into small towns strewn on both sides of the tracks and extended all the way to Monrovia. From new Varney Town up to certain parts before reaching Todee, the Kpelle of Bong Mines extended their farm villages and small towns. Gola villages are often found in similar proximity to the railroad from Todee and along the St. Paul where the train tracks crosses a bridge over the river and continues all the way to Caldwell, passing through the township before reaching Bong Mines pier at the Freeport of Monrovia.

Before the civil war, less people threaded on these paths, probably because they were rural farmers or retired workers, or staff of Bong Mining Company who had established their farms in the vicinity. Furthermore, people loathed walking along the railroad that was frequented by high speeding trains hauling long queues of buckets filled with iron ore from the pellet plant in Bong Mines to the pier in Monrovia where it is loaded on vessels and shipped abroad.

But during the civil war, more people, mostly the internally displaced, fleeing from the big towns where fighting often took place, moved along the tracks and occupied these farm villages. And as the flock of people trampled on these paths, they became wide to the extent that they could be mistaken for motor roads.

What made these paths easily usable was when local rebel fighters, returning from the battle front to visit their relatives in these farm villages and towns, soon started riding on them with motorbikes. Gradually these small towns became lively because these places were where most of these fighters brought their loot. They opened shops and entertainment centers run by their girlfriends while they headed back to the war front.

The war had ended and many of the displaced had gone back to their towns, but many still remained.

A day after Boima returned to Maila, Koikoi Pewee was riding his old Yamaha motor bike along these paths, with his belongings tied to the back carrier to make the whole day's journey to Maila. He left early in the morning from Flomo Town, one of which was situated along the tracks, some 10 kilometers from Varney Town.

Recently, he received word, through Varney Yasiah, a motor bike rider and former rebel fighter who transports people along the paths, from chief Lomeh that his old friend, Representative Barclay has a message for him and that he must go to Maila to get the message from Barclay's son who has returned from the states, and will be visiting the town.

Koikoi Pewee could not leave right away because he was undergoing a traditional medication from Mulbah Kertehme, an old herbalist for rheumatism in the joints of both of his legs that almost made him paralyzed. He had to be carried in a hammock by relatives to Flomo Town to Mulbah Kertehme.

The old man administered a traditional thermo-therapy, in which his body from wrist down was covered with dirt, dug out from a termite mound and heated with a powerful herb three times a day for more than a month, and the herbalist's treatment proved effective.

"You have only a week to fully recover before you leave," Mulbah Kertehme had advised him.

Three days ago, Varney Yasiah brought another message from Chief Lumeh that he was in Varney Town stopping at Lakay Guest House waiting for Boima to come to Bong Mines to be accompanied to Maila.

"No, old man Mulbah. I have to be in Maila tonight," he said.

The old red 1980 XT250 Yamaha, left with him by a relative who was a former employee of the Liberia County Agriculture Development Program (LCADP) in Voinjama City, Lofa County, when the 1990 war was intensifying, still looked good and strong as it moved along the path, and repeatedly crossed the train tracks without problem. This relative, Peter Koboi Bannah, was a staunch supporter of the ruling party, before the war, and many people who were opposed to the government, hated him for his harsh and verbose defense of the regime.

In May, 1990 he was attending a seminar at the Kakata Rural Teacher Training Institute (KRTTI) located behind Booker T. Washington Institute (BWI) campus in Kakata, Margibi County, when rebels overran nearby Wheala. For fear of a subsequent attack on Kakata, and be identified as a regime collaborator, he fled to Bong Mines and sought refuge at his relative, Koikoi Pewee's farm on Popota Road. He later fled to Guinea through Zorzor, Lofa County by using the bush road on foot, when most of the fighting was concentrated around Monrovia.

Koikoi Pewee took his time riding along the path and occasionally on the train tracks. While on the tracks, the bike would bounce, when the tires roll over the segments of sleepers at the base of the rail, causing him to slightly stand up to avoid his torso from being repeatedly bumped by the hard seat of the bike, or, risk reopening a scar, where a surgery to remove a hernia, he once had, was performed.

The wall of his abdomen was softened due to the thermo-therapy he underwent. Few years ago, the surgery scar reopened while he was working on his rubber farm and he had to be rushed to Bong Mines hospital where it was stitched again. About an hour and a half later, he reached an area he recognized, which told him that Bong Mines was nearby. It was one of the huge culverts under the railway which usually carry a drain or a stream.

This circular metal culvert pipe was a little distance south of the J.D.K Baker Episcopal Mission School. It was called 'Pipe 2' by the male students. On Saturdays, during the dry season they would sneak out of the campus and take almost an hour walk along the tracks to go swimming in the stream. They would compete amongst themselves to determine who would do the best frog dive, by leaping like a frog from the mouth of the high tunnel and plunged, head first into the shallow stream. The ones who did the best frog dive will be cheered while those who didn't would be jeered.

Student Benedict Mitchell of the 7th grade always won the frog dive competition from the time he joined the Junior High school in the 5th grade. That year, Jesse Kollie, a new student of the 8th grade class, having heard of Benedict's spine-chilling frog dives and how no student did it better than him, has always sought an opportunity to challenge him.

Student Kollie was from Bong Town, and had experiences diving from the high springboard at the swimming pool, and always boasted of competing with the brave and sometimes crazy German kids and on many occasions, won them. Because of this, he and Benedict often had arguments over who could do the best frog dive.

"We are tired listening to both of you arguing on who can do the best frog dive," said student Albert Blake. "We will soon be in the dry season, and 'Pipe 2' is the only place for both of you to prove yourselves."

One sunny Saturday morning, they all had their breakfast at the dining hall, and then the lads who were part of the agriculture club, in which Benedict and Jesse were members, went to work in the school's garden, a large plot of land situated south of the dining hall, bordered by a bush through which a footpath led to the train tracks.

After they completed their work for which points were going to be added to their final average at the end of the academic year, they hid their tools in the nearby bush when Mr. Gayflor, the coordinator of the Agriculture Club had called roll, added points to those present, and left. Then they sneaked out of the campus as they always did, and took the almost hour walk along the train tracks to 'Pipe 2', with excitement and enthusiasm to witness the competition between Benedict Mitchell and Jesse Kollie.

They reached the culvert in time, lucky that they did not have to jump into the bush to the blaring of the train to wait for the long queue of buckets to pass before getting back on the tracks.

After the boys managed to argue out the rules, student Blake showed the two contestants a coin for each to choose the head or the tail, to determine who will be the first to begin. Benedict chose the head while Jesse chose the tail.

Albert Blake demonstrated the 'Coco and Missy' a gambling term, by flipping the dime in the air. The coin spun and landed in his right

336

palm, just in time to cover it with the other, like referees do before a soccer match begins.

When he removed his other hand, Benedict, having chosen the head which is the 'coco' part, was the first to take the dive.

As always, he began by folding his hands and pretended like he slipped from the high tip of the culvert, allowing himself to fall like a statue, but mid-way in the air, he executed the frog leap and just in time, plunged into the water.

The boys clapped and cheered for Benedict, and sarcastically urged Jesse to do likewise, believing that he would fail just like student Henry Padmore, who challenged Benedict the previous year. For about 30 minutes, Padmore vomited a large quantity of water including all the scrambled eggs, short bread and milk he had had at the dining hall for breakfast, when the water slapped his chest and throat when he missed the timing and did not land properly.

It was Kollie's time, and to the astonishment of his doubtful friends, he performed the frog dive with ease, doing it exactly how his opponent did it. And as it is with the rules, it was his time to demonstrate his own version, if any.

At the tip of the outer cage, he balanced himself with his feet, halfway at the edge, adjusting his spider man swim shorts. He put his hands on his waist and pretended like he was meditating. Then he scooped over and took the dive, somersaulting, and executing the forward roll with a perfect timing just before plunging into the water to the cheering of the once doubtful boys, immediately prompting some of them to shift their doubts to the champ.

"Benedict! You have met your match his year. You cannot do what Jesse just did," student Martin Coleman, the smallest in the group exclaimed.

"Jesse has won," declared student Wilmot Harris, observing Benedict's nervous composure.

Not sure that he could, Benedict reluctantly took his position at the edge of the culvert, waiting for Jesse Kollie to come out of the water, but for a while, the Bong Town Swimming pool diving board champion, didn't. The boys became concerned when they saw a pool of blood floating on top of the water near the bottom of the submerged culvert.

Then Kollie suddenly emerged almost lifeless, with his forehead covered with blood. He had landed too closed to the jagged edge of the bottom of the culvert and gashed his forehead.

Koikoi Pewee, who once had a farm village nearby, was walking in that direction when he heard the boys crying in the midst of the unfortunate situation. He hurriedly rushed to the scene and saw Kollie, who was helped out of the water lying on his back with blood oozing out of his forehead.

He quickly calmed down the boys who were pointing fingers at each other as to who orchestrated the competition in the first place, and told them what to do. He hurried back to his farm and brought a herb of pounded leaf, wiped the blood, and cleaned the wound.

Then he tied it with a thick country cloth with the herb. When the bleeding somewhat reduced, he hurried into the nearby bush with his cutlass in his hands and chopped off some sticks and palm thatches. He then built a stretcher in the form of a ladder, covered it neatly with the thatches and carefully laid the severely injured kid on it. Jesse Kollie was rushed to the school's clinic.

The whole campus was suddenly plunged into disarray when two girls, students Doris Williams and Hawa Shaman who often went down to a little creek at the left of the girls' dormitory to wash their clothes, around the same place where the boys often pass to go to Pipe 2", saw Kollie lying on the stretcher carried by his friends. They left what they were doing and raced up to the dormitory.

"A hunter shot Jesse Kollie," cried Hawa Shaman. "They are bringing him to the clinic, along with the hunter that shot him.

"What?" suddenly screamed Jebbeh Brown. "I hope the hunter did not take him for an animal."

Mrs. Marshall, the nurse, administered some first aid to try to stabilize his condition and called the Bong Mines Hospital for the ambulance.

Mr. Nyantee Woart, the principal was very nervous, after hearing first from Albert Blake and then from Koikoi Pewee what happened. He summoned the boys' dormitory prefect, and asked him to take down the names of all the boys who have been breaking the school's rules by going to 'Pipe 2' to swim.

That day, as Kollie lay in the clinic unconscious, waiting for the ambulance, there were heavy arguments in the boys' dormitory when Momo Gibson, the dormitory prefect attempted to write the names of only the boys that went swimming that day.

"That list will not leave this dorm until you include every one, I mean everyone who has been going to 'Pipe 2' to swim, including you, Momo," opposed Albert Black when he and only the names of the boys that went to swim that day were on the list.

Immediately Joseph Satiah, one of the big and muscular boys whose little brother, Thomas, name was on the list, raced to the dormitory door and shot it.

"There will be no dormitory prefect business inside here today. Every one name must be on that list," he said, and took off his shirt. "Put all friendship aside, you will have to pass through me, before that list leaves this dorm."

The whole of J. D. K. Baker was upside down. A group of girls have gathered at the clinic with some of them quizzing and scrolling Hawa Shaman for providing mis-information, when they understood what actually happened. Two of them, whose brothers were amongst the boys that went to Pipe 2 that day, were rolling on the ground, crying. If Jesse Kollie dies, their brothers will be expelled from the school and probably sent to jail.

A group of boys huddled under the plump tree at the right of the boys' dormitory and the road to the entrance of the campus, arguing, suddenly cheered when they saw the ambulance turned in on the road that led to the campus, from the main road in one swing, with the left front and back tires in the air and almost flipping the beach Volkswagen bus over.

There was another roar of cheers, when Mr. Adolphus Williams, the ambulance driver who was widely regarded as Bong Mines chief driver swung the car in similar fashion right in front of the boys' dormitory. When told that the patient was at the clinic, he drove the ambulance there and Jesse Kollie was taken to the hospital. He stayed there for about three weeks and was given stitches on the forehead.

It was at the hospital that Koikoi Pewee and J. Boima Barclay Sr met for the first time, and both became friends afterwards. He was introduced to Mr. Barclay by Mr. Frederick Kollie, the father of Jesse as the brave farmer who saved his son's life. Mr. Barclay had gone to the hospital with Mr. Kollie when they heard the news.

The old representative and Mr. Kollie were both mine geologists working up the Mountain, before Barclay became the General Administrative Officer. In fact, they were the only two Liberian Mine Geologists amongst the team of German geologists and mining engineers responsible for laying dynamites in large crates dug into the mountain to blast it for the ore.

That day, Barclay got to know that Koikoi might be an asset as he was about to retire from the company and run as representative for Fuamah District. Throughout the conversation that followed after the introduction, he learned that Koikoi Pewee had vast knowledge of the entire district.

Years ago, Koikoi Pewee worked with a group of German Missionaries, teaching the Holy Bible in almost all the towns and villages in the district and some parts of lower Lofa County and so he was well known throughout Lower Bong. He was very instrumental in translating the Bible into Lorma and Kpelle, from English, and taught the locals how to read it, thus earning him the nickname 'Siegie', meaning Pastor in Lorma, his native language.

Their friendship grew further when Mr. Barclay finally retired and began preparing for his campaign, despite some people telling the old representative that Koikoi would be a liability because of a problem he once had with the Kpelle and Lorma people for almost orchestrating a conflict between both tribes, involving Yanwolo, the canoe man.

Mr. Barclay did not even budge, when some of his powerful supporters who were mostly members of the Masonic craft told him that Koikoi Pewee was a dangerous character who also led a group of people that ransacked the grand lodge at Keleku Town, and the only thing that stopped him from burning it to the ground was that the fire could have spread to the surrounding houses.

Despite all of these, Koikoi Pewee ran a very successful campaign and Barclay won, claiming 55% of the votes. Coming close to him with 27% of the votes was David Lorkpaylay, his surname meaning 'drink wine', in Kpelle. Lorkpaylay was a very successful businessman who owned a fleet of Toyota stout transport pick-ups that plied the road from Gbarnga through Kakata to Hendii, competing with giants in the business like Sekou Baid-Baid, Mamadee Kamara, Old man Farkollie, and others.

In the third place with 22% of the votes was Thomas Farlo, a lawyer from the Belle tribe who was credited for his advocacy that led to Bong Mining Company further extending its corporate social responsibility to include more of the rural villages and towns in its environs to have access to the hospital and at a low cost. People blamed his defeat on his campaign messages, mostly seeking the interest of the Belle people who were mostly in the minority.

As he approached Varney Town, Koikoi Pewee was not only happy that he had covered the first half of his journey, but he mused at an Irony he reflected once during Barclay campaign. They had entered Mahwah and one of the old representative powerful supporters, who he learned had been advising Barclay to get rid of him, came out to speak to the people.

"We will only listen to Siegie," the crowd shouted, when a man among them recognized the member of the Masonic craft.

That evening, for fear of losing votes, Barclay was contemplating on dropping this individual and others like him from his team.

"We must keep them, Barclay. But they must be behind the scenes since they are important and can be useful in other aspects of our campaign," advised Siegie.

He reached Varney Town and rode to the bus stop. Mulbah Kertehme had advised that when he gets to Varney Town, he must rest a bite and take some medicine, which was some sliced roots in a bottle, he had prepared for him.

He parked his Yamaha, locked the wheel and went walking past Cecelia Dolo's shop. He glanced in her direction. She was sitting in front of her shop yelling into her phone like she and someone were having a heated exchange.

As he passed and pretended like he did not see her, he imagined the goods on her shelves covered with clouds of dust. Cecelia Dolo knew how to purchase goods of many varieties, and had the patience to sit all day in front of her shop to sell. But, coupled with her bad ways, she lacked basic customer service skills. She did not know how to treat and talk to people, and for this reason, those who knew her, even little kids, did not venture into her shop. They would prefer buying from Alpha Barry's shop because he was the exact opposite.

During the war, she was famous amongst the fighters of the main rebel group. Because of her beauty and charm, they trusted her with their loot, and this earned her lots of money. For this reason, she respected no one; she ordered the dragging of people who were indebted to her and could not pay on time.

When Hendii was attacked, and Bong Mines was under threat, some rebel fighters confronted her for their money, but she used her affair with one of the vicious and feared commanders to intimidate them. The night before Bong Mines fell, a group of armed men broke into her place, held her at gunpoint, pillaged her shop and made away with a huge quantity of money.

She later knew that this had only occurred, when her boyfriend, this vicious commander, six months pregnant for him at the time, was killed in an ambush on the road from Hendii to Bong Mines by the opposing rebel fighters. The group that ransacked her place was most of his retreating men. Now a single mother, she had managed to re-establish herself, but people still remembered the things she did.

Koikoi Pewee stood before a local liquor shop, owned by the son of one of his late friends, George Kermue. He forced a smile as he struggled not to remember a particular encounter with Cecelia Dolo, when he saw Kleeme, George's son, busy serving his customers who were mainly motorcyclists.

It was once during the heyday of the rebel government that controlled greater Liberia including Bong Mines when the country was divided. Some Varney Town market women sought his intervention to prevail upon Cecelia to stop humiliating some of their members, who she had ordered to sit on the bare ground, under the scorching sun like criminals because they could not repay money owed to her.

The elderly man immediately rushed to the scene and saw the women sitting on the ground, surrounded by armed men.

"These are your mothers. How will you treat them like this for money business?" disgusted and pitying their situation, he tried to persuade her. "Please accept the little time the women were proposing to pay your debt. Business is rough, and the civil war has made things more difficult and unbearable."

"Siegie. Mind your own business. If you don't stop talking, I will order my boys to make you sit on the floor with them. In fact, leave now," Cecelia blasted.

The elderly man refused to leave and insisted. But he was ruffled and made to sit on the bare ground with the women, like criminals caught right in the act, as people passed by.

Reflecting on that fateful day, Koikoi Pewee stood at the door of the liquor shop for a while. He was almost sobbing when he looked towards Varney Town market at the spot right on the main road. He composed himself and wiped a tear that ran down his face.

Acknowledging how it is indeed easy to forgive but hard to forget, he had since forgiven her. He looked across the road at the late rebel commander' girlfriend who also looked at him and turned her face unremorsefully and went inside her shop. He snorted back up a slime that was about to run down his nose and finally entered the shop. There was a serious argument amongst the customers.

"Fuamah District has seen the weakest law marker in the history of lower Bong County," said one of the motor cyclists who was drinking a bottle of Jumping Deer gin. "Why will Representative Kpankpalah sit there and allow the new concession areas to center around Salala, rather than Bong Mines?"

"And if that happens, Bong Mines will not benefit from any Corporate Social responsibility," added another customer, an elderly man.

"Representative Kpankpalah was the one that ordered the police task force from Kakata to arrest and flogged people children here in Bong Mines on the false allegations that they were looting Botota," said Kleeme Kermue who has just served the elderly man with a half-bottle of cane juice. "Oh! Thank God!" he exclaimed, upon seeing Koikoi Pewee entering his shop. "Siegie is here. He was one of those that convinced us to vote for Henry Kpankpalah."

Koikoi Pewee greeted the customers and sat on one of the long benches made of planks. He scanned the place as he struggled to conceal the disappointment on his face. The once well decorated shop, run by his friend George Kermue now looked almost dilapidated. The ceiling tides were all hanging and one could see straight through the roof, the now termite-eaten planks, and the penny size holes in the zinc allowing the sun rays through. The once cement floor was full of cracks, and the white paint on the wall now covered with soot, due to years of neglect.

George Kermue was one of his many friends he referred to as his brother. Kermue always called him nephew while Siegie called him small uncle because he was older. Both men strictly followed the Kpelle-Lorma tradition.

When Siegie led the Lorma men to Hendii, in an attempt to arrest Yanwolo, George Kermue was one of those who dispelled the notion that Siegie carried men to wage war. He had only gone to apprehend a Kpelle man for allegedly having a hand in the drowning of little Yassah, which was different from instigating a tribal war between the two groups.

During the civil war, George Kermue got ill due to a strange smallpox-like disease and died in Nyeabla, a town on the road to Hendii. Had his wife, a young and beautiful girl not abandoned him and ran off when Bong Mines was attacked, he was going to live. Kleeme's mother, his first wife, was an elderly woman.

"Welcome, Siegie. I heard that you were sick. Happy to see you on your feet again," Kleeme came over to Koikoi Pewee and said, extending his hand for a handshake.

"And you did not send a word to me. But attacked me as soon as I entered my late friend and brother's shop."

"Oh. Sorry, Uncle. But I haven't laid eyes on Varney Yesiah since. And he's the one who knows Flomo Town."

"And he is always in this parking, right next to your shop."

"He does not visit my shop."

"Kleeme stop the argument and just tell Siegie sorry," interrupted the elderly man who was drinking the cane juice.

"That man is supposed to be like an uncle to you. Except you have forgotten how close he and your late father were."

"Thanks, old man Galawolo. Don't hurt your head over Kleeme. These are the children we have inherited after the war," said Koikoi Pewee, and then handed the bottle with the chopped roots inside to Kleeme. "Just fill that bottled up with cane juice and tell me how much I will pay."

"Ah Uncle. I will not take money from you."

"You will take money from me, until you apologize to me properly."

"Okay. Uncle I am very sorry," Kleeme finally gave in, scooping over Koikoi Pewee and holding him on his knees with one hand while the other held to the bottle he had been given. Then he looked to his left and his right at his customers and continued. "Gentlemen please help beg my uncle, Siegie, for me."

Some of them who were brought out in the tradition and still cared to be bordered about it came over and scooped likewise and held Koikoi Pewee's feet. The elderly man then parted his friend's son on his back, symbolizing that he had forgiven him. The customers who came forward thanked him and went back to their seats.

Kleeme went behind his counter and poured from a large jar, a quantity of cane juice into the bottle. After shaking it several times, he poured a little tip of it in the bottle's top and took a sip as it is customary to show clear heart and good intention when serving someone a drink.

"I heard all of your arguments," Koikoi Pewee said, after he was handed the root bottle of cane juice and a small glass and had taken a shot. "Henry Kpankpalah has made all of us ashamed. Lots of bad things are happening in our district and he is doing nothing about it; look at the hospital. No medicine, and the doctors are threatening to leave. Before I got sick, some elders and I met with a few doctors and appealed with them and the staff to stay for the sake of saving lives. As our representative, Kpankpalah was not around to add to our voices. And that same day he was here in Bong Mines.

When I got sick, he was informed about it, but he sent no word to me after all that I did to have him elected. But what is even more worrying to me who is sitting here, is that he is telling people that the first six years is for he and his family and the next six year will be for the district."

"But who will vote him back in office in the first place?" suddenly shouted one of the customers.

"I heard that too," added Kleeme. "He says he will use money to win for the second time."

"Hold on gentlemen," Koikoi tried to calm down the heated argument that erupted. "We will simply vote Kpankpalah out. And I am sorry to plunge this district into the embarrassment it is facing now. But I can promise you that pretty soon, we will have a redeemer."

"Who is that person?" asked the customers who were drinking the Jumping deer, after much cheering and a little jeering when Koikoi Pewee ended his statement.

"It's too early to disclose the person now," he responded, thinking of Boima as he had it in mind to discuss the possibility of running in the next election when he had developed Maila and when the people had seen what he could do. After all, his father has made a name for himself and so the legacy still continues. "But on the part of sending people to arrest the youth who looted Botota, I frown on that, but Botota should not have been looted in the first place. When the Chinese company comes, where will their staff reside? Botota was the only place still intact until it got looted."

"The company will not be operating here in Bong Town," said Kleeme. "That's some of the reason we are vex with Kpanpkalah."

"Look, my son. The concession agreement has not been reached yet. The government and the Chinese are still negotiating, so no one must tell you that the company will operate in this place or that place," countered Koikoi.

Another round of argument ensued and again, after going back and forth trying to explain to the increasingly hard to believe customers, Koikoi Pewee got up to leave. He had checked his time. It was after 2pm, and he needed to be in Maila before nightfall. While the heated discussion was going on, he had almost emptied the root bottle, but Kleeme had re-filled it back to the brim.

What was now on his mind was to tap his gas with at least two gallons. As he stood up looking in the faces of the concerned Fuamah District youth before him, he saw that they were eager to hear his parting comments.

"Let me say this before I leave you all," he began. "We will redeem Fuamah District. A son, who is developmental oriented will soon come to our rescue. And if that does not happen, I will resign from Fuamah District politics, and die with the woe that will follow me."

He got out of the shop with Kleeme accompanying him. They stood for some time and talked. After that, the young liquor shop owner escorted him to his bike. Next, he was before Binda gas selling spot and bought two gallons.

He paid the gasoline seller and left. Passing Catholic Field, he noticed that the road was too bumpy, and decided that he will not continued with it to avoid his torso being repeatedly hit by the hard seat. Moreover, the cane juice he drank from the root bottle was having a little effect, and may cause him to run off the road. So, he turned around and headed back to Varney Town to use a longer but much better road.

He waved to Kleeme who was standing outside his shop as he passed by it, but still refused to look to Cecelia Dolo way, upon seeing from the corner of his right eye that she was now standing along the road in front of her shop. He got to the bus stop, turned left and entered Benuma. He rode past Zaweata School junction and continued with the road that led to the mountain.

A team from the Chinese company who was negotiating with the Liberian government to operate the Bong Range had done some work on the road. He rode on for some time, surprised that he was accelerating due to the smoothness of the road. Before reaching what was the pellet plant he turned left, leaving the plant and the range to his right. He headed on, enjoying the gravel road.

Koikoi Pewee waved to a few people he suspected were returning from their farms, rather early, and were walking along the side of the road who recognized him and waved back. It was past 3pm. He hoped to reach an intersection where he would turn further left to connect to the road that led to Wheala while the other headed back towards the Bong Range.

Within time, he was there and began to take the 30 minutes ride to to get to Wheala Road and head back to Maila Junction, which would take him another one and a half hours. He would then get to the junction from the north unlike Boima and others who got there from the south.

He was on high speed, descending a steep hill full of gravels, when the Yamaha engine suddenly cut off. He applied the brakes but they were not holding properly. Koikoi Pewee fought to control the handlebar as the gravel hauled him from one side of the road to another, thank God for the hill borders on both sides. Whenever the gravel hauled him to one side, he would use his leg to step the wall to prevent him from colliding with it.

He passed the hill borders, descending and managing to control the bike, until he reached an area where there was a steep valley on both sides of the road. With the switch still on, and the Yamaha still in running gear, he tried several times to ignite the engine by simultaneously releasing the clutch and engaging the accelerator, but the bike could not start.

He looked in awe, struggling to remain calmed, as the gravel was now dragging the bike to the left side of the road where the valley was the steepest. If he did not manage to control it, he would crush land on the trees in the valley below. And it was going to be disastrous. But he was determined to maneuver his way out of the gravel as he descended all the way down the hill.

He was able to stabilize the bike, when the speed was gradually reducing. He continued to hold on to the brakes, and to his delight, the Yamaha continued to slow down, but not slow enough to lean sideways so he can put his foot on the ground to stop it. Instead, he steered it towards a tree on the right side of the road after he passed the valley and hit it with less impact..

The bike finally stopped. Koikoi Pewee got down, with a sense of pride, crediting himself for averting the danger. He could smell the gasoline, and scooped over to inspect the gas line. The carburetor was overflowing, and it might be a reason why the engine cut off. From previous experiences, tempering with the carburetor in an attempt to detach the gas lines and blow out the excess gas was going to make things worse. He had heard many good auto mechanics admitting that Carburetors of XT250 Yamahas are very complicated to handle, and so he decided to wait for a while, until the gas in the chamber dried up.

He looked at his watch-it was going to 5pm. With luck, and when the excess gas in the carburetor dries up in time, he would reach Maila before night fall, or, worst case scenario, early after night fall. To kill a little time, while he waited for the gas to dry up in the carburetor, he took the root bottle from the side pocket of his bag, attached to the small carrier at the rear of the Yamaha. Then he found a clear spot under a tree where the shade was perfect for relaxing and sat down with his back leaning against the trunk of the tree.

He rolled up the legs of the brown dungaree trousers he was wearing and felt both knees. He was happy that there was no pain and wondered why, because he was stepping the walls of the hill borders on the sides of the hill when the gravel was hauling him left and right. Then he again laid his back against the tree trunk and started sipping on the root bottle.

Next, Koikoi Pewee suddenly jumped to his feet, frightened. He was shaking his pants, and stamping his feet when he felt something crawling into his trousers. Angry that it was nothing, but realized he had been dreaming because he had been sleeping for hours, he hissed something which sounded like a curse in Lorma.

He felt so foolish for allowing a little nap under a tree to turn into a long and deep sleep, which lasted until it was dark. He cursed again when he looked at his watch and it was past 11 pm. Displaced, he inspected the carburetor and the gasoline. Satisfied that all the excess gas had somewhat dried up, he mounted the Yamaha and kicked the starter. The motor ignited in a roar, echoing through the silent dark night after three attempts. When he had made sure all his things were intact, Koikoi Pewee resumed his journey to Maila.

The head light of the bike was good enough to brighten the dark road suitable for his eyesight to enable him to make up the bad parts in time to avoid them. If all goes on well, that is, if the bike did not give him any more problems, he would reach Maila before 2 am which will not be bad after all.

Unfortunately, the bike started jerking when he soured up a small hill, but as he descended, the jerking stopped. Though the Yamaha did not cut off as he descended, he began to smell the gas again. Then it occurred to him that because he engaged the hill usually with heavy gear, more gas had entered into the chamber. The hill was not long and the bike had sat for long while he slept under the tree, so the carburetor did not overflow.

What was worrying him now was how he would manage to engage a longer hill without overflowing the carburetor when he had to accelerate. The route he was using was fairly better than the one from the Catholic Field side in Bong Mines but it has many hills.

With a quick split decision, he opted to continue on the road, where there were no hills and hoped to reach a certain point where some tracks occasionally veered off to the left. This will allow him to connect to the other part of the road from Maila Junction. This means he will not have to go all the way to where he will connect it closer to the Weala side, thus leaving the district on his right.

His once thoughtful expression suddenly transformed into a grin; he was using his vast knowledge of the terrain to his advantage. Just before reaching a particular hill, he left the main road and turned into a track on his left and began to gradually descend. With the motor still sounding good and working perfectly, he continued along this track halfway to where it will connect to the main road from Maila Junction side when he suddenly engaged a hill he had not expected. Before he could cut off the bike to prevent it from overflowing again, it cut off. But he was lucky enough to apply the brakes and leaned to his right and got down.

Displaced with himself, again, for missing this little detail that a hill could have been nearby, just before he connected to the main road, Koikoi Pewee put the gear in neutral and was rolling the bike up the hill. The effort was a little strenuous but he could make it, as he was taking his time. He hoped that by the time he covered the hill and got on the main road, the overflow would have receded and the bike would start again.

By then, Maila Junction will not be far. With a renewed vigor, he applied a little more effort rolling the bike up the hill and dimming the headlight to save the battery. Why he did not use the Popota-Maila Junction route in the first place, the thought ran through his mind, but he quickly brushed that aside. He needed to focus on the task of rolling the bike up the hill.

"Gbeh vey?" he suddenly asked, 'who is it? in Kpelle, and brightened the head light, upon seeing the emergence of a shadow he could make up from the trees to his left. But he saw no one, only the trees and a low bush beyond. He had almost asked for help when he saw it or thought he saw what he assumed could be a farmer who might be spending the evening at his nearby farm and taking a usual cold night walk.

He was sure that it was someone. It was not a shallow cast by a tree standing alone, which usually trick the eyes like someone is standing, waiting in the dark. He had always been out in the bush at night, from the time he was a little enfant on his mother's back returning from the farm, up to the time he was a toddler walking behind his parents, and as an adult, returning from his own farm. He has mastered how to make up a shadow cast by a tree standing by itself or a shadow cast by a figure. And the one he saw was definitely a figure.

Maybe whoever it was, was afraid. There were many evils committed during the civil war, and people did not trust each other anymore.

He had almost reached the top of the hill, and he could see the main road a few meters ahead of him. The beam of relief and delight appearing on his face quickly disappeared as soon as he started to descend, slightly holding on to the brakes of the Yamaha so that it should not roll with him all the way down, when he saw the same shadow of the figure again, emerging from the bush to his left and approaching him. For every step it took, he could hear what sounded like tinkles from the distance.

"Gbeh vay?" he stopped and asked again, this time with traces of apprehension in his voice, as he was making an effort to hold on to the bike because it was weighing him down.

The makeup of the figure was identical to the one he saw amongst the trees to where he had passed. Strangely, it was not possible to be the same figure approaching him from the front. No one can be that fast, or ubiquitous, prompting him to quiver with a sudden fear in reaction to his thoughts. Whosoever it was, was out for tricks, so he gently laid the bike against his hip and drew out his cutlass hidden underneath the carrier in a sheath made of goat skin and hung it across his chest.

He waited until the tinkling got closer. He brightened the headlight to see who it was, but a stone was thrown and he heard the glass of the headlight shattered and went off, after a spark. Koikoi Pewee immediately threw the bike down and quickly hauled out his cutlass from the sheath.

"GBEH VAY?!" alarmed and furious, he demanded, with the cutlass raised. "Not everyone can be taunted like this, least you are mistaken and it will be too late to regret it."

There was a sudden gust of wind shaking the bushes and trees on both sides of the road like a powerful storm was coming. Becoming increasingly apprehensive, he was turning in circles, readying himself to strike at anybody who would emerge from either side of the bush. Then he heard what sounded like someone was felling a tree. The next moment he heard it falling.

When he looked, there it was; a huge tree coming down and was landing right where he stood. "Aie, Gala!" Koikoi screamed, calling the name of God in Loma as he dodged the tree, just before it landed.

Thanks to years of felling trees himself and getting out of harm's way whenever they were falling.

Koikoi Pewee immediately raced down the hill in the direction he had ascended when he heard, and then saw huge logs rolling down his way. Whosoever was doing this intended for the logs to roll over and smash him dead.

He looked back, as he ran and saw that he was not going to make it. The logs were spinning and rolling very fast. With one giant leap, he jumped into the bush on the right side of the road, just in time the logs almost caught up with him and passed, rolling all the way down the hill. Had he not jumped in time, he was going to be smashed dead.

"Gbeh Vey: gbeh vey; gbeh vey," he lamented with fear as he wandered aimlessly into the bush.

"Hey gbolo," he screamed, uttering a malicious curse, in a common Guinea Kpelle expression when a wild vine suddenly entangled his right leg and pulled him to the ground.

The tinkling was rapidly advancing towards him, as he fought to disentangle his leg. He sat on the ground, drew the tangled leg and used the cutlass to chop off the vines, almost chopping off his own foot. He then got up and continued to run aimlessly in the dark bush.

He hit his face on the trunk of a large tree he did not see standing before him. He cursed again and felt his forehead. It was bruised and swollen.

Koikoi Pewee got out of the bush and entered into a clearing where he could see clearly. The moon was up, lightening his view. Then again, he saw the figure appearing from the bush in the distance ahead, taking giant strides towards him, as the tinkling echoed throughout the surrounding bushes. Breathing heavily with confusion and fear and at the same time sweating profusely, he stopped and raised his cutlass in striking position.

The African Vai shirt he was wearing was torn up on both sides, including the dungaree trousers, ripped from both sides of the front pockets, partially exposing his underwear. On his right foot was one of the pair of the rubber sanders he usually liked to wear while none was on the other foot. He had lost it while struggling to free himself from the vine.

"Gbeh Vey!!" he demanded, again, this time with all his might in an almost hoist voice, echoing into the night.

The figure continued the giant strides and stopped about six yards before him. Koikoi Pewee was standing face to face before a man, 6 feet tall, very muscular with broad shoulders and large arms and legs. He had on no shirt. Around his waist was what looked like the skirts the culture dancers wear, bedecked with cowrie shells. Around his large neck hung large Snail shells attached to what looked like robes made of neatly plaited palm branches.

He was wearing the dancer's mask, and Koikoi could see through it, the scarlet eyes of the man, looking straight into his eyes. Hanging on his back was a large bag made of woven sackcloth. Koi Koi looked down the man's feet and saw the tinkles tied around his ankles.

The man threw the sackcloth bag on the ground and gently removed the mask from his face. "Sengbeh Gbelema?" Siegie asked, quivering, and at the same time finally answering his own question. The question he had been demanding at the beginning of the encounter.

The old black smith advanced closer to him, looking straight in Koikoi Pewee's face with an expression that compelled Siegie to remember Sengbeh's threatening remarks, many years ago. 'You all must pray to die before the wrath that will come upon you,' the strong warning he issued on the night when old Chief Lumeh and the council of elders gave representative Barclay the green light to explore Maila, was about to become a reality.

He suddenly felt something warm running down his legs. Quivering out of extreme fear, he was urinating on himself. Echoing in his memory was the threatening remarks the black smith made the night the people of Maila pissed him off. *'All of you must pray to die before the wrath that will come upon you.'*

With the dreaded intention of the black smith, which was meant to inflict severe harm to those that undermined him and overlooked his threats that night sinking in, Koikoi Pewee wasted no time to charge at him, at the same time screaming.

Using his remarkable expertise with the cutlass, a trait he had mastered, growing up in Zigida, Zorzor District, Lofa County where he always won the trees felling and sticks chopping competition, he went for Sengbeh's head to chop it off, but the machete bounced.

Still screaming, he struck again, this time with a more vicious swing, but again it bounced off the chest of the black smith. Then he reverted to Sengbeh's both legs, scooping over and repeatedly using the side swing, first aiming for both ankles and then the feet, but again, that was to no avail; the black smith simply stood, looking at him.

Breathing heavily with exhaustion, he was grappling with a new round of fear he had never experienced, when he raised the cutlass in the air, towards the reflection of the moonlight to inspect the blade. The edge of the cutlass he sharpened several times at Flomo Town, and had never been used, was jagged.

Realizing that Sengbeh's skin was charmed, making it impenetrable to objects, Koikoi Pewee stood helplessly before the black smith, still breathing heavily with exhaustion.

Sengbeh Gbelema, with his broad arms stretched, slowly took one step after the other towards Koikoi Pewee like when someone was about to pounce on a cornered chicken he had been chasing. Frightening of all was the expression on his face, telling the right-hand man of Representative Barclay that it was time to face his wrath and accept his doom.

Still holding his cutlass, Koikoi Pewee took steps backwards as Sengbeh advanced closer to him. He felt his back against a tree standing behind him. Before he could move away from the tree, the black smith was on him, grabbing his neck with his powerful right hand and squeezing it, at the same time pressing him against the tree truck.

Gasping for air and stretching his eyes like they were going to jump out of their sockets, Siegie managed to also grab Sengbeh's neck with both hands and made an effort to hold him back, but the black smith was too strong for him.

Realizing that he was not going to suceed, Koikoi released Sengbeh's neck with his right hand and felt around his waist for a small knife he remembered to always carry on his side. He found and pulled it out and went straight for Sengbeh's left eye in an attempt to gouge it out and then the other one, since eyes are the only parts of the body the charm of knife proof does not protect. But Sengbeh grabbed his hand just before it could land.

When the black smith overpowered him and took the knife from his hand, Koikoi Pewee managed to dodge a vicious counter strike, meant for his left eye, by managing somehow to free himself, by slipping out of Sengbeh's grip and sliding down on his buttocks.

He noticed that Sengbeh's legs were spread apart as he struggled to remove the knife from the tree truck. He wasted no time crawling between them and got up to run for his life. He shivered with fear when he looked back and saw how the six inches knife pierced the hard tree trunk all the way to the handle and imagined what that was going to do to him when it was going to pierce his eyes.

"Ay Gala, E vee veh," he cried in Lorma, begging God as he ran aimless into the bush. "Sengbeh is evil. He's after killing me, after all these years."

He stumbled and fell, got up in no time and continued to run from one part of the bush to the other. Why did he not listen to Mulbah Kertehme to stay for at least a week to continue his treatment?

Maybe Boima and Chief Lomeh were going to look for him and they would have all gone to Maila together and all of this would not have happened, Siegie blamed himself.

It pained him more when he pondered the question why he used this route in the first place? He reeled in pain when his left foot stumbled upon a rock, bruising his big toe. He sat on the ground and briefly inspected it, and saw that his toe nail was partially removed as blood oozed from beneath.

He again shivered with fear when it occurred to him that he would not be able to run faster due to the injured toe. Weeping for his predicament, he tore a piece of cloth from the hem of his Vai shirt with his teeth and tied the affected toe and immediately hopped his way out of there when he heard the tingles approaching, again.

Struggling to ignore the pain from his injured toe, Koikoi wandered into the bush hoping to find a suitable place to hide as he could no longer move faster and the tinkling was getting louder and appeared to be echoing in all directions.

He came across a path that went down a valley and took it. He crossed a little brook, hopping on some rocks that laid across the water, and continued to follow the path.

Suddenly, a tree branch slapped his face and he fell to the ground on his back, partially unconscious. He could hear the faint tinkles getting closer to him and then stopped. Next, he felt being pulled by the neck of his Vai shirt and dragged, and then he had a blackout.

Siegie could not remember how long he was unconscious. But he suddenly came to himself, when what smelled like fume from a cigarette lighter filled his nostrils. He opened his eyes and found himself tied to a tree. When he looked a few meters ahead of him, the black smith was seated on the little stool behind the furnace, blowing the orange—green flames with the animal hide air sacs.

Siegie tried to free himself from the vines binding him to the tree but they were too strong; he could not move his hand, or his shoulders or his legs. Sengbeh Gbelema had severely strapped him to the tree.

The black smith suddenly jumped from the stool when he saw that Kio koi Pewee had regained his consciousness. He made his giant strides towards him and circled four times around the tree he was strapped on. Then he stood before him, took a knife from his side and began to violently strip off his clothes by tearing them from his body. He removed all the clothes off Koikoi Pewee except the brown Hanes briefs he was wearing. Then he took the chalk and began to rub it all over Siegie's body, at the same time mummering his usual incantation.

"Ay God! what's happening to me, so?" Koikoi Pewee, a grown man who has never known fear and was afraid of no one, cried like an infant, as tears profusely ran down his cheeks.

Sengbeh Gbelema took his giant zig-zag strides towards the now heavily blazing furnace and again sat on the stool. After a while, he took the orange-green hot cutlass from the fire and raised it into the air. He then got up and resumed his zig-zag strides towards Koikoi Pewee who was now crying bitterly. He again stood before the 'Siegie' with the molten steel raised.

"Your innocence is betrayed by your woe," chanted the black smith in his melodiously eerie tone as Koikoi Pewee violently shifted his head, the only part of his body he could move, from left to right in a vain attempt to release himself from the tree.

Siegie's efforts increased, especially when Sengbeh tried the steaming steel on himself and then continued with the ordeal verdict's code.

"But your woe is the source of your fear, for the radiance of the steel on your flesh for the abomination you have brought upon yourself."

Koi koi uttered a loud cry, calling for help as his voice reverberated through the dark night when Sengbeh pressed the hot blade on his left side, churning the flesh from under his armpit down to his waist. This time he screamed and screamed when the manic brought the hot cutlass down on his left thigh, the radiance consuming his flesh all the way to his thigh bone and down to the flesh around his knee cap. Koikoi looked at his side and saw the skeletons of his rips, thigh bone and knee cap with horror-stricken disbelief.

The black smith had taken his giant zig-zag strides back to the furnace and had put the cutlass he had just used on Koikoi into the fire. He blew it for some time and got out another one.

"Sengbeh. Just kill me quickly," cried Koikoi, upon seeing that the black smith had raised the other cutlass in the air. "Please don't suffer like this before you kill me. Whatever wrong you thought I did to you was only intended to seek the interest of the people of Maila. Please don't suffer me like this."

Sengbeh again took his giant zig-zag stride towards him and pressed the hot cutlass on Koikoi's right shoulder blade, the hot steel took the flesh with it and around the neck as he extended it. Air gushed out of his throat when it was also consumed by the steaming blade, and finally shutting his screaming voice.

Koikoi's eyes were stretched wide open and his tongue was hanging out of his mouth, but he wasn't dead. His eyes stretched wider in bewilderment as he struggled to open his mouth to scream when Sengbeh pressed the hot cutlass to the front of his neck, burning all the flesh around it until his neck bone was showing.

Koikoi Pewee's head fell on his chest which was still moving up and down as life was still in him. Then Sengbeh chopped off his head in one swing while the rest of Siegie's body convulsed for some time as his life gradually extinguished.

CHAPTER 8

"**W**HO'S SHINING THAT KIND of bright light in my face like that?" asked Gotolo, in the dark, sitting on his bench at his usual spot, in front of his house. He had on his lapper tied around him from his waist down and he had no shirt on. "That kind of light can make people blind," he complained.

"Gotolo-Gotolo," chuckled Tonola Wuamah, walking to him, with Boima and Chief Lomeh behind, at the same time dousing the powerful torchlight in his hand. "This kind of light is good for you to scan the whole town to see who will be escorting who or who will be coming from whose house, especially when Maila is in its festive times."

"Oh! Wuamah! Boima! Chief Lomeh! Welcome. But what brought you to my place at this time of the night?" exclaimed Gotolo and got up from his bench to greet his visitors.

"We thought you came to see Boima earlier this evening at the chief's compound, but as the night wore on, you just disappeared. We were wondering and so we came to look for you," responded the young chief.

"And we also brought you this torchlight which we all know is going to be good for you," added Wuamah, handing Gotolo the torchlight. "You need to thank Boima. He brought it for you."

"And because you the one that suggested it, since you always claim that I act like the town's cop."

"Gotolo. You were very close to my mother. I just want you to tell us where you think she might be," Boima went straight to the point.

"Let me bring the long bench for you," he said, after a long thought and hurried into his house and came back outside with a long bench which Boima, Wuamah and the young chief sat on. "Let me tell you the truth," he continued when he had sat opposite his three guests, looking them straight in their faces. "I have since felt uncomfortable, giving people information about other people. Because of it, I have gotten lots of funny names. At my age now, people still call me all kinds of names; man-woman, woman-man, woman tongue and all. What hurts me more is that when they need the information for their benefit, they will not call me by these names, but when the information is not in their favor, then they start to call me all these kinds of stupid names."

"It's the complicated world we live in, Gotolo," offered the young chief.

"Wuamah needs to know that," Gotolo said. "He has since avoided me."

"That ended the day I embraced you. The same day Boima came," Wuamah assured him, leaning over and extending his hand for a handshake.

"Only because you want something from me? Wuamah?"

"I desperately want something from you, Gotolo," Boima came in. "Remember the same way I used to be appealing to you to walk me down Nyenen to buy Ma Sonnie Kayan, because I was always afraid of the Gbatu, and you would do it because you did not like to see me cry?"

"I will never forget that," Gotolo responded, suddenly full of memories and wanting to cry.

"Then help us find your friend, and sister," urged Boima, full of anxiety as he shifted his torso on the bench.

Gotolo nodded and finally accepted Wuamah's hand shake. Then he received the touchlight, at the same time trying to hide the glee on his face. Suddenly, they heard giggling in the dark. This was coming from behind them. Gotolo quickly turned and flashed the torchlight in the direction.

"Gotolo you will never change," Yenpulu, a young girl walking hands in hands with her friend, Gee shouted at him.

"Maila is about to change for good, but I am afraid you will still remain the same," added Gee.

With the glee now visible on his face, indicating his satisfaction with his first demonstration of the powerful torchlight, he said nothing to the two young couples and turned it off.

"Gorpue was the only person that did not have a problem with me. She never showed her dissatisfaction with some of the things I told her, or, whenever I asked her certain personal questions, I had no business asking her. I think that was why we were very close," Gotolo explained. Then he shoved the torchlight between his legs, folded his hands and continued, "Esther remained in Sugar Hill after we heard your father had taken you to America. She did not want to come to Maila because she could not face the gossips that your father fooled and left her in the war and fled with you."

"How did she hear about the gossips?" inquired Wuamah, looking at Gotolo suspiciously.

"That is not important, now," grunted Gotolo. "Trying to figure out where she might be is what is more important."

"Okay," Wuamah agreed.

"So. She was still at Sugar Hill when the main rebel group occupied Bong Mines, but she was always indoors. She did not like the sight of the fighters. More especially, the way they were just having affairs with girls and sometimes getting them pregnant. It was then that she sent for me to be in the house with her to run her errands like going to the market or going to the drug store to buy her medicine.

When things were tough, I would come to Maila and get some produce from my farm. I had come to Maila to get some food stuff when Bong Mines was attacked by the other rebel faction. When the tension cooled down, I went back to Sugar Hill, but she had left. Ma Klubo told me that she fled with some display people to Kakata. It was in kakata that I learned that she was in an internally displaced camp between Kakata and Wheala, organized by Koikoi Pewee. I went there and met her.

But again, she was always indoors because some of the rebel boys frequented the displace camp. More especially, a rebel commander called 'Rebel Genie one day saw her and immediately started making advances at her. He brought her loot from the frontlines, which she did not accept. Some friends she had on the camp advised that she should stop refusing the things that Rebel Genie was bringing for her or else, one day, someone will lie that because she sympathizes with the enemy, is the reason why she always refused the items. So, when Gbarnga fell, Rebel Genie was part of the group that was sent to retake it. When he left, Esther fled to a village in Weala, with one of her friends who is from this village. It is far from the road and was not frequented by the fighters. But this girl later left her there and went to Monrovia.

Your mother remained in that village for some time. That was where she met a man named Johnny Vapilah. He used to work for the Central Agricultural Institute (CARI). Vapilah was old, and he had his wife who was also old. But he liked Esther and did things for her. He had a large farm and the food business was not difficult. When I saw that she was okay, I came back to Maila. It was then that I told her brother, the chief, where she was. I heard that he went there to look for her but didn't see her. And it was the last I heard from Esther."

"This Rebel Genie," Boima came in, still shifting his torso on the bench with anxiety. "Did he threaten my mother?"

"No," answered Gotolo, turning his head repeatedly from left to right and frowning. "But there was a strange thing about him. He was the quite opposite of the name he bore, and again no one knew his real name. But he was good, especially to your mother."

"Where is he now?" asked Boima, feeling a bit relieved, hearing that his mother was not threatened by this Rebel Genie.

"I learned that he was seriously wounded on Kokoya Road, trying to clear the rebels that attacked Gbarnga from that end, during the operation to liberate the city. I am told that an RPG blasted both of his legs; from the knee-caps down. But he managed to survive. People say he's currently somewhere in Nimba, now a very depressed man."

"Uncle. You went to look for your sister in this village, right? And it was the villagers that told you that she left, and they don't know her whereabouts. Did you see this Johnny Vapilah man?" Boima turned to the young chief and asked.

"What I learned was that Vapilah's wife got sick. She went mad and he took her somewhere for a cure, and that a relative of his wife who may know where he took her, no longer lives in the town, and may not be in Liberia.

They said this relative had some money a big rebel fighter gave him to keep, but thinking that the rebel was killed in the Bomi Hills attack, this relative ate the money, but later learned that the fighter was alive and was looking for him. So, he had to flee to the Ivory Coast. But I did not have the time to inquire more about this relative because the old chief sent word to me to go to Monrovia to pick up some things your father had sent for the town."

"I think we need to visit that village and see whether we can get the location of this relative of Vapilah's wife or Vapilah himself, if both may not be dead by now," suggested Wuamah.

"I think so," agreed Boima. "And Gotolo can come along with us, because he visited this village more than once."

"I will be ready to go with you any time," Gotolo agreed.

"Thank you very much, Gotolo," Boima said and got up to shake his hand. Gotolo also got up, smiling and extending his hand. "I brought some things for you. You can come to the chief quarter later in the morning for them." Gotolo looked surprised, as both of them shook hands. "Oh, come on, Gotolo," sensing that, Boima continued. "Did you believe Wuamah that I only brought Esther Lumah's right hand man a torch light?" There was laughter as Gotolo shook Chief Lomeh and his friend, Tonolah Wuamah's hands.

"So, Chief," Boima said while they were leaving Gotolo's house. We will find a day to visit this village where my mother went. But we got to first finish the boat ramp and land the boat in the water. Remember we got to go see this cliff Wuamah discovered. My friend Sam will be able to tell us exactly what happened there. He studied a bit of forensics back in the states."

"Oh! Wuamah discovered a cliff in Maila and something happened there?" asked Gotolo, who was escorting his visitors back to the chief's quarter, shining his torchlight ahead of them, and sometimes where he thought people were standing or moving about. "Wuamah. Was it not that same night I saw you pass by my house and looked scared?"

"You wanted me to look scared," Wuamah denied, slowing his steps to remain in the dark, in order to hide away from the flashlight so Gotolo must not detect how surprised and embarrassed he was, now that Boima had said something about the night he passed by his nosey friend's house, spooked and pretended that all was well.

"Yes. Wuamah discovered a cliff in Maila," Boima said, noticing how embarrassed Wuamah was and wanted to explain further but paused, when his uncle held his hand and squeezed it lightly. Then he quipped. "The thing that happened there is one of Maila's wonders."

CHAPTER 9

T HE FIRST FEW DAYS after he arrived, Boima started identifying and executing some quick impact projects in the town. Maila was laid out to construct roads and alleys. He made several tours in and around the town to identify suitable spots to construct a clinic, to relocate the Maila Elementary School, and build a youth center.

Logs were cut from the nearby bushes, to construct a huge water tower on a hill east of the town to mount 4 polyester water tanks, with the capacity to store up to 500 gallons of water. A 300HP Water Master pump with rollover frame that Boima brought will be used to pump water from the nearby tributary up the tanks, where they will be chlorinated to provide safe drinking water for the town's people.

Early the next morning after the boat ramp was completed, the townspeople gathered along the shallow creek at the edge of the town to witness the launching of the boat into the water. The old chief, his son, the young chief and some of the town's elders were also at the banks, watching as Sam drove the Ford pickup truck, hauling the boat behind it on a new road that was constructed to where the ramp was built. The four-seater gray 2003 aluminum Tagar V-18 multipurpose boat was then detached from the carrier and lowered on some rows of logs extending all the way to the edge of the water.

Everyone was cheering and jubilation as Tonola Wuamah directed some of the town's male youths to help slide the boat over the logs, until it landed into the water with a splash. Then Sam got down from the pickup and climbed into the boat from the right side of the ramp. Boima and Valarie joined him, including the old chief, his son, and Tonola Wuamah.

Sam started the engine and powered the beautiful V bass boat, less than a knot off shore in an exhibition ride and turned around and got back to the ramp. The people were amazed as they gathered around the boat and cheered the old chief who was helped to climb out of it. Boima, Sam, Valerie, Wuamah and the young chief waved to the crowd as they also disembarked.

"Siegie is not here yet. Its three days now," observed the old chief, turning to his Son.

"Maybe he is still taking his treatment in Flomo Town," replied young chief Lomeh. "Boima and I will go to look for him if we don't see him here tomorrow."

"That will be good," the old chief said, nodding. "At least he is one of those who is still alive to witness this."

"Guys," Boima called his grandfather, Chief Lomeh, and Tonola Wuamah aside, "We will sail for the cliff in two hours," he informed them, almost whispering.

"Yes. Sounds good. And my blessing is upon you all. Just be careful how you go about investigating what may have happened up that cliff. It is better whoever did it, must not suspect that we are trying to investigate, in order to catch him unaware," cautioning them, the old chief agreed.

It was a little over two hours they were embarking the boat to head for the cliff. Valerie hugged Sam for a while and then left for the chief quarter. Boima and Sam were dressed in a black and gray skin tight Puma fitness track suit with shorts and with life jackets.

The young chief and Tonolah Wuamah were both wearing Adidas shorts and T-shirts which were among the clothes Boima brought for them and also with their life jackets on.

Boima and Tonola Wuamah sat at the two-front seats while Sam sat near the engine and also sitting by him was the young chief. Some of the navigational buoys and Signage were loaded into the boat. Sam started the engine and as Boima steered, they rowed off.

From the shallow creek where they picked up, they sailed several knots, with the town disappearing behind them and reached the mouth of a tributary that flowed straight into the St. Paul. Sam was studying the sketch the old representative and Zeptter made at the same time taking pictures of the scenery while Boima steered the boat close to the banks and stopped.

Sam took one of the sign boards with the inscription 'Tributary #1: from Maila to greater St. Paul' while the other side read, 'Tributary #1: From greater St. Paul to Maila'. It was attached to a long steel pole with a pointed edge and was planted at the edge of the banks. When he had taken the GPS of the mouth of Tributary 1 with a water proofed T-Mobile Palm Pilot, the size of a small tablet, they entered the St. Paul and sailed to their right.

They covered several knots, before entering another estuary to their right as Wuamah directed. Again, the boat was inched closer to the banks. Another sign board was libeled 'Tributary #2: From greater St. Paul to Palm Wine Island with the opposite of the inscription on the other side of the sign board. Boima steered the boat closer to the edge of the banks, but they realized that it was far deeper than Tributary # 1 to plant the pole. So, Sam and Wuamah jumped into the water and swarmed with the Signage closer to the edge of the banks, where the water was not too deep.

Sam held the board while Wuamah held the steel pole. Remaining afloat, they detached a segment of the pole and attached others that were handed to them from the boat, until it was long enough to reach the bottom of the shallow edge. Then they planted the sign board into the water until the nose of the pole was inserted about 4 feet deep into the river bed.

When they had tested that it was strong enough for the current, they swarmed back to the boat. Sam and Boima referred to the sketch again, and then the GPS was taken when Sam raised the Palm Pilot Device above his head until the coordinates of this spot were captured.

They resumed rowing, eastward along Tributary 2, leaving the St. Paul at their real, and now facing the beautiful scenery before them. Taking pictures, Boima and Sam marveled at the magnificent scene while they headed for the Island where Wuamah always tapped his special palm wine.

In a couple of minutes, they reached where the tributary split into two halves and circled around the island. As Wuamah directed, Boima steered the boat into the shallow creek that runs through the Island. After several meters inward, he landed the V bass watercraft on the edge to his right with about a quarter of the keel hitting the hard ground. They all disembarked and followed Wuamah to where the palm trees were.

A three-gallon container full of fresh palm wine was brought before them and some were poured into two flask-like cups Boima and Sam took from their backpacks.

"Damn it! This is refreshing," mused Boima after taking a sip.

"Yeah. When this place is finally opened for business. Tourists will like this. It tastes good. And this place is really blessed," observed Sam, after he had also taken a sip.

"A small resort will be built here for tourists to come and enjoy the scene, taking pictures and drinking such refreshing palm wine. The surroundings and the wine are both appetizing," Boima said, extending the flask to Wuamah to pour a little more after he had taken a long drink.

"Wuamah. you can show us around a little while we finish your palm wine. And then we can go see this cliff," Sam said, looking around him with amusement as he sipped on the wine. "It seems like you are going to be the one producing this palm wine for the visitors when this place is opened."

They roamed the island for a while with Sam and Boima, first taking the GPS and then pictures. As Wuamah led, they reached the far end to where Tributary 2 rejoined and headed as a single stream southeast wards of the Island. Boima and Chief Lomeh waited, and watched from a little high rise, where the two halves of Tributary 2 re-joined, while Sam and Wuamah hurried back to the boat and returned with a sign board.

"Do you see the direction of the stream? "Asked Boima, Pointing down to where the two halves of Tributary 2 re-joined. "I think it heads south eastwards towards Maila."

"Yeah, it continues all the way to where it joins a creek full of reefs at the outskirts of the town." Wuamah agreed. "I have used it several times."

"So, we should label the Sign Board 'Double Stream: From Palm Wine Island to Reef Creek,'" Sam suggested.

When the Sign Board was labeled, and the steel poles were attached, Sam and Wuamah took careful steps on a steep path that led down to the edge of the Island where the two halves of Tributary 2 rejoined, and planted the informational signage.

Back at the entrance of Palm Wine Island, three other sign Boards were planted; one at the mouth of the creek that runs through it with the inscription, 'Welcome to Palm Wine Island' while the other two were planted at each half of Tributary 2 with the same inscription; 'Double Stream-To Reef Creek'. Then they got back into the boat and slowly rowed out of Palm Wine Island.

Few meters after the mouth of the creek, they dropped a buoy into the water with the inscription: 'ATTENTION! Strong current :Enter Island Through Narrow Creek'. When that was done, they turned left and entered one of the halves of Tributary 2 to cruise around Palm Wine Island to have a look at its perimeter.

It was the size of about two and a half soccer fields, mostly with smooth edges on both sides of Double Stream, except the steep edge on the southern tip where the two halves of the river rejoined and headed southeastwards to Reefs Creek. They were amazed to observe that the creek that runs through the island enters the other half of Tributary 2, on the left by rolling down layers of rocks, reaching half way before cascading into the water.

"Well. That's a good place to build a mini dam to electrify Palm Wine Island," Boima said, after taking a snap of the place.

Chief Lumah and Wuamah's eyes sparkled with excitement.

"I think so," Sam agreed, taking a sip of the Palm Wine as they rowed past it. "The force of the cascading water seems strong enough to produce enough power."

It took them about ten minutes to cover the entire perimeter of Palm Wine Island. And as Wuamah continued to direct them, they took the tributary ahead of them and sailed straight for the cliff. There was no reason to label this one, because they were still sailing in Tributary 2. From St. Paul, it headed north and south. The southern part further split and flowed around Palm Wine Island while the north, as Wuamah remembered, headed straight for the cliff.

Overwhelmed with the beautiful scenery bedecked with the colorful foliage that characterized the vegetation at both sides of the banks on this part of Tributary 2, as different species of birds flew overhead, Boima and Sam continued to take pictures. They maintained course, until they reached a mouth of a small but navigable distributary that flowed eastward.

"That's the route I remembered using when I fled the gruesome scene up that cliff. It also joins a creek at the northern edge of Maila," Wuamah said.

"Then let's label it," suggested Sam. "What do you think, Guys?"

"I guess you are right," Boima answered, cruising close to the mouth of the distributary.

Another sign board was then labeled 'Single Stream 1: Flows Eastwards to Maila', just like they did the others. Like the other navigational sign boards, segments of steel poles were attached in accordance with the depth of the shallow edge and were planted.

Then they sailed along Tributary 2 for a couple of minutes until they reached an inlet on the left that headed westwards towards the greater St. Paul.

"I think I missed this one," Wuamah said as Boima slowed down the boat. "I was probably asleep while my canoe passed it and drifted towards the cliff."

"Which means you don't know where it is heading," Boima said. "Upon our return, we will check it, guys."

They passed the inlet, with Boima powering the V Bass Multipurpose boat at full throttle, as the propeller displayed magnificent splashes of waves which Wuamah enjoyed seeing as they continued to head in the direction of the cliff. About thirty minutes later, Wuamah pointed ahead when he saw the rapids in the distance, except that they were more visibly protruding out of the water unlike the last time he paddled here.

Boima was forced to reduce speed and they gently glided towards the rocks to try to figure out the safest way to pass them. Few minutes later, the cliff appeared in the midst of a fog in the distance, but they could not sail through the rapids, and they did not have the inflatable mini boat to paddle through.

"I think the tide on this side has reduced a bite so we need to go back to that inlet and figure a way to get to the cliff from the right," suggested Boima, and before they turned around and went back to the inlet, they threw a buoy into the water with the inscription: Attention! Rapids Ahead.

They witnessed another beautiful scene when they entered the inlet and cruised several meters inward. It later turned out that it did not head straight into the greater St. Paul as they previously thought, but rather, it flows parallel to it, separated by a strip of land, covered with trees with healthy and magnificent foliage adorned with the effulgence of autumn-like green yellow and orange colors.

At some point, it would display a partial few of the St. Paul to their left, and then the strip of land with the trees and thick foliage will continue to extend. On their right was a thick vegetation of average height, enabling them to catch a glimpse of the cliff in the distance.

They continued until they suddenly got to what looked like a pond of beautiful species of water lilies. The water was clear to the extent that they could see varieties of cold-water fishes swimming about in a frenzy and disappearing between the bottom stem of the lilies in an apparent reaction to the sound of the boat engine.

"Why did we fight this war in the first place," wondered Sam, taking a few snaps of the scene.

"We were just lucky," Boima offered, also taking a few snaps. "The war didn't come this way or else this place would have been destroyed."

From the deep-water pond, they entered a large lake where they could clearly see the cliff to their right. The strip of land that separated the inlet from the St. Paul was now far to their left. They maintained their course to their right, looking for a stream or a creek that would lead them down to the cliff.

Not quite long they discovered one, a shallow creek that flows eastwards. The entire west side of the cliff was now before them, as they sailed down the creek. They passed through where some parts of the wall of the steep side of the cliff partially cascaded over the water, making it look like an arc way of a water tunnel.

They got out on the other side and as it became familiar to Wuamah, Boima landed the boat on the smooth part of the edge of the cliff. Sam and Boima got their backpacks, and they all got down, hopping on the rocky edge, looking around while Sam and Boima continued to take pictures.

Further along the edge, as Wuamah led them to where he landed his canoe, he suddenly stopped when he saw an old and strange looking worn out one. The rest of them got closer to it and looked inside. There were two paddles lying on the floor. The stern has been eaten up due to years of water and moist reaction.

"More proof that you were not the only one here, Wuamah," observed Boima, taking pictures.

"Yeah, I had thought the victims got here by land, but it now seems they got here by this canoe."

"As worn out as it is, this does not look like an ordinary canoe," observed Chief Lumeh. This is longer and wider inside than the ones our people make."

"I have taken enough pictures of it," Boima said. "I 'll show this to my grandfather. He might know something."

"The remains you say you saw up there might also give us a clue," Sam said, looking up the cliff. "I think we need to get going."

They reached the place where Wuamah remembered landing his canoe. He pointed at the direction he had come, and they could see the rest of the rapids to their right, where they would have come through when the tide was high enough for the boat to pass. Then he led them to where he had climbed the cliff, cautioning them to take careful steps as they followed him. Boima stock closed behind him, followed by Chief Lumeh, and then Sam.

Taking pictures as they ascended, Sam and Boima observed that it was a cliff, covered with grass and trees. Half way up they looked down and saw the beautiful vegetation below, including small rivers and streams that navigate through the forest glades.

Wuamah led them to the part where he descended the rocks and discovered the waterfall pool. But they found another way to descend with ease. After a minute or two of walking, they were led to the waterfall pool. Marveling at the exquisiteness of the place, Sam and Boima again took pictures of the pool, and the other surrounding places.

"Where's the gruesome scene?" Boima asked.

"Few yards behind us," answered Wuamah, looking in the direction, and suddenly becoming perplexed. "Here they are," he said, when he had composed himself and had led them to the first tree where the human remains were tied and scorched.

They were frightened for a moment when they saw it, and the other one, pitying the dreadful fate of the victims. Wuamah showed them what was left of the furnace.

"This made me believe that this was committed by the black smith," he reiterated his suspicion.

"What do you think, Sam?" Boima asked.

"Just a second," he responded, first looking around and studying the scene, and then took his backpack. Squatting, he unzipped it.

"Well. This is what I think happened," he said, after taking a deep breath with his expression still pitiful, when he had counted the piles of bullets Wuamah showed him lying on the ground with a pair of pincers he took out from a small case he got out of his bag. "Almost two magazines of AK-47 rounds were fired from the direction of the waterfall pool at a particular target. Strangely though, it was a hell of an aim for anyone to survive that," he paused, studying the remains before him for some time while Wuamah and Chief Lumeh looked on, scared of what they were hearing. "But the remains of whosoever that was shot at, should be lying right where these piles of bullets are."

"Or maybe whosoever it was, must have staggered with the remaining bullets in him and may have fallen dead somewhere around here," suggested Boima, looking around. "We need to look around."

They began looking within the immediate perimeter of where the skeletons were. "Hey guys," Sam alerted them, scooping over when he saw an object lying close to his feet. "Found something," he informed the others. "It's a magazine."

"Found something too," Also informed Chief Lumeh. "A skeleton of an animal, maybe a black deer."

Wuamah went to where the furnace was and got samples of the special wood. They continued to search the place, further expanding the perimeter, but they didn't see any other human remains.

It's kind of Strange," wondered Boima, when they had assembled where the two-skeletons were tied to the trees. "There are two AK-47 rifles; one lying a few meters from the first remains while the other is right beside the other one. And there's an emptied magazine and an animal skeleton. What really happened here?"

"With luck. I think we can try to patch together some explanation," responded Sam, and got out from his bag a pair of gloves and wore them.

He went to where the old and rusty Ak-47 rifle was lying, scooped over and took it. After inspecting it, he tried to pull out the magazine, but it couldn't' due to years of rust. So, he got out of his bag a canister and sprayed oil on the magazine. He waited for some time and tried to pull it out again. After some effort, the Magazine came out. He inspected it, there were few bullets inside. Then he went over to the other one lying close to the other skeleton. After oiling it, he removed the magazine and saw that the bullets were intact.

"I think I got it," he said, bringing Boima, Wuamah and Chief Lumah to attention. "It was the first victim that fired all these rounds. There are some bullets left in the magazine of the first rifle, which means the bullets did not enter into whosoever that was shot at. But the rifle lying by the other victim is intact. I think these two rebel fighters came here to rest for the night or something like that, when they encountered whosoever, it was that they did this to them. The one who did the shooting was probably on guard. You know this was war time and I would have done the same. But here's the mystery; the one who was shot at, did not get hit. And he may have done this to them."

"And I think this animal was shot, too," Chief Lumeh informed them, pointing to a dent in the skull of the animal skeleton.

"Probably," nodded Sam, studying the skull. "But not with either of these rifles," he said when he had taken one of the Ak-47 rounds and inserted it into the dent in the skull. "The bullet that killed this animal is bigger."

"It must be a fine shot, fired from a hunting gun," guessed Wuamah.

"Then the person who did this had a hunting gun, too," added Sam.

"Sengbeh will not kill an animal," Wuamah disagreed.

"So how do you think he's been surviving in these bushes?" asked Boima.

And there was silence.

"It's definitely him, Sengbeh Gbelema," Chief Lumeh said, breaking the silence as he looked at the remains on the trees, the furnace and the sample of the special wood in Wuamah hands. "He's the only surviving blacksmith in Maila that can do this. He inherited the craft from his grandfather, but he is now using it to perpetuate evil."

"This happened a long time ago. You think he's still around?" asked Sam. "This was committed during the war, and it has been some 13 years now. Maybe he might be dead or lying somewhere sick. But if he is still alive, he will be stopped," Boima said. "We have to go to Bong Mines to report this to the authorities."

"We need proof that this Sengbeh Gbelema is responsible for this," said Sam. "If I heard right, no one has seen him since the quarrel with the old chief and your dad, years ago."

"Then we stick to the old chief's advice." offered Chief Lumeh

"Yeah, Uncle," Boima agreed. "We hope to catch him in the act."

They left the scene and went looking around other parts of the cliff. Wuamah saw the path that ascended to the highest point to the east. Sam, Boima and Chief Lumeh followed him. When they got there, they had a clearer view of the land. In the mist far beyond, was the Bong Range. Sam and Boima, again captivated by the beautiful scene, took more pictures.

"This part is good for mountain climbing." Boima said, looking down the steep and sometimes rough slope with crevices on its sides and what appeared like the entrances of caves. "Tourists flock to places like these."

"Yeah," nodded Sam. "One can carve out a trail from here to the Bong Range. Could be good for camping."

"Another resort can be built here, and we can also introduce cable cars transport systems like what they have in the Scandinavian mountains and other places around the world. Through them, we can link this cliff to certain parts of the Bong Range. Tourists would enjoy viewing the beautiful scene from above and will be willing to pay lots of money for it," explained Boima, very excitedly, and at the same time taking pictures.

"You got yourself a beautiful place, uncle" mused Sam, looking at chief Lomeh and then taking more pictures.

They found their way to the Western part, where they could see other rivers and streams, and the outline of a large one that they assumed to be the St. Paul. "Indeed, this is a beautiful place where a resort can be built and can attract an influx of Tourists," Boima marveled at the splendid scenery below, further solidifying his determination to make Maila a tourism hub.

After that, they left the cliff and were back cruising through Fish Pond Lake. It was now late in the afternoon. The sun was setting and as usual, the surface of the water and the surrounding vegetation displayed a magnificent gold-like scenery as the sun cast its rays. Boima and Sam, filled with relief and amusement, after investigating the gloomy scene up the cliff, continued taking pictures. They poked around for some time, referring to the sketch, as well as making some modifications on the map. More waterways were named, and their GPS were taken. Satisfied with the day's work, they returned to Maila just before sunset.

"The canoe you saw has strange markings like those used by the water witch," said the old chief after viewing the pictures taken from the cliff, while he and his grandson were taking a late evening walk towards the boat ramp hours after they arrived from the cliff. "And it was probably used by the victims who were rebel fighters."

"My mother told me stories about them when I was a kid. There were incidents of the water witch in the Hendii area," Boima told his grandfather when they both were now walking on the boat ramp. "How can it be connected to what happened up that cliff?"

"When your ancestors finally defeated the Gola, the practice was strongly discouraged in Maila. After an incidence, some were apprehended, but many of them fled and settled along the Hendii belt."

"So, grandfather," sighed Boima, also sitting near the old chief who now sat at the edge of the boat ramp, facing the water. "How come rebel fighters used the canoe of the water witch to ferry them all the way here to Maila?"

"Well," the old chief raised his shoulders. "Maybe the fighters were fleeing from Hendii. The town was overrun during the civil war. My wild guess is, one of the victims or both may have had knowledge of the St. Paul River and were trying to connect to Gbarnga. They were probably natives of Hendii."

"And the canoe?" Boima asked, studying his grandfather.

"Probably found, ceased or stolen." Also studying his grandson, the old chief continued, "Sengbeh Gbelema, the black smith felt like they trespassed his ancestors' land, and so he killed them using the Sassaywoo ordeal. But the one he is using is not for justice. It's for reprisal."

"Then it seems we were wrong to break the pack between the Maila and the Gbelema," Boima said, shuddering a little.

"No," responded the old chief, holding his grandson on his left shoulder, in a bid to assure him. "I had no cause to risk your father's life or yours. Or else, I would have never allowed you to come here, Boima." The old chief now stood up and held his grandson's hands. "It was once on this very shore of this water, the exact spot you have now built this ramp, Sengbeh's father, now an aging man felt that the time has come to develop this land. He felt that the spirits of our ancestors who bled to preserved Maila were entrapped in its continual underdevelopment for decades. He was supposed to state his support openly at the meeting that night, but he died of mysterious circumstance few days before the meeting."

"But like you said, he died."

"Yes, but this is where he swore, before me and the spirits of the ancestors to give his blessing for your father to open up this place, like what you are doing now."

"Which means he was killed by his own son, who probably did not like the idea, and I don't think he likes you, either. According to uncle, his father was found dead under a tree he himself had cut down on his farm after they both had a quarrel," Boima said. "And knowing this, you did nothing about it."

"I had to uphold the sanctity of the pack," lamented the old chief. "Kerkula Maila and Sengbeh Gbelema vowed to never hurt each other, and that vow still extends to the generations after them. And we from the Maila lineage have to keep our part. Sengbeh's father kept his, though his son has refused to. So, I had to be tolerant, more especially to a Gbelema to strengthen our position regarding our plan to transform this beautiful land."

"Then his charm or whatever ritual he uses won't harm us, grandfather. Maila will be built, even if he will steam my flesh to the bone."

The old chief looked at his grandson for a while. After a brief thought, he said "It was never a mistake when you were born."

CHAPTER 10

ADDITIONAL TWO DAYS HAVE passed, and Koikoi Pewee has not yet come to Maila. The old chief, concerned that he may not still be well, urged Boima and Chief Lomeh to pay him a visit just as they discussed, the day the boat was launched into the river. Also, Gotolo will go along with them to Weala to visit Mr. Vapilah or his wife's relative to see whether they can get any other information concerning the whereabouts of Esther Gorpue Lumeh.

Tonolah Wuamah had left for Nathaniel Kpaingkpa's farm, the day before, to break the good news to his uncle, John Dolmayan, about an employment opportunity with Lakay Construction Company. With urging from his mother, he talked to Boima to recommend him to Lakay to join the team of workers that will be rehabilitating the road to Maila.

Chief Lomeh added his voice to convince Boima that Dormeyahn was an able heavy-duty mechanic and would be very helpful in maintaining the yellow machines. From there, Wuamah will join Boima, Chief Lumeh and Gotolo in Varney Town, first to visit Koikoi Pewee at Flomo Town. From there, they will go to Weala.

That morning, Sam and Valerie planned to go out, boating, and to take pictures. She could not wait to see with her own eyes the images of the beautiful scenery Sam had shown her on his lab tap. Sam himself, while looking at all the pictures, mainly the ones he took up the cliff, saw what looked like a beautiful glade to the north, and was also eager to go take a physical look at the place. He studied the pictures carefully and figured out how to get to this place.

He and Valerie were excited when both discussed having a nice picnic there. Since they arrived in Maila, both of them have not had quiet time together as Sam was busy helping to build the boat ramp and other things.

"Are we set for the great sail, now?" asked Valerie, wearing sky blue skinned tight leggings slightly stopping above her knee with a half-demi polo singlet; Sam had parked the things they agreed to carry along with them in the boat.

"We need to refer to the list we made before we forget something important," he said, counting the things with his eyes.

"Okay. Let me see," she crooned, taking a piece of paper from her waist. "As for the picnic, we got the grail, the fishing line, the quilt to spread on the ground, and the ingredients."

"How about the list for the photo shoot?"

"Yes. You got everything into the boat. The camera and the stand, spare batteries, the PC, etc.,"

"I think we are good, except for one thing."

"What?"

"The medic kit."

"Medic Kit?" Asked Valerie, with her eyebrow raised.

"Yep," chirped, Sam. "It's essential for camping out in the woods. One could slip and fall and get hurt. I think it is in the compartment, on the floor behind the pilot seat."

"And the life jackets?"

"Oh, Wow. I almost forgot that too. Let me check the other compartments."

"And don't forgot about signboards, poles, some navigational aids, and your backpack, too."

"You got it. Thanks for the reminder, Valerie."

The boat slowly left the ramp with Sam sitting next to Valerie while she piloted.

"Take your time. Look ahead of you, and then left and right to watch for the signs. Do not cut too deep or else you will throw us overboard," he said as the boat sailed toward Tributary 1.

They entered the greater St. Paul, and Sam encouraged Valerie to increase the speed a bit. At first, she was hesitant, but after a few knots, she grew confident and increased the speed, and as she did, her gold silver braided hair was flipping in the direction of the wind. She veered into Tributary 2 when Sam pointed to the signboard, and they moved forward, until they turned left, leaving Palm Wine Island to their right, and rolled all the way, until they turned into Fish Pond Lake.

Valerie was so amazed as Sam took pictures of her piloting the boat. He stopped the engine and angered the boat. After that he told her to get into the water, and when she did, holding the side of the hull right beneath the gunwale with her life jacket on, he took her pictures.

"This is going to be a nice photo," he said, giving her the thumbs up. "Fishes are swimming below you."

"What?!" yelled Valerie, looking in the water and seeing some fishes swimming below her. "Help me up, Sam."

"Don't worry. They won't harm you," he said, pulling her out of the water into the boat. "You will be in our tourist gallery, swimming in a lake with varieties of fishes beneath you."

"You and Boima will pay me for this," joked Valerie, wiping her skin with a big towel Sam threw to her at the same time in a fixed gazing, smiling.

"Well. I don't know about Boima, but that's not going to be my worries."

"What will be your worries, then?" She asked, laughing and throwing the towel over his face when he kept staring at her enticing body.

"The male tourists that will be chasing after you."

"Sam you are very funny," she said, continuing laughing as her voice echoed into the vegetation surrounding Fish Pond Lake.

They left the lake with Sam now piloting. And after a few minutes, they entered the larger lake where the stream led to the cliff. But figuring out from the photo, the direction of what looked like the glade, they sailed further west of the lake towards the St. Paul with hope to find a water way that would take them into the larger river. They did, and found an inlet. Just like he had been doing, Sam labeled a signboard 'Inlet 2: From Fish Pond Lake to Greater St. Paul'.

After planting it at the edge of the strip of land that divides the lake from the river, they rode along the St. Paul with Sam, now very attentive to look for the narrow waterway at the right, that snaked its way around the north of the cliff and flows all the way to the glade as seen in the photo.

"There is it," Valerie suddenly shouted, when she discovered another inlet to their right.

Oh, yeah," crooned Sam, slowing down and turning into the inlet. "You got it, baby."

Another signboard, labeled 'Inlet 3: From Greater St. Paul to Maila Glade', was planted at the edge, and then, they went cruising right into it. Sam steered the boat downstream, following the course of Inlet 3 eastward, and keeping an eye on the cliff at his distant right. After some time, they entered an area where the water was narrowed and completely cascaded on both sides by branches of trees with beautiful foliage. The temperature here was cooler and refreshing, and the aroma was pleasant. Sam stopped and took some pictures of only the scenery and others with Valerie and the foliage in the background.

After that, they rolled to another area where the water flowed left at an elbow, and continued for some time, and there it was, the glade as Sam compared the scenery with the photo on the laptop. It is a clearing with low grass like a lawn with scattered trees with yellowish red foliage. The area stretched some acres further north, dotted with ponds. Sam found a suitable place and landed the boat near a tree.

"Valerie," he called her attention in a soft tone, suddenly interrupting her gaze as she marveled at the place. "Welcome to the paradise of Maila."

"This place is beautiful, Sam," she said, watching him disembarked with another signboard in his hand he had labeled ' Maila Paradise Glade'. "Can't believe this is Liberia."

"Yeah," he said, after planting the sign board at the edge of the water, a few feet from the boat. "This is Liberia. The people of Maila managed to preserve this place for many years, and it's going to give them a lot of fortune." Looking around the quiet place except for the melodious chirps of birds in the distant trees and the occasional slapping of the ripples on the edge of the water, he spotted what looked like a gorge ahead of him. "Let's get our things. We might find a nice place to set up over there."

Beyond the gorge, the place looks perfect, with its low grass and scattered trees with naturally decorated foliage. The ground was dotted with smooth grayish looking rocks in the shape of a dome with some of them about three to four meters high, and more ponds whose surfaces reflected the foliage.

They found a spot under a flower tree with nicely spread branches, not far from a large pond. Valerie liked the spot for its perfect shade and pleasant aroma of the blossoms overhead and the ones that fell from the trees and littered the ground around them.

Quite fascinating was the manner in which the aroma filled the immediate surroundings with the fragrance filling the air and filtering into the nostrils of Sam and Valerie, with the scent on their clothes. Sam left her and went to the boat for the rest of the things while she arranged the picnic spot.

"There are ponds where we can go fishing and there are other ones, nice and safe for swimming," he informed her when he returned with the rest of the things.

"Okay," she said, taking a selfie as he watched her, admiringly.

"Time's up for taking pictures," he said after taking some more pictures of her and the surroundings. "Time to go fishing."

With sets of fishing rods in their hands, Sam led her to a dark water pond covered with water lilies with wide leaves. They stood at the edge and Sam threw the fishing line in the pond, after inserting a bait on the hook. Watching, and positioning herself like the way he did, she also threw hers into the water and made a face like she would not be able to pull out the line when she made a catch.

After a few minutes, she suddenly felt a jerk and got a bit frightened, almost dropping the fishing rod.

"Sam!" she exclaimed. "I feel something jerking the line and wants to pull me into the water."

"Don't let go, Valerie. It might be a catch. Pull it backwards or roll the coil with the small winder on the side."

"I can't, Sam. It's heavy. Maybe it's a shark!" she screamed, after attempting to wind the reel, but stopped when she heard splashes at the end of the line.

"Shark?" laughed Sam, suddenly pulling his fishing rod out of the water, dropping it down and hurrying to help her.

"Okay. At the count of three, we pull."

A very large cold-water fish like a tuna of about 15 inches long, weighing about two pounds was jerked out of the water. Sam dragged it at a safe sport away from the pond, and pounced on it. With the giant fish still fighting, he managed to hold it on the ground, shouting and jubilating, as his voice echoed through the glade.

"You did good, Valerie" he said, now holding the fish by its gills with both hands. "It's a big catch, and it is going to be enough for us."

Amazed and partially covering her face with both hands, she could not believe what she caught. She had never gone on a boat wide and fishing in her entire life and she could not stop marveling at her catch. Back under the tree where they spread the picnic quilt, Sam set up the small grill and went looking for firewood while she prepared the fish.

He returned with some, after some minutes.

"On my way back, I saw a pond that looks nice for swimming and, near the edge, looks good for taking exercise. It has been days I haven't done any."

"Don't get lost," joked Valerie, smiling as she watched Sam walking to the pond, and then resumed cleaning her monstrous catch.

At the pond, Sam found a spot between two rocks. He placed both legs on top of them and closed his eyes and began to meditate. After a few minutes, he executed some karate drills intended to relax his muscles. Then he changed to a kick boxing style drill, by jumping down from the rocks and stretching his legs far apart until his buttocks rested on the ground.

From that, he executed some other mixed martial arts drills for about 30 minutes. After this routine, he was now ready for the breath control drill. He again stretched his legs far apart and meditated for some time. Then he got up, took off his black armless Nike skinned t-shirt, exposing his impressive athletic body, and when he closed his eyes and had taken a deep breath, he plunged into the water in a splash and made a dive.

He emerged, standing up where the water reached the level of his chest and began to slowly slide back underneath, as he stretched both legs until he was completely submerged. Valerie had completed grilling her well spiced catch, and had set it in a silver tray of fresh mixed vegetables she had also prepared. She then reached over to a small red cooler, and got a bottle of Cavin Villa red wine, and sat it into another silver tray.

Satisfied with the setup, she looked ahead of her, in the distance to signal to Sam that dinner was ready. But she could not see him. He may have plunged into the water and swam further, she thought and so she covered the grilled fish with another silver tray and went sauntering to the pond.

"Sam," she called, suddenly becoming concerned after waiting at the edge for about 5 minutes and there was no sign of him. "Sam," she shouted, this time frightened, with her thrilled voice reverberating beyond the stretches of acres of the glade.

She stood quivering, looking around, and gasping with fear. She was about to shout his name for the third time, when he suddenly emerged, walked out of the water to her, breathing heavily.

"What, baby?" he asked, still breathing heavily, standing before her, and holding his waist.

"You got me scared," she complained, wiping a small drop of tear from her eyes with the stroke of her little finger.

"Sorry, baby," Sam apologized, holding her hands. "It was just a breath control drill."

"Okay. There's a lot I got to get used to. By the way, dinner is ready."

"Thanks. But let's have a swim, first," he said, and then turned around, wading his way back into the water and making a plunge. "Come on," he called to her, when he had emerged, wiping the water off his face with his hands.

Valerie first hesitated, with the expression on her face like she wasn't sure. But she suddenly thrust her shoulders, telling herself to 'hell with it' and then slowly took a few steps into the water. When it reached the level of her breasts, she threw herself into it, throwing her arms as she swam towards him in an awkward manner. Sam laughed and also swam towards her, as soon as the water reached the level of her neck and held her by her hands.

"Come on. Just swing your legs. I got you," he said as he gently thrust himself backwards at the same time, gently pulling her to him.

"We are going to the deep part," she yelped, flapping at the ripples and holding him tight, when her feet were no longer touching the bottom.

With her arms clenched around his neck and her legs wrapped around his hips, they became quiet for a moment, staring at each other intensively. Reading the hunger for her in his appealing eyes, she smiled and bought her face closer to his and immediately, they were kissing.

Still in the same position, Sam managed to swim with her back on shore. He carried her all the way under the flower tree and laid her down on the picnic quilt. Still kissing, now ferociously, they were in full romantic mood. Sam could feel the urging intensity to make love, from the way she was breathing rapidly, whenever they paused and looked at each other in the face. He liked the pleasant smell of her breath, encouraging him to kiss her more.

She inched her back slightly upwards to allow him to remove her polo demi singlet with ease, which he gladly did, exposing her firm breasts. Her body quivered when he gently held them like two delicate bulbs. Indeed, Valerie had told him the truth; for a long time, no man had touched her.

She gasped with pleasure, softly whispering his name, when he moved his lips over her nipples. For a time, he held them between his lips, one after the other and slowly brought his face down, first between her breasts.

She trembled in responds to the erotic reaction of the touch of his lips, as he moved his face away from her chest down to the middle of her stomach and then her naval.

Valerie held onto his head firmly, in an attempt to prevent him from working his lips further down her navel, as she anticipated that she would be unable to withstand the pleasure that was coming.

However, she slowly let go, and reverted to rubbing his head, the sides of his face and increasingly gasping and whispering his name more audibly when he went down and worked his longue ferociously. At one time she held onto his ears, pulling them as she reeled with an unimaginable pleasure.

Mindful not to let her explode too soon, Sam worked his lips back up her navel, and then her face and resumed kissing her. She suddenly grabbed his hands, pulled it down her hips, in a move to help her pull down her leggings.

Sam got on his knees, gently pulled it down her legs and flung them behind him. As she lied down, positioning herself and welcoming him, he stood up and also took down his shorts. Then he eased his way back on top of her, and slowly worked his way into her, feeling satisfied that he was right to believe her, that she had not made love in a very long time.

As he thrust, at the same time gradually increasing his rhythm, Valerie reflected the erotic world of the men she made love to, before meeting Sam. She remembered nothing special about Jeremy Doe. All she could record was that he was kind of gentle, but wasn't romantic, and never paid attention to her sensitivity like the way Sam was doing.

Something was always on his mind even when he made love to her. He was always worried about his position on the team he was playing for in South Korea, complaining how racist the people were towards African players. Though he graciously accepted the pregnancy, it became worse after that.

As for Victor Karr, he was an ignorant brute, always rough on top of her or when he took her from behind or when he confusingly turned her in all kinds of positions, thinking that it would demoralize her, so she would feel inferior to him, and turning her against another man. That was just stupid jealousy, she thought.

But with Sam, it was extremely different. He wasn't eager to make love to her when they met. So, she had no regret for now breaking her vow that the man she will make love to will be the man she will marry. It has been over a month and a half since she met him, but the care he showed her and Promise has changed everything.

She could not resist him. His sense of humor and gentleness, and never caring about her past, about how a foolish man like Victor Karr had used her, abused her in the open, have captivated her.

Suddenly Sam began to groan with pleasure at the same time calling her name as he increased his rhythm. She herself began to convulse more violently as she sensed that they were both going to climax together. And before she could think of it, they started calling each other names as loud as they could. She was the first, then Sam, seconds after.

"You made me feel so good," he confessed, rolling from on top of her.

"Me too," she admitted, slightly rolling on top of him with her head in his chest. "I have no regrets, Sam."

"Oh. I am hungry," he said. "What have you prepared for us?"

"Hungry?" laughed Valerie, getting up and wrapping a large white towel around her waist "First for the feesh, and now for the fish?"

"Derm, Valerie," Sam also laughed. "Never knew you were this rude. I know you cut lots of grass at Haywood."

"Haywood got no grass."

"Well, I am not surprised."

Laughing, she went for the tray and then the wine. Sam popped the cock and poured two paper cups full, while she cut a portion of the fish from the area around the head with a knife. She put it in a white paper plate with some of the mixed vegetables and served him.

After eating the delicious grilled fish with fresh mixed vegetables, she suggested that they go swimming again, and Sam agreed, with full alacrity. Back in the water, they made more love, and then they got back under the tree, ate and drank some more, and then relaxed for some time, viewing the pictures they took. Sam had imported them from the Camera's SD card to the laptop.

It was now approaching the evening hours. She was sitting on top of Sam, massaging his back. "Your skin is white, Sam," she observed.

"Yeah, we stayed in the water for a long time. There's an after-swimming lotion in one of the compartments in the boat. I think it will be the one under the steering wheels."

"Let me go and get it," she offered, and got up, found her leggings and her singlet, put them on and went hurrying to the boat.

She took careful steps on the rocks in the small water that passed through the gorge, sometimes stepping into the water, where it reached her heel and enjoyed its warmth. Right before coming out of the gorge, she suddenly froze. Someone was standing near the sign board Sam had planted, and was uprooting it.

'Who are you?" she called, and instantly became apprehensive when the person had uprooted it, and dashed it on the ground. The intruder turned, staring at her, breathing heavily with rage. It was Sengbeh Gbelema.

In his hands was a long rope attached to a large and rusty fishing hook. In the next moment, he was swinging it at the same time walking slowly to her.

"S-A-M," she screamed and turned to run, but the black smith sent the hook. She screamed again, this time louder, when it caught her between her neck and her right shoulder and tore into it. In one jerk, she fell on her back, screaming as he pulled her towards him. The blood from the wound of her torn flesh, gushed out and flowed into the water.

Sam was now sitting with his legs crossed, and had resumed viewing the pictures. He had just taken a sip of the wine, when he heard Valerie screamed his name. He immediately got up and ran towards the direction of the gorge. Getting there, he was shocked to see Valerie frantically clinching on to a rock, as Sengbeh pulled the robes towards him.

"Va-le-rie!" Sam screamed with all his might and ran towards the black smith.

He thrust forward and gave Sengbeh a very powerful spear, the impact sending both of them to the ground and forcing the black smith to let go of the robes. In no time the mixed martial arts fighter was on top of him, first securing a side control to his right, giving him the leverage to land some vicious elbow smashes across Sengbeh's face.

"I will fuck you up too bad," raged Sam, in his American accent and continued to inflict Sengbeh with nasty elbow smashes, including some hard knees on the side of his head.

Sengbeh used his strength to push Sam off, but before he could get up. Sam had taken hold of the signboard lying on the ground and detached the steel pole. Sengbeh sprung to his feet, looking very surprised at the ferocity of the adversary standing before him.

"You just fucked with the wrong person, mehn," Sam snarled and advanced to him, sweeping his 2 feet off the ground with a swing of the steel pole. Sengbeh landed on his back with a very loud thud, but before he could get up again, Sam was on top of him, pressing the steel pole across his neck in a bite to strangulate him.

Sengbeh Gbelema suddenly grabbed the steel pole and tried to push it off his neck, but Sam continued to press it down to the extent that the black smith's eyes were stretching out in reaction to the effort he was making to get the pole off his neck.

Sengbeh however succeeded to raise it about an inch and a half from his neck, thus relieving some pressure off him. But Sam, acknowledging the strength of his adversary, and how he was succeeding to pull the steel pole all the way off his neck, gave Sengbeh a nasty elbow smash into his left eye, causing the black smith to utter a faint whimpering sound and let go of the pole. In no time Sam pressed it against his neck again, until it was almost bending.

Sengbeh struggled for some time but finally gave up. His eyes were stretched wide open and he was breathing little by little, and then he finally stopped breathing. Sam jumped from on top of him and ran to Valerie who had managed to pull out the rusty hook from her flesh and crawled out of the water. She had found a rock and rested her back against it, holding her wound while it bled.

"Sam!" she called his name, breathing heavily with her eyes stretched wide open with fear. "I am bleeding too much. I don't think I will make it."

"Oh God I am so sorry," cried Sam, kneeling down beside her. "Let me take a look at it."

He easily took off her polo singlet, gently pressed it on the wound until it was soaked with blood to give him the chance to clearly see how bad it was.

"Oh, thank God," he breathed with relief. "It did not cut any artery. You will live. Hold the singlet and gently pressed it on the wound while I go and get the medic kit from the boat."

Valerie screamed when Sengbeh suddenly appeared and grabbed Sam from the back, pressing the steel pole against his chest. Sam cried as the black smith pulled him to his feet and swung him around. Becoming increasingly dazed due to the loss of lots of blood, Valerie was crying for Sam.

As it appeared, he was not going to free himself. But the mixed martial artist stepped on Sengbeh's toe with the back of his left heel and gave him a swift and ferocious back head butt. Sengbeh staggered backwards, dropping the pole. Sam then gave him a back heel in his groin forcing the black smith to scoop over, holding his testes.

"You really don't know what I am capable of, Mehn," Sam ground his teeth with rage, facing the black smith and thinking what next to do to him.

For a moment, breathing heavily, both of them stood, looking at each other. Roving in Sam's mind was how to quickly and finally disable the man standing before him. It had now occurred to him that he was probably the Sengbeh Gbelema Wuamah and the young chief talked about, and may possess magical powers to have managed to resuscitate himself when he strigulated him with the steel pole. He opted to first compose himself and remain focus to avoid a stupid rage which will cause him to make a careless move. He needed to preserve all the strength to figure out a way to overpower a very determined enemy like Sengbeh Gbelema. Through the corner of his left eye, he glanced quickly at the water, where the boat was and estimated the distance from there to where he and Sengbeh stood, facing each other. He then reverted to circling around Sengbeh, boxing style, when an idea came to him.

He moved to Sengbeh's left, forcing the Black smith to turn and facing him, with his back facing the water. Sam threw some jabs and kicks which compelled Sengbeh to dress backwards towards the water. Realizing what Sam was up to, Sengbeh attempted to get away from the edge of the water by charging at Sam to grab him by his waist and wrestle him to the ground, but Sam was swift enough to give him a tiger claw finger jab in his eyes, slipped under his arm and held him from the back with a neck choke.

He stepped the black smith at the back of both knees, which buckled outward, bringing him down to the ground, while still firmly holding his neck. By the time Sengbeh and Sam were completely on the ground, Sam had expertly converted what was a simple neck choke to an anaconda neck choke by curling his legs around Sengbeh's torso and squeezing his neck and torso at the same time.

He rolled with Sengbeh into the water to keep both of them submerged, a move to drown him. Sengbeh tried to prevent this, but the grip was too firm for him to disentangle himself. Sam rolled with him all the way to the deep part and held him under.

Sengbeh tried to hold his breath to avoid taking in water as he struggled to free himself and hurried back to the shore, but after two minutes, he couldn't'. He was taking in a lot of water as Sam observed the bubbles forming around his nose and mouth. In the next two minutes, Sengbeh was motionless.

Hearing about who he was, Sam held him under for another 3 minutes. He could have kept him under for a little longer than that, he thought, had he not earlier done his breath control drill which had reduced his underwater endurance. But it was enough for the black smith.

Sam let go of him and watched the current roll him further away. He made his way to the surface, emerging and deeply inhaling fresh air. He hurriedly swam to shore, and rushed to Valerie who had suddenly regained a little strength when she saw him. He lifted her up into his arms and hurried with her to the boat. Then he laid her on the floor.

He opened the compartment near the pilot seat and got out the medic kit. His eyes beamed with relief when he found a syringe and some medicine vials.

"I am going to give you a shot to stop the bleeding," he said, when he had inserted the needle into a vial labeled 'Tranexamic Acid' and drew about 3ml in the syringe. "Then I will give you another one for tetanus."

After that he cleaned the wound, dressed it and tied the affected area with a bandage around her neck and across her chest. He found a T-shirt in one of the compartments and helped her to put it on. He gently helped her up on the seat and ignited the boat engine.

"Need to get you to the hospital," he said and powered the boat in a roar.

Just a few meters away from the shores of the glade, the boat suddenly jerked, tilting the bow in the air, just when Sam was about to engage the motor at full throttle, and it dashed back into the water with a huge splash. The upward thrust was so high that it almost unexpectedly threw Sam and Valerie at the back. Sam wasted on time to start the engine, but it couldn't'.

Racing against time to hurry with Valerie to Maila and then use the Ford Pickup truck to drive her all the way to Bong Mines hospital, he tried the starter three times, but it dragged.

"Damn it!" roared Sam, slamming the steering wheel with both hands.

"What happened again?" inquired Valerie, in a faint and apprehensive voice.

"I don't Know," breathed Sam. "Maybe we are stuck. Let me take a look."

He walked to the rear of the boat to inspect the motor. When he looked down into the clear water to take a look at the propeller, what he saw startled him; Sengbeh Gbelema was clung onto the propeller firmly holding it in his chest. Sam quickly regained his composure, and slowly took a few steps backwards. He quietly opened the compartments and searched for some tools he could use.

"Valerie," he then reached over to her, looking at her firmly. "This is what I want you to do. You will have to carry the boat to go and get some help. Take the wheels, and wait till I tell you to start the engine and pull off. Don't care to look back. Just go."

"What about you?" she asked, at the same time expecting the answer and began to cry. "No Sam. No."

Sam suddenly covered her mouth before she could shout.

"Listen to me," he said convulsing. "He's holding on to the propeller and won't let us leave. Got to go and stopped him. If you don't go and get help, he will kill us both."

"No Sam. I love you too much," cried Valerie. "I just can't leave you here."

"I know, baby. I love you too. But you need to go when I tell you to. And the only way is to hold him off."

Valerie resisted and attempted to yell at him telling him no, but he covered her mouth again.

"Listen to me, Valerie," he insisted, gently shaking her. "I don't want to see you die, neither do you want to see me die. Follow the sign boards that will direct you back to Maila. Tell Boima its Sengbeh. Do you understand me? I am going to hold him off."

She nodded and grabbed his face, pulled it towards hers and kissed him.

"I love you Sam," she wept. "Please don't die on me. Please baby. Please don't die on me"

She eased herself over to the pilot seat, looking back and watched Sam tipped toe as he took careful steps towards the motor, holding a huge plier about 20 inches in striking position. With tears running down her face, Valerie cried when she watched Sam plunged into the water. She could hear huge splashes and noise down at the back of the boat. The disturbances lasted for some time until Sam, partially submerged from waist down, suddenly grabbed the left side of the stern close to where the motor was.

"Valerie. You can start the engine and leave now," he yelled, with urgency in his voice.

"No! I will not leave you, Sam," she yelled back at him, crying bitterly.

The black smith suddenly emerged a few inches from Sam and held onto the gunwale near the stern and started rocking the boat violently so that it would turn over. Frightened, Valerie held firmly to the wheel, balancing herself and finding it difficult to start the engine when she realized what was going to happen.

Sam charged at the black smith, grabbing him from the back and landing some punches and occasional head butts at the back of his head in an attempt to force him to leave the gunwale. Then he went for his face, clawing his fingers until he reached for his eyes. He dug his fingers into them to plunk them out. Sengbeh quickly let go of the boat to protect his eyes and they both fell back into the water and went under.

Valerie managed to balance herself when the rocking had stopped. She turned on the start button, and the boat engine finally ignited. She looked back and only saw the black smith emerging out of the water a few feet from the boat and swimming to it. She began to cry for Sam, just like that fateful day, standing alone, at the SKD

Boulevard Junction in 1990, when she lost Veronica and her mother into the crowd, when everyone was running heather scatter from the raining down of rockets, fired by the rebels.

She powered the boat in full throttle, almost running into the banks and hitting the trees on the edge, but managed to dodge in one hell of a swing, almost sending her overboard. The next moment she was out of danger, speeding on Inlet 3 and heading for the greater St. Paul. Sengbeh watched with rage when the boat slipped out of his sight at the elbow.

A disturbance in the water at his rear caught his attention. He looked and saw Sam emerged and was swimming back to the glade. Increasingly raged that he did not drown, which was a ploy to convince Valerie to escape, he swam after him.

Sam reached the shore, exhausted and breathing heavily. He waddled his way out of the water and rushed to the Sign Board lying on the ground. Looking back into the water and seeing Sengbeh in the distance making his way to him, he grabbed it and ran for the steel pole. He detached a segment and attached it to the Sign Board and planted it back in the ground. He wanted it there so as to allow Boima and others to find the glade when help comes.

He held the other part of the steel pole, about 30 inches long and readied himself for Sengbeh who was almost out of the water.

Also breathing heavily, but not looking exhausted, Sengbeh came out of the water, looking at Sam who stood ready for him and then at the Sign Board. He made an attempt to get to the signboard, but Sam blocked his way, displaying the steel pole, Kung Fu style. For a moment, both of them stood looking at each other.

"I am not going to let you take it down," Sam said. "And here's your surprise," he continued, advancing towards the black smith. "I am not going to let you do me like the way you did those fighters up that cliff. We both will die here today."

Sengbeh charged at Sam with furry, but the mixed martial artist slammed the pole on his left side with a swing, forcing the black smith to stumble, holding his side. Kunfu style, Sam lunged forward, with the pointed part of the steel pole intended to pierce Sengbbeh's eyes, noticing that it is his weak spot, but the black smith quickly grabbed it with both hands. This resulted into a scuffle when Sam tried to pull the pole off his grip while Sengbeh could not let it out of his hands.

Sam stumbled upon a rock while moving backwards and fell on his back. Sengbeh fell on top of him, gaining an advantage on the steel pole. Before he could use it, Sam caught him in an arm bar, and expertly executed it with all his might, until Sengbeh's left shoulder snapped, and was badly dislocated.

For the first time he heard the black smith uttered a sharp cry, and remained motionless. Surprised that he had finally had him, and had neutralized the danger, Sam held it for some time, applying more pressure to the affected arm to ensure that he is further weakened by the excruciating pain.

Not satisfied, he let go of the arm, and rolled over for Sengbeh's left leg, and executed a leg lock. This time, the black smith uttered a loud cry, when Sam swiftly converted the led lock into a kneebar, and dislocated it. After that, Sam jumped to his feet, while Sengbeh remained on the ground reeling in pain and was unable to get up. Then, he jerked the pole from under Sengbeh and stood over him, pointing the sharp part over his face, just how he had anticipated; to keep him down and disabled until help could come.

However, Sengbeh struggled to roll on his stomach and started dragging himself away from him. Sam raised the steel pole in the air to slam it on his back or on his head, but he suddenly became aware of a standing rule of the Mix Martial Arts world; 'Never terminate a fallen opponent'. So, he followed closely behind as Sengbeh dragged himself all the way to a rock where he hid his bag. Sam watched closely as Sengbeh laid his back against the rock and looked into the bag.

He readied himself to finish him off, if the black smith made any silly attempt to take any object or something from the bag to harm him. But what he saw was a white clay chalk he got out of the bag, and without paying attention to Sam, he rubbed it in his palm and applied it on his dislocated shoulder and knee. Then he again looked in the bag and got out a small black bottle with a concoction inside, and unscrewed the top.

He opened his mouth and stretched out his tongue. Then he gently dabbed the mouth of the bottle on it. A thick and dark liquid dropped on his tongue, which he swallowed, squeezing his eyes shot like it was something bitter.

"Oh God. He has poisoned himself out of shame," Sam lamented, when suddenly, Sengbeh started convulsing in a violent manner as the whiteness of his eyes appeared.

Sam noticed that Sengbeh was no longer convulsing and stopped breathing. He stood over him for about ten minutes, shook his hand and then he went walking to the Signboard, holding the steel pole in his hand. He looked up at the sky, and saw that it was getting dark. By now, Valerie may have safely reached Maila and had informed Boima who himself may have left Bong Mines and had come back to Maila. So, he will have to wait a little while for them to come and get him and collect Sengbeh's corpse.

While observing the sign board and looking in the direction of inlet 3, his attention was suddenly drawn to a jingling sound coming from where he left the corpse of Sengbeh Gbelema. He turned and saw that it was the black smith, coming towards him. Few feet away, Sengbeh stopped. Apart from the white clay chalk he rubbed on his dislocated shoulder and knee, his entire body was covered with yellow chalk. A chain of large snail shells was hanging around his neck, and he was now wearing the culture dancer's skirt around his waist. On his feet were tiny belts tied together around ankles.

Sengbeh Gbelema was standing before Sam, in his full Sassaywoo attire.

'It's time to face the Sasaywoo,' Sam read the ominous and dreadful grin in Sengbeh's eyes.

Sengbeh moved towards him, in his usual manner like he had cornered a prey and was about to pounce on it. For some time, Sam lost concentration as he struggled to ward off his gradually creeping fear. He had thought Sengbeh had poisoned himself and died, but he was mistaken and misled himself to have assumed so. Sengbeh was using his magical herbs to enable him to take the fight to an extraordinary level. He should have finished him once and for all, when he had the chance. Sam was now grappling with this harsh reality.

As expected, Sengbeh pounced, but Sam dodged, springing and rolling sideways to avoid his grip. He slammed the steel pole on the left side of Sengbeh's face, but it bounced off. He again went for his eyes, the only possible soft spot, but Sengbeh grabbed the steel pole in time, and just before they could begin tussling to take control of it, Sam gave him a powerful dropped kick.

Unlike falling to the ground when Sam had given him the same kind of drop kick, during the first encounter, the black smith staggered a few steps backwards, but did not fall. Sam sprung back on his feet and went for the steel pole that dropped to the ground as the result of the drop kick. Before Sengbeh could brace himself for another charge, Sam suddenly raced out of there.

There was no point in facing a charmed opponent, he thought, as he ran through the gorge to where he and Valerie had their picnic. The concoction the black smith swallowed and the yellow chalk he had rubbed all over his body, made the steel pole less effective on him, thus, accounting for why there were many bullets fired at a particular target which remains they did not find up the cliff.

The best option that ran through his mind was evade and concealment; to buy some time, until help comes. Sengbeh will not be able to handle it, if more men from Maila come for the rescue.

At the picnic sight, he rummaged through his back pack to ensure that his survival tools and accessories were intact. They included a roll of climbing ropes, a torchlight, an insulated water bottle, a small Axe, a knife, and some cans of beef.

He slipped on his black leather Timberland utility sneakers, and then his grey thick long sleeves Nike sweatshirt. Satisfied, he zipped the bag, flung it on his back, looked around and raced to an area behind the flower tree when he heard the sound of the jingles fast approaching.

He reached an area that looked like a woodland with scattered semi deciduous trees and natural lawn. This was another beautiful part of Maila Glade, but there was no time to stand and marvel at anything. The sound of the jingles was fast approaching. Sam raced into the woods, hoping to find a perfect place to conceal himself or lie in wait for an ambush.

Suddenly appearing ahead of him, at a considerable distance from the woods, was a mountain. Sam did not hesitate to race in that direction. He reached a spot where a small, but fast running river about 50 feet wide flowed north to south of the foot of the mountain, making it impossible to get to the other side.

Sam raced up the banks, hoping to find where the river is narrower to take a leap or to swim across it. He soon heard the jingles fast approaching, suggesting that Sengbeh was very close. He glanced at his real and saw him in the distance, also racing towards him.

Fortunately, he saw a dead tree lying across the river and forming a bridge. In no time Sam was taking his time skipping over it. Across the river, he whisked his back pack from his back, unzipped it and got out the axe. As Sengbeh approached the banks, and was racing to the tree bridge, Sam started chopping off the tree. Fortunately for him, it was the head of the tree, the narrow part of the tree trunk, and so it wasn't difficult to chop.

He made more efforts with all his might, chopping the tree trunk in time to fall into the water to prevent Sengbeh from using it to cross over to him. The black smith was now skipping on top of it, and was fast reaching him.

Sengbeh was in the middle, when Sam landed a few strokes and the tree trunk was finally chopped off. Sam stepped on it and as it began to slide into the river, Sengbeh turned and ran back towards the banks. He took a long leap, just in time the tree dashed into the water and was swept downstream, with the fast-moving current. Exasperated, Sengbeh stood looking at Sam, from the other side of the river. The mix martial artist looked back at the fuming black smith with a glee of triumph, then he turned and headed towards the mountain.

It was nearly dark when he reached the mountain top. The temperature was cold and the mountain was foggy, making it impossible to see ahead of him, but he was soon able to find his way-thanks to his torchlight. With thick weeds and shrubs blocking his way, he managed to thrust further, using the long knife he got from the side pocket of his back pack to brush and create his own path. Sometimes white droplets of liquid from chopped vines growing overhead entered into his eyes, causing inflammation, and forcing him to use the back of his palm to rub his affected eyes.

He finally reached the highest point, at an altitude of about 1000 feet or more, where there were layers of huge rocks covered with grass at the top. He observed that on some of the walls of these huge rocks, were cave-like crevices which entrances were covered with thick vines.

But first, he opted to make his way to the top of the highest layer, by using the climbing robes he got out of his back pack to see what lies beyond. Standing on top of the tallest rock, he could see the chain of a mountain peak in the distance ahead, which he assumed to be the Bong Range, stretching from the south to the north of his position and disappearing into the misty horizon. Pointing his touch light, he looked down, and noticed that there was a steep surface extending all the way down a deep valley on the side of the rock.

When he had scanned around him for some time, he descended and hurried to one of the cave-like crevices and shone the torchlight through a thick vine that grew at the entrance to make sure no snake or other wild animals was sheltering inside. This crevice seemed like a perfect place to conceal oneself and or to lie in wait.

Satisfied, he used the long knife to clear the vine from the entrance. Fortunately, the odor was okay. When he entered, he carefully observed around him, and was glad that the temperature inside was manageable.

He squeezed himself closer to the wall of the crevice, removed the back pack from his back and dropped it on the rocky floor. Then he sat, with legs drawn, resting his back against the wall of the crevice. The inside of the crevice was so quiet that it began to inject a series of thoughts into his mind.

His stalker has vast knowledge of the terrain, and like a hunting dog, the black smith was going to sniff him out of wherever he will hide. What would he do, if he was found? What would be his options? Would it be to continue to fight, until he is eventually subdued and be subsequently strapped to a tree and burned? or, would it be to throw himself down the steep side of the mountain, and be smashed on the rocks at the bed of the valley, just to avoid the Sasaywoo? Sam soon realized that from this vantage point, he had definitely trapped himself for reaching this part of the mountain.

Tears ran down his eyes when he considered the last option. He thought about what would happen to Boima when he died. Will he still have the guts to continue the Maila Project? What about his parents? How would they live with the fact that he had to throw himself down a steep valley for fear of being subdued by a black smith with strange traditional powers who performs the Sasaywoo with an evil intent?

What about Valerie? If he dies, how will she live with it that it was just after breaking her vow by defiling her spiritual life by making love to him? Though he promised himself that she would not regret it, he felt bad and sorry for her. The first time they met, she told him that she will only make love to the man that she was sure will marry her. For the fact that she made love to him, she trusted her heart, that given the way he portrayed himself to her, he was the man to spend the rest of her life with.

Unfortunately, here he was, grieving over a serious predicament, and thinking about committing suicide. He wiped the tears from his eyes, got up and went to inspect the place where he will have to jump down the valley to end his own life, if Sengbeh finds him.

Sam shined the light down the steep wall of the mountain again, blaming himself for his predicament, when he had the chance to finish Sengbeh once and for all as he contemplated more on the last option. If these thoughts were going to occur to him, when he had had him, he could have killed him when he stood over him holding the steel pole.

He closed his eyes and reflected deeply, weighing the thoughts and probability of a version of the last option that suddenly occurred to him. Following that, he took a deep breath and went back to the crevice to wait for what benefits him.

He had waited for little over two hours, fighting not to doze off and be caught unaware. He was hungry and was eating a can of Luncheon meat he took from his backpack, when he suddenly froze. It was the sound of the jingles, coming his way, just as he had anticipated. Sengbeh Gbelema had scented his hideout.

He stopped eating the luncheon meat, and quickly stood up. With the ropes in his hands, he scurried out of the entrance. The jingles had gotten more audible and were getting close to the entrance.

Sengbeh had appeared and was looking around, using a cutlass to clear his way. A scent caught his attention. It was coming from the top of the highest layer of the rocks surrounding him.

Quickly, he started climbing up the rocks, following the scent. Immediately reaching the top, he saw it; the source of the scent. It was the half-eaten luncheon meat in the can. He reached over to it and took the can and brought it close to his nose, sniffing, to make sure it was really the source of the scent.

Then he saw the long knife Sam had, lying at the edge of the rock with the blade partially overlooking the steep side of the rock, and the deep valley below. Facing the steep slope and the valley below, he raised the knife in the air to examine it, his large red eyes sparkled as he admired the silver blade.

Before he could realize why it was left on the rock in such a manner, Sam, standing on top of the next rock, with the climbing rope tied around his waist, suddenly leapt and gave Sengbeh a powerful spear, sending both of them down the steep wall of the mountain. Few meters down, Sam uttered a sharp cry. He was caught mid-way, as the robes jerked him up and squeezed his rib cage. He had tied the other end around a sharp rock to prevent him from falling all the way down, and was glad that his trick worked. But Sengbeh continued to slide all the way down the wall of the mountain, rolling and hitting the sharp rocks.

Using the robes, Sam managed to climb back at the top of the rocks, and rested. He loosened the robes from around his rib cage and felt his both sides at the same time reeling with pain.

"Oh, thank God," he sighed, and continued to rest and to gain strength, feeling assured that Sengbeh may not survive that fall, even with the help of all his magical portions. How to get back to the glade, and wait for rescue, was his next move.

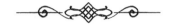

CHAPTER 11

WHEN WUAMAH WENT TO look for his uncle, John Dormeyahn at Nathaniel Kpainkpa's Farm, he was told that Dormeyahn had taken three-days off, and had gone to spend the time with a woman he had been seeing at a village across the river. Surprised, Wuamah asked for the direction to the village, and it was given. He arrived late in the evening and met his uncle in front of a house made of mud bricks, relaxing in a locally made reclining chair, sipping a cup full of fresh palm wine.

"Oh! Nephew!" exclaimed John Dormeyahn. "What brought you here? I hope there is nothing wrong."

"Nothing's wrong, Dormeyahn," standing over his uncle, Wuamah responded after a long thought, and sat down on a small bench next to him.

"How's everyone? And your precious Maila?"

"Everyone is fine, including Mamaye and Flomo. Maila is moving far-far ahead and she's not waiting for you," replied Wuamah, now looking around with curiosity. "Unless you decide to catch up with her, our little town is poised to leave you by the wayside."

"Look, nephew," Dormeyahn immediately sat up. He paused when Wuamah's attention was suddenly fixed on a young woman, fair in complexion with a nice shape, coming from in the house. She

420

smiled and waved and went into the outside kitchen at the right side of the house to check on a pot on the fire hearth. "Maila left me behind, a long time ago when people like you, Chief Lomeh and Mamaye joined others to criticize me for Rebecca Habbah business," he continued when he had gotten his nephew's attention. "But I was so glad when you yourself found your true love and felt the same way I felt about Rebecca."

Wuamah was suddenly enraged, but he didn't say anything. He suspected Gotolo to be the one who told his uncle about him and Korto. But he later calmed down. He wanted to remain focused on delivering the good news. His mother will not like it, should he be the one to jeopardize the job opportunity of her only brother. Moreover, Flomo may not be happy with him, either.

"Yes, it's true," breathed Wuamah, admitting to the affair with Korto. "She made me realize that I had been wrong about you. I now know that it can be difficult for a man to forget about a woman who knows how to give him that peculiar satisfaction all men desire. The difference between you and I was that you toted Rebecca business on your head, until you lost Gayduo, while I kept my longing for Korto to myself, when I realized that I was missing her."

"I agree, but Rebecca's business is out of my mind now. And I see that you are growing up, but you need to grow more. Just what you said, I knew something was eating you up. You kept denying to yourself that Korto is the peculiar one. Because you openly criticized me concerning Rebecca, you struggled to suppress it. Korto still loves you. You need to look for her. Don't bother about the way you met her. Since she met you, she has not been into other men. Even up to present."

Wuamah was astonished to hear his uncle tell him about this. He indeed likes and misses Korto a whole lot, but was ashamed to show it because he openly criticized Dormeyahn for showing great love to a woman who had never cared about him. With the way he treated Korto, he didn't think she could still be thinking about him, and he regretted why he abandoned her when Gotolo broke the news that they were having an affair.

He assumed that given her history with other men, she may be with someone else in Salala and no longer thought about him. But he now sensed that his uncle had met her several times, and she had always asked about him. It will be good that he abandons his foolish covertness to go and look for her. He wouldn't care what people would say.

In fact, all the men that dated Korto have now gotten their wives, and he dares if any of them will have issues with it, if he went back to her. His uncle had kept this from him all this time, because of this same foolish wall he built around himself; never wanting even the people he knows and cares about, venturing into his private life.

"I will look for her and besides that, I will send her a surprised message that she should be expecting me soon. I know Korto. She might believe it, and so she will wait," he decided, looking at his uncle and making a face that he really meant it.

"Okay," laughed Dormeyahn, pouring some of the palm wine from a small container he got from under the reclining chair into a rubber cup, handing it to his nephew. "Let's drink to that."

"You are so changed in a short time, Dormeyahn," observed Wuamah, after taking a long drink. "For some time now, no one has brought your complaint."

"Yeah," sighed Dormeyahn, offering a smile as he looked at his nephew, admiringly. "A man's character is complete not only by the noble profession endowed in him, but supplemented by the uniqueness, in all qualities, of the woman by his side. My weakness was the indelible remembrance of the satisfaction I got from Rebecca Habbah, but that lady you see in the kitchen has managed somehow to erase Rebecca's business from my mind."

"Including the pleasure she gave you?" Wuamah asked, laughing at the same time, suspicious of the sincerity in his uncle's statement.

"Yes. Unlike Flomo's mother, she never hesitates to make love to me the way I want it. She is a strong and hardworking business woman, too, and I think she likes me a whole lot."

Wuamah watched when his uncle got up and walked to the woman in the kitchen. She smiled when he told her something. He rejoined Wuamah and they continued to drink the palm wine.

It didn't take long, the woman brought a bowl of hot pepper soup with dried bush meat and fish for them. As she sat the bowl on a small stool, Tonolah kept staring at her. She caught his eyes and smiled, forcing Wuamah to nod in appreciation.

"Nephew. This is Nawoe. She has been very nice to me." Dormeyahn introduced her.

"I am happy to meet you and thanks for my uncle," responded Wuamah, extending his hand to the woman.

"I am happy to meet you, too," replied Nawoe, also extending her hand. "Your uncle has been nice to me, too."

She rubbed Dormeyahn's head and played with his cheeks.

He recounted on how It was one day, while driving from Nathaniel Kpaingkpa's Farm in the old Toyota double cabin farm pick-up, the one used to haul cup lumps and mostly dried latex bought from smaller rubber farms, he met her standing on the side of the road with lots of loads of garden products. Right next to her was a moto cyclist struggling to start his bike which had broken down.

Dormeyahn asked where she was going, and she said she was going to Varney Town, but the motorbike carrying her broke down. So, he helped her with her load and the motorcyclist with his bike and took both of them all the way to Varney Town. There, he also helped her to find a transport vehicle to take her and her goods to Gorbachev Market at Paynesville Red-light, outside Monrovia.

Since then, he had been helping her to transport her market products to Varney Town whenever she was taking them to Monrovia.

Later that evening, Dormeyahn showed Wuamah around the village and where Nawoe had her large garden of sweet potatoes, cucumbers, fresh tomatoes, corn and pineapples.

The village comprised three big houses and four huts with thatched roofs. The two other houses and the huts were occupied by the men and their family who worked in the garden.

"The people who live in this village are Nawoe relatives, from her father's side," he explained.

At night, they sat outside, under the moonlight and talked. Nawoe joined them, but later went to bed while Wuamah and his uncle continued to talk late into the night.

"I highly knew Barclay's son," Dormeyahn said when his nephew finally broke the news about the possible job opportunity with Lakay's Construction Company.

"Before the war, he was never frequent in Maila, just like you," said Wuamah.

"Yeah, but I know his mother, Esther. It's been a long time now she has not returned home to see her old man."

"We are trying to locate where she may be. I will join he, Chief Lomeh, and Gotolo early tomorrow morning in Varney Town to make the trip, first to Flomo's Town to see how Siegie is doing and then we head straight to Weala to talk to a man who we hope will know her whereabouts."

"Okay," sighed Dormeyahn. "I will go and thank him for the offer. Make sure you let me know when you return from Weala, or, better still I will be in Maila waiting for you. I need to go and thank Mamaye for always being there for me."

That night, while he lay in bed in the stranger room Nawoe had prepared for him, he was thinking about Korto and how foolish he had been to her, with all the good times they had together. He was right to admit that all men desire that peculiar satisfaction a woman gives, but he had also come to realize that some men like him are enthralled and aroused by a woman who wouldn't' mind making love anywhere.

Because of his very secretive nature, he and Korto did it in the bush, sometimes in the kitchen on his mother's farm, and once on Palm Wine Island. When Korto left, it was difficult to fend around the other girls in the town.

Later on, he noticed that Lela was giving him the looks. She was beautiful and had a nice height, but he avoided her because she was always in company with the likes of Gotolo. Moreover, she was kind of conservative and the type who will not only want a serious relationship, but will want to get pregnant, as well.

Getting pregnant for him was not part of his agenda. He saw it as a distraction to his dreams for Maila. Though Korto showed seriousness, she did not have or show him the slightest thought of wanting to get pregnant for him and he liked and appreciated her for that.

He had always thought when Maila became the way he always dreamed about it, then maybe, he can start thinking about having children. So, having an affair with Lela would jeopardize his dreams for his beloved town.

As the night wore on, the incident that occurred, years ago, between he and Rebeca Habah, when he spied on her and his uncle, also filled his memories. He anticipated hearing the same strange noises John Dormeyahn was making that night.

But this night seems different; Dormeyahn and Nawoe were quietly sleeping in a room adjacent to his. Maybe they decided to control their moans, screams and grunts to avoid being heard, if they were doing something, because the room had no ceiling. Or maybe his uncle suggested that he and Nawoe should wait, until their stranger was far as sleep. But there was absolute quietness in the room.

However, Tonolah did not know how he even dozed off. Probably it was due to the effect of the palm wine he and his uncle were drinking. At dawn, he was awakened to the noise of controlled growling's filtering through the naked roof. Surprisingly this time, it wasn't Dormeyahn's voice, and comparing it to the night he was frightened when he saw Rebeca Habbah on top of his uncle, the thought of it, almost made him laugh at himself.

The next morning, after having breakfast of dry country rice with fried fish and Palm Kernel oil along with a mixture of mashed bitter balls, okra and benne seeds, eagerly prepared by Nawoe, Tonolah Wuamah left for Varney Town. He was happy that his uncle was excited to be part of rehabilitating the road leading to their town, including laying out and constructing other roads throughout Maila.

At about 10:00 that morning, Boima, Chief Lomeh and Gotolo had also arrived and met Wuamah and Varney Yasiah coming from Mahammad Barry Tee-Shop, where the motor bike rider always had his Tee and bread with fried eggs. He greeted them, and introduced Varney Yasiah to Boima.

"Varney told me that Koikoi Pewee left Flomo Town five days ago," Tonolah informed them.

"Mulbah Kertehme told me that Siegie was heading straight to Maila the very day he left Flomo Town," explained Varney Yasiah when he was quizzed. "Even Kleeme saw him off. He told me Siegie took the road towards the pellet plant."

"But it has been five days now. Hope he wasn't still feeling well when he left," wondered Boima.

"Maybe," sighed, Varney Yasiah. "Kertehme told me that he had almost completed his traditional thermotherapy for his rheumatism, but Siegie could not wait for another week before leaving."

"Maybe he passed on his farm to rest a little before coming to Maila," Suggested the young chief. "But that's not like Siegie," he concluded, becoming concerned, at the same time looking at Boima.

"He may have decided to rest a while at his old rubber farm near Popota. I suspect that was why he took the Pellet Plant Road," offered Wamah, buttressing the young Chief.

"So? What do we do now?" asked Gotolo.

"Just a minute," said Boima, getting down from the jeep, stepping aside and dialing his phone. "Let me call the old honorable man."

Boima called his father to brief him of his activities in Maila, but not mentioning the gruesome scene up the cliff, which they believed was perpetuated by Sengbeh Gbelema. Then he called his fiancée, Diana Rice. They talked for some time and then he sent her some of the pictures he had uploaded to his phone. He made the last call to Veronica, telling her that her sister was okay, and she and Sam are happy in the town and had gone for a little picnic.

After that he walked to his uncle, the chief, Gotolo, and Wamah who had gotten down from the car and were conversing with Varney Yasiah.

"So," he said when he joined them. "Since we know that Koikoi Pewee is not in Flomo Town, we can drive to Weala to look for Johnny Vapilah." Then he turned to Varney Yasiah. "Can you go to his old rubber farm and tell him we are looking for him? I will pay for your gas."

"Yes," agreed the motorcyclist, who then received a US$ 20.00 bill from Boima.

In the next few minutes, Boima, Chief Lomeh, Wamah and Gotolo got back into the Range Rover. As Boima drove while his uncle sat in the front passenger seat, they crossed the train tracks, drove past Varney Town Market and soon they were on their way to Weala. They made a stop at Lakay's Town and spoke to the old man. After that, they were in Kakata in about 13 minutes and heading to Weala.

About a kilometer after the city, Gotolo suggested that they stop at the old internally displaced center, where Esther Lomeh briefly stopped, during the war. Boima agreed and branched off the Kakata-Weala

Highway to his right and entered the place which now looked like a little town, with an elementary school, a clinic and a market.

There was also a Lutheran Church, established by the displaced people who fled from the fighting in Bong Mines and surrounding towns, during the civil war. The church was built by Koikoi Pewee and some of the Lutheran men. At the edifice, they met Pastor Harris Lavala who was now in charge. He told them he was a young deacon, when they built the church. He explained how Koikoi Pewee was very instrumental in building the church and ran after the establishment of a relief center for the displaced people.

"Can you remember seeing this woman here in this displaced camp? She's also from Bong Mines," Boima showed the picture of him and his mother, after the Pastor mentioned also being a recording clerk, at one time, at the relief center.

"I don't think so," said Pastor Lavala, in a heavy Lorma accent. "That was years ago and I can't remember the faces of every one that came to this camp, and benefited from the relief center. But Siegie will be the best person to ask. He knew everyone from Bong Mines that came to this center."

"I recognized your face now," said Gotolo. "I came here twice to see Easter and I saw you recording the names of new displaced people. It was the time Gbarnga fell. Actually, I don't think she was frequent around the center where rebel fighters always gathered. But she did register here. I can remember she showed me her ID Card."

"Then there must be a photographer who took her picture," suggested Chief Lomeh.

"Yes," agreed Pastor Lavala, handing the picture back to Boima. "It's this boy, Siakor. But he left when he and Siegie fell out over some money business and he took all the records with him. Mr. Pewee hired another photographer, his nephew Sumo Pewee and we had to refill many of the forms. And I don't think this woman you are looking for came back to be re-registered.

"Why do you think so?" asked Boima. "You said you can't remember seeing her."

"Yes, because I was at the full front when we did the re-registration. By then there were more displaced people and people were rushing to have themselves re-registered by showing us their ID Cards. If I had seen her old ID, I would remember."

Pastor Lavala took from a bible lying on his office desk, an old ID card and showed it to his guests.

"Well, it makes sense," said Boima. "But any idea where we can find this Siakor or Sumo Pewee?"

"I am told Siakor died in a sick bush, somewhere near Palala. They say he had lassa fever. As for Sumo, Siegie will be the best person to ask. But the last time I heard; he was running his uncle old rubber farm on Popota Road."

"But we can look through the forms and see whether we can find hers, and continue with the information she may have provided," suggested Boima, looking at piles of files arranged alphabetically in dusty box folders on wooden shelves on the wall behind the Pastor's desk. "We will pay for your time, Pastor."

After a long thought, Pastor Harris Lavala agreed and they went through the boxes one after the other, flipping through the forms. It took them about an hour until Gotolo suddenly recognized a picture on a form with the name Marie Zaowolo. They read through the information and they found out that she was from Weala.

"She was Esther's friend," cried Gotolo. "She was the one who took her to Weala when she wanted to get away from Rebel Genie."

"I know Marie very well," the Pastor informed them. "She now lives in Monrovia on 12th Street and every now and then she goes to Conakry, Guinea for business. But I can't remember seeing this particular Esther girl with her."

Pastor Harris Lavala guests thanked him for his time after spending additional 30 minutes with him, going through the records. Boima gave him a USD 100.00 bill, encouraging him to keep looking and asking around the old camp and promised to come back.

They left the church and drove around what was left of the displace camp with Boima taking some pictures of the place, of themselves with the Pastor and some of the people who were still living in the camp. From there, they left for Weala. It was about 2pm when they got to Weala Junction. Before reaching the checkpoint, they turned left on Seekie Town Road. They drove about 25 minutes on the dirt but fairly good road, and after climbing a steep and rocky hill, they reached a town, passed it and branched off the road to their right.

"Humm. The last time I came to visit Gorpue here, this was a path. I am surprised that it is a motor road now," said Gotolo as they drove on the road leading to Vapilah' s village.

"When I came here, the interim government representative at the time mobilized the people to do some work on it," Chief Lomeh explained.

They drove three miles before reaching Johnny Vapilah's Farm. They stopped by a house made of mud bricks with zinc roof, wooden windows and a wooden door at the front, when they saw an older and a young woman pounding rice seeds in a mortar. Another young girl was funneling the pounded rice taken from the mortar as chicken scurried around them.

"Katua," the young chief greeted them in Kpelle, using the salutation meant for the afternoon, when Boima wound down the front window glass.

"Humm, katuah ay," they responded in Unisom.

"Mr. Vapilah still lives in that big house over there?" inquired Chief Lomeh.

"No," replied the young woman who was helping the old lady to pound the rice seeds. "He no longer lives there, but at a compound he built right after it."

They drove to the compound after thanking the women. It was a big house made of bud bricks and plastered with cement with a big porch. There were four smaller houses of similar designs like the big one. The yard was littered with mango trees, with a hammock hanging on two of them. At the center was a palaver hut made of concrete walls and zinc roof.

Behind the big house was what looked like a small valley planted with plantain. To the left of the big house was an outside kitchen with an old lady sitting on a stool, cracking palm kennel.

"There he is," informed Gotolo as they approached a man who looked to be in his early 50s lying in a hammock, negotiating with a boy who was holding a dead groundhog, by one of its hind legs.

"Hello," greeted Boima. "Mr. Vapilah?"

"Yes, I am Johnny Vapilah. Who's asking? And what can I do for you?" replied Mr. Vapilah, getting up and sitting upright.

"We are from Maila, Fuamah District. We came to you concerning Esther Lomeh who once lived here during the civil war. We were told you were nice to her, and helped her a lot," Boima explained.

"Yes. I will never forget Esther. What happened to her?" Johnny Vapilah asked, suddenly becoming concerned and jumping down from the hammock.

Before his guests could answer, he told the boy standing with the woodchuck in his hand to carry the dead animal to the old lady in the outside kitchen, and come back for his money later in the evening. Then he called out several times into the big house, asking who was inside to bring four chairs for his guests but no one answered.

So, he excused himself and hurried into the house. He came back outside, bringing the first two beautifully made dining room chairs and went back to get the other two.

Boima observed that Mr. Vapilah was slim and tall, fair in completion, and spoke a very good and accent-free English.

"So, gentlemen," he said, when he had brought the last two chairs and had sat back in the Hammock, nervously rocking it when his guests had taken their seats. "Let me get to know you all, first."

"I am Chief Peter Lomeh, the Town Chief of Maila. The man who spoke to you is my nephew, Boima Barclay, Esther's Son. The other man is Tonolah Wuamah, a confidant and childhood friend, and Gotolo Nyagoi, who is also from our town, and a close friend of Esther," Chief Lomeh Introduced them and signaled Boima to show Mr. Vapilah the picture of him and his mother.

"Yes," said Mr. Vapilah, nodding, when he took the picture from Boima and looked at it. "Your mother spoke about you a lot."

"We came to find out from you where you think she might be," said Boima.

"If you can still remember me, I came to visit her once when she was here," added Gotolo.

"Not exactly. But I remembered once a man visited her and she told me that he was from her town," said Mr. Vapilah, who then continued after he bowed his head, closed his eyes and reflected for a while.

"Shortly before Gbarnga fell, her friend, Marie, brought her to our village," Mr. Vapilah began. "She used to come along with Marie to my sugar cane farm, where I have my sugar cane mill to buy cane juice, and Marie will take them to kakata to sell.

That was how I got to know Esther, and I liked her. I offered her one of my small houses, and told her to be free around me. But she was afraid of my wife, the old lady you see in the outside kitchen over there. But I told her that she will not have a problem. She was old and we had grown up children. Some of them are even living abroad. My wife even encouraged her to move to the house, which she later did, and of course, reluctantly."

"I think my mother was right," Boima cut in. "I guess you got to know how she had me in the first place."

"Yes, but in my case she was wrong. I was a little boy in 11th grade at BWI when I met my wife, a market woman who sold at Kakata Market. She supported me up to the University where I earned my first degree in General Agriculture. We had our last son just before I went to the States to obtain my Masters. By the time I started working, she was way older than me, but I did not abandon her like most of us in such a situation will do.

Knowing that she had gotten too old for me, she always encouraged me to find someone young as she could no longer give me the comfort every young man desires. I didn't give it a thought until I met your mother. My wife and I promised her the many acres of land we have, and to convince her, I told her I was going to make a will, but your mother was always skeptical or she did not even like me. But I was still good to her as your uncle said."

"We thank you for that, Mr. Vapilah," said Boima. "We are just trying to locate her, since no one said she died during the war."

"That's the mystery about your mother. We who are interested in her have not been able to figure that out, up to now. Even her friend Marie still ponders about this.

I had gone to Gbarnga on business and was there for some days when the town fell to the opposing rebel forces. There was no way to come back to Weala, so, I fled with the displaced people to Kpai, right after Palala. When Gbarnga was liberated, I got back here and did not see your mother. She left no message. She just took off like that.

I first had my suspicions with my wife, a thing I had never done before. What she told me was, during that period, rebel fighters were frequent here and one of them saw her and had interest in her. During the day, for fear of being seen, my wife will take her to our farm village, a day's walk from here, where they would stay until the late evening hours.

It came at a time, according to my wife, that Esther did not want to come back here-she would rather remain there. This lasted until Gbarnga was cleared. One day when my wife went there, she did not see your mother again. She had left.

When I came back, we looked everywhere; in all the towns and farms we knew in this part of Weala, but no one saw her.

My wife later got sick, and so I along with her nephew took her somewhere in Nimba County, near the Ivorian border to a herbalist who we learned could cure her. I stayed with them for some time, and I left her with her nephew to come back to look for Esther.

I even risked my life to confront the rebel commander whose business she had to leave my yard, but he himself expressed his shock and disappointment in why a woman would just take off two days after he met her and told her that he likes her.

When I did not see or heard from Esther, I went back to see how my wife was doing and stayed there until the war ended. When we got back, no one told us she came here looking for us. Marie also tried her best to look for her, but to no avail. She wanted to take her to Guinea for her wedding, but she did not find her friend. Up to present, my wife who had forgotten a lot of things due to her old age, and her health, still asked about her, sometimes."

"Was anybody else on that farm village of yours?" asked Boima, his face full of discouragement.

"No. That was a farm where my wife grew a variety of crops like cassava, Eddoes, pepper and corn. But there were lots of palm trees in the vicinity. I built a house of sticks and mud there. It was a two,bedroom house. That place was mainly used by my wife for making her kennel oil."

"Okay," sighed Boima, looking at his time. "We might come back next time to take a look at that farm. Maybe we might get a clue."

"Well," breathed Mr. Vapilah. "It might just be to satisfy your curiosity. I have turned that place upside down to see whether I can find something, but I got nothing at all. The only thing I could guess on was that she may have gone back to her people. The road you came on leads to Bong Mines. I could have gone to look for her, but it seems not many people know your town, and secondly, I did not want to pursue a girl who I thought had already run away from me, even with what all I did for her. And trust me. Never a day I asked her to sleep with me."

When Mr. Vapilah had answered all the questions he was asked, the visitors thanked him and got up to leave. While accompanying them to the jeep, they met his wife who had come from the Kitchen. She looked frail, but appeared to be strong, and had gray hair. She could pass for Vapilah's mother, observed Boima.

Mr. Vapilah might be a good man, he mused. And indeed, he must have been very young when he met this woman. She came close to Boima, stared at him for a while and said something in Kpelle.

"She said you look just like your mother," interpreted Gotolo.

"She hears and understands conversations from a distance," Mr. Vapilah explained, as Boima looked puzzled. "So, gentlemen," he continued when they reached the jeep. "I am sorry I could not give you some of the cane juice I produce here, to carry. Production is slow these days, as most of my productive workers have left me for the renewable energy company that was just established in Salala. The money they offer over there is good; for every old rubber tree you cut down, it gives you lots of bonuses, and I don't blame them. Anyway, I will make some available the next time you come here."

Back on their way to Bong Mines, Boima began to sense that he may never find his mother. So far no one has said she died, but no one has given a clue as to where she might be. Moreover, the people he had spoken to never seem to think that she may be dead, but the idea he has gotten was that she may have disappeared.

He wondered how a woman, in a bid to avoid the lust of rebel fighters, ended up hiding on a farm alone, and had not been seen since. He quickly brushed the hideous thought out of his mind, that maybe, she may have fled further into the bush and may have gotten sick, died, and her corpse eaten by scavengers.

But again, this may be possible, but in another sense: Johnny Vapilah had said he searched every village and town in the Weala belt for her. Was he telling them the truth? Or was he trying to cover up for his wife who may have poisoned his mother out of jealousy and buried her somewhere on that farm they said she was hiding. The morbid thoughts flooded Boima's mind as he struggled to focus on the road.

Vapilah also told them that the old lady got sick as a result of some mental illness, and maybe, one day while only two of them were on the farm, she may have snapped when Esther, out of trust, may have finally agreed to Vapilah's proposal, prompting his wife to hit his mother in the head with something and managed to somehow bury her when she died of concoction.

On the contrary, the old lady looked frail, and innocent. He will have to talk to Marie and maybe he will get some clues from his mother's friend. Women share each other's secrets.

At about 4:30pm they arrived back in Bong Mines and met Varney Yasiah and Kleeme at the Bus Stop in Varney Town waiting for them. They looked apprehensive.

"Siegie is not on his farm," informed the motorcyclist. "But his bike was found on a road that leads to the Popota Highway. It's at the Police station."

"But Siegie told me that he was going to his farm," added Kleeme, increasingly becoming puzzled. "He first took the usual route, but he turned around and took the Pellet Plant Road."

"Where's the police station?" asked Boima, a streak of consternation ran through his face.

In no time they were at the Police Station in Zaweata, not far from the school. Varney Yesiah and Kleeme, who were ahead of them on Varney's bike, showed them the Yamaha when they reached the police station. The head light was burst, and his belongings, attached to the carrier at the back of the Yamaha were still intact.

"I carried this bike to him in Flomo Town, last week when he sent Varney to me that he wanted it," said a young man who came out of the police station, and later introduced himself as Sumo Pewee, Koikoi Pewee's nephew.

"Did he say he was going to his farm?" asked Chief Lomeh.

"No. He told me he was going to Maila and would stay there for some time before coming to check on his farm."

"Which means he was on his way to us, then," Boima concluded, looking at his uncle and Wuamah seeking from the expressions on their faces that he was right. "Anyway, let's talk to the commander."

Lieutenant Jusu Kamara, the commander of the Bong Mines Police Detachment was sitting behind his desk in a tight office when Boima, Chief Lomeh, Wuamah, Gotolo, and Sumo Pewee were ushered in by a female officer. Kleeme and Varney Yasiah were seated on a bench at the door because they all could not fit in Jusu's office. But they could hear what was discussed.

The Lieutenant was dark in completion and tall. He spoke softly with occasional smiles.

"From the statements we have received so far suggest that he was riding on that road at night and someone threw a stone at the headlight," Lt. Kamara informed them, at the same time adjusting his seat. "What's strange is whosoever did it was not after robbing him. It might most likely be an enemy."

"So, we can rule out that it was not an accident, right?" asked Boima.

"I am definitely sure about that. Infect whoever threw the stone had cut a tree and laid it across the road, preventing Siegie from going wherever he was going. And according to his nephew, he was not going to his farm. If that was where he was going, then he took the long route. It doesn't make sense at all."

"Also, according to the old man that saw the bike, there were piles of logs further down the hill Siegie may have ascended, "added Varney Yasiah, who got up and stood at the door of the Lieutenant's office.

"That's correct," admitted Lieutenant Kamara. "The logs appeared to have rolled down the hill from where the bike was discovered."

"And we have been expecting him at our town for five days now," said Chief Lomeh, worried.

"So," the lieutenant suddenly stood up, with expression on his face like he was done with his briefing and had other matters to attend to. Extending his hand for a handshake, he continued. "We can't readily conclude anything concrete until we find him. Maybe he may be somewhere in the bush. We will shortly organize a search party and inform you all when we come up with something."

CHAPTER 12

L ATER THAT MORNING WHEN Tonolah Wuamah left his uncle for Varney Town, John Dormeyahn had gone to Nathaniel Kpaingkpa's Farm. It was the day he had completed his three-days off which he used to spend the time with Nawoe, and he was returning back to work.

Quite recently, the old rubber farmer had given him the foreman job, after his nephew had refused the offer. Since then, he had been doing well in his duties, and there has been no complaint against him. People who knew him credited his newly refined attitude to Nawoe.

Having performed his duties for the day; getting the tapers ready and dropping them in the fields to tap rubber and supervising others to brush under the bud-graph and the new seedlings that were recently brought from firestone, and also driving to nearby farms to haul latex and cup lumps, he went to the old man to ask him for an advance on his pay.

He told Kpaingkpa he will be going to Maila to see his sister, Mamye. It had been a long time since he had not seen her and it wouldn't look good to continue to stay away from his oldest sister who also took care of him and now taking care of his son, Flomo.

"I also want to go and thank Barclay's son, Boima, for taking care of my nephew. I am told he has re-conditioned our house and other houses in the town. So, I need the money to get some things for my sister and my son. I don't want to go there empty-handed," he explained to the rubber farm owner.

"Is Barclay's son here?"

"Yes, my nephew, Tonolah told me yesterday."

"And he's here to do some good things for Maila?"

"I think so," Dormeyahn answered the increasingly concerned rubber farmer.

Nathaniel Kpaingkpa was one of those Representative Barclay helped to own his own farm. The people of Maila and other citizens of Fuamah District who supported the representative, did not like it when they found out that it was Barclay who assisted him.

He was a staunch supporter of David Lorkpalay on grounds that the then candidate, who came second to Barclay in the elections, was a true son of Fuamah District, not James Boima Barclay, and so he campaigned vigorously against his candidacy.

A year after Barclay's victory, the successful transport businessman continued to recuperate from his loss of finance due to an elaborate campaign he ran, and could not fulfill promises made to Kpaingkpa and others who were part of his campaign team. To the surprise of everyone, Kpaingkpa extended an olive branch to the representative, and they became good friends afterwards.

The people did not blame their beloved representative directly but his trusted aid, Koikoi Pewee, for being the mastermind and the middleman between Kpaingkpa and Barclay. But Siegie managed to convince them that it is better Barclay is not seen as a representative full of personal vendetta, especially to productive citizens of the district like Nathaniel Kpaingkpa. The likes of him, joining the

Barclay team, will bring much development, and scoring the chance for a re-election for the incumbent.

"Then let me go along with you to thank his father through him, too," he told Dormeyahn, who agreed, but fought to hide his reluctance.

He did not want Kpaingkpa to know his main intent for going to thank Boima and his sudden urge to visit his hometown. Nawoe, his new found love, also encouraged him to go see his people right away, after his nephew had left.

"But we must first stop at Benedict Gbakoyah's farm. I heard that he wants me to finance the development of his seedlings so that whenever he was they are full grown trees, he can sell the latex to me."

They left Benedict Gbakoyah Farm late that night, and were driving on a feeder road that Dormeyahn often used when hauling latex from village to village. The one they were using was a two-tires trail that took an hour drive to connect to the road that led to Maila where they will have to take a similar trail at the old orange farm, before joining the newly rehabilitated road to Maila.

But because it was at night, it would take them about an hour and forty minutes. The trail was dark and narrow and enveloped by the cascading branches of trees. As Dormeyahn drove while Nathaniel Kpaingkpa sat at the front passenger seat of the double cabin white Toyota Hilux pickup with his right hand outside, the engine of the old pickup roared, and it's thundering sound echoed into the dark bush.

The meeting with the young rubber planter was fruitful, and Nathaniel Kpaingkpa was full of life. Gbakoyah, a University of Liberia graduate in Agriculture, and a former employee of the International NGO, Tree of Life, had cleared hundreds of acres of his father's land, left with him by the former agriculture instructor at BWI, to plant his rubber. He was determined to do so with his experience in tree planting and its preservation, which knowledge he acquired while working with the Non-Governmental Organization. With such expertise, Kpaingkpa was optimistic that Gbakoyah's trees will produce quality latex which he will buy relatively cheaply and sell at a higher price.

"Dormeyahn. You are speeding like you are trying to catch up with Maila like the town is running away from you," quipped the rubber farmer, as Dormeyahn, who had been quiet, was stepping on the accelerator at the same time dimming and brightening the headlights.

Nathaniel Kpaingkpa suddenly pulled his hand back inside when a cascading branch of a small tree on the side of the road, lashed the area around his elbow.

Dormeyahn remained silent as he sped on. His employer looked at him for a while, rubbing his elbow, and then swung his arm back outside.

"Why are you quiet?" he asked. "Is it because I am dealing with Gbakoyah who is contemplating on running in the next election while you assume young Barclay will also be running?"

"No," Dormeyahn shook his head, denying. But he was not going to be bothered by that since in fact he will soon bid Kpaingkpa farewell for a more meaningful job.

"You are lying, Dormeyahn. I know that is exactly what you are thinking. But you see, I am a businessman and a principal stakeholder in our district now. So, I am also going to strike a deal with the young Barclay and his father to offer my support, if they can agree to my terms just what I told Gbakoyah. Then I will support the one with the best deal," he said, but maintaining in his heart that he will obviously end up supporting Benedict Gbakoyah, instead of Boima, who he thinks may want to follow in his father's footsteps; Fuamah District is not a dynasty. "And if I am successful," he continued, "No matter if he or Gbakoyah wins, you will also benefit. The only thing is, that your town chief, Peter Lomeh who doesn't like to see me will have to cry and die."

Dormeyahn turned to look at Nathaniel Kpaingkpa, now struggling to conceal his reaction to the rubber farmer's illusion. He wondered whether the old man knew what was on his mind.

Just then he suddenly gasped, stretching his eyes in bewilderment, when he saw a figure dashed out of the bush, and with such swiftness, grabbed the rubber farmer's hand and pulled him through the window. In the view mirror, a huge man was standing over Nathaniel Kpaingkpa whose right arm was pulled from its socket. The old man was lying on the ground, convulsing and groaning softly. Nathaniel Kpaigba was jacked from the ground and swung into the bush to the cracking of the branches.

Dormeyahn felt his head rising when what looked like a familiar face with its pair of large red eyes appeared in the view mirror. The rubber farm foreman, overwhelmed with fear, quickly focused back on the road. He pressed his right foot on the accelerator, until it reached the floor, and as he expertly controlled the steering, swinging it left and right with both hands, the Toyota Hilux rumbled through the dark bush.

For every time the pickup would bounce the front tires would lift up in the air, tilting the front and would bounce back on the track. As the engine continued to roar, the shrubs in the middle of the road scrubbed the front bumper and the under carrier.

He had gone a little far away from where the incident occurred, after taking a series of curves, and looked in the view mirror again. This time he saw no one and was relieved; thank God, he was not the one who was pulled through the window of a moving car, Dormeyahn reflected on the brief encounter.

But he was surprised at himself for harboring such a feeling for someone who he considered a father and friend; he should not have been elated for the unfortunate circumstance of Nathaniel Kpaingkpa. But that is always the case in such situations. He had heard former rebel fighters, recounting their experiences during the civil war, expressing similar glee, especially when a close comrade was killed on the battle front.

Hearing about that brief joy that occurred when a friend or relative was shot dead when in fact it should have been you, always made him question the mental state of such persons. Now, as he had experienced the same thing, he understood that there are certain things one does not have control over.

Dormeyahn had now veered into the old orange farm, overwhelmed with fear and profusely sweating as he drove on. It would take him about 30 minutes to join the road to Maila. But he opted to branch west of the farm, where he will drive parallel to the road to Maila for some time before joining it. Only a thick bush was between him and the main road.

The part of the track he was on will lead him some kilometers west, and will pass through a wide gravel field before joining the road to his right. By then, he will be less than 10 minutes' drive from Maila. He wanted to reach his home town as fast as he could to alert the people of what happened to the rubber farmer. And that their surroundings have recently become dangerous.

When he had dimmed and brightened his headlight, a surge of fear, like a feverish chill suddenly ran through his body, upon seeing from the distance ahead, what looked like a big black monkey swinging on the branches that cascaded the two-tire tracks, and was coming his way. The tempo of his fear began to rise to the extent that his heart was pounding rapidly, when it occurred to him that all the time, he used these tertiary roads hauling latex, he had never seen a monkey in this part of the bush.

Before he could realize it, a wooden light pole with a circumference of about 27inches, sliced into a log of about 5 feet was swinging on ropes like a pendulum. Before he could dodge it, the pole smashed the windshield, and shattered it into glass fragments.

The pole landed into Dormeyahn's chest, but with less impact due to its first contact with the windshield. The glass fragments covered his body and his chest with some, gashing his face and splattering blood. The smelly oily scent of the pentachlorophenol leashing from the old light pole filled his nose and made him dizzy.

Dormeyahn lost control and ran into the bush to his left and hit a tree, the impact damaging the front bumper and the radiator. And because he was not wearing his seat belt, the impact sent him through the shattered windshield and he landed on the ground on his back with a heavy thud. As he groaned in agony, he realized that the light pole was one of many planted on the old orange farm by Dr. Fasou and his wife when they were electrifying the farm.

Then he heard the sound of jingles coming toward him. He quickly looked up, unable to see clearly ahead of him due to the blood that covered his face. He gasped again, as if to say his breath had cut when the jingles stopped. The huge man with the similar face he saw in his mirror was standing over him.

"Gbeh vay?" he asked, in a whimper. "Sengbeh Gbelema!" He answered his own question, now fully weeping, when the black smith grabbed him by the collard from the double breast pockets of the Khaki shirt he was wearing and pulled the frightened foreman up so that he should see his face.

Paralyzed with fear, John Dormeyahn was in the firm grip of the bogie man whose name he has always used to frighten the little children in his hometown, even his own son, Flomo.

The kid, going to three-years, refused to leave breast milk, and he would cry hysterically for it. He would throw himself on the ground and roll all over the dirt floor whenever his mother refused to give it to him. One day, his father warned him that Sengbeh Gbelema will catch him, and have him circumcised if he doesn't stop crying, and leave breast milk.

Upon hearing the name 'Sengbeh Gbelema', little Flomo, who was born years after the black smith left Maila, and often listens to scary tales about him, ran to Mamaye and immediately stopped crying. From that day, he never cared about breast milk. Other kids in the town, especially the uncircumcised little boys would be told that the black smith will catch and circumcise them with his hot cutlass, if they continued to misbehave and give their parents a hard time.

"I have done nothing," cried Dormeyahn, with tears running down his eyes. "Please let me go."

Sengbeh became enraged and swung the former heavy-duty mechanic around and flung him. Dormeyahn cried out loud when he landed on the right side of the track with some of the dead tree stumps almost piercing his side. Groaning in agony, he started to crawl as Sengbeh slowly took one jingling step after the other, behind him.

Dormeyahn felt himself grabbed from behind. Fortunately, his khaki shirt had ripped open from the front with most of the buttons cut. In a brief struggle for refusing to be pulled back on his feet, he managed to slip out of the shirt, sprang back to his feet and ran towards the main road to Maila. Sengbeh stood looking with the khaki shirt in his hands.

Dormeyahn continued with an impressive speed sometimes leaving the tracks and entering into the bush. Sawgrass and other thorny weeds lacerated his bare upper body, and ankles, leaving bloody scars. Still crying out loud, and blaming himself for allowing his nephew, Tonolah to convince him to return to Maila, and how he might never see Nawoe or even his son and other relatives again if Sengbeh caught him, he got out of the bush and was now on the main road racing towards the town.

He reached the entrance of the town and was right under the arc made of palm thatches that was erected to welcome Boima. Sweating profusely and breathing heavily, after running for about 45 minutes without looking back, he felt his lungs were going to explode, thus, compelling him to bent over, holding his knees to catch his breath. He rested for a few seconds, and was about to race to the town chief quarter when he heard the jingles again. Then he heard the sound of a rope swinging. Next, it was thrown around his neck. Now trapped like a young calf caught by a cowboy, Dormeyahn suddenly dropped to his knees and looked up at the skies of Maila. Then he looked at the town. It was past midnight and it was quiet, only the silhouette of the houses and threes he could see in the dark. He suddenly stretched both hands in opposite directions, and looked up at the sky again.

"Ngaa-nuahn ayy. Sengbeh a par ooo," he shouted with all his might, meaning 'O my people. Sengbeh has returned.'

It was going to 7pm when Boima and the others left the Police Station and got back to Varney Town. He had gotten more frustrated when he had ventured to ask Sumo Pewee about his mother, and he admitted he remembered seeing her briefly at the displaced center with Marie Zaowolo.

"She and Marie then moved to a village way behind Weala," Sumo had said. "But the last time I saw her was when she accompanied Maire to sell cane juice at the market in Kakata. That was when Gbarnga was attacked and the majority of the fighters had gone to the front line to defend it."

It was now clear that most of the people he asked concerning his mother pointed to Weala, the last place they either saw or heard she was. But none of them could say that she was dead. When they return to Weala, maybe he will talk to Vapilah's old lady himself, thought Boima, as they were on their way back to Maila, late that evening.

By about 9:00 pm, the road was dark and foggy, and he seemed to be paying less attention as the jeep bounced into gutters and on the rocks on the road. His uncle attempted to caution him to be careful before he ran them into the bush, or down a ditch, but he decided against it.

The chief knew what was going on in his nephew's head. He understood the mind of someone who loves his mother and is trying to find her. He hasn't seen her in more than 14 years.

Boima continued to figure out the mystery surrounding her disappearance. If no one, even Gotolo who was very close to her, could not determine where his mother might be, then it meant that she may be dead. But if she's dead, and they managed to identify where she was buried, he would have the body exhumed and give her a proper burial.

While he detested thinking about this, he opted that the best place he will bury her will be Maila. But annoyed with himself for harboring such a thought, he quickly erased that of his mind. What to do next is to talk to Johnny Vapilah's wife, himself. Maybe his mother may have gotten sick while hiding on that farm and was afraid to come to Kakata to seek medication since she would have to get back to Vapilah's village where frequented the rebel fighter who was interested in her. Or, she may have probably remained on that farm and eventually died and was buried there.

"She will definitely remember something," with tears running down his cheeks, he murmured, as he drove recklessly on the road.

Wuamah also looked perplexed as he sat quietly at the back, but his thought was different. He shyly looked at Gotolo who was sitting next to him to determine whether his inquisitive friend was also looking at him to read what he was thinking about.

Why was Koikoi Pewee's Yamaha found on the road with its headlights bust, which according to Lieutenant Jusu Kamara, someone, who might be an enemy, may have thrown a stone at it? Why were there logs on the road? And puzzling of all, why a tree was lying across the road near the spot where the bike was found, and going to six days now, why has there been no word from Siegie himself?

CHAPTER 13

LATER THAT NIGHT, THE council of elders had just left the chief's quarter. Every evening, they would visit the old chief to discuss the progress made so far, including other things. Then they would eat and drink, and would remain at the chief's quarter, until it was late before returning to their various homes. This was the routine, since the day Boima returned to Maila.

Whenever necessary, they would convene a meeting with Chief Lomeh and Boima to convey their impression of what was happening in their town and they would make some suggestions. And whenever the council of elders leave, the music will play for some time and stop, and the people, mainly the youth who would still be around, would also retire to their various homes, and the chief quarter, and most of Maila would be quiet.

The old chief had just gone to bed, shortly after he had asked Kafia, one of his nephews who live in the chief quarter, whether Sam and Valerie had returned, and also Boima and the others who had gone to Weala earlier that morning.

He had gotten a little concerned, why Sam and his friend were staying too long, but he later thought that maybe they had returned and were at the boat ramp, and as usual, talking under the moonlight. As for his grandson and the others, they were probably in Bong Mines, and were on their way back to Mala.

Johnny Colomea Lomeh did not remember the time he fell as sleep, but could only remember that the music Ka Pao, another track from David Grualee Collections, was the last he heard, amidst a roar of jubilation from the youth who always went into a frenzy whenever this popular song was played. He listened to it for some time, before he became sleepy and went to bed.

He was suddenly awakened by wailing and screaming in the houses around him, disrupting the melody of the famous song that was still playing in his heart. He heard people yelling and the voices of women screaming the names of their husbands, and calling for help. He heard footsteps rushing towards the chief quarter, and the voices of men desperately yelling, giving each other instruction on what to do.

Then he heard what appeared like a commotion, followed by whimpering and groans. Disturbed, he jumped out of his bed, found his woven country cloth gown and hurried to his window. He opened it and saw the houses around the compound ablaze and with women and children inside, screaming. Before he could figure out what to do, the light bulbs in the chief quarter and the ones on the poles, which Sam and the youth had planted were popping and blowing off one after the other, immediately turning the surrounding into darkness.

The old man heard the same whimpering and groaning, and squinted his eyes in the dark to see what was that. Sitting on the ground not far from the entrance of the quarter, were some of the town's men with no shirt on with their hands tied behind their backs like warriors captured in war.

His attention was avertedly drawn to the roofs of the houses that were burning, and saw that the flames were heavy and unusually orange-green, but the fire was not consuming them.

Moreover, there were more yelling and screaming of men, women, children, and most frightening of all, with the desperate cries of babies when more of the houses in the town were mysteriously set ablaze, as the fire with the strange flames lighted the skies above his town.

He trembled with fear when he heard a young baby screaming in a nearby house that was ferociously blazing and thought that the fire had entered the house and into the room where it was. And then a woman yelled and sounded like she was rolling on the ground crying for her baby.

She may have probably come outside to urinate in the outside bath room and meet the house ablaze upon her return and was unable to enter the house to save her baby.

The old chief managed to compose himself and remained calmed. He slowly closed the window when he noticed what looked like more men were being rounded up and dragged towards the chief's quarter. He hurried to his bed and knelt before it. Looking under, he pulled out an old black and rusty iron trunk with red flowery drawings, and flipped the lid open.

He quickly changed into a woven sleeveless V-neck traditional suit with brownish tar dye designs. He also put on a small hand-woven hat, designed with thread with varieties of colors, and searched at the bottom of the trunk, found a beautiful sculpture like a walking stick, carved out of dark red wood.

The old chief closed the lid of the trunk, shoved it back under the bed and then got up and looked into the ceiling. He muttered something. After that, he put on a pair of sandals made of animal skin. He met his nephew, Kafia and the other children who live in the house with him in the hallway and told them to follow him outside.

In the yard around the platform on which the welcome ceremony for Boima was held, the old chief was appalled to see the town's council of elders strapped to stick poles, and partially stripped naked, except for their underclothes. Johnny Colomea Lomeh's heart suddenly leapt when the platform was suddenly set ablaze and unlike the roof of the houses, the wooden stage began to burn down very fast.

"Who did this?" he demanded, catching the terrified eyes of old man Grualee Tartee, one of the council of elders.

Before Grualee Tartee could answer the old chief, the old man became more frightened when he swung his head to the right, upon hearing the jingles. The old chief also heard it and looked in the direction of the sound.

Then he saw who it was. Sengbeh Gbelema suddenly emerged from the plumes of smoke that was enveloping the town, dragging along with him, John Dormeyahn.

Shaken, the old chief watched how the Black smith looked at him for a while and pulled Dormeyahn from the ground and shoved him on one of the poles and began to strap him mercilessly while the heavy-duty mechanic cried out aloud.

At a house not far from the platform that was now burning like a bond fire, Naitee, a woman who lived in the house suddenly burst her wooden window open, screaming with her young grandson in her hand calling for help as her roof was blazing ferociously.

The old chief attempted to rush there to pull her and the baby out of the house through the window, but a chunk of fire fell from the roof on the opened window and set it ablaze, forcing Naitee to rush back inside the house with her grandson, screaming.

"Gbeh vay?" demanded old Chief Lomeh, calling out very loud.

Sengbeh had finished tying John Dormeyahn to the pole and turned to his old rival. Then he took a few steps forward and stopped. The old chief watched with horror as the black smith took something wrapped in a country cloth from his bag hanging across his chest and dropped it on the ground.

Old Chief Lomeh, the council of elders strapped to the poles, and the men bonded together on the ground, gasped with fear as the head of Koikoi Pewee rolled out of the country cloth, and landed at the feet of the old chief.

"He has returned to Maila for revenge," cried old man Grualee Tartee, whose brother, Mulbah Tartee was found in the bush strapped to a tree, many years ago. "He had not been satisfied with the decision we took, the night we authorized Barclay to build Maila. That's why he left unceremoniously, and had hardened his heart to blame us."

The old chief stood staring at Sengbeh Gbelema. The black smith was destroying his town because he blamed him for going against the park made between Kerkula Maila, Sengbeh Gbelema and Tokpa Toto Kolleh. And now he is going to perform his vengeful Sassaywoo ordeal on the descendance of the ancestors of those who were there the night the park was made.

The old chief suddenly became determined and eliminated all fears and looked at his elders, gesturing with his expression that they must not panic.

"We have no regrets for our decisions, old chief. Even if he kills us," cried Yallah Sumonlor, a council of elder who was picked up, and dragged all the way to the chief quarter, while on his way from his young rubber farm he had gone to inspect, when Boima who he had asked, agreed to get him some rubber cups from firestone, to begin his first harvest.

"Sengbeh Gbelema," old chief Lomeh suddenly called out loud, firmly holding his walking stick and slowly taking steps towards the black smith who remained standing, with an expression, masking his determination to complete whatsoever he came to do. "Yes, we are responsible for this woe that has come back to haunt us."

"Colomea," interrupted Grualee Tartee. "We stand by our word. We have no regret for the decision we took that night. You know that this man was the cause of my brother's loneliness and humiliation, which led him to banish himself from his own home town and died in shame. Mulbah Tartee was never himself after that incidence. Let Sengbeh kill all of us. Let him kill us and our children and burn Maila down. We are prepared to die, if this is sanctioned by the spirits of our ancestors, so be it."

The old chief suddenly turned to Grualee, and pointed his walking stick at him ordering him to stop talking. Then he again faced the black smith, and continued his slow steps towards him.

"This woe, Sengbeh Gbelema, we now face was a noble duty our forefathers once faced and transferred to us their sons," he continued. "When brave warriors make their pack, they swear to uphold it, no matter the consequences. The genesis of the woe for which you are blaming us did not start few years back when we gave this land to be explored against your ill-fitted will, or, the action of my daughter or my matrilineal lineage to Kerkula Maila for which you denounced my legitimacy to the chieftaincy of Maila.

Neither did it start when our forefathers finally defeated Lamine Ganganma and made this park you are so keen to uphold. It started right after the battle of Fissibou, when the French were halted in their advances to capture what is Lofa County today. Hope the descendants of Zubah Keleko were here at this very moment to bear us witness.

I am constrained to tell you, O Sengbeh, that the noble duty to brace ourselves for the woe of Maila that was handed down to us by our forefathers is what has kept you alive. You may think that because of the power you process, you were untouchable whenever you committed crime, since the day you were born, but it was due to an unexpected addendum to the park, when the forefathers of those you have dragged and tied here tonight, made a commitment with your forefather that the blood of a Gbelema must never be shed unless it is absolutely necessary. Or unless that person lays his hands on Maila, the land his forefather bled for.

After the victory of Fissibu in which our forefathers bravely fought alongside our Lorma nephews, and halted the advances of the French, your forefather, Sengbeh Gbelema returned to Maila with Sonnie Vagurah, a beautiful woman and made her his wife. Sonnie Vagurah belonged to Guowola Acquoi, a brave warrior and blacksmith who was a close friend of your ancestor, Sengbeh. He took the wife of a nephew and brought her here.

As a result, the brave and powerful Acquoi felt betrayed and died a broken man, after making several unsuccessful attempts to locate Maila, having roamed all Kpelle land to find his wife.

Guowola Acquoi vowed to break the taboo to kill his nephew if he ever sees him, but he was strongly warned by the highest order of the Zoes that straight adherence to the taboo must be preserved no matter what, and they must find a way to bring back his beloved wife without wasting the blood of an uncle.

Very sick and distressed, and at the point of his death, lying on his death mat, Guowola Acquoi, out of anguish, swore that if Vagurah ever produces a child for Sengbeh, that child will be the source of a seed that will one day destroy Maila. Maila will one day be destroyed by its very own just like the way a son of Maila had destroyed his life and all that he had labored for. That child will be the woe of Maila that will one day rise up to haunt it.

Your forefather Sengbeh Gbelema consulted the best soothsayers and Zoes in Kpelle land to verify and revert the curse. But he was troubled when they confirmed that the curse was legitimate, and reversible, only if Sonnie Vagurah is returned back to her home land, and be given to a brother, who is next to the late Guowola Acquoi.

Your ancestor, Sengbeh Gbelema cried out loud and threw himself before his friend and brother, chief Kerkulah Maila begging to order his execution first, before sanctioning the return of the woman he loves back to the house of Guowola Acquoi. Out of solidarity and brotherhood, Kerkula Maila refused to send Vagurah back. That curse also extended to chief Kerkulah Maila, my forefather and manifested itself when his son did not have a son to succeed him. It was then that the chieftainship was transferred to his nephew, Kpakolo Lomeh, my grandfather.

On the day you were born, The zoes discerned that you were the curse, that woe who was going to one day lay waste to Maila, but again my father Chief Gee Lomeh and some of the elders you have tied here today, upheld the addendum made by their fathers that never the blood of a Gbelema must be shed, in recognition of the sacrifices the old black smith made in the founding, the defense, and the liberation of Maila. So, you were spared.

And that duty was passed on to me, to uphold, to protect you, when you did that evil to Mulbah Tartee, and even when you shed the blood of a citizen of Maila, by killing your own father. I and the elders were not stupid to believe that your father died as the result of an accident when the tree he was felling on his farm, fell on him. Knowing this, we did not opt to take you to the law, because we had our share of that noble duty to honor the addendum of our forefathers, which I am sorry you did not know, until now."

Upon hearing this, the black smith suddenly dropped to his knees. He wrung his head left and right like he was going through some emotional pains. As everyone watched, he then bowed his head like he was in a state of deep remorse.

Old chief Lomeh, upon seeing this, quickly held the walking stick in both hands and pulled it apart. To the surprise of the elders and everyone who were watching, the old chief was holding a very black and pointed dagger in his right hand while the wooden outer covering which was the walking stick was in his left hand. He then dropped the wooden outer covering and held the dagger with both hands.

"O our ancestors," he cried out loud, raising the dagger with both hands. "We have executed our duty, the duty you successfully handed from ages past and passed unto us to keep the park, until this day the town you found and bled to defend is on the verge of being destroyed by its very own for the curse that was betrothed upon him.

To you, O our forefathers. As a seed of Sengbeh Gbelema has portrayed himself like a cub, who thought he was a full-grown leopard, but finds himself in a python's belly, we therefore execute the verdict to finally put to end to the woe of Maila."

Old chief Joseph Colomea Lomeh brought the dagger down on the right side of Sengbeh's neck, straight to the spot between the shoulder and the base of his neck to pierce his jugular vein. The pointed blade landed, but to the surprise of the old chief, it bounced off. In a sudden desperate move, he again raised it in the air and brought it down again, this time at the same spot on the left side. But again, the blade bounced off. Frightened and becoming more desperate, he continued to strike at the sport with all his might, yelling at the same time, until the dagger broke from the handle and fell to the ground.

Sengbeh Gbelema, who all that time was still kneeling, suddenly jumped to his feet.

Old chief Lomeh stood quivering, and the elders strapped to the poles and the men tied on the ground began to cry, when they saw that nothing happened to Sengbeh. The dagger was to pierce the black smith's skin and sink down deep beneath his collar bone, and instantly kill him, but that did not happen.

The walking stick and the traditional suit the old chief was wearing were prepared by an old zoe, the day Sengbeh was born, and when the infant was thought to be the woe Guowola Acquoi had cast upon Maila. Since then, it was handed down to the old chief by his father, and he had been observing the necessary rituals intended to preserve its powers.

A custodian should never do woman business for three months, every three months. A young rooster that has not yet climbed on top of a hen must be killed, cooked in pepper soup and eaten before the abstinence from the pleasure of women can begin, and during this period, no food with palm oil must be eaten. Also, the walking stick must be touched, only when it is about to be used. Additionally, a bearer must first lick a paste of pure white rice mixed with honey to signify that it must be used out of a pure heart, but not for a malice, harbored against anyone.

What went wrong? Consumed by his worst fear, ever, the old chief pondered. Just how his father was sure he was matured enough before the walking stick was transferred to him, he did not turn it over to his son, Peter Lomeh, who was relatively young, when he turned over the chieftainship to him.

In fact, since the unceremonious departure of Sengbeh from Maila, he had since observed straight adherence to the rituals. When the civil war ended, and reasoning that it is only when the woe will come back to haunt their town, he turned over the chieftainship to his son, so he should focus more on preserving the power of the walking stick.

He had reinforced his abstinence by always making his mind blank of thinking about woman business, and made sure he ate the required rooster paper soup every day, from the day Tonolah Wuamah discovered skeletons strapped to trees up the cliff, and upon the expected return of his grandson.

"O Maila. I have failed you. What have I done?" old Chief Lomeh suddenly cried out loud and dropped to his knees when he realized that he wasn't sure whether he licked the paste of pure white rice mixed with honey, before he took the walking stick from the trunk Once, his father strongly warned him that the power of the walking stick is weakened when one is doubtful as to whether one has fully observed the necessary rituals.

The town people were screaming louder, fearing for the worst, when the black smith stood over the old chief who was still kneeling with his face bowed to the ground, lamenting for committing a grievous error, after all the efforts he had made. His nephew, Kafia and the other children who live with him had all thrown themselves to the ground, rolling and crying, when Sengbeh grabbed the old chief by the back of the collar of the V-neck shirt and began to drag him through the aches of the wooden platform that was burned down.

Johnny Colomea Lomeh resisted, by clinching to the left leg of the black smith, like a small boy who is afraid to be taken to the native doctor to be circumcised. His whole body was covered with soot. But Sengbeh pulled his leg out of the old chief's grip, and continued to drag him towards a pole he had planted for him.

Gbatou Zaowolo, one of the young men who was sitting on the ground with his hands tied behind him, managed to drag himself on his butt and reached for the black smith's legs, by wrapping his around Sengbeh's feet, thus, preventing him from moving. But Sengbeh let go of the old chief, grabbed one of Zaowolo's legs and violently twisted it. The brave man uttered a painful cry when his knee fractured with a loud sound like when a large tree is hit with an axe and about to fall.

Sengbeh then scooped over the old chief who was now trying to crawl away from him. He grabbed his legs and resumed dragging him all the way to the pole he had planted before the ones the elders were tied on.

He pulled the old chief from the ground and smashed him on the pole, the impact rattling the stick that was firmly planted deep into the ground.

Johnny Colomea Lomeh cried out loud at the pain it caused. The old chief lamented more, as Sengbeh began to strap him mercilessly to the stick pole; he had failed Maila and its people. He had failed the sweat and blood of his forefathers, and painful of all, he had brought disgrace to the Maila-Lomeh blood lines for his inability to revert the woe.

The whole scheme to lure Sengbeh back to Maila was a plan that failed. Had he known this, he was not going to allow his grandson back to the town, even if it was the only way Sengbeh was going to resurface and be finally stopped.

But he had used his only grandson, a resourceful and determined young man, as bait, snatched from the hook without catching the fish. He prayed in his heart that Boima must not return from Weala until morning when everyone was dead, and Sengbeh had left.

Meanwhile it was around 1am when the Range Rover was driving in the vicinity of Maila. Just before entering the town, Boima and the others in the jeep saw the orange-green light above the skies of the town.

"I have never noticed this about our town," observed Gotolo, leaning forward between the driver and the front seats.

"Maybe you missed that one, all the time you used to be out at night, poking and spying on other people," quipped Wuamah, and they all laughed.

"Don't mind your friend, Gotolo," said the young chief. "Maila is gifted with many strange unknowns."

Their amusement from the thought of the young chief's statement, were short lived when they entered the town and saw the roofs of the houses ablaze, with people crying and yelling in them. Suddenly apprehensive, Boima sped towards the chief's quarter. He gasped with fear when he saw ahead of him, the old chief strapped to the pole. He also saw the council of elders, tied to poles facing the old chief's, with their hands tied behind.

"He's here!" cried Tonolah Wuamah, extremely bewildered upon seeing the orange-green flames on the top of the houses, blazing aggressively, but still not consuming them.

"Who?!" demanded Boima.

Before Tonolah could answer, Boima swung the Range Rover to a halt. He jumped out of the car, and ran to his grandfather with heavy speed.

The young chief also jumped out of the front seat and ran after his nephew. Tonolah Wuamah and Gotolo also got down and ran after them. The old chief lifted his head and saw with horror, his grandson, Boima and his son, Peter Lomeh racing towards him.

"No. Don't worry about us," cried the chief. "You boys got to get out of here. Get out of here now."

By then, they had reached the pole and began to look around for something to cut the robes that were tied around the old chief while he was crying bitterly, urging them to leave.

Wuamah and Gotolo suddenly joined them, but they hurried to the poles where the council of elders were strapped and tried to free them. But Wuamah saw his uncle, John Dormeyahn also tied to a pole and ran to him, crying bitterly.

"No!" suddenly screamed the old chief when Boima and the young chief were suddenly pulled from the back and swung to the ground. "Get out of Maila now or else he will do you like us," he cried, with tears running down his eyes as Sengbeh Gbelema, exasperated, walked to Boima and the young chief.

"Who the fuck are you?" cried Boima, when the black smith stopped and looked down at them.

"He's Sengbeh Gbelema," said the old chief. "I could not stop him. I am so sorry I failed you both and our beloved town."

Boima suddenly composed himself and stood up, facing the black smith.

"I don't get for fuck what they say you can do, mehn. But I will not let you destroy this town or harm any of us," he said, grinding his teeth, speaking in his American accent.

Sengbeh stared at him for a while and took from his bag a filthy African lapper suit in rags, and threw it at his feet. Then the black smith searched inside again, got out what looked like a bundle of human hair, with the country plait still intact, and threw it at Biome's face, forcing him to sneeze from inhaling the strong and foul odor of the hair.

Still sneezing, Boima took it from his face and looked at it. It was the hair of a woman and he remembered the kind of plait very well. With his heart suddenly racing uncontrollably, he looked at the rags of the African lapper dress at his feet, and suddenly knew what it was. It was the same dress his mother wore when they took that picture. The picture he has always kept with him.

"Gorpue?! O God! He killed Gorpue!" Gotolo cried out loud and threw himself to the ground, at the same time hammering it with his fists. "O my sister, Gorpue."

"My mother was innocent, you sick fuck," Boima screamed.

Like a salvage, he leapt, aiming for the black smith's neck, and grabbed it with both hands. With all his might he began to choke Sengbeh, with his thumbs pressing beneath his Adam's apple to bore his throat. Sengbeh grabbed Boima's hands to pull them apart to free his neck, but he held on, applying more pressure on his esophagus.

Demonstrating his powers, Sengbeh freed his neck with a decisive pull. He swung Boima in a 360 degrees fashion a number of times and flung him. He flew in the air spinning, and went dashing into the corridor before his grandfather's house. He landed on a big tools box, with screwdrivers, wrenches, and pliers scattering all over him.

With his eyes red with rage, and still weeping for his mother, Boima ran back outside with an 18 inches long diagonal cutting pliers in his hands. Ignoring the pain when he fell, he charged at Sengbeh, this time going for his neck. But the black smith blocked the tool with his right hand, but it was caught between the cutters. Boima wasted no time to squeeze the handles to cut Sengbeh's hand off.

Unfortunately, Sengbeh drew him closer by folding his trapped arm, and landed a heavy left upper cut under Boima's chain, sending him to the ground. The black smith now stood over him, throwing the plier down and rubbing his right hand. Boima was convulsing on the ground. But Sengbeh scooped and pulled him by the collar of the Tee shirt he was wearing.

Puffing with rage, Sengbeh stared at the grandson of Johnny Colomea Lomeh.

"You have to save your nephew and yourself," cried the old chief, turning his head to his son, Peter Lomeh.

Immediately the young chief, who was still lying on the ground reeling with pain, jumped to his feet and charged at Sengbeh with a ferocious spear intended to hit him from his left side. But just in time, the black smith dashed Boima back to the ground with a chokeslam, and caught Peter Lomeh, mid-way before it landed.

As Boima fell to the ground on his back with a loud thud, which sounded like his vertebrae columns were splintered, causing him to cry out loud, Sengbeh had given the young chief a bear hug.

With a loud voice echoing into the night, Peter Lomeh screamed as Sengbeh squeezed his ribs with his large and powerful arms. Locked in his grip, Sengbeh continued to squeeze him, until he heard his rips rattling. Then he threw the chief on the ground and stepped on his already injured thorax.

While chief Lomeh lay on the ground holding his chest and waist, moaning, Sengbeh again grabbed and pulled Boima from the ground, and carried him to a pole, right next to the old chief.

Johnny Colomea Lomeh watched with trepidation as Sengbeh strapped his grandson to the pole, and was violently ripping his T-shirt and trousers off him. At one point, old chief Lomeh was violently squirming on the pole when he could no longer bear seeing his son and grandson being strapped to the pole to facing Sengbeh's vicious ordeal, the Sassaywoo, a version in which the innocent is automatically guilty and must bear a brutal punishment.

He cried out loud when it occurred to him that after killing his only daughter, Sengbeh wanted to let him watch his son and grandson, scourged before his very eyes.

All hope was lost as Wuamah sat on the ground, overwhelmed with fear and bewilderment helplessly watching Sengbeh preparing the furnace to perform the ordeal of his evil trial of the council of elders, the old chief and his son, the current chief, his beloved uncle, John Dormeyahn who was tired weeping and had become weak and looked spooked.

He looked at the direction of his house and whimpered at the thought of his mother, Mamaye, and little Flomo trapped in inside as the roof blazed.

"O Esther. I blamed myself for your death," Gotolo, looking transfixed, continued to cry. "I should not have been giving you information about what some of the town people were saying about you, when Barclay took your son to America. O Esther, you kept asking me to bring you news from our town, and that's why kept you in Weala. Ay Gorpue. Please forgive me. Please forgive me. I feel too guilty."

The black smith had prepared the furnace and had inserted a bunch of cutlasses into the gradually blazing fire as he began his giant strides, zig zagging his way between the poles on which his culprits were tied. For every pole he reached, he would rub his chalk all over the person tied on it, at the same time chanting in his usual eerie manner.

When the furnace was fully ablaze, he raced towards it, in his zig zag strides and got out one of the cutlasses which had turned orange-green.

"Your innocence is betrayed by your woe," he began to recite the ordeal's verdict code in his usually loud and raspy voice, when he got back to the poles of infliction, and facing Boima.

"Boima!" suddenly screamed Valerie, who had earlier reached Maila with the boat, but fell off due to an unbearable and sustained pain from the wound she sustained during her encounter with Sengbeh at Paradise Glade. She had jumped out of the boat, when it landed near the ramp, and suddenly became dizzy and fell to the ground and remained unconscious until now.

She had come to herself, gotten up and raced to the chief quarter, only to see Boima strapped to the pole and was about to face some strange ordeal.

"Oh God. He did the same thing to Sam," she wept, sinking to her knees when she saw Sengbeh Gbelema standing with the orange green-hot object in his hand. "O Sam. I am sorry I got here too late," she continued to cry hysterically.

"But your woe is the source of your fear; for the radiance of this steel to consume your flesh; for the abomination you have brought upon yourself," Sengbeh had finally completed reciting the verdict code, and raised the steaming cutlass in the air to bring it down, on the left side of Boima's jaw.

"Y-A-H!" suddenly, a powerful voice sounded, reverberating through the dark, rattling all the trees in the town, to the extent that everyone, including those trapped and screaming in their houses, the men bundled on the ground with their hands tied behind them, Gotolo, who had stopped weeping and lying on the ground motionless, Wuamah, the chief and his father, froze to the sound of this unrecognizable, but authoritative voice, meaning 'you there.' in Kpelle.

Valerie who had shot her eyes and had covered her ears screaming, because she could not bear seeing what was going to happen to Boima when Sengbeh raised the hot orange-green cutlass in the air to bring it down on his face, also stopped when she heard the voice.

Sengbeh had brought the hot cutlass down as Boima screamed and was using invectives, but also froze just in time the hot steel was near the left side of his skull. As everyone looked, spell bond, he turned towards the direction of the voice, including the old chief and Peter Lomeh who turned their heads in the same direction.

Valerie looked on the ground and saw a shadow that appeared to be emerging from behind her. Then it got bigger as it approached. Still on her knees and sobbing, she turned to look and saw a figure, and when it got closer, she noticed that it was a man, dressed like a traditional hunter.

"Gbeh vay?" to everyone's surprise, Sengbeh Gbelema, for the first time in many years was forced to speak, asking, when the man looked Valerie in the face, nodded and passed by her and continued walking to the chief quarter.

"I am Sergeant Sackie Binda, otherwise known as Sackie Dirty Water. The great grandson of Moie Laynumah who once roamed these lands. I commanded the Bush Dog Squad organized to defend Hendii, my home town from enemy forces during the Liberian civil war. When we were overrun during the Hendii's attack, I escaped with two of my colleagues by way of the St. Paul to connect to the Bong Range to make our way through Weala to get to Gbarnga for reinforcement, when we stumbled upon you up that cliff.

That fateful night, I watched how you murdered my colleagues by using your evil ordeal. When it was my turn to burn my flesh at the stick, you thought I was dead before your hot steel could touch my skin, and left me tied on that tree. But I was rescued by the spirits of your ancestors, and have since prepared me to confront you, today."

Upon hearing this, the old chief looked up at the sky and shouted in a loud triumphant voice, thanking his forefathers. Sengbeh stood, suddenly breathing heavily. He tried to control it, when a fear suddenly swept through his body; for the first time in his life, he felt his power left him-he was feeling the cutlass turning hot in his hand.

He looked at it and then at Boima, with his face masking a stubborn hate for the grandson of Johnny Conlomea Lomeh. Then he looked back at Sackie, who now looked slim, with dreadlock bedeck with cowrie shells and a long beard also encrusted with the traditional dice. He still had his old hunting gun, the one he used to kill the black backed duiker up the cliff, the night he, Sergeant-Major Eric Gonpue and Takpor Due encountered Sengbeh.

"You remember me now?" asked the former Bush Dog Commander. "We've met again."

As the cutlass got hotter in his hand, Sengbeh quickly turned to Boima and attempted to slap it on his face and pressed it against his flesh until he died, but a shot was fired. Sengbeh froze, again.

"Step away from the young man," demanded Sackie, putting another round in the Single barrel hunting gun, and advanced it. "I will be forced to shoot you, if you try that again."

"He's already cursed. He won't listen," cried old chief Lomeh as Sengbeh, who would rather die along with Boima, raised the cutlass in the air again.

Sackie fired another shot, this time aiming at Sengbeh's shoulder, the one whose arm held the cutlass. Everyone was shocked with another dose of surprise, when they saw the red flame of the bullet, traveling through the dark and hit Sengbeh on his shoulder and pierced his skin. It came out through his right shoulder blade with a remarkable force that sent the black smith to the ground.

Sengbeh cried out loud, holding his shoulder, with the cutlass lying far from him.

Sackie moved closer to him. He put another round into the gun, and advanced it. Before he could point it at Sengbeh, the black smith got up and grabbed his bag lying near the furnace and ran across the town to the northside, and jumped into the bush.

The man from Hendii was about to chase after him, but he noticed that the fire had started burning down the houses with thick plumes of smoke billowing over the skies of Maila. He hurried to Boima, who was looking at him strangely, and reached over for the cutlass on the ground and cut the ropes from around him.

"Save your town and its people," he said. "I am going after him, and will be back before day breaks to give you your justice."

Rubbing his arms to ease the tension from the firm grip of the ropes, when he was released from the pole, Boima watched the strange man race across the town after Sengbeh.

"Wuamah, Gotolo. It's not over yet. We must hurry up to untie the others and put out the fire," he said, and immediately Wuamah who still looked transfixed as he tried to figure out what had just happened, came to himself and helped Gotolo up. Both of them ran to the other poles to untie the elders.

Boima hurried to the poles where his grandfather and chief Lomeh were tied. After loosening them, they embraced each other with cries of joy.

"Boima," Valerie called and ran to him, weeping.

"Where's Sam?" he asked, looking at the wound on her neck, bleeding again.

"I left him where we had the picnic. He had to hold up the man who did this, to allow me to come and get help," she cried. "Oh God. I am afraid for him. I pray that nothing happens to him."

"Oh God," wept Boima, still looking at her shoulder. "Let me check your shoulder first. When day breaks we will go look for him, okay?"

By then the whole town was busy putting the fire out and rescuing those who were trapped in their houses. Boima raced towards the water pump, as chief Lomeh, Gotolo and Tonolah Wuamah, who had loosened his uncle John Dormeyahn, told him to hurry to their house to help put the fire out.

He, along with some of the town's men, ran up the tower to the water tanks and detached the hoses. They brought them down, and Boima started the water pump. They were now extinguishing the fire, using the huge hoses as they sprayed water. Some of the town's people were racing up and down the tower with buckets, and tubs while others ran back and forth to the nearby tributary where the boat ramp was, and the creeks with buckets of water on their heads.

CHAPTER 14

I T WAS DAWN. DAYLIGHT was slowly appearing in the skies. And one by one, the birds were trooping out of their nests, chirping as they flew from one tree to another, swooping down after the early morning worms. The distant crows of roosters echoed from nearby farm villages, including the cries hens make when chased by roosters.

But it was still dark in the forest, as Sengbeh Gbelema waddled through the young bush, a cutlass in one hand and his bag clinched under his arm. Leaves and low branches brushed his face, as he left a footpath and went docking under the thick undergrowth.

He could no longer bear the pain of the gunshot wound on his shoulder. He was bleeding profusely and feeling dizzy. He found a large tree and rested under it for a while, wincing, as the pain became more unbearable. Sitting on the ground with his legs spread, and his back leaning against the tree, he looked into his bag and got out a chalk, and licked it. He checked inside again and got out a neatly folded bundle of wide leaves, tied with red thread.

He tried to loosen the thread from around the folded leaves, but he couldn't. The pain had gotten too severe, and so he used his teeth to cut the thread and removed it from around the leaves. Then he opened it. What looked like a layer of traditional medicine made of pounded herbs was wrapped with leaves. He took some and rubbed them on his gunshot wound, first on his upper left breast, where the bullet entered and the big wound at the back of his shoulder blade where it came out. He cried out loud to the excruciating pain caused by the herb. After a few minutes, the pain stopped.

His face suddenly became serious when the thought of what happened ran through his mind. He must finish what he came to do, whether the spirits of his ancestors like it or not, he will return again, just like he did, to destroy Maila once and for all. If he is the cursed one, then Maila is bound to be doomed, as will.

He felt he was still inexorable, even with the setback he had just encountered with the strange man. But just how the dagger could not harm him, he will find a means to subdue the man from Hendii, when he faces him, again. But he would first heal his wound.

After that he would study whatever herbal power that was used for the bullet to penetrate him and determine the anti-dote for it. And when he had given the man from Hendii a fatal blow, he would return to Maila for the second and final time to lay waste to the doomed land, when its people would have totally forgotten about him and least expected.

He contemplated resting under the tree for a while, and later make his way to a secret cave further north of his direction where he would remain until nightfall, at which time he would head east for the uninhabited vicinity of Mount Zaweah, which is part of the Bong Range. There he will remain for some time to recuperate, learn his mistakes and more adequately prepare himself to administer his judgement.

He suddenly sprang to his feet when a stick unexpectedly cracked. Before he could reach for his cutlass lying by his feet, Sackie Dirty Water suddenly appeared and hit him on his forehead with his gun butt. Sengbeh Gbelema cried out and fell to his knees holding his foreface as it bled. Surprised that he was easily found, he slowly raised his head to look at Sackie.

"It is time you face the true ordeal; the Sassaywoo of pure justice," said the former bush dog commander, with his gun pointing at Sengbeh's forehead. "The people you have afflicted are waiting for you."

He cocked his hunting gun and gestured to Sengbeh to get up and move or he will shoot him. As the black smith led, with his hand on top of his head, Sackie followed closely behind, with his gun pointed at his back. They were heading back to Maila.

The people of Maila had worked all through the early morning hours to put out the fire, and save those who were trapped in their houses. They were happy that they managed to save about 90% of the houses, and no one was left in the fire. Most of the people had minor injuries like light burns and running eyes caused by the smoke and asphyxiation of non-life-threatening proportions.

Exhausted, they all gathered at the chief quarter. Some of them were in groups talking among themselves. They were recanting the events of the night, while others, like the youth, were debating what led to Sengbeh Gbelema's unceremonious disappearance and return.

Mothers, and grandmothers with their children or grandchildren on their backs had formed a circle, playing Sasa, singing and dancing songs of praises.

But many of them were crying and mourning the death of Koikoi Pewee and Esther Lomeh. Some women who heard Gotolo lamenting, were blaming him for the gossips he took to Esther, which discouraged her from returning to her hometown.

"Some of you hypocrites in that group must stop blaming me, or else, I will name all of you who said the worst things about Esther," he blasted when he heard what they were saying. "And if any of you deny it, I will quote the exact words and where you said them."

The anxiety of what was going to happen next was building up. Sengbeh Gbelema had fled again from the town, some of the brave men, proposed to the young chief to organize a search party to help the stranger to capture and bring him back to Maila. But Chief Peter Lomeh, in consultation with his father, refused.

"Let's wait and see what will happen, since the man from Hendii had said he will bring him back for justice," said the town chief.

Instead, he organized a team headed by John Dormeyahn and Tonolah Wuamah who had returned from putting the fire out from their house and rescued Mamaye and Flomo. Their job was to tour the town to conduct an initial assessment of the fire damage and report back to him.

Boima was holding Valerie in his arms, after he had dressed her wound, and had given her some pain killers. He was mourning his mother and at the same time telling her to stop crying for Sam as he will only believe that his friend had died when he sees his body.

They both watched how old man Dalamue, the town's healer, was forced to remove a splint made of bamboo he had earlier placed around the injured leg of Gbatou Zaowolo, the brave man whose knee Sengbeh fractured, when the affected area kept swelling. Chief Lomeh had urged that it remain like that to wait and see what will happen next, when the man from Hendii returns.

In the midst of all of these, the entire quarter became quiet when someone pointed towards the north of the town, when they saw Sengbeh Gbelema walking towards them with his hand on his head with the man from Hendii walking closely behind him with his gun pointed.

Immediately, the women who knew Sengbeh ran towards him and fell at his feet crying and asking while he killed Esther Lomeh, and Siegie. Naitee also ran to him with a broom in her hand and knocked it on Sengbeh's head for almost burning her and her grandchild alive. She attempted to stick it in the wound on his shoulder, but suddenly stopped, when the man from Hendii looked at her and shook his head in disapproval.

Sackie, along with the group, marched with Sengbeh towards the chief, the old chief and the council of elders, including Boima and Valerie who were also marching towards them, amidst a sudden roar of jubilation.

"I have returned to serve you the justice for your affliction, as I said. Here is your witness," Sackie addressed the chief and the council of elders, and shoved Sengbeh Gbelema forward with a toss of the barrel of his gun.

"Thank you, O son of Hendii," responded the young chief, after having a brief discussion with his father and the council of elders.

He then gestured with his right hand towards the poles Sengbeh had planted and continued, "we shall now proceed."

Sengbeh fought, and tried to free himself, as he was led to one of the poles, but he was restrained by some of the town's men, who dragged him to a pole, coincidentally the same one Grualee Tartee, the brother of Mulbah Tartee was strapped on.

"O Justice. Sometimes your delay does bring forth the right timing to heal the wound of the long afflicted," said Grualee Tartee. "The spirit of my brother will now rest well."

There was a sudden silence as those around the poles watched, except for the women who chose to stay behind in the circle, dancing, singing and playing the sasa, when Sackie Dirty Water began strapping Sengbeh to the pole, while the black smith continued to fight to release himself.

When Sackie had finished tying him, he walked to the furnace Sengbeh had built, which was still intact. He sat on the stool, inspected it, and took a cutlass hanging on his side to clear the aches and the remaining special wood that were still in the fire chamber. All the other cutlasses Sengbeh had put into the fire when the furnace was blazing have melted due to overheating.

"Bring me charcoal made of iron wood," he ordered, and looked towards the chief. "Where's the man with the injured leg?"

To everyone's surprise, Gbatou Zaowolo was brought before him while some other men raced to other parts of the town asking for those with the charcoal made of iron wood. The man from Hendii took from a small bag hanging on his waist, put his hand inside and got out what looked like a black paste with the odor of a strong mint. He first muttered something, turned his head to his right shoulder and spat, and then repeated the same thing to his left. He then applied the black paste on the injured knee, and began to rub, pressed, and hauled it for some time.

"You can now put it into the split," he told the town's healer, who nodded and looked inquiringly at the man from Hendii. "And don't forget to break the rooster's leg and continue with the rest of the required remedies. As you are aware, he will walk again, as soon as the foul's leg is healed and start to walk again."

When the fire in the furnace was built after a bag of charcoal made of the iron wood was brought, Sackie put the cutlass inside and continued blowing it with the air sacs. After some time, the cutlass became red-hot, unlike the charmed orange-yellow or the orange-green one Sengbeh used, depending on the gender. Sackie then took it from the fire and brought it before the chief and the council of elders.

"Here's the executioner. A witness from the side of the afflicted can step forward," said the man from Handii, holding the hot blade in one hand while his other hand held a small black plastic bottle sealed with a cock with a big feather of brownish red color stock into it.

The young chief and the council of elders including his father began to hang their heads, again. Before they could decide who could be the best witness, Boima stepped forward. Chief Lomeh held him by his hand to prevent him, but his father, the old chief, shook his head in disapproval.

His grandson was a suitable witness on the side of the afflicted; the trouble with Sengbeh Gbelema all started when the town agreed to allow his father, representative J. Boima Barclay and the German, Zepter, access to the wonders of Maila, and it was partly because his daughter, Esther, had had a child for the then representative, which engendered the trust in the two explorers. Additionally, the blacksmith's return to Maila was precipitated on the return of Boima to complete the work his father and the German had started.

The man from Hendii, looking at Boima in the face, nodded and gestured that he must wait a second as he hurried back to the furnace and put the cutlass back into the fire. He came back with the small bottle, pulled out the cork and asked Boima to stretch his right hand.

Afraid, Valerie rushed to him, and clinched on his left shoulder, worried that something would happen to him when Boima had stretched his arm. But Tonolah Wuamah hurried after her, urging her to step back.

Sackie turned the bottle upside down and gently dabbed the mouth in his palm. A dark green liquid, inundated with pounded herbs flowed out of the bottle and filled his palm. Then, he muttered something and robbed the liquid herb on Boima's hand, from his shoulder down to his fingers.

"Let the arm remain stretched as I go and get the executioner," Sackie instructed and hurried to the furnace, blew the fire for some time with the air sacs and returned with the hot red cutlass.

"You can now state your innocence and the consequence if the oracle detects that you lie," he said, and then raised the cutlass in the air.

The whole town became quiet and tensed, when Boima facing Sengbeh Gbelema, who was still stubbornly twisting on the pole to loosen himself. He stretched his hand before the black smith, looked in his eyes and took a deep breath as he fought to eliminate any trace of hate and malice for the man who killed his mother.

"If I J. Boima Barclay Jr. or my father, Representative J. Boima Barclay Sr. or my grandfather, Johnny colomea Lomeh or the council of elders of this great town, have ever defiled the park made by our ancestors for allowing access to and for venturing into the wonders of Maila for the purpose of bringing development to improve the lives of our people, let this hot steel consume by flesh and turn my bone into aches."

"So, let it be," suddenly shouted the man from Hendii and as everyone gasped with fear, including Valerie who turned away and bowed her head in Wuamah's chest, Sackie brought down the red-hot cutlass on Boima's arm and rubbed it up and down his shoulder and his fingers, several times.

Boima turned towards the crowd and raised his hand in the air and soon there was an uproar of jubilation when the people saw that nothing happened to his hand. The women who were singing, dancing and playing the sasa all trooped around him with more singing and dancing.

Valerie ran and hugged him at the same time weeping with joy, but she soon broke away from him when some of the young boys broke their way into the circle of the dancing women and lifted him into the air, jubilating, as the man from Hendii watched, patiently.

"My people. Please let us wait a little. It is not over yet," cried the young chief, running to disperse the crowd from around Boima, with Tonolah following closely behind.

When the crowd finally settled town after some efforts, the man from Hendii cried out loud, raising the cutlass into the air and began taking some drunken strides towards Sengbeh. He circled around him several times and raced up and down the chief quarter, four times, and extended his strides towards the middle of the town with children running behind him.

He returned to the furnace and placed the cutlass inside. He held the two-air sacs in his hands and blew the fire for some time until the metal became hot and red again. From sitting on the small stool behind the furnace, he suddenly sprang to his feet and commenced his drunken strides towards Sengbeh, with the small black bottle in his hand. He circled around the black smith four times and stood before him, looking in his face.

"It's your time to state your innocence and the consequence, if the oracle detects that you lie," said the man from Hendii when he had rubbed the dark green liquid herb on Sengbeh's right leg from the thigh down to his foot.

The black smith didn't say a word after he was allowed some time to make his statement.

"Silence means consent," quoted the man from Hendii, and continued his drunken strides towards the furnace.

He came back with the red-hot cutlass and appeared before Sengbeh again. He stretched it to his right, in the direction where Boima was standing. The just acquitted grandson of the old chief stepped forward, took the red-hot metal by its handle, and walked to Sengbeh, who upon seeing Boima with the hot red cutlass in his hand, became very aggressive on the pole.

"O ye spirits of our ancestors and to you, the Great One, who has created us all," Boima began again and paused, making sure that he said the right words, free of malice and revenge while the onlookers remained attentive, even the women who were singing, dancing and playing the sasa as this was the most crucial part of the trial; it might be logical after all, that Sengbeh could also be acquitted as the root cause of the hideous swear that was cast on him was as a result of an injustice done by his forefather, the ancestor Sengbeh Gbelema, according to the narration by the old chief.

"If Sengbeh Gbelema is justified for taking the innocent lives, some of whom were members of this great town, and for attempting to lay waste to the land you bled for, let the oracle close its eyes on his doing. But if his actions went against your commitment to protect this town and its people, even after you have long gone, let this cutlass burn his skin and consume his flesh."

Everyone held their breaths when Boima slowly laid the cutlass on Sengbeh's thigh and slowly pressed it against his skin. But the black smith gave him an eye that he was wasting his time, as the hot steel rested on his skin, steaming but not burning him. Boima remained calmed as he noticed the redness of the metal diminishing, suggesting that it was losing heat. Many onlookers were becoming uneasy and again gasping with fear that this would mean that Sengbeh Gbelema would be acquitted.

Out of a sudden, the redness began to reappear, and Boima, who had attempted to remove the cutlass from Sengbeh's thigh, felt a force against his hand, pressing the now extremely hot steel against the black smith's skin.

The next moment the cutlass had burned his skin and was consuming Sengbeh's flesh to the extent that it was reaching all the way to his thigh bone. The black smith uttered a loud cry of an unimaginable pain, and again the soon to be terrified crowd burst into an uproar of jubilation. Sengbeh Gbelema has been proven guilty.

"The spirits of his ancestors had just decided his fate," muttered the man from Hendii.

Boima, weary of the screams Sengbeh was making, as he could no longer stand imagining the pain the black smith was going through, tried to pull the cutlass away from Sengbeh's legs, but the force kept it pressed into his flesh. He then let go of the cutlass, breathing heavily, in reaction to his encounter with the strange and invincible force. Just in that time the redness disappeared and the cutlass fell from this burned flesh to the ground.

"Your ancestors have listened to you for the wise decision you have just made," holding him by the shoulder, Sackie told Boima.

The jubilating crowd had gathered around the pole to witness the most powerful Sengbeh Gbelema reeling in pain as blood profusely oozed out of his thigh. Chief Lomeh and the elders, including his father, the old chief were watching Sengbeh helplessly hanging on the pole with his head bowed in his large chest. Boima then raised his hand in the air, calling for attention. Then he held Sengbeh by his lower cheek and tilted his head upwards.

"I have decided, which I believe my uncle the chief, the council of elders, including my grandfather, the old chief have also agreed that we will not spill the blood of a descendant of our dear ancestor, Sengbeh Gbelema," Boima said, amidst nodding and whispers of concurrence from the chief and the elders. "But we will take you to the law. It will be to our satisfaction that you do not only feel that everlasting wound on your leg as a reminder for the pains you inflicted on those you tortured to death. We will prefer that you live to see or hear the development of Maila, which we believe will be the pain you loath bearing. As you rot in prison, you will bear these pains. The development of this town will be your worst nemesis."

After that, Boima turned to the chief and gestured that he had finished saying what he had to say and it was their turn to do the rest as by tradition. Then he went to Valerie and asked her whether she was feeling better and strong enough to lead them to where she left Sam, and she said she was.

Just before reaching the chief's house, they met his grandfather and the man from Hendii having a little conversation. The old chief was holding the dagger in one hand and the handle in the other hand. 'How the hell did I forget to lick the paste of pure white rice mixed with honey?' Still wondering, he said to himself.

"I guess you know what to do with them," he told the man from Hendii, who took it, walked to the furnace and put them inside to burn.

He stood looking as Sackie threw the walking stick into the fire after blowing the furnace, and watched it burn. After that he came back to the old chief.

"It is done," he said. "And the furnace must be disposed of now." When the old chief nodded, the man from Hendii then turned to

Boima. "I will be waiting by your boat to join you in the search of your friend," he said and then went walking in the direction of the boat ramp.

"He must be a messenger sent by the spirits of our ancestors," the old chief told his grandson when Sackie was out of ear-shot, and as they both hugged and held firmly to each other for a while, weeping for Esther, "We have finally put to end to the woe of Maila," he said.

Chief Lomeh and the elders held a brief meeting to decide how to proceed with Sengbeh Gbelema and it was concluded that he and Tonolah Wuamah must go to Varney town to inform the police about what happened. John Dormeyahn and the other men who were selected to access the fire damage went back to conclude on the exercise. Boima, Valerie, Sackie and three of the town's men had gotten into the boat and had set off to look for Sam.

"This is the same way we paddled, the morning we arrived here," the man from Hendii told Boima, just as they turned right from the St. Paul at the mouth of Tributary 2. "No one navigating south or north of the St. Paul will get here, unless you are able to see the twilight or the early morning sun with the right timing. My grandfather told me his father was the one who discovered this. That's how he was able to return to Hendii, after the expedition to honor calls for the French campaign. But many of his compatriots, some of whom were his relatives, got mesmerized by the wonder of this land and got lost. And since then, no one has heard of them."

"I guess that was why you were able to get here and ended up on that cliff," thought Boima. "By the way, we think we saw the canoe you and your colleagues used to get here. My grandfather told me it was a strange canoe, used by the water witch."

"He was right. I stumbled upon one of their secret abodes, a small abandoned village not far from the river. But it shockingly revealed to me a century old secret. No one up to the time I discovered that shrine could have ever known where their loved ones the Water Witch snatched away from them were kept."

"So, what are you going to do about that," asked Boima.

"Well," sighed the man from Hendii. "I don't know yet."

"Look! There's the signboard," Valerie interrupted, pointing to the signage 'Inlet 2 from Fish Pond Lake to Greater St. Paul'.

As Boima turned the boat into the inlet leading into the St. Paul, and leaving the one that headed east to the cliff, Sackie looked at the high rise and closed his eyes as he reflected on the gruesome incident he encountered the night up the cliff.

After 30 minutes, they reached Paradise Glade when they left the greater St. Paul and entered Inlet #3. Boima saw the sign board and landed the boat near it. They got off and as Valerie led, they raced through the gorge shouting Sam's name as their voices echoed through the glade. She took them to the place under the flower tree where they had the picnic, but only met some of the things she and Sam brought, still intact, thus causing a little stir.

They all spread out and continued to shout Sam's name. This continued for some time, but to no avail and just when they were getting frustrated, except the man from Hendii who was looking around and, on the ground, studying the place, they heard his voice, loud and clear, telling them that he survived.

"Oh my God! he's alive!" astonished, Valerie, who could not believe her eyes, yelled and ran to him.

Boima looked up at the sky and took a deep breath of relief. He dropped down on his knees, sobbing and at the same time thanking God and the spirits of his ancestors that his friend is alive-he had managed to survive the vicious onslaught of the Black smith.

Valerie had reached Sam and jumped on him, catching the mix martial artist off balance and sending both of them to the ground. Sam winced when his rib cage hurt, which Valerie ignored and firmly held him to herself, weeping with joy.

"You are a real man, Sam," she cried. "For what I saw that man did, tying people to sticks, including Boima, the old chief and his son, and almost burning the town, I thought that was what he did to you."

They remained clung on the ground for some time with Sam managing to bear the pain from his rib cage, allowing time for Valerie's overwhelming relief to ebb. When he noticed that the over joyfulness of seeing him alive had subsided, he gently tipped her on her back, kissed the side of her forehead and slowly eased her off him. He got off the ground and also held her up and brought her close to him. Then he held her by her lower cheek.

"He almost had me," he told her. "And you did good to come back for me."

She smiled and hugged him again.

"Love you," he whispered in her ears.

"You were in a hell of a fight, buddy," Sam said, with tears in his eyes when he reached his friend, who released himself from Valerie's grip and embraced him. "I saw it, mehn; the sick fuck survived my choke."

"The dude almost had me, mehn," Sam admitted. "I managed to find a way to give him a spear from a mountain a few klicks east of here. And I am thrilled that he survived that fall. That dude isn't real."

"But we have him," Boima informed Sam. "Had it not been the case, he was going to wipe us all and burn down our town. And maybe come back to finish you."

"That's good to know, buddy," Sam said and hugged his friend, and then caught the eyes of the man from Hendii. "Who's this other dude?"

"He's the one who came from nowhere and rescued us from Sengbeh. His name is Sackie Binda, from Hendii. A former fighter who organized a group composed of mainly local lads to defend their town from an opposing rebel faction during the heydays of the civil war. He and two others fled, when the town was eventually overrun and made their way by the St. Paul up to that cliff. The remains we saw tied to those trees were his friends murdered by Sengbeh, but he managed to survive, which according to him, it was due to his rescue by the spirits of the ancestors of Maila."

"Jesus!" Sam exclaimed, leaving Boima and facing Sackie. "So, you are the one with the hunting gun, right? The one whose fragment we saw in the skull of the animal that was shot. That must have been a terrible experience up there. But thanks for Saving us," he held Sackie's both shoulders in an expression of gratitude.

The men from the town that came along with them, went back and forth, hauling the picnic things Sam and Valerie brought the day before, into the boat.

"So how did you survive all these years," inquired Valerie, turning to the man from Hendii while they were on their way back to Maila.

Sackie Dirty Water closed his eyes and took a deep breath.

"When Sengbeh murdered by friends, the way you saw what he was going to do, I was also tied to that tree. Before he brought the hot blade to my face, I was already unconscious, and his version of the ordeal only works, when one is awake.

He tried to bring me back to consciousness, but he was unsuccessful. He waited until morning, but I wasn't still breathing and so he got frustrated and left. It was about noon when I suddenly came to myself when I felt the feather of a woodpecker which may have swooped down the tree I was tied to, brushing my face. Then it went and picked the vine binding me to the tree and I was able to loosen myself. It flew over my head several times gently picking at my skull, and as soon I got up to leave, it suddenly flew off.

I left the cliff. Stayed five days in the bush making my way to the Bong Range, and got to the old Julia Slocum Mission school, located at the other side of the mountain and headed straight for Belemu Town, south of the old mission school to my parents. Just before entering the town, I had left the bush to cross the motor road when I saw a truck full of rebel fighters returning from the village with my parents in the back. I made some enquiries when I entered the village and I discovered that my parents were taken to Gbarnga for questioning about my whereabouts on allegations that I and my friends sold Hendii to the opposing rebel faction, and I killed Sergeant-Major Eric Gonpue and Takpor Duo to covered up for the conspiracy.

"Did you do that? I mean selling your town to the other rebel faction?" interrupted Sam.

"No," breathed the man from Hendii. "What we did was prevent some of our own fighters who were not from our town from harassing our people; they were being accused by nervous intelligent officers for conniving with the enemy and some of them were confiscating food and the belongings of our people. So, we resisted, and it was settled by Gonpue.

I was shocked to learn of all this, and I became a figurative. I fled back into the bush, and that's where I have been, living by hunting and farming and at the same time was being prepared to save your town and its people."

It was just about noon when they returned to Maila. Chief Lomah and Tonolah Wuamah have returned with the police. At the chief quarter, they met Lieutenant Jusu Kamara questioning the old chief and the elders. Jusu brought along with him five well-armed police officers dressed in their Emergency Response Unit outfits, standing by the marked double cabin Mitsubishi Pickup that brought them. Huddled at the back, partially under the bench where officers riding the trunk sit, was Sengbeh Gblema with his hands cuffed.

"Good afternoon, Officer Jusu," greeted Boima, extending his hand for a handshake. "Thanks for coming."

"You're welcome, Mr. Barclay," complimented the Bong Mines Police Commander. "We got your suspect now and we will be on our way when our CID officer has gotten some initial statements."

"He beheaded Koikoi Pewee and possibly my mother," stated Boima, pointing to Sengbeh at the back of the police pick up.

"Allegedly so," breathed Lieutenant Jusu Kamara. "We have that as evidence and the clothes, supposedly your mother wore at the time of her death. I am sorry."

"Excuse me, Mr. Barclay," interrupted a woman, who looked to be in her mid-forties wearing blue levi jean trousers and a white collared

T-shirt with a police cap on her head. She had in her hands a small notepad and a pen. "I am Captain Julie Swen, the Chief investigator of the Criminal Investigation Division (CID) in Bong Mines. Can I ask you a few questions?"

"Sure," Boima agreed, excusing himself from the Lieutenant and stepping aside to talk to her.

"We noticed that there's a gunshot wound on the right shoulder of the suspect. Some of the town's people who witnessed the incident told us that a strange hunter shot him when he had tied you to the poles like he did the others and was about to perform the Sasaywoo on you. Is that correct?" Asked the CID officer.

"That's correct," responded Boima.

"Where is this hunter now? We need to take his statements, too."

"Well. He accompanied me to help find my friend who was also attacked in the bush earlier yesterday by the suspect. He went his way when we were able to find my friend. But he promised to be a help to the trial when the time comes."

Officer Swen wrote something on the note pad, and made a thoughtful face and then asked again. "What can you say about the wound on his right thigh? The people say you will be the best one to know."

"Yes. They are also correct. The suspect's ordeal simply turned against him. This is a traditional town that still observes its traditional practices. Out of malice, Sengbeh came to perform the Sasaywoo on people he perceives are his enemies, but it just turned against him."

Officer Swen looked at him for a while and again jogged that down in her notepad. Then she walked over to Lieutenant Jusu Kamara and both of them discussed something, briefly. Boima watched, as they walked back to him.

"Mr. Barclay," Officer Kamara said. "We will take the suspect to Bong Mines, and then we will give you time to assess the damage done to your town and those who were injured. After that, you can come to the police station and then we can conclude the preliminary investigation. The suspect will have to be taken to Gbarnga to be charged based on what we find and be placed at the detention center there, until a full court trial."

"Okay. But please ensure that he tells you where he's keeping my mother's remains and that of Koikoi Pewee."

"We are on it. Though he's refusing to say anything now."

As the police pickup left for Bong Mines with Sengbeh Gbelema, the kids ran behind it at the same time throwing jabs at the black smith.

While on his way back to the chief quarter to talk to his grandfather and the chief, he met Tonolah, John Dormeyahn, Mamaye and little Flomo. Dormeyahn was introduced to Boima and they talked about the role the heavy-duty mechanic will play in the reconstruction of the town. After that he joined his grandfather and Chief Lomeh who were standing with the man from Hendii.

"Be assured that I will also be watching the prison," Sackie told them. "And whenever I see the need to, I will return. But I must leave now."

"Hendii is still waiting for you. The town hasn't changed much," said Chief Lomeh.

The man from Hendii closed his eyes and took a breath. He looked to the south, in the direction of his home town and reflected for a while.

"Hendii will always be there. But first, I must see my parents who I haven't seen in 18 years. And when the spirits of our ancestors are willing, I will return to Hendii."

Boima, his grandfather and chief Lomeh accompanied the man from Hendii to the boat ramp. They watched as he climbed into his canoe, and paddled in the direction of the St. Paul. Sam and Valerie joined them as they saw the canoe, heading to the mouth of Tributary 1, disappearing from their sight.

"I have checked the town's people. Majority of them have minor injuries and I have applied some first aids, but I advised that we need to get some medicine for them, and also, Valerie and I need to go to the Bong Mines Hospital to have ourselves checked and to give proper treatment to Valerie's wound," Sam informed them while they were walking back to the town.

"I will go with you guys," Boima said. "I talked to Veronica yesterday and I told her that both of you are doing well. And I am so happy it is the case, now."

End.

ACKNOWLEDGEMENT

My special thanks and appreciation to the following persons:

Thomas M. Sako, for encouraging me to pursue my calling as an author. I can recall in the winter of 2018, when I visited Philadelphia, while vacationing in the states, we had this conversation about my calling in fictional writing. I still remember how you evoke this noble gift I possess by constantly reminding me about my unique story telling abilities. And since then, you have been supportive when I embarked on this journey.

My sister Mrs. Ruth Hanson Thomas, and my niece Mrs. Samaria Massoud Greene for your support. Also, to my niece, Miss Natasha Batsmen who I always referred to as the family-oriented type, for your frank opinion along with your sister Samaria, after reading the manuscript. All of you made sure that "SASSAYWOO: Trial by Ordeal" was published.

To Mr. Varney Arthur Yengbeh, Chairman of the Board of Trustees, Bomi Community College, Tubmanburg, Bomi County, thanks for your technical advice.

Mr. Sabastian Neufville, Head of the Language Arts Department, Levi C. Williams High school for your advice on the ingredients of Liberian Literature.

Mr. Thomas Kaydor, a publishing author, and Associate Professor at the University of Liberia for believing in my work and for ushering me into the publishing world.

To Commissioner Saa Saamoi, and my colleagues at the Department of Policy, Statistics & Strategic Planning of the Liberia Revenue Authority, who have in one way or another contributed to the success of my work. I benefited from your encouragement, assistance, and inspiration.

Finally, to my loving and caring wife, Mrs. Mosesetta Bedell Zeze for your understanding and patience and all the sacrifices we made to have SASSAYWOO published.

SPECIAL WORDS

1. Tar-bay

   A painful way rebel fighters tied people they suspected as enemies by pulling their arms behind them until the two elbows locked and tied them at their wrists.

2. Zaygay

   a magical charm rebels used as bulletproof, during the Liberian Civil war.

3. Attaya Center

   A place where Attaya, a green tea made of Chinese gunpowder, is sold, usually located around street corners which attracts lots of youth who engage in organized intellectual debates.

4. Sasa

   A musical instrument made up of calabash and beads played by women in the traditional setting of Liberian.

5. Peking

   A common Liberian colloquial used to refer to a little boy.

CPSIA information can be obtained
at www.ICGtesting.com
Printed in the USA
VHW040237050423
1734BV00006B/208

9 781958 434857